S/L		
P/L		
V.A.T.		
D/B		

THIS edition, issued in 1956, is for members of The Companion Book Club, 8 Long Acre, London, W.C.2, from which address particulars of membership may be obtained. The book is published by arrangement with the original publishers, Methuen & Co., Ltd.

Also by
PEARL S. BUCK

★

THE HIDDEN FLOWER
COME, MY BELOVED
GOD'S MEN
KINFOLK
PEONY
FAR AND NEAR
PORTRAIT OF A MARRIAGE
THE PROMISE
DRAGON SEED
TODAY AND FOREVER
OTHER GODS
THE PATRIOT
THIS PROUD HEART
A HOUSE DIVIDED
THE MOTHER
THE FIRST WIFE
SONS
THE GOOD EARTH
EAST WIND: WEST WIND

★

MY SEVERAL WORLDS
THE CHILD WHO NEVER GREW
AMERICAN ARGUMENT
HOW IT HAPPENS
TALK ABOUT RUSSIA
TELL THE PEOPLE
WHAT AMERICA MEANS TO ME
AMERICAN UNITY AND ASIA
OF MEN AND WOMEN
FIGHTING ANGEL
THE EXILE

IMPERIAL WOMAN
JOHNNY JACK
and his beginnings
THE MAN WHO MADE CHINA
ONE BRIGHT DAY
THE BIG WAVE
YU LAN
THE DRAGON FISH
THE WATER-BUFFALO CHILDREN
THE CHINESE CHILDREN NEXT DOOR
STORIES FOR LITTLE CHILDREN

★

THE CHINESE NOVEL
(*Nobel Prize Lecture*)

ALL MEN ARE BROTHERS
(Translated from the Chinese)

★

PAVILION OF WOMEN

"A blessed companion is a book" - JERROLD

PAVILION OF WOMEN

*

PEARL S. BUCK

THE COMPANION BOOK CLUB
LONDON

*Made and printed in Great Britain
for The Companion Book Club (Odhams Press Ltd.)
by Odhams (Watford) Limited
Watford, Herts
S.1056.ZSA.*

I

It was her fortieth birthday. Madame Wu sat before the tilted mirror of her toilet case and looked at her own calm face. In her mind she was comparing it with the face she had seen in this same mirror when she was sixteen. On that day she had risen from her marriage bed early, for she had always been an early riser, and putting on her new chamber robe she had come into this same room and had taken her place before the toilet table. She had sat in her quiet fashion, easily motionless, and had gazed at her young face.

"Can it be that I look the same to-day as yesterday?" she had asked herself on that first morning after her marriage.

She had examined her face minutely, broad low forehead, yesterday stripped of its girlhood fringe, long eyes, delicate nose, the oval of cheeks and chin and the small red mouth, that morning very red. Then Ying, her new maid, had hurried in.

"Oh, Miss—— Oh, Madame," she had faltered. "I thought to-day you would not be so early!" Ying's cheeks had been bright with blushes.

Madame's own cheeks were as pearly pale as usual, above the red mouth. "I like to get up early," she had replied in her usual gentle voice, the voice which in the night the young man whom she had never seen before had told her was like the voice of a singing bird.

At this moment, twenty-four years later, as though she knew what her mistress was remembering, Ying spoke from behind the heavy redwood chair. Her hands were busy with the coils of Madame Wu's shining, straight black hair, but she had now made these coils for so many years that she could lift her eyes from the task and look at the beautiful face in the mirror.

"Lady, you have changed not at all in these twenty-four years," Ying said.

"Are you thinking of that morning, too?" Madame Wu replied. She met Ying's eyes in the mirror with affection. Ying had grown stout in twenty years of being married to

7

the head cook, but Madame Wu was as slender as ever.

Ying laughed loudly. "I was more shy than you that morning, Lady," she said. "Ai-ya, how shy I was then—with how little cause, eh, Lady? It's only natural, what goes on between men and women, but then it seemed some sort of magic!"

Madame Wu smiled without reply. She allowed Ying complete freedom in all she said, but when she did not wish to carry on the conversation she made her smile fleeting and kept silence after it. Ying fell silent, too. She pretended dissatisfaction with a coil of the smooth black hair under her fingers, and pursing her lips, she let one strand down and put it up again. When it was finished she put two jade pins into the coil, one on either side, and wetting her hands with an oiled perfume, she smoothed Madame Wu's already sleek head.

"My jade ear-rings," Madame Wu said in her clear pretty voice. It was a voice so feminine that it concealed everything.

"I knew you would want to wear them to-day!" Ying exclaimed. "I have them ready."

She opened a small box covered with flowered silk and took out the ear-rings and fastened them carefully through Madame Wu's little ears. Twenty-four years ago young Mr. Wu had come into this room at the exact moment when she had dressed her mistress freshly in a soft wide-sleeved red satin coat over a pleated black satin skirt whose panels were embroidered, front and back, with birds and flowers. In his hand Mr. Wu had held this box. His handsome eyes were full of sleepy content. He had handed the box to Ying, being too well-mannered to speak to his bride before a servant. "Put these in your mistress's ears," he had said.

Ying had cried out over the flawless clarity of the jade and had held them before the bride's eyes. Those eyes had lifted to her husband for one moment before she dropped the lids with graceful shyness. "Thank you," she had murmured.

He had nodded, and then while the maid fastened them into her ears he had stood watching. Madame Wu had seen his face in this very mirror, the handsome full face of a wilful and proud young man.

"*Ai*," he had said, in a sigh of pleasure. Their eyes met in the mirror and each took measure of the other's beauty. "Go and fetch me hot tea," he had said abruptly to Ying, and at the sound of his voice the maid had been startled and scuttled away.

They were alone again, as they had been in the night. He had leaned over her and put his hands on her shoulders. He stared into her face in the mirror.

"If you had been ugly," he said, "I would have killed you last night on the pillow. I hate ugly women."

She had smiled at this, without moving under his hands. "But why have killed me?" she had asked in her pretty voice. "To have sent me home would have been enough."

She had been deeply excited that morning. Would he be intelligent as well as handsome, this husband of hers? That would be perhaps too much to ask. But if he were?

At this moment twenty-four years later, Ying now said, "Jade is as beautiful as ever against your skin. What other woman of forty can say this? It is no wonder that the master has never wanted another wife."

"Do not speak quite so loudly," Madame Wu said. "He is still asleep."

"He should wake early on your fortieth birthday, Madame," Ying replied. She rubbed her nose with the back of her hand. After all these years she felt she knew Mr. Wu, and of one thing she was certain: in spite of his fondness, he still did not appreciate enough his beautiful wife whom the whole house loved. Yes, of the sixty-odd souls under this roof, who did not love Madame Wu, from Old Lady down to the smallest grandchild and lowliest servant? If in the servants' quarters a new maid dared to grumble because the mistress saw the dust swept behind the door, Ying jerked her ears.

"This is the house of the Wu family," she said in her loud voice. "This is not a common house like Wang or Hua."

The head cook always grinned at this. All his life as a husband he had known that against the mistress, he was nothing in Ying's eyes. But indeed in this house even the two sons' wives had no evil to speak. Those narrow hands which Madame Wu held so often lightly clasped on her lap, were firm and kind while they ruled.

"I will have my breakfast," Madame Wu now said to Ying. "After I have eaten I will speak with my eldest son. You will dress me for the feast at noon. But keep watch over your master, and when he wakes let me know."

"That I will do, of course, Lady," Ying replied. She stooped to pick up a comb she had let fall. It was made of the fragrant sandalwood which was the scent Madame Wu used for her hair. Ying plucked a few long hairs from the comb and curled them carefully round her finger and put them in a small blue porcelain jar. She was saving these hairs against the day of her mistress's great old age, when it was possible she might need to thicken even her coil with a switch.

Madame Wu rose from the chair. She was ready for this day. A woman's fortieth birthday in a rich and old-fashioned family was a day of dignity. She remembered very well when her husband's mother had passed such a day, twenty-two years ago. On that day Old Lady had formally given over to her son's wife the management of the big house with its many members. For twenty-two years Madame Wu had held this management in her own hands, skilfully maintaining its outward habits so that Old Lady did not notice changes, and at the same time making many changes. Thus before Madame Wu had decided to do away with the overgrown peony bushes in the eastern garden, just outside these rooms, she had allowed the peonies to die one winter. When their strong red shoots did not push up as usual in the spring she called Old Lady's attention to this and helped her to decide that the peonies must have exhausted the soil and air in this garden, and therefore something else had better be planted here for a generation or two.

"Narcissus?" Madame Wu, then eighteen, had suggested gently. "Orchids? Flowering shrubs? I am only anxious to please you, Mother." But she had put orchids in the middle of the sentence. They were her preference. By putting them in the middle, Old Lady would think she did not care for them.

"Orchids," Old Lady said. She was fond of her daughter-in-law, but she liked to show her own authority.

"Orchids," Madame Wu had agreed. Within five years she had the finest orchid garden in the city. She spent a great deal of time in it. Now, in the early part of the sixth month of the year, the delicate silver-grey blossoms of the first orchids were beginning to bloom. By the eighth month the dark purple ones would be at their height, and by the ninth month the yellow ones.

She went from her own sitting-room into this garden and plucked two of the scentless grey flowers and took them back

10

with her into the room, where her breakfast was waiting. It was a slight meal, for she had never been able to eat much in the morning. Tea, rice congee in a small closed bucket of polished wood bound in silver, and two or three little dishes of dried salt meats stood on the square table in the middle of the room. She sat down and lifted her ivory chopsticks that at the upper end were held together by a thin silver chain.

A maidservant came in smiling. She carried in both hands a plate of long-life steamed rolls of bread, very hot. They were made in the shape of peaches, the symbol of immortality, and each one was sprayed with red dye.

"Long life, long life, Mistress!" the maidservant called in a coarse, hearty voice. "Mistress does not like sweet in the morning, I know, but we who are servants must bring these for good luck. The cook made them himself."

"Thank you," Madame Wu said mildly, "thank you all."

Out of courtesy she took one of the steaming rolls and broke it open. A dark sweet filling was inside, made of crushed beans and red sugar. "It is delicious," she said, and began to eat.

The woman was encouraged and leaned forward. "I ought not to tell you," she said in a loud whisper, "but I do it because I think of the good of the house. That old head cook, he is charging our Mistress three times the price in the fuel grass. Yesterday at the market I heard the price—it is high now, true, because the new grass is not in yet—but eighty cash a catty will buy as good as can be found. Yet he charges two hundred cash! He thinks he can do anything because Ying is your maid."

Madame Wu's clear black eyes took on a look of distance. "When he brings in the accounts, I will remember," she said. Her voice was cool. The woman remained an instant, then went away.

Madame Wu put down the roll at once and with her chopsticks picked up a bit of salt fish. She resumed her thoughts. She had no intention on this day of resigning her position to Meng, the wife of her eldest son. In the first place, she had four sons, two of whom already had wives. Old Lady had had only the one, and so there had been no question of jealousy between young wives. Her eldest son's wife, moreover, was very young. Liangmo had been married according to old-fashioned ways. She had chosen his wife for him, and this wife had been the daughter of her oldest friend, Madame

11

Kang. It had not been her intention to marry Liangmo so quickly, since he had been only nineteen; but her second son, Tsemo, who had gone to a school in Shanghai, had loved a girl two years older than himself, and had insisted upon marriage at eighteen. This meant that Rulan was older than her sister-in-law, who was nevertheless her superior in the house. Out of this embarrassment, for which Madame Wu blamed herself in not having kept better watch over Tsemo, her only refuge now was to keep her own place for another few years, during which time anything might happen.

She would therefore announce no changes in the house to-day. She would accept their gifts and the great feast which was planned. She would be kind to the grandchildren, whom she warmly loved, and in all that was done she would defer to Old Lady, who was getting out of bed at noon especially to be at the feast.

For Madame Wu herself this was a day to which she had long looked forward with a strange mingling of relief and quiet sadness. The first part of her life was over and the second part about to begin. She did not fear age, for age had its honours for her. She would with each year gain in dignity and in the respect of her family and her friends. Nor was she afraid of losing her beauty, for she had allowed it to change with the years so subtly that it was still more apparent than her years. She no longer wore the flowering colours of her youth, but the delicacy of her face and skin were as clear now as ever against the soft silver blues and grey-greens of her costumes. The whole effect of age upon her was one of refining and exalting rather than loss. Because she knew herself still beautiful she was ready to do to-day what she had planned to do. A woman who had lost her looks might have hesitated through feelings of defeat or even jealousy. But she had no need to be jealous and what she was about to do was of her own clear, calm will.

She finished her breakfast. Everyone else in the family was still sleeping except the grandchildren, whom the amahs would be amusing in some corner of the vast compound until the parents awoke. But the children were never brought to her except when she called them. She was a little surprised, therefore, when in a few minutes she perceived something like a commotion in the court just beyond her own. Then she heard a voice.

"It is not every day that my best friend is forty years old! Does it matter if I am too early?"

She recognized at once the voice of Madame Kang, the mother of Meng, her elder daughter-in-law, and she made haste to the door of the court.

"Come, please," she exclaimed, and held out both her hands, in one of them the two silver-grey orchids which she had taken again from the table.

Madame Kang lumbered across the court towards her friend. She had grown fat in the same years during which Madame Wu had remained exquisite, but she was too generous not to love her friend in spite of this.

"Ailien!" she exclaimed. "Am I the first to wish you long life and immortality?"

"The first," Madame Wu said, smiling. Servants, of course, did not count.

"Then I am not too early," Madame Kang said and looked reproachfully at Ying, who had tried to delay her. It was a rule in the house that no one should disturb Madame Wu while she took her breakfast, because at a disturbance she would eat no more. Ying was not abashed. No one was afraid of Madame Kang, and Ying would have defied even the magistrate to gain an hour of peace for her mistress in the morning.

"I had rather see you than anyone," Madame Wu said. She linked her slender fingers into her friend's plump ones and drew her into the orchid garden with her. Under a drooping willow-tree two bamboo chairs stood, and towards these the ladies moved. A small oval pool lay at their feet. At its bottom a clump of water lilies were rooted. Two blue lilies floated on the surface. Madame Wu did not care for lotus. The flowers were too coarse and the scent was heavy. Very minute goldfish darted in and out among the blue lilies, and paused, their noses quivering at the surface. When they found no crumbs there, they snatched themselves away and sprang apart, their misty tails waving behind them in long white shadows.

"How is your eldest son's son?" Madame Wu asked her friend. In the years when Madame Wu had borne her four living sons, and three children, who had died, of whom only one was a girl, Madame Kang had borne eleven children, six of whom were girls. There was none of the peace in Madame

Kang's house that was here in this court. Round her fat, good-natured person was a continuous uproar of children and bondmaids and servants. Nevertheless, in spite of everything, Madame Wu loved her friend. Their mothers had been friends, and when one went to visit the other, each had taken her small daughter along. While the mothers had gambled all day and late into the night, the two little girls had come to be as close as sisters.

"He is no better," Madame Kang said. Her round red face which had been beaming like a lit lantern was suddenly woeful. "I am considering whether I should take him to the foreign hospital. What do you think?"

"Is it a matter of life and death?" Madame Wu asked, considering the matter.

"It may be, within a few days," Madame Kang replied. "But they say that the foreign doctor does not know how to tell what a sickness is without cutting people open to see. And Little Happiness is so small—only five, you know, Sister. I think his life is still too tender for him to be cut open."

"At least wait until to-morrow," Madame Wu said. "Let us not spoil to-day." Then, fearing lest she were selfish, she added, "Meanwhile I will send Ying with a bowl of broth made after an old recipe of my great-grandmother for just such a cough as he has. I have used it often on my first and third sons and more than once on their father. You know he has been troubled with a cough for the last two winters."

"Ailien, you always are kind," Madame Kang said gratefully. It was early and the garden was cool, but she took a small fan from her sleeve and began to use it, laughing while she did so. "I am hot as soon as the snow is gone," she said.

They sat for a moment in silence. Madame Kang looked at her friend lovingly and without jealousy. "Ailien, I did not know what to bring you for a birthday gift. So I brought you this——"

She reached into the loose bosom of her wide blue satin robe and brought out a little box. This she handed to her friend.

Madame Wu recognized the box as she took it. "Ah, Meichen, do you really want to give me your pearls?"

"Yes, I do." Across Madame Kang's plain good face a flicker passed as of pain.

"Why?" Madame Wu asked, perceiving it.

Madame Kang hesitated, but only for a moment. "The last time I wore them, my sons' father said they looked like dewdrops on a melon." Madame Kang smiled. Then tears came to her eyes. She paid no heed to them, and they rolled slowly down her cheeks and splashed on the thick satin over her bosom without penetrating it.

Madame Wu saw them without appearing to do so. She did not move in her chair. In her hands she held the box of pearls. She had often let Madame Kang talk of her difficulties with Mr. Kang. Neither of them had ever talked of Mr. Wu beyond a word or two put in by Madame Kang.

"Ah, Ailien," she would say, "your sons' father is so little trouble to you. So far I have never heard of his even entering a house of flowers. But my man—well, he is good too. Yes, only——"

At this point Madame Kang always paused and sighed.

"Meichen," Madame Wu had once said many years ago, "why not allow him to enjoy himself so long as he always comes home before morning?" She had never forgotten the look of shame that came into her friend's honest eyes. "I am jealous," Madame Kang had declared. "I am so jealous that my blood turns to fire."

Madame Wu, who had never known what jealousy was, became silent. This was something in her friend which she could not understand. She could understand it less when she remembered Mr. Kang, who was an ordinary wealthy merchant and not even handsome. He was shrewd but not intelligent. She could not imagine any pleasure in being married to him.

"I have been wanting for a long time to tell you something," she said now after a moment. "At first, when I began thinking about it I thought I would ask your advice. But—I have not. Now I think it is beyond advice. It has already become certainty."

Madame Kang sat waiting while she fanned herself. The slight breeze from the fan dried her tears. She wept and laughed easily out of the very excess of her goodness. In this friendship she knew humbly that she took the second place.

It was not only that she was not beautiful, but in her own mind she did nothing so well as Madame Wu. Thus with all her efforts her house, though as large and as handsome as this one, was seldom clean and never ordered. In spite of her every endeavour, the servants took charge of it, and convenience rather than good manners had become the habit. When she came here she felt this, although living in her house she did not see it. But she often told herself that anyone who came into Madame Wu's presence grew better for it, and this was perhaps the chief reason why she continued to come ten times to this house to Madame Wu's one visit to her own house.

"Whatever you want to tell me," she now said.

Madame Wu lifted her eyes. They were long and large, and the black irises were very distinct against the white, and this gave them their look of ageless youth. She spoke with cool clarity. "Meichen, I have decided that to-day I shall ask my sons' father to take a concubine."

Madame Kang's round mouth dropped ajar. Her white small teeth, which were her one beauty, showed between her full lips. "Has—he—has he, too——" she gasped.

"He has not," Madame Wu said. "No, it is nothing like that. Of course, I have never asked what he does at his men's feasts. That has nothing to do with me or our home. No, it is only for his own sake—and mine."

"But how—for you?" Madame Kang asked. She felt at this moment suddenly superior in her own relationship to Mr. Kang. Such a step would never have occurred to her, nor, she was sure, to him. A concubine always in the house, a member of the family, her children fighting with the other children, she contending with the first wife for the man—all this would be worse than flower houses.

"I wish for it," Madame Wu said. She was gazing now into the depths of the clear little pool. The orchids she had plucked an hour ago lay on her knee, still fresh. So quiet was she that in her presence flowers lived many hours without fading.

"But will he consent?" Madame Kang asked gravely. "He has always loved you."

"He will not consent at first," Madame Wu said tranquilly.

Now that she had received this news, Madame Kang was full of questions. They poured out of her, and the fan dropped from her hand. "But will you choose the girl—or he? And, Ailien, if she has children, can you bear it? Oh, me, is there not always trouble in a house where two women are under one man's roof?"

"I cannot complain of it if at my wish he takes her," Madame Wu said.

"Ailien, you would not compel him?" Madame Kang asked with pleading.

"I have never compelled him to do anything," Madame Wu replied.

Someone coughed, and both ladies looked up. Ying stood in the doorway. On her round cheerful face was a mischievous look which Madame Wu at once recognized.

"Do not tell me that on this day of all days Little Sister Hsia is here!" she exclaimed. Her lovely voice was tinged with rueful mirth.

"It is she," Ying said. She stopped to laugh and then covered her mouth with her hand. "Oh, heaven, she will hear me," she whispered. "But Lady, I swear she does not understand a no. I told her you were having guests——"

"Not that it was my birthday!" Madame Wu exclaimed. "I do not want to have to invite her."

"I am not so stupid as that," Ying replied. "But I told her that Madame Kang was here."

"I am going," Madame Kang said with haste. "I have no time to listen to foreign gospel to-day. Indeed, Ailien, I came here when I should have been directing the affairs of the house, only to give you my gift."

But Madame Wu put out her slender hand. "Meichen, you may not go. You must sit here with me, and together we will be kind to her and listen to her. If she does not leave at the end of a half an hour, then you may rise and say farewell."

Madame Kang yielded, as she always did, being unable to refuse anything to one she loved. She sat down again in great good nature, and Ying went away and came back bringing with her a foreigner, a woman.

"Little Sister Hsia!" she announced.

"Oh, Madame Wu—oh, Madame Kang!" Little Sister Hsia cried. She was a tall, thin, pale woman, now nearly middle-aged, whose birthplace was England. The scanty hair on her head was the colour of sand, and she had fish

17

eyes. Her nose was thin and high, and her lips were blue. In her Western dress of striped grey cotton she looked older than she was, but even at her best she could never have been pretty. Long ago the two Chinese ladies had come to this conclusion. But they liked her for her goodness and pitied her for her lonely life in the city where there were so few of her kind. They did not, as some of their friends did, put her off with excuses when she came to see them. Indeed, in this both Madame Wu and Madame Kang were much too kind. But since Little Sister Hsia was a virgin, there could be no talk in her presence of concubines.

"Please sit down, Little Sister," Madame Wu said in her pretty voice. "Have you eaten your breakfast?"

Little Sister Hsia laughed. She had never, in spite of many years of living in the city, learned to be wholly at ease with the ladies. She laughed incessantly while she talked. "Oh . . . I get up to box farmers," she said. She studied Chinese faithfully every day, but since she had a dull ear she still spoke as a Westerner. Now she confused the sounds of two words. The two ladies looked at each other with a faint bewilderment, although they were accustomed to Little Sister's confusions.

"Box farmers?" Madame Kang repeated.

"Resemble farmers," Madame Wu murmured. "The two words are much alike, it is true."

"Oh, did I say that?" Little Sister cried, laughing. "Oh, please, I am too stupid!"

But Madame Wu saw the red rush up from her neck and spot her pale skin, and she understood the tumult in this uneasy foreign heart.

"Ying, bring some tea and some little cakes," she said. "Bring some of the long-life cakes," she added, and relented. "Why should I not tell my foreign friend that it is my birthday?"

"Oh, your birthday!" Little Sister Hsia cried. "Oh, I didn't know——"

"Why should you know?" Madame Wu asked. "I am forty years old to-day."

Little Sister Hsia gazed at her with eyes that were wistful. "Forty?" she repeated. She fluttered her hands and laughed her meaningless shy laughter. "Why," she stammered, "why, Madame Wu, you look twenty."

18

"How old are you, Little Sister?" Madame Kang asked politely.

Madame Wu looked at her with gentle reproach. "Meichen, I have never told you, but it is not polite, according to the Western custom, to ask a woman's age. My second son's wife, who has lived in Shanghai and knows foreigners, told me so."

"Not polite?" Madame Kang repeated. Her round black eyes looked blank. "Why not?"

"Oh, ha, ha!" Little Sister Hsia laughed. "It doesn't matter—I have been here so long, I am so used——"

Madame Kang looked at her with mild interest. "Then how old are you?" she asked again.

Little Sister Hsia was suddenly solemn. "Oh—thirtyish," she said in a low, quick voice.

Madame Kang did not understand her. "Thirty-six," she repeated amiably.

"No, no, not thirty-six, not so much," Little Sister Hsia was laughing again, but there was protest in the laughter.

Madame Wu heard this protest. "Come," she said, "what does age matter? It is a good thing to live life year by year, enjoying each year." She understood, by her gift of divining others, that the matter of age touched this Western woman because she was still a virgin. An old virgin! She had once seen this before in her own mother's family. Her mother's mother's youngest sister had remained an old virgin, because the man she had been about to marry had died. The family had admired her and at the same time had been irritated daily by an elderly unmarried woman withering under their roof. At last, for her own peace, she had become a nun. In a fashion this Western woman was also perhaps a nun.

In her great kindness Madame Wu now said, "I have guests coming in a short time, Little Sister, but before they come preach a little gospel to us." She knew that nothing pleased the foreign woman so much as to preach.

Little Sister Hsia looked at her with gratitude and reached her hand into a deep black bag she carried with her always. Out of this she brought a thick book with a worn leather cover and a black spectacle case. She took out the spectacles and put them on her high nose and opened the book.

"I was guided to-day, dear Madame Wu," she said in an

earnest and touching voice, "to tell you the story of the man who built his house on sand."

Madame Kang rose. "Excuse me," she said in her loud, somewhat flat voice. "I left my family affairs unsettled."

She bowed and walked out of the court with her heavy, solid footsteps.

Madame Wu, who had risen, sat down again as soon as she was gone, and calling Ying to her side she gave direction that the broth she had promised was to be sent after Madame Kang for her grandson. Then she smiled faintly at Little Sister Hsia. "Tell me what your lord said to this man who built his house on sand," she said courteously.

"Dear Madame Wu, he is your Lord too," Little Sister Hsia breathed. "You have only to accept Him."

Madame Wu smiled. "It is very kind of him, and you must tell him so," she said, still courteously. "Now proceed, my friend."

There was something so unapproachable in Madame Wu's dignity as she said this that Little Sister Hsia began to read nervously. Her broken accent made the story difficult to follow, but Madame Wu listened gravely, her eyes fixed on the darting goldfish. Twice Ying came to the door of the court and made signs over Little Sister's bent head, but Madame Wu shook her head slightly. As soon as Little Sister Hsia was finished, however, she rose. "Thank you, Little Sister," she said. "That was a pleasant story. Please come again when I have time."

But Little Sister Hsia, who had also been planning a prayer, rose unwillingly, fumbling with her bag and her spectacles and the heavy book.

"Shall we not have a little prayer?" Her mistaken accent really said 'cake' instead of 'prayer,' and for a moment Madame Wu was confused. They had had cakes, had they not? Then she understood, and in kindness did not smile.

"You pray for me at home, Little Sister," she said. "Just now I have other duties."

She began walking towards the door of the court as she spoke, and Ying suddenly appeared and took over Little Sister Hsia, and Madame Wu was alone again. She returned to the pool and stood looking down in it, her slender figure reflected in it quite clearly from head to foot. The orchids,

20

she discovered, were still in her hand, and she lifted that hand and let the flowers fall into the water. A swarm of goldfish darted up and nibbled at the orchids and swerved away again.

"Nothing but flowers," she said, and laughed a little at them. They were always hungry! A house built on sand? But she could never be so foolish. This house in which she lived had already stood for hundreds of years. Twenty generations of the Wu family had lived and died here.

"Mother, I should have come before to wish you long life." She heard her eldest son's voice from the door. She turned.

"Come in, my son," she said.

"Long life, Mother!" Liangmo said with affection. He had bowed before his mother half playfully when he came in. The Wu family was not quite old-fashioned enough to keep the ancient custom of kneeling obeisance to elders on birthdays, but the bow was in memory of that old custom.

Madame Wu accepted his greeting with a graceful receiving bow. "Thank you, my son," she said. "Now sit down. I want to talk to you."

She sat down again in one of the bamboo chairs and motioned him to the other, and he sat down on the edge of it in deference to her.

"How well you look, son," she said, examining his handsome young face. He was, if possible, more handsome than his father had been at the same age, for she had given him something of her own delicacy too.

He wore this morning a long robe of summer silk, the colour of pale green water. His dark short hair was brushed back and his dark olive skin was smooth with health and good food. His eyes were quiet with content.

"I have married him happily," Madame Wu told herself. "And the little child, my grandson?" she asked aloud.

"I have not seen him this morning," Liangmo replied. "But had he been ill I would have heard of it."

He could not keep from answering his mother's smile. There was great affection between them. He trusted her wisdom far more than he did his own, and because of this when she had asked him to marry in order that there would not be confusion in the family because of the marriage of

21

his younger brother ahead of him, he had said at once, "Choose someone for me, Mother. You know me better than I know myself." He was completely satisfied with Meng, his pretty wife, and with the son she had given him within a year of their marriage. Now she was pregnant again.

"I have been saving some good news for this day, Mother," he said at this moment.

"It is a day for good news," Madame Wu replied.

"My son's mother is to have her second child," he announced proudly. "Her second moon cycle has passed, and now she is sure. She told me three days ago, and I said we would wait until our mother's birthday to tell it to the family."

"That is good news indeed," Madame Wu said warmly. "You must tell her that I shall send her a present."

At this moment her eyes fell on the little box of pearls that she had put on a small porcelain table. "I have the gift," she exclaimed. She took up the box and opened it. "Her own mother gave me, an hour ago, these pearl ear-rings. But pearls are for young wives, I think, and it would be fitting for me to give them to our daughter. When you return to Meng—no, I will go to her with you. But first, my son, is there anything I should do in regard to our guests to-day and the feast?"

"Nothing, Mother," he replied. "We are doing everything for you. Your children want to give you a day of idle joy. You shall not even ask about anything—only enjoy. Where is my father?"

"I doubt he can rise before noon even on my birthday," Madame Wu said, smiling. "But I told him he must not, indeed. He enjoys the day so much more when he does not get up early, and he will be fresh and happy at the feast."

"You are too good to us all," Liangmo said.

She surveyed him with her steady beautiful eyes as though she did not hear this. "My son," she said, "since doubtless we will be interrupted soon, I will speak at once of what I am planning to do. I have decided upon a thing, and yet I feel it is due you, as my eldest son, to tell you what I plan. I have decided to invite your father to take a concubine."

She said these stupendous words in her calm, pretty voice. Liangmo heard them without understanding them. Then

22

they crowded his mind and deafened him like thunder. His handsome full face paled to the colour of cream.

"Mother!" he gasped. "Mother, has he — **has** my father——"

"Certainly not," she said. But it struck her with a touch of pain that Liangmo too, had first asked this question. Was it possible that her husband could so seem to all the sort of man who might . . . ? She put away the unworthy thought. "Your father is still so youthful, although forty-five years old, and he is still so handsome, that it is no wonder that even you, his son, should put that question," she said. "No, he has been and is most faithful."

She paused, then with the nearest to diffidence that her son had ever seen in her calm manner, she went on, "No, I have my own reasons for the decision. But I should like to be assured that you, my eldest son, would accept her coming and help the house to accept it when it is known. It is natural that there will be talk and some disturbance. I must not hear the disturbance. But you must hear it and maintain the dignity of your parents."

By now, although his cheeks were still cream pale, Liangmo had recovered himself. His black eyebrows settled themselves above his eyes, which were like his mother's. "Of course, the matter is between you and my father," he said. "But if you will let me step beyond my place, I beg you that if my father has not this wish you will not ask it of him. We are a happy family. How do we know what a strange woman will bring into the house? Her children will be the same age as your grandchildren. Will this not be confusing the generations? If she is very young, will not your sons' wives be jealous of her position with my father? I can foresee many sorrows."

"Perhaps you cannot understand, at your age, the relationship between men and women of my generation," Madame Wu replied. "But it is because I have always been happy with your father, and he with me, that I have decided upon the step. Please, my son, return to your place. I require of you only to obey your mother in this as you have in all things. You have been the best of my sons. What you say will influence your younger brothers. What Meng says will influence the young wives. You must help her, too."

Liangmo struggled against this in his own mind. But so

deep was his habit of obedience to his mother that he obeyed her now. "I will do my best, Mother, but I will not pretend that what you have told me does not sadden this day."

She smiled slightly. "I am really saving you greater sadness on other days," she said. And then she saw that what she said was an enigma to this man so much younger than she, and so she rose and took up the box of pearls. "Come," she said. "We will go and see Meng and I will make my gift."

He had risen when she did, and now he stood beside her, young and strongly built as his father was, head and shoulders above her. She put out her little hand and rested it on his arm for a moment in a gesture of affection so rare that it startled him. She did not easily endure the touch of another human being, even her own children's. He looked down at her and met her clear upward look.

"In you," she said distinctly, "I have built my house upon a rock."

.   .   .

Meng was playing with her little boy in the courtyard of her own house within this great house. She was alone with him except for his wet nurse, who squatted on her heels, laughing and watching. Both young women, mother and nurse, adored this little boy all day long. At night he slept in the nurse's arms. In this common adoration the two women found a deep companionship. They poured out, in happy sacrifice, the love and attention the child demanded.

Meng's body was made to bear children, and her breasts had been full of milk. But no one, not even she herself, had thought of allowing the baby to pull at her lovely small breasts and spoil their firmness. Lien had been hired to provide milk. She was the young wife of one of the farmers on the Wu lands. Her own child, also a boy, had been fed flour and water and rice gruel by his grandmother instead of his mother's milk. For this reason he was now thin and small and yellow, while Lien's nursling was fat and rosy. Lien was allowed to go home once a month, and when she saw her child she wept and put him to her great breast. Her full nipples dripped milk, but the child turned away his head. He had never tasted this milk, and he did not know how to suckle. Lien could never stay out her day because of her aching breasts. By mid-afternoon she must hasten back to the

24

Wu house. There her nursling waited for her, shouting with rage and hunger.

At the sight of him she forgot the thin yellow child. She opened her arms, laughing, and the big fat boy screamed for her from his mother's knees. Then Lien ran to him, snatching open her coat as she ran. She knelt beside him at Meng's side, and with both hands the child grasped her breast like a cup and drank in great gulps. Together Meng and Lien laughed, and each felt in her own body the child's satisfaction.

Now, to see the two women as they watched the child, it would have been hard to tell from the two faces which was the mother. Indeed, the child made no difference. He smiled radiantly on both. He was learning to walk, and he took the few steps from one to the other, laughing and falling upon each in turn.

Meng was always happy, but she had been deeper in happiness the last few days than she had ever been. She had told no one except Liangmo of the coming of the second child. Servants, of course, knew it. Her own maid had first reminded her that her second moon cycle had passed without sign. In the servants' rooms there was already secret rejoicing. But in a great house servants were like furniture, used without heeding.

Lien knew, and knowing it was more gay than ever. A house with many young wet nurses was a lucky house. She had gradually ceased to love her own child. All her rich animal love was transferred to her nursling. Her own home was poor and hard, the food scanty. The mother-in-law had a bitter tongue and a hand greedy for the wages Lien brought home. Although Lien had loved her home once and had wept all day and all night when her husband's mother had sent her to the Wu house, now she had come to love the good food, the ease, the idleness. Beyond nursing this healthy boy, nothing was asked of her. She was urged to eat, to drink, to sleep. Her young, pleasure-loving body responded quickly. This was now her home, and she loved her nursling more than her child.

She longed, in the soft fullness of her content this morning, to tell her young mistress how rejoiced she was at the promise of a second birth, but she hesitated. These rich, idle, soft, young women allowed anything, it seemed, and yet sometimes they flew into anger not expected and causeless. She continued only to laugh, therefore, and to praise the little boy.

"A little godling," she said fondly. "I never see one like him anywhere, Mistress."

Before Meng could do more than smile, they heard footsteps. The child ran to Lien, and from her arms stared at his grandmother and father. Meng rose.

"Here you are, Meng," Madame Wu said. "Sit down, child. Rest yourself, please. Come here to me, son of my son."

Lien pushed the little boy forward and inched herself along on her heels so that he was always in the shelter of her arms. Thus he stood at Madame Wu's knee and stared at her with large black eyes whose corners were tucked in. He put his fingers in his mouth, and she took them gently away.

"A lovely boy," she murmured. "Have you raised a name for him yet?"

"There is no haste," Liangmo replied. "He does not need it until he goes to school "

She looked down at the little boy. He stood in their midst, the centre of them all. And yet, she thought musingly, it was not he himself, not this simple creature, who so held their hopes in him. Were he to die, another would take his place. No, he was a symbol of continuing life. It was the symbol which held all their dreams.

She turned her eyes from the charming little face and remembered why she had come.

"Meng, Liangmo tells me you have added happiness," she said. "I have come to thank you and to bring you a gift."

Meng blushed her ready peach bloom and turned her little head. The one defect in her beauty was her hair, which tended to curl in spite of the fragrant wood oil with which she continually smoothed it. Now her pleasure was mingled with fear lest her hair was curling again before Liangmo's mother's eyes. She loved Madame Wu, but she feared her. No one ever saw a hair misplaced on Madame Wu's graceful head. Then she put out both hands to receive the gift and forgot her fears.

"My mother's pearls!" she breathed.

"She gave them to me, but I am too old for pearls," Madame Wu said. "Now everything happens for good in this

26

house. You declared your happiness to-day, and I had these pearls ready to give you."

"I have always craved these pearls," Meng said. She opened the box and gazed down at the jewels.

"Put them on," Liangmo commanded her.

Meng obeyed. Her soft cheeks blushed more deeply. They were all watching her, even the little boy. But her slender fingers did not fumble as she fastened the pearls in her ears.

"I used to put them in my ears and beg my mother to let me keep them," she confessed.

"Now you have earned them," Madame Wu said. She turned to her son. "See how rosy the pearls have become. They were silver-grey."

It was true. The pearls looked rose pink against Meng's soft flesh.

"*Ai ya,*" Lien cried. "She must not look too pretty or the baby will be a girl!"

They laughed, and Madame Wu closed the laughter by saying as she rose to depart, "I would welcome a girl. After all, there must be female in the world as well as male. We forget it, but it is true, is it not, Meng?"

But Meng was too shy to answer such a question.

.   .   .   .   .

It was the hour of the birthday feast. Madame Wu had taken her place at the left of Old Lady, who because of her age and generation had the highest seat. Mr. Wu sat on his mother's right, and on the other side of him sat Liangmo. Tsemo, the second son, sat on Madame Wu's left, and on Tsemo's left the third son, Fengmo. Yenmo, the fourth son, was still a child of seven. But he had come to live in his father's rooms, and now he stood in the circle of his father's arm. Thus one by one each member was in his place, and below the sons the two sons' wives sat, Meng with her child on her knee, and a maidservant stood near to take it away if it became troublesome. Old Lady was proud of her great-grandchild but easily impatient, whereas Madame Wu had endless patience.

Indeed, nothing seemed to fret her. Her smooth pearl-coloured face looked with pleasure on this great gathering of her family. At six other tables, of eight places each, there were uncles and aunts and cousins and friends and their children, and at one table Madame Kang presided. All had sent gifts to Madame Wu before this day. These gifts were of many kinds—pairs of vases, packages of dates, boxes of soft cakes and sweets, scrolls of silk upon which were pasted characters cut out of gold paper, each carrying a good wish. There were many other gifts. Mr. Wu had added two bolts of heavy brocaded silk, and Old Lady had added two boxes of fine tea for her personal gift.

The family gift had been expensive. They had ordered a painting, by the best artist in the city, of the Goddess of Long Life. All the guests agreed as to its beauty when they came to offer their first greetings to Madame Wu. The picture hung in the place of honour, and even its details were correct. The goddess held the immortal peach in her hand. By her side was a stag, red bats flew about her head in blessing, and from her girdle hung the gourd containing the elixir of life. Even long-lived herbs were not forgotten by the artist; he had tied them to her staff.

On the wall behind Madame Wu hung a square of red satin upon which were sewn the characters for long life cut out of black velvet. Against this bright satin Madame Wu's dark head was dainty and austere.

To all the greetings and good wishes of the guests Liangmo responded for Madame Wu. Before the guests were seated, he and Meng had gone to each table and thanked the guests, for their mother, as the eldest son and daughter-in-law of the house.

Everything, that is, had been done with ease and yet with some formality, which showed that the Wu family valued the old ways and understood the new. Every now and again Madame Wu rose from her seat and moved among the guests to make sure that all had been properly served. Whenever she did this the guests rose and begged her not to trouble herself, and she in turn begged them to be seated again.

When she had so done twice, the third time Mr. Wu leaned across the corner of the table and said, "I beg you not to rise again, my sons' mother. I will take your place when the sweet is served."

Madame Wu bent her head and smiled slightly in thanks, and then she saw that Old Lady had taken too large a piece of fowl and was dripping the broth from it upon her gown.

28

She took her own chopsticks and held the bit until Old Lady could encompass it all in her mouth. As soon as she could speak Old Lady did so with her usual vehemence. "Ying!" she cried loudly.

Ying, waiting always near her own mistress, came near at once. "Ying!" the Old Lady cried, "you tell that piece of fat who is your man that he must cut the fowl smaller. Does he think we have the jaws of lions and tigers?"

"I will tell him, Ancient," Ying replied.

But Old Lady felt quite happy now, being full of food, and she began to speak to everybody in her loud, flat old voice.

"Foreigners eat huge pieces of meat," she said, looking round the room. "I have never seen it, but I have heard that the whole leg of a sheep or a lump of cow as large as a small child is set on their tables, and they hack it with knives and cut off pieces from it. They take it up with iron prongs and thrust it into their mouths."

Everybody laughed. "You are in good spirits, Mother," Mr. Wu said. He had never tried to correct the mistaken statements of his mother. In the first place, he did not wish to make her unhappy, and in the second place, it made no difference anyway and so was not worth the trouble.

At this moment the sweetened rice with its eight precious fruits came in, which was a sign that the feast was half over, and everyone looked pleased at the sight of the delicacy. At the door Ying saw her husband standing half hidden in order to hear the praises of the guests. Madame Wu saw him too, and leaned towards Ying.

"Tell him to come here," she commanded.

Ying's pride rose in a flush to her plump cheeks, but out of good manners she pretended to belittle her husband.

"Lady, do not trouble yourself with my good-for-nothing," she said in a loud voice.

"But it is my pleasure," Madame Wu insisted.

So with false unwillingness Ying beckoned to her husband, and he came in and stood before Madame Wu, smoothing his filthy apron with pride, for no good cook has a clean apron, and he knew it.

"I must thank you for this sweet rice and its eight precious fruits," Madame Wu said in her kind way. "It is always delicious, but to-day it is better than ever. This I take as a sign of your faithfulness and goodness of heart. I will remember it before the day is over."

The cook knew that she meant she would give gifts to the servants at the end of the feast, but in good manners he pretended otherwise. "Please do not think it good," he said. "I do not deserve mention."

"Go away, oaf!" Ying whispered loudly while her eyes shone with pride. And so he went away, well pleased, and behind his back Ying tried not to look too proud and beyond her station.

And now Mr. Wu must rise to fulfil his promise, and he went to every table and begged the guests to eat heartily of the sweet. Madame Wu followed him thoughtfully with her eyes. Did she imagine that he lingered a moment at Madame Kang's table where the pretty young third daughter sat beside her mother?

"Pudding, pudding!" Old Lady complained, and Madame Wu put out her slender arm and, holding back her sleeve, she took up a porcelain spoon and dipped the pudding generously into Old Lady's bowl.

"Spoon—where's my spoon?" Old Lady muttered, and Madame Wu put a spoon into the old hand.

Then she continued to watch Mr. Wu thoughtfully while everybody at the table was silent in enjoyment of the dish. Mr. Wu was beyond doubt lingering beside Madame Kang's pretty daughter. The child was modern, too modern, for her hair was cut to her shoulders and curled in the foreign fashion. She had been to school for a year in Shanghai before that city was taken by the enemy. Now she frequently made her mother and father wretched by her discontent in living in this small provincial city.

Madame Wu watched her as she lifted her head and replied pertly to something Mr. Wu had said. Mr. Wu laughed and went on, and Madame Wu took her spoon and dipped up a fragment of the glutinous sweet. When Mr. Wu returned she looked at him with her long clear eyes.

"Thank you, my sons' father," she said, and her voice was its usual music.

The feast went on its long pleasant course. The sweet was followed by meats, and then at last by the six bowls. Instead of rice the cook had made long fine noodles, because it was a birthday feast and the long noodles were a symbol of long life. Madame Wu, always delicate at eating, refused the meats, but it was necessary that she eat some of the noodles. They were made even longer than usual by the zealous cook, but she wound them with graceful skill round her chopsticks.

But Old Lady had no such patience. She held the heaped bowl to her mouth with her left hand and pushed the noodles into her mouth with her chopsticks, supping them in like a child. Old Lady ate everything heartily. "I shall be ill to-night," she said in her penetrating old voice. "But it is worth it, daughter, on your fortieth birthday."

"Eat to your own content, Mother," Madame Wu replied.

One by one guests rose with small wine bowls in their hands, and toasts were drunk. To these Madame Wu did not reply. She was a quiet woman, and she looked at Mr. Wu, who rose in her place and accepted the good wishes of all. Only Madame Kang, catching her friend's eye, silently lifted her bowl, and as silently Madame Wu lifted hers, and the two drank together in secret understanding.

By now Old Lady was full of food, and she leaned against the high back of her chair and surveyed her family. "Liangmo looks sick," she declared.

Everybody looked at Liangmo, who indeed smiled in a very sickish fashion. "I am not ill, Grandmother," he said hastily.

Meng gazed at him with troubled eyes. "You do look strange," she murmured. "You have been strange all morning."

At this, brothers and brothers' wives all looked at him, and he shook his head. Madame Wu did not speak. She quite understood that Liangmo was still unable to accept what she had told him to-day. He looked at her at this moment with pleading in his eyes, but she merely smiled a little and looked away.

It was when she turned her head away that she caught the shrewd, too-intelligent gaze of her second daughter-in-law. Tsemo's wife, Rulan, had not said a word all during the feast, but speech was never necessary for this girl's comprehension of what was happening about her. Madame Wu perceived that she had seen the son's pleadings and also the mother's reply. But Tsemo himself paid no heed to what went on. He was an impatient young man, and he sat back

31

from the table, tapping his foot restlessly. For him the birthday feast had lasted long enough.

Somewhere an overfed child vomited suddenly on the brick floor with a great splatter, and there was a fuss among the servants.

"Call in the dogs," Madame Kang advised, but Ying, hastening to the scene of the disaster, begged her pardon.

"Our Lady will not allow dogs under the tables," she explained.

"You see, Mother," Madame Kang's pretty third daughter pouted. "I told you nobody does—it's so old-fashioned. I'm always ashamed when you do it at home.'

"Well, well," Madame Kang said, "be quiet now about your shame in the presence of others."

"Too much talk from girls," Mr. Kang said, but he was fond of this Linyi, because she was the prettiest of all his daughters, and he smiled at her.

Old Lady staggered to her feet. "I am going to bed," she said. "I must prepare to be ill."

Madame Wu rose. "Do go, Mother," she said. "We will remain with the guests in the other room."

She waited while two servants led Old Lady out, and all the guests stood. Then she looked at Mr. Wu.

"Will you take your guests to the main hall?" she directed gently. "The ladies will come into my own sitting-room." She moved away as she spoke, and the women followed her, and the men went with Mr. Wu in dividing streams. Children were taken to the courts and held by their nurses while they slept.

Madame Wu paused at the door. "Take the sick little one to the bamboo bedroom," she directed its nurse, "it is cool there. He must sleep a while." The child who had been wailing stopped suddenly at the sound of her voice.

The feast was over, but in her sitting-room Madame Wu maintained her delicate dignity over the women. She spoke little, but her silence was not noticed because she was by habit a silent woman. Only when some decision had to be made did they turn to her by instinct, for they knew that in this house she made all decisions. Then whatever she had decided she made known in a few simple, clear words, her voice always pretty and smooth and gentle as water slipping over stones.

32

Round her the talk ebbed and flowed. A small troupe of actors had been hired for entertainment, and they performed their tricks. The children watched with pleasure, and the elders watched while they talked and sipped hot tea of the finest leaves plucked before summer rains fell. In the presence of younger women there was no talk possible between the older women, and Madame Kang slept a little. Once Madame Wu said to Ying, "Go and see if our Old Lady is ill."

Ying went away and came back laughing. "She has been ill and has cast up everything," she told Madame Wu. "But she says it was worth it."

Everyone laughed, and at the sound of the laughter Madame Kang woke. "It is time we went home," she said to Madame Wu. "We must not weary you, Sister, for you are to live a hundred years."

Madame Wu smiled and rose as one by one the guests came to her to say good-bye. Packets of sweetmeats and gifts and money from the guests had been prepared for the servants, and now Ying brought these in on a tray and servants came in to receive them. They bowed before Madame Wu, their hands clasped politely on their breasts, and Madame Wu replied to each one courteously and gave him his gifts. All these servants had feasted, too, in the kitchens.

So at last she was alone again, and she allowed herself to be weary for one moment. Small muscles that held her bones gracefully erect relaxed at throat and breast and waist, and for a moment she looked wilted as a flower and now almost her age. Then she straightened her slender shoulders. It was too soon to be weary. The day was not yet ended.

. . . . . .

An hour later, after she had rested, she rose and walked up and down the room seven times. Then she went to the window and leaned on the low sill. The window was long and wide, and the lattices were thrown back. Outside was the court where she had sat this morning with Madame Kang and then with Liangmo. She recalled their horror at what she was about to do, and unconsciously she smiled her pretty smile which was neither sad nor gay.

Ying at this moment appeared at the round moon gate of

the court and she caught the smile. "Lady, you look like a young girl there in the moonlight!" she called.

Madame Wu's smile did not change, but she turned and sat down at the toilet table. Ying came in and took off her garments down to the fine white silk of her innermost ones. Then she let down Madame Wu's long hair and began to comb it in firm strong strokes with the fine-toothed sandalwood comb. She saw the quiet face in the mirror and saw how large and black the eyes looked to-night.

"Are you tired, Lady?" Ying asked.

"Not at all," Madame Wu replied.

But Ying went on, "You have had a long day. And now, Lady, you are forty and beginning another kind of life, and I think you ought not to work so hard. You should give over the government of the house and shops to your eldest son, and you should let your son's wife direct the kitchens, and even your second son's wife could attend to the supervision of the servants. Now you should sit in the court and read and look at your flowers and remember how good your life is under this roof, and how your sons' wives are bearing sons."

"Perhaps you are right," Madame Wu replied. "I have been thinking of such things myself. Ying, I shall ask my sons' father to take a small wife."

She said this so calmly that for a moment she knew it was not comprehended. Then she felt the comb stop in her hair, and she felt Ying's hand holding her hair together tighten at the nape of her neck.

"It is not necessary for you to speak," Madame Wu said. The comb began to move again too quickly. "You are pulling my hair," Madame Wu said.

Ying threw the comb on the floor. "I will not take care of any lady but you!" she burst forth.

"It is not asked of you," Madame Wu replied.

But Ying went down on her knees on the tiled floor beside Madame Wu, and she sobbed and wiped her eyes with the corner of the new sateen jacket which she had put on for the day. "Oh, my mistress!" she sobbed. "Does he compel you, my precious? Has he forgotten all your goodness and your beauty? Tell me just one thing——"

"It is my own will," Madame Wu said firmly. "Ying, get up from your knees. If he comes in he will think I have been beating you—"

34

"You!" Ying sobbed. "You who could never put your hand to pinch a mosquito, even when it sucks your blood!" Neverthless, she rose and took up the comb from the floor and, sniffling in her tears, again she combed Madame Wu's hair.

Madame Wu began to speak in her quiet, reasonable voice. "I tell you first, Ying, so that I may tell you how to behave among the servants. There is to be no loud talk among you and no blaming this one and that. When the young woman comes——"

"Who is she?" Ying asked.

"I do not know yet," Madame Wu said.

"When does she come?" Ying interrupted again.

"I have not decided," Madame Wu said. "But when she comes she is to be received as one honoured in the house, a little lower than I am, a little higher than my sons' wives. She will not be an actress or a singing girl or any of those persons, but a good woman. Everything is to be done in order. Above all, there is not to be a word spoken against my sons' father or against the young woman, for it is I who will invite her to come."

Ying could not bear this. "Lady, since we have been together so many years, is it allowed for me to ask you why?"

"You may ask, but I will not tell you," Madame Wu said tranquilly.

In silence Ying finished combing the long hair and scenting it and braiding it. She wound it into a coil for Madame Wu's bath, and then she supervised the pouring of the water in the bathroom. There stood a deep round jar of green-lined pottery, and two water-carriers brought in great wooden buckets of hot and cold water through an outer door and poured it in and went away again. Ying tried the water with her hand and dropped in scent from a bottle and then, holding fresh soap and silken towels, she went into the other room.

"Your bath is ready, Lady," she said as she said every night.

Madame Wu took off her last garments and walked, as slender as a young girl, quite naked across the room and into the bathroom. She took Ying's hand and stepped into the tub, and sat cross-legged in the water while Ying washed her as tenderly as though she were a child. The water was clear,

35

and Madame Wu's exquisite flesh was ivory white against the deep green of the porcelain. The water was about her shoulders, and as she thus sat submerged she reflected on her own wisdom. Her body was actually as beautiful as it had ever been. Mr. Wu had not allowed her to suckle her children, and her little breasts looked like lotus buds under water.

When she stepped out Ying wrapped her in the silken sheet and pressed her flesh dry and put fresh silk night garments upon her, and tended the nails of her hands and her feet. Then when all was finished she opened the door of the bedroom. It was still empty, for Mr. Wu never came in until Ying had gone away. There were, of course, some nights when he never came at all, but these were few. Madame Wu stepped upon the long carved stool at the bedside, and from this into the high, silk-canopied bed.

"Shall I not draw the bed curtains?" Ying asked. "The moonlight is too bright."

"No," Madame Wu said, "let me see the moonlight."

So the curtains remained behind the big silver hooks, and Ying felt for the teapot and for the little silver pipe which Madame Wu smoked sometimes in the night if she were sleepless, and she saw that the matches were beside the candle.

"Until to-morrow," Madame Wu said.

"Until to-morrow, Lady," Ying said, and went away.

Madame Wu lay very still and straight under the silken sheet and the soft silk-stuffed summer quilt. The moonlight shone upon the wall opposite her bed. It was bright indeed, so bright that she could see the outlines of the picture on the scroll which hung there. It was a simple picture but painted by an artist. He had used space instead of much paint, and with only a few strokes of his brush he had suggested a cliff and a crest upon a mountain, and a small bent figure struggling upward. None could' tell whether this was a man or a woman. It was only a human creature.

Sometimes, or so it appeared to Madame Wu, this small figure seemed higher on his climb than he did at other times. Sometimes he seemed to have fallen back many miles. She knew, of course, that this depended entirely upon how the light fell from the window. To-night the edge of the window cut the picture with shadow and then light so that the human creature seemed suddenly to be very near the top of the mountain. But still she knew that he was exactly where he had always been, and neither higher nor lower.

She lay, not thinking, not remembering, but simply being all that she was. She was neither waiting nor expecting. If he did not come to-night she would presently fall asleep and tell him at another time. Times were chosen and appointed. If one forced them, they were wrong. All the quiet strength of her decision would gather round the opportune moment, and then it would become actually right.

At this moment she heard the footsteps of Mr. Wu coming solidly through the courtyard. He came through the outer room and into her sitting-room. Then the door opened and he stood there in his bedroom. He had been drinking wine. Her sensitive nostrils caught the smell of heated wine as the alcohol distilled through his breath and his skin. But she was not disturbed, for he did not drink to excess at any time, and to-night of course he had been drinking with friends. What was more natural at the end of a feast day than such drinking? He had his pipe in his hand, and he was about to put it on the table. Then he delayed for an instant and stood holding it in his hand.

"Are you tired?" he asked abruptly.

"Not at all tired," she replied tranquilly.

He put the pipe down and, loosening the curtains from their hook, he got into bed behind them.

After twenty-four years, there was, of course, a certain routine in their life. She would like to have varied it somehow, since this was the last night that he would spend with her. But she had already considered such variation and had decided against it. It would only be harder for her to convince him of the wisdom of her decision—that is, if he needed convincing. She had tried to prepare herself for the possibility that he might even be pleased. In that case it would be easier. But he might not be pleased. There was also the possibility that he would refuse to the end to accept her decision. But she thought he would not refuse, certainly not to the end.

She was careful, therefore, to be almost exactly the median of what she always was. That is, she was neither cold nor ardent. She was pleasant, she was tender. She saw to it that nothing was lacking, but that nothing was over and above.

Fulfilment and not surfeit was her natural gift in all things.

She was, however, somewhat disconcerted to find that he himself was not quite as usual. He seemed disturbed and a little distracted.

"You were more beautiful to-day than you have ever been," he murmured. "Everybody said so."

She smiled up into his eyes that were above hers as she lay on the pillow. It was her usual pretty smile, but in the half-light of the single candle on the little table by the bed, she saw his dark eyes flicker and burn with a flame certainly more intense than she had seen for a long time. She closed her eyes, and her heart began to beat. Would she regret her decision? She lay as soft as a plucked flower for the next two hours, asking herself many times this question. Would she regret? Would she regret?

At the end of the two hours she knew she would not regret. When he slept she rose and went silently into her bathroom and bathed herself again in cool water. She did not go back to the bed where he lay outflung, sleeping in deep-drawn breaths. She picked up her own little pipe and filled its tiny bowl with sweet tobacco and lit it. Then she went to the window and stood watching the sky. The moon was almost down. In another five minutes it would have sunk behind the long lines of roofs of this ancient house. Peace filled her being. She would never sleep in this room again as long as she lived. She had already chosen her place. Next to Old Lady's court was the empty one where Mr. Wu's father had once lived. She would take that one, on the pretext that she could watch Old Lady by night as well as by day. It was a beautiful court in the very centre of the great house. She would live there, alone and at peace, the single heart in all the life that went on about her.

From the big bed Mr. Wu suddenly yawned and woke. "I ought to go back to my own rooms," he said. "You have had a long day and you should sleep."

Whenever he said that, and he always said it, being a courteous man in love as well as in business, she always replied, "Do not move, I beg you. I can sleep very well."

But to-night she did not say this. She replied, without turning her head, "Thank you, father of my sons. Perhaps you are right."

He was so astonished at this that he climbed out of the bed

38

and fumbled for his slippers on the floor. But he could not find them, and then she came quickly and knelt and found them and still kneeling she put them on his feet. And he, like a big child, suddenly leaned his head on her shoulder and twined his arms about her body.

"You are more fragrant than a jessamine flower," he murmured.

She laughed softly in his embrace. "Are you still drunk?"

"Drunk," he murmured, "drunk—drunk!"

He drew her towards him again, and she grew alarmed. "Please," she said, "may I help you to rise?" She rose, suddenly steel-strong, and pulled him upward with her.

"Have I offended you?" he asked. He was now wholly awake. She saw his dark eyes clear.

"No," she said. "How can you offend me after twenty-four years? But—I have come to an end?"

"Come to an end?" he repeated.

"Today I am forty years old," she said. She knew suddenly that this was the moment, now, in the middle of the night when around them the whole house lay sleeping. She moved away from him as he sat there on the bed and lit the other candles with the one that burned. One after another they flared, and the room was full of light. She sat down by the table, and he sat on the bed, staring at her.

"I have been preparing for this day for many years," she said. She folded her hands on her knees. In her white silken garments, in the moonlight, her hands on her knees, she summoned all the strong forces of her being.

He leaned forward, his hands clasped between his knees, still staring at her.

"I have been a good wife to you," she said.

"Have I not been a good husband to you?" he asked.

"That, always," she replied. "As men and women go, there could not be better than we have had. But now the half of my life is over."

"Only half," he said.

"Yet the half of yours is far away," she went on. "Heaven has made this difference between men and women."

He listened as he listened to anything she said, as though he knew that her words always carried a weight of meaning beyond their bare frame and beyond, perhaps, his comprehension.

39

"You are a young man still," she went on. "Your fires are burning and strong. You ought to have more sons. But I have completed myself."

He straightened his lounging body, and his full handsome face grew stern. "Can it be that I understand what you mean?" he asked.

"I see that you do understand," she replied.

They looked at each other across the twenty-four years they had spent together in this house where their children now slept, where Old Lady slept her light, aged sleep while she waited to die.

"I do not want another woman." His voice was rough. "I have never looked at another woman. You have been more beautiful than any woman I ever saw, and you are still more beautiful now than any woman."

He hesitated, and his eyes fell from her face to his hands. "I saw that young girl to-day—and I thought when I saw her, how much more beautiful are you than she!"

She knew at once what young girl he meant. "Ah, Linyi is pretty," she agreed. Inwardly she renewed her decision. When the talk had proceeded to the matter of who should choose another woman for him, she would choose. It would be ill for the house if the generations were mingled, and Liangmo was already married to Meng, the sister of Linyi, who were both daughters of her own closest friend.

He pursed his smooth, full lips. "No," he said, "I will not agree to your plan. What would my friends say? I have never been a man to go after women."

She laughed softly and was amazed as she laughed that she suffered a small pang in her breast, like the prick of a dagger that does not pierce the skin. If he could begin to think of how it would seem to his friends, then he would be soon persuaded, sooner than she had thought.

"It looks very ill for a woman over forty to bear a child," she said. "Your friends would blame you for that too."

"Is it necessary for you to bear a child?" he retorted.

"It is always possible," she replied. "I should like to be spared the fear of embarrassing you."

He spoke of friends and she of shame. They had not yet come together. She must dig into his heart and pull her roots out of him, unless they were too deep.

He looked at her. "Have you ceased altogether to love me?" he asked.

She leaned forward towards him. This now was heart to heart. "I love you as well as ever," she said in her beautiful voice. "I want nothing but your happiness."

"How can this be my happiness?" he asked sadly.

"You know that I have always held your happiness in my hands," she replied. She lifted her two hands as though they held a heart. "I have held it like this, ever since the moment I first saw your face on our wedding day. I shall hold it like this until I die."

"My happiness would be buried with you if you should die before me," he said.

"No, for before I die I will put it into other hands, the hands which I will prepare for it," she said.

She saw her power over him gaining its way. He sat motionless, his eyes on her hands. "Trust me," she whispered, still holding her hands like a cup.

"I have always trusted you," he said.

She let her hands fall.

He went on doggedly, "I do not promise, I cannot, so quickly——"

"You need not promise anything," she said. "I shall not force you even if I could. When was force ever my way? No, we will put this aside now. Go back into the bed and let me cover you. The night is growing cool because it is so near dawn. You must sleep and do not wake early."

She guided him by quick, soft pressures on his shoulders, on his arms and hands. He obeyed her unwillingly, and yet he did obey her. "Mind you that I have promised you nothing," he kept saying.

"Nothing," she agreed. "Nothing!" And she drew the covers over him and put back one curtain for air and let down the other against the morning light when it came.

But he held her hand fast. "Where will you sleep?" he demanded.

"Oh—I have my bed ready," she said, half playfully. "To-morrow we will meet. Nothing will be changed in the house. We will be friends, I promise you, not separated by fears and shames——"

He let her go, lulled by her promising, beautiful voice.

41

She could always lull him. He never believed the fullness of all she meant.

And when he had dropped into sleep she went away and walked softly alone through the courts to the court next Old Lady's. By her order it had been kept clean and ready through the years since Old Gentleman had died, and only a few days ago she had seen to it that fresh bedding was laid ready upon the mattress of the bed. Into this new bedding she now crept. It felt chill and too new, and she trembled for a moment with the chill and with it a strange, sudden deathlike fatigue. Then, as though it were a sort of death into which she had come, dreamlessly she fell asleep.

BUT it is morning which sets the seal upon what the night has made. Right or wrong is clear only by the sun. Madame Wu woke on this day after her fortieth birthday with a new feeling of lightness. Her eyes fell upon the known but unfamiliar room. This room was very different from the one in which she had slept for years. That one had been decorated for a young woman, a woman who was wed to a man and was expected to bear him children. The embroideries upon the curtains of that bed were of fruits and signs of fecundity. That room she had left last night was just as it had been when Old Lady had sent her into it as a bride for her only son. Old Lady had bought such strong satins and such fast-coloured silks for the embroidered canopy that there was still no excuse after twenty-four years to buy a new one. The only object which Madame Wu had added to the room was the picture of the human creature struggling up the mountain. She missed this picture now. To-day she must have it brought here with her clothes and her toilet articles. Beyond that, her old room would be very suitable for a new young concubine. Let the fruits and fecund signs be for that one!

Madame Wu lay in her new bed alone. It was an even vaster bed than the one she had left, and as she lay in it she delicately probed her heart. Did she suffer to think that another would lie under the rose-red satin covers of her marriage bed? She did feel some sort of faint, distant pain, but it was neither close nor personal. It was a large pain, the pain which one must suffer when Heaven in its impenetrable wisdom decrees against the single soul. Thus she knew it would have been ineffably good and comforting to her had it been possible for Mr. Wu to have been ready to enter into the latter half of life with her. It would have been a miracle of content for her if out of his own fulfilment, and without sacrifice, he could have reached the same point of life that she had at the same time that she did.

She pondered for a long time. Why had Heaven not made

women twice as long-lived as men, so that their beauty and fertility might last as long as man lived and fade only with the generation? Why should a man's need to plant his seed continue too long for fulfilment in one woman?

"Women," she thought, "must therefore be more lonely than men. Part of their life must be spent alone, and so Heaven has prepared them.'

Her reason recalled her from such futile questioning. Could anyone change what Heaven had decreed? Heaven, valuing only life, had given seed to man, and earth to woman. Of earth there was plenty, but of what use was earth without seed? The truth was that a man's need went on even after his bones were chalk and his blood water, and this was because Heaven put the bearing of children above all else lest mankind die. Therefore must the very last seed in a man's loin be planted, and that this last seed might bear strong fruit, as the man grew old the seed must be planted in better and stronger soil. For any woman, therefore, to cling to a man beyond the time of her fertility was to defy Heaven's decree.

When she had thus reasoned, the distant large pain melted away in her, and she felt released and calm. She felt, indeed, restored to herself and almost as she had been as a girl. How strange and how pleasant it would be to lie down at night and know that she could sleep until morning, or if she were wakeful that she could be wakeful and not fear waking another! Her body was given back to her. She pushed up her sleeve from her arm and contemplated her flesh. It was as firm and as sound as ever. Nourished and cared for and infused now with new freedom, she would live to be a very old woman. But that she might live happily she must be careful in all her relationships, but most of all with him. She must not allow herself to be cut off from him. Certainly this would not be easy when the tie between them would no longer be of the flesh, but of the mind and the spirit. Then she must consider new ways of his dependence upon her, yet ways which would not in fairness divide him from the new-comer.

"I must somehow do my duty toward all," she murmured, and pulled the sleeve down again over her pretty arm.

Who was this young woman to be? Madame Wu had thought a great deal about her. Now she began thinking about her again. Clearly she should be someone very different from herself. She must be young, yet not younger than the daughters-in-law, for that would bring trouble into the house. The proper age would be twenty-two. She must not be too well-educated, for Madame Wu herself had learning. She must not be modern, for a modern young woman would not be satisfied to be a concubine and in a short time she would be pushing Madame Wu out of the way and demanding Mr. Wu's whole time and heart, and this would be shameful in the house before the sons. An older man may take a concubine in dignity, but he must not be possessed by her. Pretty of course she must be, but not so pretty that she would distract young men in the house, or indeed Mr. Wu himself. Pleasantly pretty would be enough. And since Madame Wu's own beauty had been of one sort, this young woman's should be of another. That is, she should be plump and rosy, and it would not matter if she were somewhat thick in the bones.

All this, Madame Wu reflected, pointed to a young woman country bred. Moreover, a country woman would have health and no bad habits and would be likely to have sound children. Children, of course, must be had, for no woman is content without children, and where there are none the woman grows peevish and dwells upon herself and fastens her demands upon the man. Mr. Wu must not be made less happy, certainly, by his concubine. "And she must be a little stupid," Madame Wu reflected, "in order that she will be content with what he gives her, and not wonder what is between him and me."

She now began to have a clear picture in her mind of this young woman. She saw a healthy, slightly stupid, pretty young woman, one fond of food, one who had not lived before in a rich house so that she would be a little fearful of this house, and one not stubborn or proud, so that she would not seek to overcome her fear by temper and noise.

"There must be many such common young women," Madame Wu thought cheerfully.

She decided as soon as she had risen and had tended to the duties of the day that she would send for the old woman who had been go-between for Meng. For Madame Wu had employed a go-between even with her friend, lest Madame Kang in her kindness demand too little, and later the

45

marriage would suffer because it had not been just. "This old Liu Ma must be called hither," Madame Wu thought, "and I will tell her plainly just what is wanted. It is as definite as an order for merchandise." So she thought and without cynicism.

Then she let her mind drift to these rooms in which she now would live the rest of her life. She would make very few changes here. She had always been fond of the old man who had been her father-in-law. Since he had never had a daughter, he had been good to her and when he found that she was intelligent and learned as well as beautiful, he had been very pleased indeed. He had put aside the convention which forbids an old man to speak to his son's wife. Many times he had even sent for her that he might read to her something from the old books in his library. She had learned to come to this library herself during his lifetime and read the books. Certain of these books he had put aside as unfitting for a woman, and she had never touched them. Now, however, since the first half of her life was over and she was alone, she could read them all.

It gave her pleasure to think of the library full of books now hers. She had not had time in these middle years of her life to look much into books. Mr. Wu did not enjoy reading, and therefore he did not like to see her with a book in her hand. To-day, after years of giving body and mind to others, she felt that she needed to drink deeply at old springs.

These rooms became every moment more her own. Old Gentleman had been so long dead that he had ceased to exist for her as flesh and blood. To-day when she thought of him he was a wise old mind, a calm old voice. There was therefore nothing in these rooms which she wanted changed, since she felt no flesh and blood were here. The bed curtains were of a thin dark-blue brocaded silk, speaking neither of passion nor of fecundity. The walls were whitewashed and creamy with age. The beams of the roof were unceiled. Doors and windows, chairs and table were heavy and smooth and of plain, polished wood dark with Ningpo varnish, that stain and oil which last generations in a house. The floor was of big square grey tiles, so old that they were hollowed beside the bed and at the door into the library. The bedroom was one of the three rooms, and the third was the long sitting-room which opened upon a court. Only in the court would she perhaps make a little change. The trees had grown together and did not let enough sun through, and the stones beneath them were slippery with moss.

Someone knocked at the door. "Come!" she called.

Ying came in, looking frightened. "I did not know where you were," she stammered. "I went everywhere. I went into your old room and waked the master, and he was angry with me."

"You will find me here now every morning until I die," Madame Wu said calmly.

．　　　．　　　．　　　．　　　．

The news filtered through the household while the day went on. Son told wife, and one wife told another, and Ying told the cook, and the head cook told his undercook, and so by the end of that day there was not a soul who did not know that Madame Wu had moved into Old Gentleman's rooms. Through servants the news was taken to Old Lady's own maid, and so to Old Lady, who would not believe it. Madame Wu had purposely not told Old Lady. She knew that Old Lady would hear it from her maid, and this was well, for then Old Lady's first temper would be spent on someone who was only a servant. After this was over, Old Lady would be torn by not knowing whether to quarrel first with her son or with her son's wife. If she came first to Madame Wu, this would mean she blamed her. If she came first to her son, this meant she felt her son was at fault.

Towards noon, when Madame Wu was reckoning the month's accounts in the sitting-room which was now hers, she saw Old Lady's maid leading her across the court. The trees had already been cut and carried away, and the moss-covered stones were scraped and cleaned of moss. Old Lady paused to see what had been done. She leaned on her maid's arm with one hand, and in the other hand she held her long dragon-headed staff. The sun poured down into the once shadowy court, and the fish in the central pool, blinded by the light, had dived into the mud, so that the water was empty. But a pair of bright blue dragon-flies danced above the water, drunk with the new sun.

"You have cut down the Pride of China tree," Old Lady said accusingly.

47

Madame Wu, who had risen and come to her side, smiled. "Those trees spring up so easily," she said, "and they grow so quickly. This one was not planted. It had only pushed itself up between two stones."

Old Lady sighed and walked on towards the door. When Madame Wu took her elbow she pushed her half-spitefully. "Don't touch me," she said peevishly. "I am very angry with you."

Madame Wu did not answer. She followed Old Lady into the sitting-room. "You didn't tell me you were moving in here," Old Lady said in her harsh high old voice. "I am never told anything in this house." She sat down as she spoke.

"I should have told you," Madame Wu agreed. "It was very wrong of me. I must ask you to forgive me."

Old Lady grunted. "Have you quarrelled with my son?" she asked severely.

"Not at all," Madame Wu replied. "Indeed, we never quarrel."

"Do not make words for me," Old Lady commanded. "I am able to hear the truth."

"I will not make words, Mother," Madame Wu replied. "Yesterday I was forty years old. I had long made up my mind that when that day came I would retire from my duties as a female and find someone for my lord who is young. He is only forty-five years old. He has many years left him yet."

Old Lady sat with her lean hands crossed on the dragon's head and peered at her son's wife. "Does he love someone else?" she demanded. "If he has been playing in flower houses, I will—I will——"

"No, there is no other woman," Madame Wu replied. "Your son is the best of men, and he has been nothing but good to me. I am selfish enough to want to keep fresh between us the good love we have had. This cannot be if I am ridden with fear of a belated child, and surely it cannot be if my own fires slacken while his burn on."

"People will say he has played the fool and you have revenged yourself," Old Lady said sternly. "Who will believe you have of your own will withdrawn yourself—unless indeed you have ceased to love him?"

"I have not ceased to love him," Madame Wu said.

48

"What is love between a man and woman if they don't go to bed together?" Old Lady inquired.

Madame Wu paused for a long moment before she answered this. "I do not know," she replied at last. "I have always wondered, and perhaps now I shall find out."

Old Lady snorted. "I hope that we will not all suffer from this," she said loudly. "I hope that a new trouble-maker will not come into this house!"

"That must be my care," Madame Wu admitted. "I should blame myself entirely were such a thing to happen."

"Where is this new woman?" Old Lady demanded. She was still aggrieved, but she felt anger melting out of her against her will. It was true that no woman wanted to conceive after she was forty. She herself had had this misfortune, but luckily the child had died at birth. Yet she remembered with clarity, as though it were yesterday instead of more than twenty years ago, her deep shame when she knew that at such an age she was pregnant. She had longed for more children until then, and yet when she was forty she wanted no more, and she had quarrelled with her husband through all those months of discontented waiting.

"Go and find yourself a whore," she had told the distressed man. "Go and find yourself some young girl who is always ready!"

Old Gentleman had been deeply pained at such remarks, and he had never come near her again. But he had never loved her so well again, either. She had often been teased by his reticence, for he was gentle and shy as too many books can make a man, but after that he became almost totally silent towards her. Yet she knew that the whole thing had been only an accident, and that he wanted a child of her no more than she did of him. Even now when she remembered her anger against him she felt a vague guilt. What had happened had been merely an act of nature, no more, and why should she have blamed her good old man?

Old Lady sighed. "Where is this woman?" she demanded again, forgetting that she had already asked this.

"I have not found her yet," Madame Wu said.

The bondmaid was listening to everything while she pretended to serve her old mistress by now pouring tea and now fanning her and now moving a screen so that the sun did not fall on her. But Madame Wu had considered this and

49

had told herself that it was well that all the servants should know everything from the source.

"She will be hard to find," Old Lady said stubbornly.

"I think not," Madame Wu replied. "I know exactly what she should be. It remains only not to take any other."

"Nevertheless," Old Lady went on, "I still feel I should blame my son."

"Please do not," Madame Wu begged her. "To blame him for anything would make him feel he is at fault in some way, and indeed there is no fault in him. He must not be made to feel self-reproach merely because I am forty years old. It would be most unjust."

Old Lady groaned. "O Heaven, that has made man and woman of two different earths!"

Madame Wu smiled at this. "You may blame Heaven, and I will not deny it."

There seemed nothing to say after that. Old Lady kept remembering the acuteness of her own like situation many years ago. She would have been angry if her son's father had taken a younger woman, even when she had cried at him to do so. This woman, her son's wife, was perhaps wiser.

Her mind slipped a little, as it did often now that she was old, and she looked about her. "Are you changing everything in these rooms?" she asked.

"I shall change nothing," Madame Wu said, "except that I have brought in that painting from my old room. I was always fond of it." The picture already hung opposite where she sat, for this morning immediately after she had eaten, she had bade Ying tell a manservant to bring it and hang it here. She had decided not to put it in the bedroom where it had hung before. In this bedroom she would only sleep.

Old Lady rose and went to the scroll and stood before it, leaning on her staff. "Is that a man or woman climbing the mountain?" she asked.

"I don't know," Madame Wu said. "It does not matter, perhaps."

"Lonely!" Old Lady muttered. "Lonely in the midst of all those mountains! I have always hated mountains."

"I suppose the person wouldn't be there if he minded loneliness," Madame Wu said.

But Old Lady whenever she felt sad immediately felt hunger also. The picture had made her sad.

She turned to Madame Wu with a piteous look. "I am hungry," she said. "I haven't eaten anything for hours."

Madame Wu said to the maid, "Take her back to her own rooms and let her eat anything she wants."

When Old Lady had gone, she sat down again to her reckoning. For the rest of the day no one came near her. The household was unhappy and silent. She wondered whether Mr. Wu would come to see her, and was surprised to find in herself some sort of shyness at the thought of him. But he, too, did not come near her. She understood exactly what was happening in the great house. The sons and sons' wives would have been talking half the day, arguing as to what should be done and said, and consulting with cousins and cousins' wives. Since they had reached no agreement none had come to her, and since elders did not come, children were kept away. As for the servants, it was only natural prudence which kept them quiet and at work until the air in the house had cleared. Only Ying served her all day long, and she said little, although her eyes were freshly red every time she came in. But Madame Wu pretended to see nothing. She spent the entire day on her accounts, which she had allowed to gather in the preparation for her birthday.

Now she studied one book after another, first the house accounts which the steward kept, then the clothing accounts, repaired and new, then the house repairs and replacements, always heavy in so large a family, and finally the land accounts. The ancestral lands of the Wu family were large and productive, and upon them and the shops the family depended. Neither Mr. Wu nor any of his sons had ever gone away to work. Some of the remoter cousins, it is true, had settled in other cities as merchants or in banks and trade, but even these, if they were temporarily out of work, came back to the land for a while to recover themselves. Madame Wu administered these lands as she did the house. It had been many years since Mr. Wu did more than read over the accounts once a year just before the old year passed into the new one. But Madame Wu studied the house accounts twice monthly and the land accounts every month. She knew exactly what the harvests of rice and wheat, eggs, vegetables and fuel were. The land steward reported to her any change or disaster. Sometimes she talked this over with Mr. Wu and

51

sometimes she did not. It depended on how tired she was. If she were tired she settled a matter herself.

This day she had spent in such work from early morning until dark, pausing only to supervise the hanging of the picture and the cutting away of the trees. Round her the house was as silent as though she were the only soul in it. The silence was restful to her. She would not, of course, want it every day. That would have been to enter too soon into death. But after forty years it was pleasant to spend one day entirely alone, without a single voice raised to ask her for anything. The accounts were accurate and satisfying. Less had been spent than had been taken in. The granaries were still not empty, and soon the new harvests would be reaped. The larders were full of food, both salted and fresh. Watermelons had ripened and were hanging in the deep wells to be cooled. The steward had written down in his little snakelike letters, "Nineteen watermelons, seven yellow-hearted, the rest red, hanging in the two north wells." She might have one drawn up to-night before she slept. Watermelons were good for the kidneys.

When the account books were closed she sat steeping herself in the sweet silent loneliness. She felt the weariness begin to seep from her like a poison breathed out of her lungs. She had been far more weary than she knew, a weariness not so much physical as spiritual. It was hard to define even where in the spirit it lay. Certainly her mind was not weary. It was hungry and alert and eager to exercise itself. It seemed to her that she had not really used her mind for a long time except in such things as reckoning accounts and settling quarrels and deciding whether a child should go to one school or another. No, her weariness was hid somewhere in her innermost being, perhaps in her belly and in her womb. She had been giving life for twenty-four years, before the children were born and after they were born, and now they would themselves give birth to other children. Mother and grandmother, she had been absorbed in giving birth. Now it was over.

At this moment she heard a footstep. It was clear and decided, clacking on the stones lightly as it approached. She wondered for a moment—leather shoes? Who wore leather shoes among the women? For it was a woman's footsteps. Then she knew. It was Rulan, the Shanghai wife of Tsemo, her second son. She sighed, reluctant to yield even for a moment her silence and loneliness. But she rebuked herself. No one must think she had withdrawn from the house. Rather, let them think of this as the centre of the house because she was here.

"Come hither, Rulan," she called. Her pretty voice was cheerful. When she looked up she saw the girl's dark eyes searching her face. The young woman stood in the doorway, tall and slender. Her straight, long robe was pinched in at the waist after the half-foreign fashion of Shanghai. Her bosom was flat. She was not beautiful because of her high cheekbones. Madame Wu's own face had the egg-shaped smoothness of classical beauty. Rulan's face was wide at the eyes, narrow at the chin. Her mouth was square and sullen.

Madame Wu ignored the sullenness. "Come in and sit down, child," she said. "I have just finished our family accounts. We are fortunate—the land has been kind."

The girl was plain, and yet she had flashes of beauty, Madame Wu thought, watching her as she sat down squarely upon a chair. She had none of the polish and courtesy which all the other young women in the house had. Instead, it seemed that this girl even took pleasure in being rude and always abrupt. Madame Wu looked at her with interest. It was the first time she had ever been alone with Rulan.

"You must be careful of your beautiful mouth, my child," she now said in that gentle dispassionate manner which all young persons found disconcerting, since it was neither chiding nor advising.

"What do you mean?" Rulan stammered. Her lips quivered when they parted.

"It is a lovely trembling mouth now," Madame Wu said. "But women's mouths change as they grow older. Yours will become more lovely as it grows firm, or it will become coarse and stubborn."

Her cool voice conveyed no interest, merely the statement of what was to be expected. Rulan might have declared, had there been any interest, that she did not care what her mouth became. But confused by the coolness, she merely pressed her red lips together for a moment and drew her black brows together.

"Did you come to speak to me about something?" Madame Wu inquired. She had changed her seat to one more comfortable than the straight wooden chair by the table. This one was wooden, too, but the back was rounded. Yet she did not lean against it. She continued to sit upright while she filled her little pipe. She lit it and took her two customary dainty puffs.

"Our Mother!" Rulan began impetuously. She was pent and disturbed, yet she did not know how to begin.

"Yes, child?" Madame Wu said mildly.

"Mother," Rulan began again, "you have upset everybody."

"Have I?" Madame Wu asked. Her voice was full of music and wonder.

"Yes, you have," Rulan repeated. "Tsemo said I wasn't to come and talk with you. He said that it was Liangmo's duty as the eldest son. But Liangmo won't. He said it would be no use. And Meng does nothing but cry. But I don't cry. I said someone must come and talk with you."

"And no one came except you," Madame Wu smiled slightly.

Rulan did not smile in reply. Her too-serious young face was agonized between shyness and determination. "Mother," she began yet again, "I have always felt you did not like me, and so I ought to be the last one to come to you."

"Child, you are wrong," Madame Wu said. "There is no one in the world whom I dislike, not even that poor foreign soul, Little Sister Hsia."

Rulan flinched. "You really do not like me," she argued. "I know that. I am older than Tsemo, and you do not like me for that. And you never forgive me that we fell in love in Shanghai and decided ourselves to marry instead of letting you arrange our affairs."

"Of course I did not like that," Madame Wu agreed. "But when I had thought about it I knew that I wanted Tsemo's happiness, and when I saw you I knew he was happy, and so I was pleased with you. That you are older than he you cannot help. It is annoying in the house, but I have managed in spite of it. One can manage anything."

"But if I were like Meng and the others," Rulan said in her stormy impetuous way, "I would not feel so badly now over what you have done. Mother, you must not let Father take another woman."

"It is not a matter of letting him," Madame Wu said, still

54

mildly. "I have decided that it is the best thing for him."

The colour washed out of Rulan's ruddy face. "Mother, do you know what you do?"

"I think I know what I do," Madame Wu said.

"People will laugh at us," Rulan said. "It's old-fashioned to take a concubine."

"For Shanghai people, perhaps," Madame Wu said, and her voice conveyed to Rulan that it did not matter at all what Shanghai people thought.

Rulan stared at her in stubborn despair. This cool woman who was her husband's mother was so beautiful, so perfect, that she was beyond the reach of all anger, all reproach. She knew long ago that against her she could never prevail with Tsemo. His mother's hold upon him was so absolute that he did not even rebel against it. He was convinced that whatever his mother did was finally for his own good. To-day when the women were storming against the idea of the new woman and Liangmo had only been silent, Tsemo had shrugged his shoulders. He was playing chess with Yenmo, his younger brother.

"If our mother wants a concubine," he said, "it is for a reason, for she never acts without reason. Yenmo, it is your turn."

Yenmo played without heeding the turmoil. Of all his brothers he loved Tsemo best, for he played with him every day. Without him Yenmo would have been lonely in this house full of women and children.

"Reason!" Rulan had cried with contempt.

"Guard your tongue," Tsemo had said sternly, not lifting his eyes from the chessboard.

She had not dared disobey him. Though he was younger than she, he had something of his mother's calm, and this gave him power over her storm and passion. But she had secretly made up her mind to come alone to Madame Wu.

She clenched her hands on her knees and gazed at her. "Mother, it is now actually against the laws for a man to take a concubine, do you know that?"

"What laws?" Madame Wu asked.

"The new laws," Rulan cried, "the laws of the Revolutionary party!"

"These laws," Madame Wu said, "like the new Constitution, are still entirely on paper."

She saw that Rulan was taken aback by her use of the word Constitution. She had not expected Madame Wu to know about the Constitution.

"Many of us worked hard to abolish concubinage," she declared. "We marched in procession in the Shanghai streets in hottest summer, and our sweat poured down our bodies. We carried banners insisting on the one-wife system of marriage as they have it in the West. I myself carried a blue banner that bore in white letters the words 'Down with concubines.' Now when someone in my own family, my own husband's mother, does a thing so old-fashioned, so—so wicked—for it is wicked, Mother, to return to the old cruel ways——"

"My dear child," Madame Wu asked in her sweet, reasonable voice, "what would you do if Tsemo one day should want another wife, someone, say, less full of energy and wit than you are, someone soft and comfortable?"

"I would divorce him at once," Rulan said proudly. "I would not share him with any other woman."

Madame Wu lit her little pipe again and took two more puffs. "A man's life is made up of many parts," she said. "As a woman grows older she perceives this."

"I believe in the equality of man and woman," Rulan insisted.

"Ah," Madame Wu said, "two equals are nevertheless not the same two things. They are equal in importance, equally necessary to life, but not the same."

"That is not what we think nowadays," Rulan said. "If a woman is content with one man, a man should be content with one woman."

Madame Wu put down her pipe. "You are so young," she said reflectively, "that I wonder how I can explain it. You see, my child, content is the important thing—the content of a man, the content of a woman. When one reaches the measure of content, shall that one say to the other, 'Here you must stop because I am now content'?"

"But Liangmo told us our father does not want another one," Rulan said doggedly.

Madame Wu thought, "Ah, Liangmo has been talking to his father today!" She felt a moment's pity for her husband, at the mercy of his sons for no fault of his own.

"When you have lived with a man for twenty-four years as

56

his wife," she said gently, "you have lived with him to the end of all knowledge."

She sighed and suddenly wished this young woman away. And yet she liked her better than she ever had before. It took courage to come here alone, to speak these blunt, brave, foolish words.

"Child," she said, leaning towards Rulan, "I think Heaven is kind to women, after all. One could not keep bearing children for ever. So Heaven in its mercy says when a woman is forty, 'Now, poor soul and body, the rest of your life you shall have for yourself. You have divided yourself again and again, and now take what is left and make yourself whole again, so that life may be good to you for yourself, not only for what you give but for what you get.' I will spend the rest of my life assembling my own mind and my own soul. I will take care of my body carefully, not that it may any more please a man, but because it houses me and therefore I am dependent upon it."

"Do you hate us all?" the girl asked. Her eyes opened wide, and Madame Wu saw for the first time that they were very handsome eyes.

"I love you all more than ever," Madame Wu said.

"Our father, too?" the girl inquired.

"Him, too," Madame Wu said. "Else why would I so eagerly want his happiness?"

"I do not understand you," the girl said after a moment. "I think I do not know what you mean."

"Ah, you are so far from my age," Madame Wu replied. "Be patient with me, child, for knowing what I want."

"You really are doing what you want to do?" Rulan asked doubtfully.

"Really, I am," Madame Wu replied tenderly.

Rulan rose. "I shall have to go back and tell them," she said. "But I do not think any of them will understand."

"Tell them all to be patient with me," Madame Wu said, smiling at her.

"Well, if you are sure——" Rulan said, still hesitating.

"Quite sure," Madame Wu said.

She was glad once more of the loneliness and the silence when Rulan had gone. She smiled a little to think of the family gathered together without her, all in consternation, all wondering what to do, because for the first time in their

57

knowledge of her she had done something for herself alone. But as she smiled she felt full of peace. Without waiting for Ying, since she was two hours before her usual time for bed, she bathed and put on her white silk night garments and lay down in the huge dark-curtained old bed. When Ying came in an hour later she was frightened at the silence and ran to the bedroom. There behind the undrawn bed-curtains she saw her mistress lying small and still upon the bed. She ran forward, terror in her heart, to gaze upon that motionless figure.

"Oh, Heaven," Ying moaned, "Our Lady is dead!"

But Madame Wu was not dead, only sleeping, although Ying had never seen her sleep like this. Even her outcry did not wake the sleeping lady. "She whom the flutter of a bird in the eaves wakes at dawn!" Ying marvelled. She stood for a moment looking down on the pure beauty of Madame Wu's face, then she stepped back and drew the heavy curtains.

"She is tired to the heart," Ying muttered. "She is tired because in this great house all feed on her, like suckling children."

She paused at the door of the court and looked fiercely right and left. But no one was coming, and certainly not Mr. Wu.

.   .   .   .   .

In Liangmo's court the two elder sons and their wives talked together until the water clock had passed the first half of the night. The two young husbands were silent for the most part. They felt confused and shy for their father's sake. He, too, was a man, as they were now. When they were in their middle years, would it be so with themselves and their wives? They doubted themselves and hid their doubt.

Of the two young wives, Meng was the more silent. She was too happy in her own life to quarrel with anyone for anything. Liangmo she held to be the handsomest and best of men, and she wondered continually that she had been so fortunate as to be given him for life. There was nothing in him which was not to her taste. His strong young body, his good temper, the sweetness of his ways, his endless kindness, his patience, his ready laughter, the way his lips met each other, the flatness of his cheeks, the heavy smoothness of his black hair, the firm softness of his hands, his dry, cool, palms —she knew and rejoiced in all. She found no fault in him. She was lost in him and content to be lost. She wanted no being of her own. To be his, to lie in his arms at night, to serve him by day, to fold his garments, to bring his food herself, to pour his tea and light his pipe, to listen to his every word, to busy herself with healing any slight headache, to test the flavour of a dish or the heat of the wine, these were her joys and her occupations. But above all was the bearing of his children. To bear him many children was her sole desire. She was his instrument for immortality.

Now as always when he was present she thought of him and heard the voices of others through the golden haze of her joy in him. That his father might take a concubine only made Liangmo more perfect in her eyes. There was no one like Liangmo. He was better than his father, wiser, more faithful. And Liangmo was content with her.

While Rulan talked, Meng listened, thinking of Liangmo. When Rulan demanded of her, "Meng, you are the eldest son's wife—what do you think?" then Meng turned to Liangmo to know what she thought.

Be sure Rulan knew this and was contemptuous of Meng for having no mind of her own. She, too, loved her young husband, and she declared to Tsemo often enough when they were alone that she loved him more for not being a fool as Liangmo was. Secretly she grieved because Tsemo was not the elder son. He was stronger than Liangmo, keener, quicker, thin and sharp-tongued. Liangmo was like his father, but Tsemo was like his mother. Even while she quarrelled with him she loved him well. But quarrel with him she did very often, hating herself for it while she did it. Every quarrel ended in her stormy repentance, and this repentance came from her constant secret fear, hidden even from herself, because she was older than Tsemo and because she knew that she had loved him before he loved her. Yes, this was her secret shame—that she had set her heart upon him in the school where they had met, and her heart had compelled her to seek him out with ill-concealed excuses of books she could not understand and lecture notes she had lost, and anything she could devise to bring him to her. Hers had been the first offer of friendship, and hers the hand first put out to touch his.

All this she had excused boldly to herself and to him because, she said, she was a new woman, not old-fashioned, not fearful of men, but believing, she said, that men and women were the same. But she knew, all the time, that Tsemo was the younger and that he had never known a woman before, and that he was hard pressed by her love and had yielded to it, but not with his whole being. "You are afraid of your old-fashioned mother!" she had cried.

To this he had made answer, thoughtfully, "I am afraid of her because she is always right."

"No one is always right," Rulan had declared.

"You do not know my mother," Tsemo had replied, laughing. "Even when I wish her wrong, I know she is right. She is the wisest woman in the world."

These words he had said innocently, but with them he had thrust a dagger into Rulan's heart, and there it stayed. She came to the Wu house ready to hate Tsemo's mother and be jealous of her, and was angry because she could neither hate nor be jealous. For Madame Wu's cool kindness to all alike gave no handle. If she felt Rulan's hatred she did not show it, and the young woman soon saw that Madame Wu cared neither for love nor hate.

Nor could the young wife be jealous. In one of their quarrels she had flung this back at Tsemo, "Why do you love your mother so much? She does not love you so much."

To this Tsemo replied with usual coolness, "I do not want to be loved too much."

Thus he flung the barb back again at Rulan and left it in her quivering flesh. But she was easily wounded, her heart always open and ready for hurt, and her pride quivering.

"I suppose you think I love you too much!" she had burst out at Tsemo then.

But this he would not answer. He was a debonair figure, his shoulders broad, his waist narrow. All the sons were handsome except Yenmo, who was too fat yet, but Tsemo had a certain look more noble than them all. This noble look tortured Rulan. Was it a sign of his soul or only a trick of bones fitted together in his skull and covered with fine flesh and smooth golden skin? She did not know, and he hid the truth from her, or she thought he did.

"Tell me what you are thinking," she demanded of him often.

Sometimes he told her, sometimes he would not. "Leave me a little privacy," he said harshly then.

"You do not love me!" she cried too often.

"Do I not?" he would reply, and she cursed her nagging, tearing tongue. Yet there were times when he did love her with all the kindness she demanded, and how was she to know what were those times? Alone she raged against his cheerfulness and put herself at the mercy of her own love and longed to be free of it because it made her less than he and dependent on him. But how could she be free of chains she had put upon herself? Her soul was all tempest. The dreams she had once had of her life were dead. She was in prison in the house. And yet who was her jailer except herself?

In this tempest she lived as secretly as she could, but she could not hide it all. Her temper was quick and her scorn hot. She blamed servants easily, and they were not used to discourtesy in this house and so they served her less well than the others in the family and laughed at her in the kitchens, and be sure one always told her of this laughter. And she was peevish often and thought everything inconvenient and old.

"In Shanghai we had self-come water and self-come light," she would say, and complained against baths bucket-filled and against candles and oil lamps. But who heeded her? She was only one amongst sixty-odd souls under the Wu roof, and she had not even borne a child yet.

When, therefore, she complained too long this night against his father, Tsemo grew weary of her. He yawned and stretched himself and burst out laughing.

"Our poor father!" he said cheerfully. "After all, it is he whom we must pity, if we are to listen to you, Rulan. We will only see the woman in passing, but he must have her as his burden day and night. Come, girl, it is midnight. Go to bed and rest yourself—and give me rest."

He rose, shook himself, rubbed his hands through his hair, whistled to her as though she were his dog, and went away. What could she do but follow him to their own court?

★ 3 ★

In the morning, after a full night's sleep, Madame Wu woke. This was one of her blessings, that after sleep and when she waked, before her eyes she saw the path like moonlight upon a dark sea, the path she chose to walk. It lay clear before her now.

"I must choose the woman at once," she told herself. The household could not be at ease in this waiting. She would therefore to-day send for the old woman go-between and inquire what young women, country bred, might be suitable. She had already brought to her own memory all others that she knew, but there was not one whom she wanted. All were either too high or too low, the daughters of the rich, who would be proud and troublesome, or so foreign-taught that they might even want her put away. Or they were the daughters of the poor who would be equally proud and troublesome. No, she must find some young woman who had neither too much nor too little, so that she might be free from fear and envy. And it would be better, she reflected, if the young woman were wholly a stranger, and her family strangers, too, and if possible, distant, so that when she came into the house she would take up all her roots and bring them here and strike them down afresh.

When Ying came in with the morning's tea and sweetmeats she said after greeting, "As soon as I have eaten I will talk with that old Liu Ma."

"Yes, Lady," Ying said sadly.

In silence she helped Madame Wu to rise and dress. She brushed the long satin-smooth hair and coiled it, and then she went away and came back with Madame Wu's breakfast. All this time she did not speak a word, nor did Madame Wu speak either. She let herself be dressed, her thin, beautiful body as limp as a doll's in Ying's hands. But she ate well and felt content.

She had scarcely finished the last cup of tea when Ying brought Liu Ma. Be sure Lui Ma knew already why she had been called. She had her paid spies in every rich household

62

to tell her when discontent rose between men and women. Her flat, broad nose had as delicate a scent for mating man and woman as a hound's has for wild flesh. Thus she knew that a concubine was to be found for Mr. Wu. But she was too knowing to let Madame Wu see that she had any such knowledge. Instead she pretended that of course the reason for this meeting was that Madame Wu must want to betroth Fengma, her third son.

But Madame Wu was wise also in the ways of human beings, and she was sure that Liu Ma knew everything from servant's mouth to servant's ear, and so she allowed Liu Ma to think she was deceiving.

"You are early, Lady," Liu Ma panted as she came in. She was a short fat woman who in her girlhood had been in a flower house. But she grew fat very early and found that she could earn more money by bringing other women to men than herself, and so she had married a small shopkeeper, giving him for dowry the money she had saved, and she took up the profession of go-between for good families.

"I like the early morning," Madame Wu replied gently.

She did not rise, since Liu Ma was her inferior, but she motioned the old woman kindly to take a seat, and Ying poured tea for her and went away.

Liu Ma supped her tea loudly. She made no remark on Madame Wu's having moved to this court. Instead she said in her hoarse voice, "You are more beautiful than ever. Your lord is very lucky."

This she said by way of introducing the subject of concubines. For now, she thought, Madame Wu would sigh and say, alas, that her beauty stood her in no stead. But Madame Wu only thanked her.

Liu Ma took out a square of white cotton cloth and coughed into it. She knew better than to spit on the floor in this house. Everyone knew that Madame Wu was as particular as a foreigner in such matters. Then she began again.

"I thought that you might be wanting a fine young girl for your third son, and so I brought some pictures with me."

She had on her knees an oblong package tied up in a blue cotton handkerchief. This she untied. Inside was an old foreign magazine which had pictures of motion picture actresses. She opened this and took out some photographs.

"I have now three young girls, all very good bargains," she said.

"Only three?" Madame Wu murmured, smiling.

This old Liu Ma always roused her secret laughter. Her merchandise was the passion between men and women, and she bartered it as frankly as though it were rice and eggs and cabbage.

"I do not mean to say three is all I have," Liu Ma made haste to reply. "Surely I have as good clients as any other go-between in the city. But these are my very best. These three young girls have good families who are able to give money and the finest furniture and wedding garments."

"Let me see that foreign book," Madame Wu said. Now that the moment had come to choose a woman to take her place she felt half frightened. Perhaps she had undertaken more than she knew.

"None of these young women are mine," Liu Ma said. "They are only the electric shadow of women in America."

"I know that," Madame Wu said, laughing her soft laughter. "I am only curious to see what the foreigners think is beautiful in a woman."

She took from Liu Ma the paper book she held out. It was soiled but not wrinkled, for Liu Ma prized it. Neither of them could read the foreigners' language and so the names were unknown to them.

Madame Wu turned the pages and gazed at one gay face after another. "They all look alike," she murmured, "but then all foreigners do look alike, of course."

Liu Ma laughed loudly. "Certainly Little Sister Hsia is not like these," she said. "I could marry off these, but not Little Sister Hsia!" Everybody in the city knew Little Sister Hsia, and jokes about her were told over counters, in shops, and in courtyards and teashops. All declared her good at heart, but they relished their laughter nevertheless. Only her one servant, an old man, defended her.

"Do not tell me you can understand what she says," a fish man at the market had teased the old man, while he weighed a small fish for Little Sister's noon meal.

"I can," the old man had sworn. "If I know what she is going to say, I can even understand her easily."

"Little Sister Hsia is a nun," Madame Wu replied to Liu

64

Ma. "A foreign nun. Nuns are not women. Where did you get such a book as this?"

"I bought it," Liu Ma said proudly. "A friend was going to Shanghai some five or six years ago, and I said I wanted such a book and he brought it back. I paid five dollars for it."

"Why did you want a book of foreign women?" Madame Wu inquired.

"Some men like to look at such faces," Liu Ma explained. "It rouses their desire and gives me business. Then also there are the new men who want modern women, and they point to one of these and say 'I want one like this'. I find a girl somewhere who will make herself look as near as she can to the one chosen."

Madame Wu closed the book quickly and gave it back to Liu Ma. "Let me see the three photographs," she said.

She took them without touching Liu Ma's dirty old hand and looked at them, one by one.

"But these three faces also look alike," she objected.

"Do not all young girls look alike?" Liu Ma retorted. "Bright eyes, shining hair, little noses and red lips—and if you take off their clothes what difference is there between one woman and another?" Her belly shook with laughter under her loose coat of shoddy silk. "But we must not tell the men that, my precious, else my business will be gone. We must make them think that each young girl is as different from another as jade is from pearls—all jewels, of course!" Her belly rumbled with her laughter.

Madame Wu smiled slightly and put the photographs down on the table. The young faces, all pretty, all set in smooth black hair, looked up at her. She turned them over, face down.

"Have you any girls whose families live at a distance?" she asked.

"Tell me exactly what you want," Liu Ma said. She felt now that they were coming to the heart of this hour, and she put her entire shrewd mind upon the matter.

"I seem to see the woman I want," Madame Wu said, half hesitating.

"Then she is as good as found," Liu Ma said eagerly, "if she is on the earth and not already gone to Heaven."

"A young woman," Madame Wu said, still in the same half-hesitating voice. She had not faltered at all before her

65

family in speaking of the young woman, but before this hard old soul who dealt in men and women as her trade, she knew she could hide nothing.

Liu Ma waited, her sharp small eyes fixed on Madame Wu's face. Madame Wu turned her head away and gazed into the court. It was a fine morning, and the sun lay on the newly cleaned stones, and they showed faint colours of pink and blue and yellow.

"A pretty woman," Madame Wu said faintly, "very pretty but not beautiful. A girl—a woman, that is—about twenty-two years old, round-cheeked and young and soft as a child, ready in her affection to love anybody and not just one man —someone who does not, indeed, love too deeply any man, and who will, for a new coat or a sweet, forget a trouble —who loves children, of course, good-tempered—and whose family is far away so that she will not be always crying for home——"

"I have exactly what you want," Liu Ma said in triumph. Then her round face grew solemn. "Alas," she said, "no, the girl is an orphan. You would not want one of your sons to marry an orphan who does not know what her parents were. No, no, that would be to bring wild blood into the house."

Madame Wu brought back her gaze from the court and let it fall on Liu Ma's face. "I do not want the girl for Fengmo," she said calmly. "For him I have other plans. No, this girl is to be a small wife for my own lord."

Liu Ma pretended horror and surprise. She pursed her thick lips and took out the square of cotton again and held it over her eyes.

"Alas," she muttered, "alas, even he!"

Madame Wu shook her head. "Do not misjudge him," she said. "It is entirely my own thought. He is very unwilling. It is I who insist."

Liu Ma took down the cloth from her eyes and thrust it into her large bosom again. "In that case," she said briskly, "perhaps the orphan is the very thing. She is strong and useful."

"I do not want a servant for myself," Madame Wu interrupted her. "I have plenty of servants for the house, and Ying has always taken care of me and would poison another. No, if she is a servant she will not do."

"She is not a servant," Liu Ma said in alarm. "What I mean is that she is so willing, so soft, so gentle——"

"But she must be quite hearty and healthy," Madame Wu insisted.

"That she is," Liu Ma replied. "In fact, also, she is quite pretty, and had she not been an orphan I could have married her off long months before this. But you know how it is, Lady. Good families do not want wild blood for their sons, and those who are willing to have her are somewhat too low for her. She is strong, but still she is not low. In fact, Lady, I had thought of putting her in a flower house for a while for the very purpose of finding some older man who might want her for a small wife. But Heaven must have been watching over her, that at this very moment when she is at her best you should be looking for just such a one as she is."

"Have you a picture of her?" Madame Wu inquired.

"Alas, no, I never thought of taking her picture, nor she of having a picture," Liu Ma said. "The truth is"—the cotton cloth came out and she coughed into it—"the girl's one fault is that she is simple and ignorant. The worst I had better tell you. She cannot read, Lady. In the old days this would have been considered even a virtue, but now, of course. it is fashionable for girls to read even as boys do. It is the foreign way that has crept into our country."

"I do not care if she cannot read," Madame Wu said.

Liu Ma's face broke into wrinkles of pleasure. She struck both her fat knees with her palms. "Then, Lady, it is done!" she cried. "I will bring her whenever you say. She is in the country with her foster mother on a farm."

"Who is this foster mother?" Madame Wu inquired.

"She is nothing," Liu Ma said eagerly. "I would not even tell you who she is. She found a child, Lady, one cold night, outside the city wall. Someone had left it there—a girl not wanted. The old woman was walking home after a feast meal with her brother who that day was thirty years old. He keeps a little market at—— No, I will not even tell of it. It is nothing where he is or what his market. She heard a baby cry and saw the girl. Now, she would not have taken another mouth home, for she is poor, but the truth is she had a son, and when she saw this girl she thought it might serve her one day as a wife for her son, and she would be saved the cost of finding one outside. How could she know her one son would

67

sicken and die before they could marry? Plague took him. She has the girl now and no husband for her."

Madame Wu listened to this without moving her eyes from Liu Ma's face. "Will she give the girl up altogether?" she now asked.

"She would be willing," Liu Ma said. "She is very poor, and after all the girl is not her bone and flesh."

Madame Wu turned her back to the court. The sun had crept over the wall and shortened and thickened and blackened the shadows of the bamboos on the stones. "I had better see her," she said musingly. She put her delicate finger to her lip as she did when she was thoughtful. "No, why should I?" she went on. "It would not be to your interest to deceive me, and as you say, one girl is like another, after we have decided on her nature."

"How much would you pay, Lady?" Liu Ma now inquired.

"I should have to dress her, of course," Madame Wu said thoughtfully.

"Yes, but since the old woman is not her mother she would not care what you did for that," Liu Ma said. "She would only want heavy silver in her hand."

"One hundred dollars is not too little for a country girl," Madame Wu said calmly. "But I will pay more than that. I will pay two hundred."

"Add fifty, Lady," Liu Ma said coaxingly. Sweat burst out of her dark skin. "Then I can give the two hundred whole to the woman. She will let the girl go to-day for that."

"Let it be then," Madame Wu said so suddenly that she saw a greedy sorrow shine in the small old eyes that were fastened on her anxiously. "You need not grieve that you did not ask more," she said. "I know what is just and what is generous."

"I know your wisdom, Lady," Liu Ma said eagerly. She fumbled the pictures together. Then she paused. "Are you sure you don't want a pretty wife for your son, too, Lady? I would take off some cash for two girls at once."

"No," Madame Wu said with a sort of sternness. "Fengmo can wait. He is very young."

"That is true," Liu Ma agreed. Now that the bargain was made she was half tearful with joy, and she wanted to agree with everything that Madame Wu said. "Yes, yes, Lady, it is the old that cannot wait. The old men must be served first, Lady. You are right always. You know all hearts."

She tied the picture-book into the handkerchief again and rose to her feet. "Shall I fetch the girl here at once?"

"Bring her this evening at twilight," Madame Wu said.

"Good," Liu Ma said, "good—the best of times. She will have the day in which to wash herself and her clothes and clean her hair."

"Tell her to bring nothing," Madame Wu said, "nothing in her hands, nothing in a box. She is to come to me empty-handed, clad only in what she wears."

"I promise you—I promise you," Liu Ma babbled, and bowing and babbling she hurried away on her feet that had been badly bound in her childhood and now were like thick stumps.

Almost immediately Ying came into the room with fresh tea. She did not speak, and Madame Wu did not. She watched in silence while Ying wiped the table and the chair where the old woman had sat and took up the tea bowl she had used as though it were a piece of filth. When she was about to leave with this bowl Madame Wu spoke.

"To-night about twilight a young woman will come to the gate."

Ying stood motionless, listening, the dirty bowl between her thumb and finger.

"Bring her straight to me," Madame Wu directed, "and put up a little bamboo bed for her here in this room."

"Yes, Lady," Ying muttered. Her voice choked in her throat, and she hurried away.

.   .   .   .   .

The day moved on towards the night. It was Madame Wu's habit to retire to her bedroom after her noon meal and rest for an hour. But on this day when she went into the big shadowy bedroom she found that she could neither sleep nor rest. It was not that the room was still strange to her. Indeed, she had already come to feel so at home in the rooms that she wondered at her own comfort in them. Her restlessness was not a matter of the room but of her inner self.

"I will not lie down to-day," she said to Ying.

Ying stared at her with foreboding in her faithful eyes. "You had better sleep this afternoon, Lady," she said. "I doubt you sleep well to-night with a stranger here in our house."

"I seem to need no sleep," Madame Wu said. At the sight of Ying's foreboding her mood changed. She felt mischievous and wilful. She put out her hand and gave Ying a soft touch on the arm that was half a push. "Go—leave me, Ying," she commanded. "I will find a book—I will amuse myself."

"As you choose," Ying replied, and with unusual abruptness she turned and left Madame Wu standing in the middle of the room. But Madame Wu did not notice her. She stood, her finger on her delicate lip, half smiling. Then she gave a quick nod and moved across the room towards the library. Her footfall fitted into the hollowed stone before the door where before her scores of feet now dead had fitted too.

"But they were all men," she thought, still half smiling, feeling that hollow under her foot.

She felt free and bold as she had never felt in her life before. Not a soul was here to see what she did. She belonged wholly to herself for this hour. Well, then, the time had come for her to read one of the forbidden books.

Old Gentleman had never made it a secret from her where these books were on the shelves. Indeed, after he had discovered that she could read and write, he had led her one day into the library and himself had showed her the shelf where they lay, packet by packet, in their blue cotton covers. "These books, my child," he had said to her in his grave way, "these books are not for you."

"Because I am a woman?" she had asked.

He had nodded. Then he had added, "But also I did not allow my son to read them until he was fifteen and past childhood."

"Has my lord read them all?" she had then inquired.

Old Gentleman had looked embarrassed. "I suppose he has," he said. "I have never asked, but I suppose all young men read them. That is why I have them here. I told my son, 'If you must read these books, wait until you are fifteen and read them here in my own library and not slyly hidden in your school books'."

She had then put another of her clear questions to him. "Our Father, do you think my mind will never be beyond that of my lord's at fifteen?"

He had been further embarrassed at this question. But he

was an honest old man, although a scholar, and he wrinkled his high, pale yellow brow.

"Your mind is an excellent one for a woman," he had said at last. "I would even say, my daughter, that had your brains been inside the skull of a man you could have sat for the Imperial examinations and passed them with honour and become thereby an official in the land. But your brain is not in a man's skull. It is in a woman's skull. A woman's blood infuses it, a woman's heart beats through it, and it is circumscribed by what must be a woman's life. In a woman it is not well for the brain to grow beyond the body."

Had she not been so dainty a creature her next question might have seemed indelicate. But she knew Old Gentleman loved her and comprehended what she was. Therefore she asked again, "Is this to say, Our Father, that a woman's body is more important than her brain?"

Old Gentleman had sighed at this. He had sat down in the big redwood chair by the long library table. Thinking of him, she now sat down there too, while her memory mused over that day so long gone. He had stroked his small white beard, and something like sorrow had come into his eyes. "As life has proved," he said, "it is true that a woman's body is more important than her mind. She alone can create new human creatures. Were it not for her, the race of man would cease to exist. Into her body, as into a chalice, heaven has put this gift. Her body therefore is inexpressibly precious to man. He is not fulfilled if she does not create. His is the seed, but she alone can bring it to flower and fruit in another being like himself."

She had listened carefully. She could see herself now as she had looked that day when she was sixteen, standing before the wise old man. She had put another question.

"Then why have I a brain, being only a woman?"

Old Gentleman had shaken his head slowly while he looked at her. A rare twinkle came into his eyes. "I do not know," he had answered. "You are so beautiful that certainly you do not need a brain also."

They had both laughed, her laughter young and rippling and his dry and old. Then he was grave again.

"But what you have asked me," he went on, "is a thing about which I have thought much and especially since you came into my house. We chose you for our son because

71

you were beautiful and good and because your grandfather was the former viceroy of this province. Now I find that you are also intelligent. To a pot of gold have been added jewels. Yet I know that in my house you do not need so much intelligence—yes, a little is good so that you can keep accounts and watch servants and control your inferiors. But you have reasoning and wonder. What will you do with them? I cannot tell. In a lesser woman I should be alarmed, because you might be a trouble inside these four walls which must be your world. But you will not make trouble because you also have wisdom, a most unusual wisdom for one so young. You can control yourself."

She had stood before him motionless. He had remembered this. "Sit down, child," he had said. "You will be weary. Besides, you need no more stand in my presence."

But she had scarcely heard him, so absorbed was she in what they were saying to each other. She continued standing before him, her hands clasped loosely in front of her. Her next question was formed and ready.

"Will my lord love me less because I am what you say?"

Old Gentleman had looked very grave at this. His hand wandered back to his white beard. She could see that old hand now, narrow and thin, the skin stretched like gold leaf over the fine bones.

"Ah, that is what I, too, have asked myself!" he had replied. He had sighed deeply. "This matter of intelligence —it is so great a gift, so heavy a burden. Intelligence, more than poverty and riches, divides human beings and makes them friends or enemies. The stupid person fears and hates the intelligent person. Whatever the goodness of the intelligent man, he must also know that it will not win him love from one whose mind is less than his."

"Why?" she had asked. A strange fright had fallen upon her. She was at that time a little arrogant in herself. She knew the quality of her own mind and trusted to it. Now Old Gentleman was saying she would be hated for it.

"Because," Old Gentleman said without sign of emotion in his face or voice, "the first love in a man's heart is love of self. Heaven put that love first in order that man would want to live, whatever his sorrows. Now, when self-love is wounded, no other love can survive, because when self-love

72

is too much wounded, the self is willing to die, and that is against Heaven."

"Will my lord hate me, then?" she had asked again.

Without his putting it into words, it was clear to her that Old Gentleman knew that she was more intelligent than his son, and he was warning her.

"My child," Old Gentleman said, "there is no man who can endure woman's greater wisdom if she lives in his house and sleeps in his bed. He may say he worships at her shrine, but worship is dry fare for daily life. A man cannot make of his house a temple, nor take a goddess for his wife. He is not strong enough."

"Our Father, had I not better read the wicked books?" she had asked so suddenly that Old Gentleman had started. She was surprised and then even a little shocked to see a certain diffidence in his eyes. He had been looking at her with his usual mild directness. Now to evade her he turned to the teapot on the table.

She had stepped forward. "Let me pour it for you," she had said, and did so. He sipped his tea for a moment before he answered. Then he said, still not looking at her, "Child, you will not understand me, perhaps. But believe me without understanding. It is better that you do not read these books. Men love women when they are not too knowing. You are so wise already, so very wise for your youth. You do not need these books. Apply your own mind, now fresh and pure, to the task of making my son happy. Learn love at the source, my child, not out of books."

For a moment it had seemed to her that this was no answer at all. Then, standing there by the table, leaning on her hands as he looked at him, she perceived that he was the wisest soul in all the world, and that until her wisdom matched his she had better believe him.

"I will obey you, my father," she had said, and so she had obeyed him for twenty years and more.

But to-day, alone in this room where they had once been, sitting in the chair which had once been only his, it seemed to her now that her wisdom did match his and her obedience had been fulfilled. She was free of Old Gentleman, too, at last.

So she rose and went, her heart beating strangely, towards the forbidden books. She knew the names of some of them, the names of novels and stories which she had always been taught the true scholar never reads because they are beneath him. Only the low and the coarse, who cannot bear the high either of spirit and thought, can be allowed the diversion of such books. Yet all men read them, yes, even the scholars, too! Old Gentleman himself had read them and he had allowed his son to read them, knowing that if he did not, his son would read them anyway.

"What all men know," Madame Wu now asked herself, "ought not a woman to know?"

She chose a book at random. It was a long book. Many thin volumes lay in the cloth-bound box. The name of the book she had heard. Among the many women in a house as large as her mother's and as large as the Wu house, there were always some who were coarse in their talk. The story of Hsi Men Ch'ing and his six wives all had heard in one way or another. *Plum Flower in a Vase of Gold*—the letters were here delicately brushed on the satin cover of this first volume.

"The books look often read," she thought and smiled with a fleeting bitter mirth. Generations of men of the Wu house had read them, doubtless, but perhaps she was the first woman who had ever held them in her hand.

She took them to the table and looked first at the pictures. An artist had drawn them. There was profound art in the sensuous lines. She studied especially the face of Hsi Men Ch'ing himself. The artist had outdone himself in describing through pictures the decay of man. The young handsome joyous face of Hsi Men Ch'ing, who had found the expression of his youth in love of women's flesh, had grown loathsome as the face of a man dead by drowning and bloated with decay. Madame Wu gazed thoughtfully at each picture and perceived the deep meaning of the story. It was the story of a man who lived without his mind or spirit. It was the story of a man's body, in which his soul struggled, starved, and died.

She began to read. The hours passed. She heard Ying stirring about in the other room, but she did not know that Ying looked in at the door and stared at her and went away again. She became aware of the time only when darkness stole into the room and she could no longer see. Then she looked about as though she did not know where she was.

"I ought not to have obeyed the Old Gentleman," she murmured half aloud. "I should have read this book long ago." But now she had stopped reading she did not want to begin it again. She was surfeited and sick. She bound the volumes together into the box and slipped the small ivory catch into its loop and set it on the shelves again. Then she put her hands to her cheeks, and thus she walked back and forth the length of the room. No, it was better, she thought, that she had not read this book when she was young. Now that she had put it into its cover again she saw that it was a very evil book. For such was the genius of the writer that the reader could find in this book whatever he wanted. For those who wanted evil, it was all evil. For those who were wise, it was a book of most sorrowful wisdom. But Old Gentleman was right. Such a book ought not to be put into the hands of the young. Even she, had she read it twenty years ago, could she have understood the wisdom? Would she not rather have been so sickened that she could not have gone willingly to bed at night? Old Gentleman was still the wisest soul. The very young are not ready for much knowledge. It must be given to them slowly, in proportion to their years of life. One must first live before he can safely know.

It was at this moment of her musing that Ying stood at the door again. Her solid shadow was black against the grey of the twilight. In the court behind her was another shadow.

Ying spoke. "Lady, the old woman Liu has come—the girl is here."

Madame Wu's hands flew to her cheeks again. For an instant she did not answer. Then she took her hands away. She moved to the chair and sat down.

"Light the candle," she commanded Ying, "and bring her here alone. I will not see the old woman."

Ying moved aside in silence, and at the door Madame Wu saw the girl. The candlelight fell on her full but gently. Madame Wu saw almost exactly the face she had imagined and almost exactly the figure. A healthy, red-cheeked girl gazed back at her with round childlike eyes, large and very black. Her black hair was coiled at her neck and fell over her forehead in a fringe, in the fashion of a countrywoman. She held a knotted handkerchief in her hand.

"What is that in your hand?" Madame Wu asked. "I told them you were to bring nothing." The girl looked so innocent, so childlike, that she could only speak these simple words.

"I brought you some eggs," the girl answered. "I thought you might like them, and I had nothing else. They are very fresh." She had a pleasant voice, hearty but a little shy.

"Come here, let me see the eggs," Madame Wu said.

The girl came forward somewhat timidly, tiptoeing as though she feared she might make a noise in the intense quiet of the room. Madame Wu looked down at her feet. "I see your feet have not been bound," she said.

The girl looked abashed. "There was no one to bind them," she replied. "Besides, I have always had to work in the fields."

Ying spoke. "She has very big feet, Lady. Doubtless she has gone barefoot as country children do, and her feet have grown coarse."

The girl stood looking anxiously from Ying's face to Madame Wu.

"Come, show me the eggs," Madame Wu commanded her again.

The girl came forward then and put the bundle on the table carefully. Then she untied the handkerchief and picked up each egg and examined it. "Not one is broken," she exclaimed. "I was afraid that I might stumble in the darkness and crush them. There are fifteen——"

She paused, and Madame Wu understood that she did not know what or how to address her.

"You may call me Elder Sister," she said.

But the girl was too shy for this. She repeated, "Fifteen eggs and not one is older than seven days. They are for you to eat."

"Thank you," Madame Wu said. "They do look very fresh."

She had already perceived several things about this girl as she stood near her. Her breath was sweet and clean, and from her flesh there came only the odours of health. Her teeth were sound and white. The hands that had untied the handkerchief were brown and rough but well shaped. Under the washed blue cotton coat and trousers, the girl's body

76

was rounded without fat. Her neck was smooth, and her face was innocently pretty.

Madame Wu could not keep from smiling at her. "Do you think you would like to stay here?" she asked. She felt a little pity for this young creature, bought like an animal from a farmer. She discovered in her something delicate and good in spite of her sunburned cheeks and rough garments.

The girl perceived this kindness and into her dark, clear eyes there sprang a light of instant devotion. "Liu Ma told me you are good. She said you are not like other women. She told me to please you first above all, and that is what I will do." She had an eager, fresh voice.

"Then you must tell me all you can remember about your life," Madame Wu replied. "You must hide nothing at all. If you are honest I shall like you very much." She perceived the devotion and felt, to her own surprise, a pang of something like guilt.

"I will tell you everything," the girl promised. "But first shall I not take the eggs to the kitchen?"

"No," Madame Wu said, hiding a smile at this. How astonished would the servants be at such a visitor! "Ying will take them to the kitchen. You must sit down there in that chair across from me, and we will talk."

The girl tied up the eggs and sat down on the edge of the chair. But she looked somehow distressed.

"Are you hungry?" Madame Wu asked.

"No, thank you," the girl said carefully. She sat straight, looking before her, her hands folded.

Madame Wu smiled again. "Come, you are to be honest," she said. "Are you not hungry?"

The girl laughed suddenly, a quick burst of rippling laughter. "I am a bone," she said frankly. "I cannot lie even to be polite. But Liu Ma told me I must say, 'No, thank you' if you asked me if I were hungry, lest I seem greedy at the first moment."

"Did you not eat your supper before you came?" Madame Wu inquired.

The girl flushed. "We have not much food," she said. "My foster mother said—my foster mother thought——"

Madame Wu interrupted her. "Ying!" she commanded. "Bring food."

The girl sighed. Her body relaxed, and she turned so that

77

she might face Madame Wu. But she did not look at her.

If she had a fault, Madame Wu thought, it was that she was a little too big in the frame. This must mean that she had come of northern blood. It might be that her family had been refugees from some disaster, a flood, perhaps, of the Yellow River, or a famine, and they had been compelled to put a girl child out to die.

"Liu Ma told me you were an orphan," Madame Wu said aloud. "Do you know anything of your own family?"

The girl shook her head. "I was new-born when they left me. I know the place where they laid me down, for my foster mother has pointed it out to me many times when we have come to the city market. But she told me there was no sign on me of any kind, except that I was not wrapped in cotton, but in silk. It was only ragged silk."

"Do you have that silk?" Madame Wu asked now.

The girl nodded again. "How did you know?" she asked with naïve surprise.

"I thought you would want to bring with you the only thing that was your own," Madame Wu said. She smiled in answer to the girl's round eyes.

"But how do you know the heart of a stranger?" the girl persisted.

"Show me the silk," Madame Wu replied. She had no wish to tell this girl the ways of intuitive knowledge which were hers.

Without hesitation, as though she had indeed made up her mind to obey Madame Wu in all things, the girl put her hand in her bosom and brought out a folded piece of silk. It was washed and clean, but faded from its first red to a rose colour. Madame Wu took it and unfolded it. It was a woman's garment, a short coat, slender in width but long-sleeved.

"If this was your mother's she, too, was tall," Madame Wu observed.

"You know that!" the girl exclaimed.

Madame Wu examined the embroidery. The garment was old-fashioned, and a band of embroidery was stitched round the collar and down the side opening. The same bands went round the wide sleeves.

"It is delicate embroidery," Madame Wu said, "and it is done in a Peking stitch of small knots."

78

"You tell me more than I have ever known," the girl said under her breath.

"But that is all I can tell you," Madame Wu said. She folded the garment again and held it out to the girl.

But the girl did not put out her hands to receive it. "You keep it for me," she said. "I do not need it here."

"I will keep it if you like," Madame Wu said. "But if you find later that you want it again, I will return it to you."

"If you let me stay here," the girl replied with pleading in her voice, "I shall never want it again."

But Madame Wu was not ready yet to give her promise. "You have not even told me your name," she said.

The girl's face changed as plainly as a disappointed child's. "I have no real name," she said humbly. "My foster parents never raised me a name. They cannot read and write, and I cannot either."

"But they called you something," Madame Wu said.

"They called me Little Orphan when I was small and Big Orphan when I was big," the girl said.

"That, of course, is no name," Madame Wu agreed gently. "When I know you better I will give you a name."

"I thank you," the girl said humbly.

At this moment Ying came in with two bowls of food and set them on the table. Madame Wu looked into each bowl as she put it down. If Ying had brought servant's food, she would have sent it back. But Ying had been sensible. She had brought dishes not quite good enough for the family, but certainly too good for the kitchen. She put down a bowl of broth with chicken balls in it and a dish of pork and cabbage. A small wooden bucket of rice she had brought also, and a pot of tea and a tea bowl and chopsticks. The chopsticks were not the family ones of ivory and silver nor the common bamboo ones of the kitchen. They were of red painted wood such as the children used.

"Serve her," Madame Wu commanded.

Ying had hesitated, but now she obeyed, her lips tight and silent.

But the girl noticed nothing. She accepted the bowl of rice from Ying with both hands, rising a little from her seat in country courtesy, and thinking everything was too much. Indeed, Madame Wu soon saw the girl was torn between

79

honest hunger and the wish to be polite, and so she rose and made an excuse to leave her alone.

"I shall return in a little while," she said. "Meanwhile eat heartily."

With these words she went away into her sitting-room. There stood the bamboo bed which Ying had prepared for the girl. Madame Wu looked down on it thoughtfully. She would let the girl sleep here a few nights. She ought even, perhaps, to keep her here until the girl understood her place in the family and until she, too, understood the girl. There must be some deep accord established between them before she released her from this court to enter the other, else trouble might arise in the house. She was doing a delicate and difficult thing, and it must be done skilfully. She stood, her thumb and finger at her lower lip. When she had been a girl she had liked in the spring to help with the making of silk on the family lands. After the silk-worms had spun their cocoons, there came a certain moment, sure but swiftly passing, when the cocoons must be put into tubs of hot water, lest they turn to moths and gnaw the cocoons. She could divine that moment. The farm wives had marvelled at her discernment. She remembered now the size of her certainty, out of nothing and yet of everything.

"Now," she would declare, and the sprays of rice straw to which the cocoons clung were plunged into the tubs. Then she, too, with her delicate, feeling fingers would find the wet, fine end of the silk and unwind the cocoons. The old divination stirred again. Her delicacy must not fail her, lest Mr. Wu reproach her as long as she lived.

She moved from this room into her own bedroom and walked slowly back and forth, her satin-shod feet noiseless on the smooth tiles.

The girl seemed as open as a child. All her heart and nature lay revealed to anyone. But this meant she was undeveloped, and how would she develop? She was not a fool. Her eyes were quick with intelligence. Her lips were tender in their fullness. Was she perhaps too intelligent? There was also the silk garment and the fine embroidery. Her blood was not common, unless perhaps the mother had been a maidservant in a rich family. Yes, there was a possibility that this girl was the child of a maidservant in such a family, gotten with child by one of the sons, perhaps, and this garment had been given out of the discard of her mistress. Or it might be that some tea-house girl had worn such a garment and had given it to a child, unwanted.

"It is impossible to tell what this girl is," Madame Wu murmured to herself.

Did she want to take into her house so unknown a being? She could not answer this. She went back after a while to the library. The girl was sitting there alone, looking frightened in the big, shadow-filled room. She held her hands clasped on her knees. The meal was finished, and Ying had taken away the bowls. When she saw Madame Wu she rose, and relief beamed on her face.

"What shall I do now, Elder Sister?" she asked. The name came to her lips trustfully and warmed Madame Wu against her will. She was wary of giving affection too soon.

"What do you usually do at this hour?" she asked.

"I always go to bed as soon as I have eaten at night," the girl replied. "It wastes candlelight to sit up after it is dark."

Madame Wu laughed. "Then perhaps you had better go to bed," she said. She led the way into the room where the narrow bed lay waiting. "There is your bed, and beyond that door yonder is the room where you may make yourself ready."

"But I am ready," the girl replied. "I washed myself clean before I came here. I will take off my outer clothes and that is all."

"Then I will see you to-morrow," Madame Wu replied.

"Until to-morrow," the girl replied. "But I beg you, Elder Sister, if you want anything in the night, please call me."

"If I need you I will call," Madame Wu said, and went out of the room to her own.

.   .   .   .   .

Long after she had gone to bed herself she could not sleep. Towards midnight she rose and went into the other room and lit the candle and looked at the girl while she slept. She had not tossed nor even stirred. She lay on her right side, one hand under her cheek. She breathed easily, her mouth closed, her face rosy. In her sleep she was even prettier than when she was awake. Madame Wu observed this. She observed also that the girl did not move or snore.

The covers were drawn neatly to her waist. She slept in her cotton undergarments, but she had unfastened her collar so that her round neck showed and part of her breast. One breast Madame Wu could see quite clearly. It was young and round and firm.

She slept deeply, still without stirring. This was good. Madame Wu herself had always been a light sleeper, waking instantly if Mr. Wu so much as turned in the bed and then unable to sleep again. But this girl would sleep soundly all night and wake fresh in the morning. Madame Wu shielded the candle with her hand and bent near to the girl's face. Still the same sweet breath! She straightened and went back to her own room and pinched out the candle between her thumb and finger and lay down again.

She was awakened before dawn by small sounds from the other room. The bamboo bed creaked, something rustled. She woke, as she always did, to the full, and lay listening. Was the girl preparing to run away at this hour? She rose and put on her robe and lit the candle and went out again. The girl was sitting on a stool brushing out her long hair. She was dressed, even to her shoes and white cotton cloth stockings.

"Where are you going?" Madame Wu asked.

The girl was startled by the sound of her voice, and dropped the big wooden comb she was using. Her black hair hung about her face.

"I am not going anywhere," she said. She got to her feet and stared at Madame Wu. Her dark eyes shone out of the flying shadows of her hair. "I am getting up."

"But why are you getting up at this hour?" Madame Wu asked.

"It is time to get up," the girl said in surprise. "I heard a cock crow."

Madame Wu laughed sudden and unusual laughter. "I could not dream to myself why you were getting up, but of course you are a country girl. There is no need, child, for you to get up here. Even the servants will not be awake for an hour yet. And we do not rise for an hour after that."

"Must I go back to bed?" the girl asked.

"What else can you do?" Madame Wu asked.

"Let me sweep the rooms," the girl said, "or I will sweep the court."

"Well, do as you like," Madame Wu replied.

"I will be quiet," the girl promised. "You go back, Elder Sister, and sleep again."

So Madame Wu went back to her bed, and she heard the sound of a broom which the girl had found in the corridor. She used it on court and floor, and her footsteps were light and guarded as she moved about. Then, without knowing, Madame Wu fell asleep again, and when she woke it was late. The sun was shining across the floor, and Ying stood waiting by the bed.

She rose quickly and the rite of dressing began. Ying did not mention the girl, and Madame Wu did not speak. The rooms were silent. She heard nothing.

This silence grew so deep that at last Madame Wu broke it. "Where is the girl?" she asked of Ying.

"She is out there in the court, sewing," Ying replied. "She had to have something to do, and I gave her some shoe soles for the children."

From the slight scorn in Ying's voice Madame Wu understood that she did not think more highly of this girl for wanting to be busy, like a servant. Madame Wu did not speak again. She would not be led by Ying's likes and dislikes.

Instead she ate her breakfast and then went out into the court. There the girl sat on a small three-legged stool, in the shade of the bamboo. She was sewing, her fingers nimbly pushing the needle through the thick cloth sole. On her middle finger she wore a brass ring for a thimble. She rose when she saw Madame Wu and stood waiting, not speaking first.

"Please sit down," Madame Wu said. She herself sat down on one of the porcelain garden seats.

Now as it happened this seat was placed so that she sat with her back to the round gate of the court, but the girl sat facing the door. She had no sooner taken her seat on the stool again and lifted her needle, when she looked up and saw someone in that gate. Madame Wu saw her large eyes look up and fall and the peach-coloured flush on her cheeks deepened. Madame Wu turned, expecting from this behaviour to see a man, perhaps the cook.

But it was not the cook. It was Fengmo, her third son. He stood there, his hand on one side of the entrance staring at the girl.

"Fengmo, what do you want?" Madame Wu asked. She was suddenly conscious of a strange anger because he had come upon her unexpectedly. He was the son whom, she knew herself, she least loved. He was wilful and less amiable than Liangmo or Tsemo, and less playful than little Yenmo. When he was small he had preferred the company of servants to the company of the family, and this she had thought was a sign of his inferiority. She had treated him outwardly exactly as she treated the others, but inwardly she knew she loved him less. Doubtless he had felt this difference, for he seldom came to her, after he was fifteen, unless she sent for him.

"Fengmo, why have you come?" she asked again when he did not answer. He continued to stare at the girl, and she, as though she felt this, lifted the eyelids and glanced at him and let them fall again.

"I came to see—to see—how you are, Mother," Fengmo stammered.

"I am quite well," Madame Wu replied coldly.

"There was something else too," Fengmo said.

Madame Wu rose. "Then come into the library."

She led the way, and he followed, but neither of them sat down. Instead Fengmo moved his hand towards the girl, "Mother," he said, "is that—the one?"

"Fengmo, why have you come here to ask me?" Madame Wu said severely. "It is not your affair."

"Mother, it is," he said passionately. "Mother, how do you think it is for me? My friends will laugh at me and tease me——"

"Is that what you came to tell me?" Madame Wu inquired.

"Yes," Fengmo cried. "It was bad enough before. But now that I have seen her—she is so young and my father—he's so old."

"You will return at once to your own court," Madame Wu said in the same cold voice. "It was intrusion for you to come here without sending a servant first to find if it was convenient for me. As for your father, the younger generation does not decide for the elder."

She was accustomed to Fengmo's stubbornness. She was therefore surprised when this stubbornness wavered. She saw his handsome face flush and quiver. Then without a word he turned and left the room and the court without one backward look.

But Madame Wu was deeply annoyed that these two had seen each other. In spite of many old customs which she had broken, and she did not hesitate to break them when she chose, she had steadfastly followed that one which separated male from female at an early age. In this house her sons had been separated from all women at the age of seven. She had not even rebuked the menservants for their ignorant replies to the questions of the boys. Once she had heard Fengmo ask the steward, "Why am I forbidden to play any more with my two girl cousins?"

"Boys and girls cannot play together or they will have sore feet," the steward had said half jokingly.

Madame Wu, usually so quick to correct ignorance, had let this pass.

Now Fengmo had seen this girl before she had taken her place in the house, and the girl had seen him. Who could tell what fire would blaze out of this? She walked back and forth in the library. Each time she passed the open door she could see the girl's head bent industriously over the shoe sole and her hand pulling the needle in and out. Her mind was suddenly quite made up. The matter must be decided at once. She would keep this girl. But the girl must understand exactly what her duty was. She went out with a swifter step than was usual to her and sat down again.

"I have made up my mind," she began abruptly. "You shall stay in this house."

The girl looked up, held the needle ready to pierce the cloth, but she did not move to take the stitch. She stood up in respect to Madame Wu.

"You mean that I please you?" she asked in a low and breathless voice.

"Yes, if you do your duty," Madame Wu said. "You understand—you come here to serve my own lord—to take my place—in certain things."

"I understand," the girl said in the same half-faint voice. Her eyes were fastened on Madame Wu's face.

"You must know," Madame Wu went on, "that our house is in some ways still old-fashioned. There is no coming and going between the men's courts and the women's."

85

"Oh, no," the girl agreed quickly. Her hands fell into her lap, but her eyes did not move.

"In that case," Madame Wu said in the strange abrupt way which was not at all like her usual way of speaking, "there is no reason why the matter should not be concluded."

"But ought I not to have a name?" the girl asked anxiously. "Shall I not have a name in this house?"

There was something pathetic and touching in this question, and Madame Wu found it so. "Yes," she said, "you must have a name, and I will give it to you. I will name you Ch'iuming. It means Bright Autumn. In this name I set your duty clear. His is the autumn, yours the brightness."

"Ch'iuming," the girl repeated. She tasted the name on her tongue. "I am Ch'iuming," she said.

* 4 *

MR. WU did not come near Madame Wu, and she let it be
so. After the many years, she knew what was going on in
his mind. Had he been resolute against the girl he would
have come to tell Madame Wu so, with temper and
decision, possibly even with laughter. But that he had stayed
away proved to her that he was not unwilling for the girl
to come into his court, and that he was secretly ashamed
before Madame Wu because he was not unwilling. She knew
him well enough to know that he might even be inwardly
disgusted with himself, though in a degree too small to help
him against his inclination. In short, he was what Madame
Wu knew him to be, of a nature able to know what were the
qualities of a great man, to admire and wish for all of these
qualities, and yet hamstrung in his soul by the demands
of his body.

Thus, as he was never able to resist a well-seasoned dish at
the table, so he would not be able, however he longed for
perfection, to deny himself the pleasure of a young woman.
He was not austere, although he had been able for years
to be satisfied with Madame Wu as his wife. But Madame
Wu, without conceit, knew that, had she been less beautiful
and less conscientious as a wife, he might have been led
elsewhere. She had been careful to keep him satisfied in all
things. Did he feel a desire for knowledge concerning any
matter to be found in books, she informed herself and then
told him. Did he mention a curiosity concerning foreign
things, she learned and let him know. In all their years he
had not an unsatisfied desire. But she knew without pain
that this was because she had studied his wishes, and when
they were vague, by careful discourse she helped them to
emerge clearly, even to himself, and when they were sharp
and immediate she wasted no time in satisfying him. She
had been a good wife.

Nor had she been discontented with him. She had no
sudden disappointment in him. At first she had taken his
wilful curiosities as the stirrings of a mind impeded because

his mother had indulged him from the moment he was born. Old Lady had never allowed Old Gentleman any power over their only child, unduly precious because he was the one left alive out of several births. At first Old Lady had quarrelled openly and violently when Old Gentleman wished to discipline his son. This occurred when the boy was seven years old. Until that time, after the custom of all such families, Old Gentleman had allowed the boy to live in his mother's courts. But at seven, he told Old Lady, it was time the boy came into his own court.

One excuse after another did Old Lady then put out. First the boy had a weak throat and she must have him where he could be watched at night, and next he had a small appetite and must be coaxed at meals. When Old Gentleman grew stern she wept, and when he was angry she was more angry. But Old Gentleman was harder than a rock, and she was compelled to yield. When their child was nine years old he had been moved into a small room next to his father's bedroom, and Old Gentleman undertook the teaching and discipline of his only son.

Alas that this small room had also a side door through which the handsome, wilful boy could creep at night to his mother. Old Gentleman patiently and tenderly instructed his son to no avail. For instead of the self-discipline which he taught, she, out of the excess of her love, helped him play when he should have been studying. She gave him rich and delicate foods, and when his young belly was overstuffed and ached she taught him to puff an opium pipe to relieve the pain. It was only the boy's own health and restlessness which saved him from this opium smoking. As it was, by the time he was twenty, Old Gentleman perceived that Old Lady had won over him, and with a last hour of admonition he had yielded up his son.

"My son," thus he had ended his admonition, "you have chosen woman over man, your mother rather than your father, ease rather than achievement. Let it be so. It now remains for the sake of our house to find you a wife who will give strength to your weakness."

The boy had been frightened by the gravity of his father's voice and, as he always did when he was frightened, he had hastened away as quickly as he could to his mother, and in a few minutes he had forgotten his discomfort.

88

Madame Wu had come to the house soon afterwards. On the tenth day after the marriage Old Gentleman had sent for her to come to his library, and had talked with her thus about his son, "He is what you will make him. Some men make themselves, but he will always be made by women. Yet you must not let him know this. Never reproach him with his own weakness, for then he will became wholly weak. Never let him feel that but for you he would be useless, for then he will indeed become useless. You must search for the few strong threads in him and weave your fabric with those, and where the threads are weak, never trust to them. Supply your own in secret."

She had been very young then, and her bridegroom was handsome and gay, and she was drunk with marriage. She was afraid of nothing.

"I love him," she had said simply to Old Gentleman.

He had looked startled, for it was not usual for a woman to speak so boldly. But the voice in which she had uttered these extraordinary words was very soft and pretty, and she had looked so delicate and innocent as she spoke them that he had not the heart to reproach her.

Instead of reproach he had merely inclined his head and said, "Then you have a woman's sharpest weapon in your hand."

It had been perhaps ten years before Madame Wu had come to the full comprehension of the man to whom she was married and whom she loved still, with tenderness. So slowly, so gradually that she had not felt the pain of disappointment, she had found all the boundaries of his mind and soul. The space within these boundaries was small. The curiosities and questions which had at first excited her because she had taken them to be stirrings of intelligence, she saw now had no root. They were no more than ways to pass the time. They led to no end. At any moment he might grow weary of a question and cease to pursue it, and then she must discover the way the next wind blew.

It was at this time that she herself had stepped out beyond his boundaries and had let her own spread as far as they would. But this she did not tell him. Indeed, why should she, since he would not have understood what she said? Enough of her remained within his boundaries so that he thought she was still there with him. But she had already begun to dream of her fortieth birthday and to plan for what she would do when the day came.

Now she made up her mind that she must go and tell Mr. Wu herself that Ch'iuming had been found and was ready. He would have heard it from servants, but still she must tell him. There should not be delay, since Fengmo had seen the girl. For a young man to see a young woman might mean nothing, but it might mean much. There is a moment in the tide of youth when any such meeting, however accidental, may be as dangerous as a rendezvous. If Mr. Wu were in the right mind, she would send Ch'iuming to him as quickly as she could get her ready.

Ch'iuming was happy enough on this bright summer morning. Madame Wu had sent Ying to a cloth shop for flowered cotton cloth of good quality and silk of medium quality, and a clerk had brought bolts of such goods. From these Madame Wu now chose enough to make Ch'iuming three separate changes of garments. She wished to please the girl, and so she allowed her to point out which were her favourite colours and patterns, and she was pleased that the girl chose small patterns and mild colours. She was still more pleased when the girl set to work at once to make the garments herself.

Ch'iuming stood at the square table and spread the printed cotton on the table first. Then she paused, the iron scissors uplifted.

"Shall I cut them like your garments, Elder Sister?" she asked. Her own clothes were wide-sleeved and short in the coat as country people's are.

"Ying will help you to make the proper fashion for this house," Madame Wu replied.

So Ying had measured and marked with a piece of chalky white stone and then had cut the cloth to fit Ch'iuming's slender curved body.

And while this was going on the girl stood in a trance of pure pleasure. "In my whole life I have never had a garment from new cloth," she murmured.

When the pieces were cut she threaded her needle and slipped the brass ring of her thimble over her forefinger and sat down in a dream of joy. Slowly and carefully she stitched, while Ying looked on to examine the stitches for smallness and evenness. Watching Ch'iuming, Madame Wu felt again that strange pang of vague guilt, as though she were about to do this girl a wrong. She decided at once to go and find Mr. Wu and beckoned to Ying to come aside for a moment in the other room. There beyond the hearing of the girl she said:

"You must help her. See that she has a full set of undergarments quickly, and one outer set. I may send her from here to-morrow, depending on what the day shows me."

"Yes, Lady," Ying said, guarding her face and her voice against showing pleasure or sadness.

Now Madame Wu went out of her own court for the first time since she had moved here. In duty she stopped to see Old Lady. She found her well, sitting in the sun outside her door, and unusually cheerful while a maid rubbed oil into her feet and ankles which happened that day to be a little swollen.

"It was crabs," Old Lady said. "Crabs always make my feet swell. But since I am about to descend into the grave at any moment, shall I refuse crabs for this cause? My feet and ankles are little good to me anyway. I drank much wine with the crabs too, to take away the poison."

Old Lady seemed to have forgotten entirely that she had been angry with her daughter-in-law about the concubine, and Madame Wu did not remind her. She stopped and examined Old Lady's swollen feet and bade the maid rub them upward so that the blood would ascend rather than descend. Then she went on her way.

She had expected to find Mr. Wu in her old courts rather than in his, and so there she went. In that court her silver orchids were fading. She stooped to see if there were aphids on the leaves, but there were none. It was at this moment that she saw Mr. Wu sitting inside the room in his easy garments. Because of the heat he wore a pair of white silk trousers loose round the ankles, and a silk jacket unbuttoned over his smooth chest. He was fanning himself with a white silk fan painted with green bamboos, and in his hand was a tea bowl. The empty dishes of his breakfast were on the table. She discerned embarrassment and some sullenness on his well-fed, handsome face, and out of old habit she spoke cheerfully to him, "I think it is time we planted peonies again in this court. What do you say, Father of my sons?"

"I never cared for those little grey orchids," he replied. "I like something with colour."

"I will have them taken away and peonies planted this very day," she went on. "If we buy them in pots they will go on blooming without being disturbed."

He rose and sauntered out of the room and into the court and stood at her side, looking down at the orchids. "Red and pink peonies," he said judiciously, "and a white one to each five, say, of the red and pink."

"A good proportion," she agreed. "Where is Yenmo?" she asked. Her youngest son was usually somewhere near his father.

"I sent him yesterday to the country," Mr. Wu said with solemnity. "He is too young for the turmoil in this house."

"That was thoughtful of you," she told him. "You are entirely wise." She looked up at him affectionately. He was a tall man, somewhat fat, for he was fond of food. "How are you this morning?" she asked. "You look like a prince of Chu."

"Well," he replied, "very well." But she discovered a certain impatience in him. She smiled.

"I have not forgotten you," she said. Her pretty voice was rich with tenderness.

"I feel as though you had," he grumbled. He opened his jacket and fanned his bare breast swiftly and hard for a moment. "I have been very lonely, waiting for you to make up your mind. I am a good husband, Ailien! Another man would not have stood for this separation for so long. All these days! Enough, I say!"

"I have not forgotten you for one moment," she said. "I have diligently searched, and the young woman is here."

A fine red sprang into Mr. Wu's face. "Ailien," he said, "do not speak of that again."

"You must have heard she was here," Madame Wu went on in her clear voice.

"I pay no heed to servants' talk," he said, and looked lordly. But this she knew as merely his picture of himself. He listened to all his manservant told him and laughed at his jokes, for the man was a clown and knew that his master liked to laugh.

Madame Wu moved gracefully to a garden seat. "The young woman is truly suitable," she murmured. Her delicate hands fell into their usual tranquillity upon her lap. "Healthy, young, pretty, innocent——"

"Do you have no jealousy whatever?" he interrupted her harshly. The clear sunlight fell upon him as he stood, and she appreciated the picture it made of him—shining black hair, smooth golden skin, handsome lips, and large bold eyes.

"You are so handsome," she said smiling, "that I might be jealous were she not so much a child, so simple, so less than nothing between you and me."

"I cannot understand why you have grown so monstrously cold overnight," he complained. 'Ailien, last week you were —as you have always been. This week——"

"I have passed my fortieth birthday," she said for him, still smiling. Then she motioned to the seat beside her. "Come," she coaxed him, "sit down."

He had scarcely taken his seat when she saw Fengmo pass the door. He looked in, saw his parents side by side, and went away quickly.

"Fengmo!" she called. But the boy did not hear her and did not return.

"We must marry that third son of ours," she told Mr. Wu. "What would you say if I spoke to Madame Kang at once— perhaps to-morrow—and asked for Linyi?"

"You have always chosen the boys' wives," he returned.

"Tsemo chose his own," she reminded him. "I wish to avoid that mistake with Fengmo."

"Well enough," he said. She was pleased to see that there was no interest in his voice at the thought of Linyi. He had forgotten her. He was thinking only of himself. She decided to speak directly, as though she had ordered him a new suit of clothes or a pair of shoes.

"Unless you are unwilling, I will send the girl to you to-morrow," she said.

The bright red came back again to Mr. Wu's cheeks. He put his thumb and forefinger into the small pocket of his jacket and brought out a package of foreign cigarettes, took one out and lit it. "I know you are so devilish stubborn a woman that I could kill myself beating against your wish," he muttered between clouds of smoke. "Why should I kill myself?"

"Have I ever made you less happy by my stubbornness?"

she inquired. Her voice was bright with laughter. "Has it not always been stubbornness for your sake?"

"Do not talk to me about this matter," he said. He blew a sudden gust of smoke. "Never mention the girl to me again!"

"There is no reason why we should talk about her," Madame Wu agreed. "I will send her to you to-morrow night."

She saw a second shape at the gate to the court and recognized her eldest son, Liangmo. He also was passing by, or so it seemed.

"Liangmo!" she called. But Liangmo also went and did not return.

Mr. Wu rose abruptly. "I now recall I promised to meet a man at the tea-house," he told Madame Wu. "The land steward thinks we should buy that pocket of a field that my grandfather, three generations ago, gave to one of his servants who saved his life. The man's descendants are ready to sell, and it would restore the land to its old shape."

"A very good thing," she said, "but it must not cost more than seventy-five dollars to the fifth of an acre."

"We might give him eighty dollars," Mr. Wu said.

"I shall be happy if it is no more," she told him. "We must think of our children."

"Not more than eighty," Mr. Wu promised. He turned and went into the house, and she too rose, and prepared to go on her way. But at the threshold Mr. Wu stopped and turned. He looked at her. "Ailien," he cried, "I cannot take the blame for anything!"

"Who will blame you?" she replied. "And, by the by, I have forgotten to tell you her name. It is Ch'iuming. She will be brightness in your autumn."

Mr. Wu heard this, opened his mouth, closed it, and walked away.

Madame Wu looked down at the fading orchids with thoughtful eyes. "He wanted to curse me," she thought, "but he did not know how to do it."

She suddenly felt timid and longed to return to her own quiet rooms. But she knew she must not, in duty to her sons, who would be expecting her. Son by son she must visit them all.

She found Liangmo in the next court which was his and

94

his family's own home. It was a happy, lively home. Liangmo's small son was playing with his nurse in the court, and he came to Madame Wu when she came in. She fondled his cheeks and stooped to smell his sweet flesh.

"Little meat dumpling," she said tenderly. "Ah, your cheeks are fragrant!"

Liangmo heard her voice and came out of the house. He was dressed for the street. "Here I am, Mother. I was about to go outside the city and see how the rice is growing. It's time to measure the harvest."

"Put off your going, my son," she said. He held out his arm and she placed her hand on it for support and thus he led her to a garden seat under a pine-tree that had been trained to curve over it like a canopy.

"I have come to ask that you go with your father to the tea-house. He is thinking of buying back the parcel of land that the Yang family have had these three generations. The present son is an opium smoker, as you know, and it is a good chance to secure that land again into our own holding. But you must go and see that not more than seventy dollars is offered. Your father talks eighty. But it can be had for seventy. People rob us because they think we are rich, and no one is rich enough to be robbed."

"I will go, Mother, of course," he said. She saw him hesitate and knew at once that he wished to ask about Ch'iuming. But she had made up her mind that she would not talk of the girl with any son. It was not well to allow one generation to discuss another.

"Where is Meng?" she asked. "I have not seen her since my birthday. I want to ask her—and you, too, my son—what do you think of Linyi for Fengmo's wife?"

"Linyi?" Liangmo had not thought of it. "But will Fengmo let you decide for him?"

"If he will not, then I will let him decide for himself to marry Linyi," Madame Wu said with her pretty soft laugh. "I never compel anyone to anything."

At this moment Meng came out of the house. Her chief fault was that she was sleepy in the morning and slatternly for an hour or two after she rose. This morning when she heard Madame Wu she had been sitting in her night garments with her hair uncombed. She had hastened into the inner room and made herself decent. Now she came out looking like a rose, neither bud nor full blown. Her new pregnancy made her soft and mild with lassitude. Her great eyes were liquid, and her lips were parted. In her ears she had put the pearls that Madame Wu had given her.

"Mother," she called in greeting, "are you come?"

"How the pearls suit you," Madame Wu said. She looked at Liangmo. "Go, my son," she said with the pretty authority that never seemed real because it was so light. "Meng and I will talk a while."

When he was gone she surveyed Meng from head to foot. "Do you vomit in the morning yet?" she inquired affectionately.

"I am just beginning to do it," Meng replied. "That is, I am roiled but nothing comes up."

"Another ten days and you will begin," Madame Wu said. "A healthy child. especially if it is a boy, always makes the mother vomit for three months."

"That little turnip did," Meng said, pursing her red underlip at her small son who was now riding his nurse for a pony.

Madame Wu had always to take time to approach real conversation with Meng. None of Madame Kang's children had their mother's largeness of mind and body. Madame Wu reflected upon this as she looked at Meng's little plump figure and exquisite small face and hands. It was as though her friend had divided herself into nine parts in her children. Madame Wu herself in giving birth to her own children had been conscious of no division of herself. She had created them entirely new, and they were separate from her from the moment of their birth. But Meichen was never separate from her children. She clung to each as to a part of herself.

"Meng, my child," Madame Wu now began, "I come to you for advice. What do you think of asking your mother for your sister Linyi for Fengmo? They are almost the same age—your sister is, I think, four months younger than Fengmo. She is pretty, and Fengmo is well enough. Both are healthy. I have not yet consulted the horoscopes, but I know their birth months are suitable. She is water and he is stone."

"How I would like to have my sister here!" Meng cried. She clapped her hands and her rings tinkled together. Then her hands dropped. "But Mother, I must tell you. Linyi thinks Fengmo is old-fashioned."

"But why?" Madame Wu asked, astonished.

"He has never been away to school. He has only grown up here in this house," Meng explained.

"Your mother should never have let Linyi go to that school that year in Shanghai," Madame Wu said. Severity hardened the beautiful lines of her mouth.

"Of course Fengmo could still go away to school," Meng said. She covered a yawn behind her dimpled hand.

"I will not send Fengmo away at the time when he is not yet shaped. I wish this house to shape my sons, not a foreign school," Madame Wu replied.

Meng never argued. "Shall I ask Linyi?" she now inquired.

"No," Madame Wu said with dignity. "I will speak with your mother myself."

Madame Wu felt out of sorts with Meng for a moment. But before she could consider this a startled look passed over Meng's childish face.

"Oh, Heaven," she cried, and clasped her hands over her belly.

"What now?" Madame Wu asked.

"Could it be the child I feel—so early?" Meng said solemnly.

"Another boy," Madame Wu proclaimed. "When it quickens so early it is a boy."

It would have been unbecoming to allow herself impatience with Meng at such a time, and so she controlled it. In young women one asked nothing except that they fulfil their functions. This Meng was doing.

She rose. "You must drink some warm broth, child," she said. "Rice broth is the best. When the child stirs, he is hungry."

"I will," Meng said, "even though I have only finished my morning meal. But I am hungry day and night, Mother."

"Eat," Madame Wu said. "Eat your fill and the child's."

She went away, and as she walked through the beautiful old courts she felt herself taken out of her own being and carried as she so often was upon the stream of this Wu family which she had joined so many years ago. Life and marriage, birth and new birth, the stream went on. Why should she be impatient with Meng, who could think of nothing but giving birth?

"With my own sons I, too, have carried on my share of that river of life," Madame Wu told herself. Her present duty was only to keep the flow pure and unimpeded in each generation. She lifted her head and breathed in the morning air. Beyond this duty she was free.

But now there still remained Tsemo. Fengmo she would not see until she knew Linyi's mind. Yenmo was gone. As soon as she had greeted Tsemo and Rulan she would have completed her tasks for the day.

Tsemo's court was the least pleasant of all. As she stepped into the cramped space she repented the revenge she had taken on him for his marriage. There were only two rooms, and they faced north. The sun did not warm them in winter, and in summer they were damp.

She found Tsemo inside the main room. He was mopping up some foreign liquid ink which he had spilled out of its bottle, and she saw him first and saw he was in a surly mood. This son of hers was often surly, his handsome mouth down-turned, his eyes cruel. So was he to-day.

Madame Wu stopped on the threshold.

"Well, son?" she said in greeting. "Are you alone?"

"Rulan is ill," he replied, throwing his inky cloth on the floor.

"Ill? No one told me." Madame Wu stepped over the high door sill and came in.

"She did not look well, and I told her to stay in bed," Tsemo said.

"I will go in and see her," Madame Wu said.

She put aside the red silk curtain that hung between the two rooms and went in. It was the first time Madame Wu had entered this room since Rulan came, and she saw it was changed. The bed was curtainless, and there were, instead, curtains at the window. Some foreign pictures hung on the walls, and among the books on the shelves along the walls there were foreign books.

On the bare bed Rulan lay. Her head was on a high pillow, and her short hair fell away from her face and showed her ears. They were small and pretty as little shells. Madame Wu noticed them at once.

"I never saw your ears before," she said kindly. "They are

98

very nice. You should wear ear-rings. I will send you a pair of gold ones."

Rulan turned her dark brilliant eyes upon Madame Wu. "Thank you, Mother," she said with unusual meekness.

Madame Wu was alarmed at this meekness. "I am afraid you are very ill," she exclaimed.

"I am tired," Rulan admitted.

"You have happiness in you, perhaps?" Madame Wu suggested.

But Rulan shook her head. "I am only tired," she repeated. She began to pleat the silk coverlet with her brown fingers.

"Rest yourself, then," Madame Wu said. "Rest yourself. There is nothing in this house that cannot be done by someone else."

She nodded and smiled and went out again to Tsemo. He was writing foreign letters, one after the other, a foreign pen in his hand. He rose when she came back, the pen still in his fingers.

"What do you write?" she asked.

"I am practising my English," he said.

"Who teaches you?" she asked.

He flushed. "Rulan," he replied. She understood at once that he was ashamed, and so she said something else quickly.

"Rulan is tired. She must rest."

"I shall compel her," he said eagerly. "She is too active. Yesterday she went to a meeting of the National Reconstruction Committee at the City Council House and was chosen its president. When she came home she was exhausted."

"National Reconstruction again?" Madame Wu's voice was silvery. "Ah, that is very exhausting."

"That is what I told her," Tsemo agreed.

She nodded and went away after that and walked with unwonted briskness into her own court. Ch'iuming was sitting on a stool in the court, sewing on the new garments. Madame Wu stopped beside her, and the girl made to rise. But Madame Wu pushed her down gently, her hand on Ch'iuming's shoulder. "Stay by your sewing," she commanded her. "To-morrow is the day, and you must prepare yourself."

The girl sank back and picked up the needle which had

fallen and was hanging by the thread. She did not speak one word. Bending her head, she began to sew again with quick, nimble movements of finger and hand. Madame Wu, looking down on that bent young head, saw a flush as red as peach flowers rise from between Ch'iuming's shoulders and spread up the back of her round neck and into the roots of her soft black hair.

.   .   .   .   .

Madame Wu had by the end of the next day made up her mind as to the manner of Ch'iuming's entrance into the court of Mr. Wu. The least disturbance would be caused if it were done quietly and at night. There was no reason for celebration. This was an affair of her own generation and Mr. Wu's, and to allow the younger generation any part in it would be to embarrass them.

The next day, therefore, she directed Ying to help the girl in certain small details of her toilet, of which Ch'iuming would naturally be ignorant. She herself spent the day in the library. She had no desire to take up again the forbidden books. Now indeed she felt she might never open one again. What more had she to do with man? Instead she chose a book of history and began to read from the beginning of time, when earth and heaven were not separate, but mingled together in chaos.

The day passed as though she were out of her body and travelling in space. No one came near her. She knew that all the household waited to see what would be her will, and until she had settled Ch'iuming, no one would come here. No one knew how to talk so long as affairs in the centre of the family remained confused. Her only visitor was the land steward, who sent word in the late afternoon that he would like to report the matter of the land purchase. She gave orders that he was to come, and when he appeared upon the threshold of the library she looked up from her book and without closing it bade him come in. He came in and stood before her and drew a folded paper from his breast.

"Lady," he said, "I have brought the deed of purchase for the Wang lot. We paid eighty for it. Had our lord stayed out of it I might have had it for seventy, but he remembered that the land had been a gift and he would not be hard."

"I will take the deed," she said, without answering his

100

complaint against Mr. Wu. She put out her hand and he placed in it the deed.

"Is that all?" she asked. Beyond doubt this man knew what was happening in the house. She saw him cast a quick look round as though his eye searched for a new face.

"Is that all?" she repeated.

He brought back his eyes but, being a coarse, common man, he could not hide what he thought. She saw the loosening of the corners of his thick lips, the wavering of his eyes, and read his thoughts as clearly as though she were reading the forbidden book.

"Well?" she asked sharply.

He dropped his glance at that sharpness. "There is nothing more, Lady," he said. "Except, unless you forbid it, I will plant the new land to beans. It is late for any other crops."

"Beans and then winter wheat," she directed.

"That is what I thought," he agreed.

She nodded and then knew that he expected some small gift on the purchase. She rose and took a key from her inner pocket and fitted it to a wooden chest that stood against the wall and, opening the door of this, she took out an iron-bound wooden box, opened this, and took out some silver dollars, counting ten before his eyes.

"With this I thank you," she said courteously.

He held out his hand in protest, drew back, rolled his head to deny the gift, and then took it. "Thank you, Lady, thank you," he said over and over again and then backed from her presence and so out of the door. In the court she saw him straighten himself and look right and left as he walked to the gate.

But she was pleased that Ch'iuming was not to be seen. The girl had the grace to stay hidden. That was more favour added to her. Madame Wu closed the book she had laid upon the table open and put it away into the covers and went into the sitting-room. Ying had brought her night meal and with it Ch'iuming's. Madame Wu examined the food that the girl was to eat. Then she bent and smelled it.

"You have not put in garlic or onion or any strong-smelling thing?" she inquired of Ying.

"I know what should be done," Ying said shortly.

"No pepper?" Madame Wu persisted. "It makes heartburn."

"Nothing a baby could not eat," Ying replied. She had made her kind face unfriendly and indifferent to show her mistress she had not relented. Madame Wu smiled at the angry eyes and pursed mouth of her maid.

"Ying, you are faithfulness itself," she said. "But if you would really serve me, then know that I do only what I wish."

But Ying would not answer that. "Lady, your meal is in your room," she said, still shortly.

So Madame Wu ate her own meal alone in her own room with her usual dainty slowness, and she loitered over it and smoked her little pipe. Then she walked into the court where all day a gardener had been busy transplanting the orchids. She had given him directions as to their placing, and now the work was done. He had pinched off flower and bud and had cut off the outer leaves, but to each stalk a single spire of new leaf remained. They would live. The court where they had bloomed to-day was planted with blooming peonies.

When darkness had fallen she waited an hour, and after the hour of darkness she went into the house again. Ch'iuming had bathed herself and combed her hair. She had put on the new garments. Now she sat upright on the edge of the narrow bed, her hands clasped on her lap. Her young face was fixed and told nothing. But from under her hair, smoothed over her ears, Madame Wu saw two fine streams of sweat pouring down. She sat down beside the girl.

"You must not be afraid," she said. "He is a very kind man."

The girl threw her a quick look from under her lowered eyelids, and looked down again.

"You have only to obey him," Madame Wu said. But she felt somehow cruel even as she said these words. Yet why should she feel cruel? The girl was no longer a child. The man who was to have been her husband had died. Had she lived on in the house of her foster mother, what could she have hoped as her lot except to be married, as a young widow never wed, to some other farmer whose wife had died and left him with many children? Surely this fate was better than that!

So Madame Wu tried to harden herself. But the girl put up her hand stealthily and wiped the sweat from her cheeks and remained silent.

"You had better take her now," Madame Wu said abruptly to Ying, who stood waiting.

Ying stepped forward and took the girl's sleeve between her thumb and finger. "Come," she said.

Ch'iuming rose. Her full red mouth opened, and she began to pant softly and to hang back. Her eyes grew wide and very black.

"Come," Ying said hardily. "For what else have you been brought into this house?"

The girl looked from Ying's face to Madame Wu's. Then, seeing nothing in either face to give her escape, she bent her head and followed Ying out of the room, out of the gate, and so out of the court.

Left alone, Madame Wu sat for some time without moving her body. Nor did a thought stir her mind. She sat in a state of blind feeling, and she let feeling take its course. Did she suffer pain? She knew she did not. Did she regret? No, she had no regrets. In this state of emptiness so might a soul find itself lost in death.

Then she lifted her head. Her mouth quivered. Did not a soul unborn exist also in the womb in just such emptiness? So she, too, might now be born again. She rose and went out into the court and lifted her face to the dark sky. The night was soft and black, and the square of sky above the courtyard was covered with clouds through which no stars shone. There would be rain before morning. But she always slept well on a rainy night.

Ying came back and passed her, not seeing her in the darkness. She went into the empty house and was startled by its emptiness.

"Oh, Heaven!" Madame Wu heard her mutter. "Where has she gone now? Mistress—Mistress!" Ying's voice screamed out.

"Here I am, stupid," Madame Wu said tranquilly at the door. "I stepped into the court to see if it would rain."

Ying was as green as old bean curd. She held her hand to her heart. "Oh, Mistress," she gasped. "I thought—I thought——"

Madame Wu laughed. "If you would only stop thinking, you would be much happier. You should leave thinking to me, Ying. You have no need of it."

Ying sighed, and her hand dropped. "Do you want to go to bed now, Mistress, as usual?"

"Why not?" Madame Wu asked in her pretty voice. "It is beginning to rain. I can hear it on the roof."

An hour later she climbed into the high big bed. Freshly bathed, freshly dressed in her white silk night garments, she laid herself down.

Ying suddenly began to sob. "What bride is as beautiful as you?" she cried between her sobs.

Madame Wu had laid her head on her pillow. Now she lifted it again. "How dare you weep when I do not?" she said.

Swallowing her sobs, Ying loosened the curtains and drew them across the bed. And shut behind their satin splendour, Madame Wu folded her hands on her breast and closed her eyes. Upon the tiled roof above her head she heard the steady soothing downpour of the rain.

.   .   .   .   .

Ch'iuming had stepped through the darkness in a direction strange to her. She had not once left Madame Wu's court since entering it. Now sent from it, she felt completely homeless, as orphaned as she had been when the woman who bore her had put her down outside a city wall and left her there. Then she had not known her plight. Now she knew it.

But such had been her life that long ago she had learned to be silent, for no voice would hear her if she called. Ying still held her sleeve by thumb and forefinger, and she felt this slight pull guiding her steps. But she did not speak to Ying.

And Ying, too, had kept silent as she trod the stones through one court into another. Old Lady's court was quiet, for that old soul went to bed at sunset. From somewhere to the west a child cried. It was the Eldest Son's child. To the north Ying heard or thought she heard a woman sobbing. She stopped to listen. "Hark!" she said. "Who is that crying in the night?"

Ch'iuming lifted her head.

"I cannot hear it now," Ying said. "Perhaps it was only a mourning dove."

They went on again. Ch'iuming's heart began to throb.

Every sense was quickened. She felt the air damp on her skin. Yes, she did hear a woman sobbing. But what woman wept in these courts? She did not ask. What could she do if she knew who it was? Her helplessness rose in her and frightened her, and she, too, wanted to weep. She must speak, she must reach out to some living soul and hear an answering voice, though it be only this servant woman's.

"I think it strange they wanted me," she gasped. "I should think he would want a girl from a flower house, someone, you know, who knows how to—— I have only lived in the country——"

"Our mistress would not have such a girl in our house," Ying said coldly.

Before Ch'iuming could speak again they were there. The court was full of peonies. A lantern shone down on them, and they glowed in the shadows.

"No one is here," Ying announced. She led the way, and Ch'iuming followed. She saw a large room, the largest she had ever seen. The furniture was rich and dark, and paintings hung upon the walls. In the doorways the night wind swung satin curtains gently to and fro. They were scarlet against the ivory walls. She stepped in timidly. Here she was to live—if she pleased him.

But where was he?

She did not ask, and Ying did not speak of him. In the same cold fashion Ying helped her to make ready for bed. Only when the girl sat on the edge of the bed, and Ying saw her pale face, did she take pity.

"You are to remember that this is an honourable house," she said in a loud voice. "If you do your duty here, you have nothing to make you afraid. He is kind, and she is wise as well as kind. You are lucky among women, and so why are you afraid? Have you a home to run to or a mother to receive you back again?"

Ch'iuming shook her head, and the red flooded into her cheeks. She lay down and closed her eyes. Ying drew the curtains and went away.

Behind the curtains Ch'iuming lay alone and full of terror. Within the next hour or two, what would befall her? The great house enclosed her. From somewhere she heard the clacking of mah-jong pieces. The servants were gambling —or was it the sons? Or was it *he*, with his friends? Was ever a concubine brought into such a house in this fashion without having seen him? It was as though she were a wife instead of a concubine. But the elder lady was the wife, not she. And how could she ever be so beautiful as that wife, and how could she please him after that one, whose every look was beauty?

"I am so coarse," she thought. "Even my hands!" She raised them in the darkness and let them fall again. They were rough, and the fine silk of the quilt caught at them.

She remembered the woman sobbing. Who were the others in the house? Sons and sons' wives, she must make her peace with them all, lest they hate her. And the many servants, could they be so kind as Ying? And what did one call the servants? She who had nothing to pay them when she wanted a service done, would she be allowed to serve herself?

"I wish I were in my own bed again," she moaned under her breath. She had slept all her life in a little lean-to, next to her foster mother's room. Her bed had been boards stretched on two benches, and at night she could hear the breathing of the ox and the flutter of the few fowls that roosted in its stall. On the boards had been a cotton quilt which she had wrapped round her for mattress and covering. Sometimes in the morning she was waked by the droppings of birds on her face, for the sparrows sheltered under the rafters.

Then she thought of the boy she had grown up with, her foster mother's son, but never her brother. From the time she knew anything she knew that she had been brought into the house to be his wife. She had not loved him because she knew him too well. He was a farm boy like all the others in the village. She saw his round face and fat cheeks now when she thought of him, as he used to be when she was a little girl. Then he had grown tall and thin, and she was just beginning to be shy of him when he died. She had not even made any wedding clothes. He had died so young, before she had begun to think of him really as her husband. When he died her foster mother had blamed her.

"You have brought a curse on my house," she had said. "I ought to have left you to die by the city wall. You were not meant for my son."

She remembered how these words had hurt her. The

farmhouse was her only home, the woman her only mother. The woman had not been unkind. But when she had said these words Ch'iuming knew that she was no more than a foundling again, and she did not belong to that house. When Liu Ma had come and the bargain had been struck, she had said nothing.

"So what could I do but come here?" she now asked herself.

At this moment she heard a footstep, and her blood stopped in her veins. She snatched the silk quilt and drew it to her chin and stared at the closed curtains. They parted. She saw a handsome, heavy face, neither young nor old, and reddened with drinking. The smell of wine spread into the alcove of the bed. He stared at her for a full minute, then he closed the curtains again softly.

For a long time she heard nothing at all. Had he gone away? She dared not move. She lay in the close darkness waiting. If he did not like her she would be sent away to-morrow. But where could she go? If they sent her away would they give her a little money? What happened to concubines who did not please? She grew so frightened of such a fate that now it seemed anything would be better than that.

She sat up impetuously and parted the curtains with one hand and looked out. There he sat motionless in a great chair. He had taken off his outer garments and had on only his inner ones of white silk. But how had he moved so quietly that she had not heard?

She looked at him and he at her. Then she closed the curtains quickly and lay down and hid her face in her hands. He was coming! She heard his soft, heavy footstep upon the tiles of the floor. The silk curtains opened as though they were ripped, and then she felt his hands pulling her hands away from her face.

5

MADAME WU woke out of the deepest sleep she had ever
known. It was morning, and she had slept all night without
waking once. She could not remember when she had done
this. The new candle which Ying had put on the table last
night beside her bed had still its white wick.

Her first feeling was one of complete rest. Fatigue was
gone out of her body, and out of her soul. But there was
something familiar, too, in this relief. She sent her mind
backward over her rich life and found the memory. Thus
she had felt after each of her children had been born. Each
time through the ten moon months the burden within her
had grown heavier, closer, and more invading until only
her most careful self-control had made it possible for her
to keep the gentle poise which was her atmosphere. Then
had come the birth of the child. But to her it was not birth
so much as reclaiming her own body. Her first thought when
the pain stopped abruptly and when she heard that sharp
cry of the separate child was always of her own freedom.
As soon as the child was brought to her, washed and dressed,
she began to love him for what he was, but never because
he was a part of herself. She did not, indeed, wish for any
division of herself. She wanted only to be whole again.

So this morning she felt the same wholeness, but deeper
and more complete. All her duty was now fulfilled. No one
in this house lacked anything which he needed.

. . . But her third son Fengmo came into her mind. Alas,
until he was wed she was not quite free!

She rose at this thought and put her little narrow feet
into the embroidered black satin slippers which Ying always
set on the long bench by the bed. Madame Wu's feet were
a little narrower than they might have been by nature. This
was because many years ago when she had been a child of
five her mother had begun to bind them. Her father was
then travelling in foreign countries with Prince Li Hung
Chang. She had looked at her father's pictures taken in
those foreign countries, and her nurse had told her about

his wisdom and his goodness. Her mother, too, spoke of him often, but always to correct some waywardness in her. "What would your father say to you now?" her mother had inquired often. Because the little girl could not answer this, since she did not know, she always gave up her waywardness. When the mother called the child to her one day, and the child saw the long white bandages of cotton cloth she began to cry. She had seen all this happen to her older sister, that sister who had once run and played so joyfully and now sat all day silent over her embroidery, unwilling even to stand upon the sore, bound feet.

The mother had stopped to stare at her second daughter severely. "What would your father say if he came home and found your feet splayed like a farmer's wife's feet?" she had demanded.

The little girl's sobs had sunk into a whimper, and she had let her feet be bound.

To this day Madame Wu remembered the month of that agony. Then the letter came saying her father was coming home. She endured half a month more, for her father's sake. When he came home she had forced herself to walk to him on those little feet. What joy was like to the joy that came next? Before she had had time to see his face or to call his name, he had given a harsh cry and had lifted her in his arms.

"Take these bands from off the child's feet!" he had commanded. There had been hubbub and outcry. She could never remember a single word of that battle between her elders, but she never forgot the storm. Her mother had cried and her grandmother had screamed with anger and even her grandfather had kept shouting. But her father had sat down and kept her on his knees, and with his own hands he had taken off the bandages and made her feet free. She could still remember the pain, the joy, of the freed feet. He took them in his hands, one and then the other, and rubbed them gently to bring in the blood again, and the blood running into the pinched veins had been first agony and then joy.

"Never—never," he had muttered.

She had clung to him crying. "What if you had not come home!" she cried into his breast. He had come in time to save her. She could run again in a few months. But it was too late for her sister's feet. The bones were broken.

After this there had been nothing but disturbance for three years in the household. Her father had learned new ways in new countries, and he had insisted that she be taught to read. When he died of a sudden cholera at the end of a hot summer three years later, it was too late to bind her feet again, and too late for ignorance because she already knew how to read. She was even allowed to keep on with her reading because she was betrothed, and Old Gentleman was pleased that she could read and that her feet were not bound. "We are very lucky," her mother had said, "to find a rich family so lenient."

Now she remembered her father at this moment when she put her narrow feet into her slippers. Something of that joy of freedom was in her again too. She smiled, and Ying came and caught her smiling.

"You, Mistress," Ying chided her. "You are too happy this morning!" She looked at her and against all her wish to behave decorously she could not keep from smiling. "You do look like a mischievous child," she said.

"Do not try to understand me, good soul," Madame Wu said gaily. "Why should you harass yourself? Let us only be as we always are. Tell me, is the day fair?"

"As though there had never been rain," Ying replied.

"Then," Madame Wu said, "dress me for visiting. I shall go to see Madame Kang as soon as I have eaten. I have a matter to talk about with her. What do you think of her Linyi for our Fengmo?"

"Two knots on the same rope," Ying replied musingly. "Well, Mistress, better to repeat a good thing than a bad one. Our eldest young lord is happy enough with the eldest Kang daughter. But our second lord beat his wife last night."

"Tsemo beat Rulan?" Madame Wu exclaimed.

"I heard her sobbing," Ying said. "It must be she was beaten."

Madame Wu sighed. "Will I never have peace under this roof?"

She ate her breakfast quickly and rose and went to Tsemo's court. But Tsemo had risen even earlier and was already gone. Rulan was still in bed sleeping, the servant said. Madame Wu would not ask a servant why her son had beaten his wife, and so she said, "Tell my son I will see him to-night."

She went on then as she usually did each day to inspect the kitchens and family courts, and when she had examined all parts of the house, had praised here and corrected there, she returned to her own court.

Two hours later she stepped out of the gate of the Wu house. Mr. Wu had some two years before bought a foreign motor-car, but the streets were so narrow that Madame Wu would never willingly use it. She disliked to see the common people flatten themselves against the walls of the houses while the big car spread itself across the street. At the same time she did not enjoy the openness of the rickshaw which Mr. Wu had once given her as a present. She still liked best the privacy of this old-fashioned sedan chair which had been part of her wedding furniture. She told Ying, therefore, to follow in the rickshaw. Then one of the four bearers lifted the curtain and Madame Wu stepped in and sat down and he let the curtain fall. From the small glass window in this curtain she could see enough of the streets for her own interest and yet not be seen.

Thus borne through the crowded streets by the four bearers, she felt she did harm to no one. Her weight was easy for the men, and the sedan was so narrow that none was pushed from its path. Moreover, she liked the courteous call of the head bearer as he cried out to those in his way, "I borrow your light—I borrow your light!" So ought the rich to be courteous to the poor and the high to the low. Madame Wu could never bear oppression of any sort. Since she had been mistress in the Wu house no slave had been beaten nor any servant offended. Even though it was sometimes necessary to dismiss an unfaithful or incapable servant, it was never done on this ground but on some other which, though he knew it was false, yet comforted him before his fellows. She was the more distressed, therefore, when she considered what Ying had told her—that Tsemo had beaten Rulan.

"I will not believe it," she thought, "until I have inquired for the truth." Thus she put the matter from her mind.

The distance between the houses of Wu and Kang was not short, being indeed almost across the entire city. But Madame Wu had no sense of haste. She enjoyed the sunshine falling into the streets still wet with the night's rain. The stones were washed and clean and the people gay and glad of the brightness of the sky. Markets were busy and farmers were already carrying into the city their loads of fresh green cabbages, baskets of eggs, and bundles of fuel grass. The sight of all this life going on always soothed Madame Wu. In this city the Wu family was only one house. It was pleasant to think that there were all these others where men and women lived together and brought forth their children and children's children. And in this nation there were many more such cities, and round the world many other nations where in different ways men and women lived the same life. She liked to dwell upon such thoughts. Her own life took its proportion. What was one grief among so many like it, or what was one joy in a world of such joys?

In something under an hour the sedan was set down before the gate of the Kang house. Ying had, of course, sent a man-servant ahead to tell of Madame Wu's coming, and so she was expected. The great red varnished gates swung open, and a servant was waiting. Ying hastened forward from her rickshaw to help Madame Wu out of her chair. She carried under her arm Madame Wu's small travelling toilet case, lest she wish to smooth her hair or touch her face with powder.

Then they entered the gates, but before they had crossed the first court Madame Kang herself came to greet her friend. The two ladies clasped hands.

"How good of you, Sister!" Madame Kang cried eagerly. She was anxious to hear from Madame Wu's own lips all that had happened. She knew, since the servants in the two houses came and went, that Madame Wu had fulfilled her plan. She knew even that last night Ch'iuming had gone into Mr. Wu's court.

"I have come to talk about many things, Sister," Madame Wu replied. "But I come too early—I disturb you."

"How can you say that!" Madame Kang replied. She searched her friend's fresh and lovely face. It was not in the least way changed. The tranquil eyes, the composed and exquisite mouth, the pearl-pale skin, all were at their best.

"How beautiful you always are," Madame Kang said tenderly, and was conscious, though without the least pain, of her own hair as yet unbrushed.

"I rise early," Madame Wu said. "Now let us go inside and while your hair is brushed I will wait.

"Do not mind my hair," Madame Kang urged. "I get it combed in the afternoon. Somehow the mornings pass too quickly."

She looked round and laughed as she spoke, for behind her a dozen children seemed to come from nowhere. Children and grandchildren were mingled together. She stooped and picked up the smallest one, not yet able to walk, but hung on his feet by a cotton cloth passed round his middle and held at the two ends by a little bondmaid. The child was unwashed and none too clean, although his coat was of satin, but Madame Kang smelled him with love, as though he were fresh from the tub, and held him close.

Together the two friends walked into the house and through two courts until they reached Madame Kang's own court. There she put down the child whom she had carried all this time, and waved her two plump hands at the children and small bondmaids who had followed her. "Away with you!" she cried heartily. Then, seeing their faces fall, she put her hand into her loose coat and brought out a handful of small cash. These she pressed into the hands of the eldest bondmaid. "Go and buy peanuts for them all," she commanded her. "With shells!" she called after the eager child, "so that it will take a long time for them to be eaten!"

She laughed her rich rolling laughter at the sight of the children scampering towards the street. Then she seized Madame Wu's hand again and led her into her own room and closed the door.

"Now we are alone," she said. She sat down as soon as Madame Wu was seated, and she leaned forward, her hands on her knees. "Tell me everything," she said.

But Madame Wu looked at her friend. A certain blankness mingled with surprise appeared in her eyes.

"It is a strange thing," she said after a second's pause, "but I feel I have nothing to tell."

"How can that be?" Madame Kang cried. "I am as full of questions as a hen of eggs. The girl—who is she—did you like her? Did he like her?"

"I like her," Madame Wu said. Now she knew, as her friend paused, that she had been wilfully not thinking of

Mr. Wu and Ch'iuming this morning. Did he like her? She forced herself to go on without answering this question that sprang up like a snake in her heart.

"I gave her a name—Ch'iuming. She is only an ordinary girl, but a good one. I am sure he will like her. Everybody will like her, because there is nothing about her to dislike. No one in the house will be jealous of her."

"Heaven!" Madame Kang exclaimed in wonder. "And you say all this as though you had hired a new nurse for a grandchild! Why, when my father took a concubine my mother cried and tried to hang herself, and we had to watch her night and day, and when he took a second concubine the first one swallowed her ear-rings, and so it went until he had the five he ended with. They all hated one another and contended for him." Madame Kang's big laughter rolled out of her. "They used to hunt his shoes—he would leave his shoes in the room of the one he planned to visit that night. Then another would steal them. At last, for peace, he divided his time among them equally."

"They must have been silly women, those concubines," Madame Wu said calmly. "I do not mean your mother Meichen. Of course it is natural she might have believed in a man's heart. But the concubines!"

"There never was a woman like you, Ailien," Madame Kang said fondly. "At least tell me—could you sleep last night?"

"Last night," Madame Wu said, "I slept very well because of the rain on the roof."

"Oh, the rain on the roof!" Madame Kang cried, and went into gusts of laughter so that she had to wipe her eyes with her sleeves.

Madame Wu waited, smiling, until this was over. Then she said seriously, "I do have a matter to talk about with you, Meichen."

Madame Kang grew grave whenever she heard this tone in her friend's voice. "I will laugh no more. What is it?"

"You know my son Fengmo," Madame Wu said. "Do you think I should send him away to school?"

This question she put very skilfully. If Madame Kang declared it was not necessary she would at once ask for Linyi. If on the other hand——

"It is altogether a matter of what this boy will do with

114

himself," Madame Kang answered. Her large round face fell into lines.

"He has never shown what he wants," Madame Wu said. "He has until now merely been growing up. But after seventeen a mother must begin to watch a son."

"Of course," Madame Kang agreed. She pursed her lips and thought of Fengmo, his arrogant bladelike body and proud head.

"Come," Madame Wu said frankly, "why do I not speak the truth to you? I had thought of pouring our blood into the same stream again. Fengmo and Linyi—what do you say?"

Madame Kang clapped her hands twice together. "Good!" she cried. Then she let her plump hands drop. "But that Linyi," she said, mournfully. "It is one thing for me to say good. How do I know what she will say?"

"You should never have let her go to a foreign school," Madame Wu said. "I told you that at the time."

"You were right," Madame Kang said sadly. "Nothing at home is good enough for her now. She complains about everything. She quarrels at her father when he spits on the floor, poor soul. She wants us to put jars on the floor for spittle. But the babies pick up the jars and drop them and break them. And Linyi is angry because she wants all the babies to wear cloths tied about their little bottoms. But with thirteen small grandchildren under this roof still not able to contain their water, how can we tie cloths about all of them? Our ancestors taught us wisdom in seatless trousers. Shall we flout their wisdom? We have three wash maids as it is."

"In our house she would not be troubled with any small children except her own," Madame Wu said. "And with her own a woman learns wisdom."

She was too kind to tell Madame Kang that in this matter she secretly felt sympathy with Linyi. The wet nurses and maids in this house were continually holding out the babies to pass their water on the floor until one did not know where to step. Madame Wu had never allowed these easy-going ways in her own house. The maids had always commands to take the small children into certain corners or behind trees.

Madame Kang looked doubtfully at her friend. "I would be glad for you to have her," she said. "She needs to be married and have her mind taken up. But I love you too well not to tell you her faults. I feel she will demand foreign learning in Fengmo even if she is willing to marry him. She will think it shameful that he speaks no foreign language."

"But with whom would he speak it?" Madame Wu asked. "Would she and he sit together and talk foreign tongues? It would be silly."

"Certainly it would," Madame Kang agreed. "But it is a matter for pride, you know, in these young women, nowadays, to chatter in a foreign tongue."

The two ladies looked thoughtfully at each other. Then Madame Wu said plainly, "Either Linyi must be satisfied with Fengmo as he is, or I shall have to let the matter drop. War is in the air, and my sons may not go off to coastal cities. Here we are safe, for we are provinces away from the sea."

"Wait!" Madame Kang was suddenly cheered. "I have it," she said. "There is a foreign priest in the city. Why do you not engage him as a tutor for Fengmo? Then when I speak to Linyi, I can tell her Fengmo is learning foreign tongues."

"A foreign man?" Madame Wu repeated doubtfully. "But how could we have him come into the house? Would there not be disturbances? I hear all Western men are very lusty and fierce."

"This is a priest," Madame Kang said. "He is beyond such thoughts."

Madame Wu considered the matter still more thoughtfully. "Well," she said at last, "if Linyi should insist upon this, it would be better than sending Fengmo away from us into a foreign school."

"So it is," Madame Kang agreed.

Madame Wu rose. "Then you will speak to Linyi and I will speak to Fengmo."

"If Fengmo will not?" Madame Kang asked.

"He will," Madame Wu said, "for I will choose the right time. With a man, young or old, the important thing is the choice of the time."

"How well you know," Madame Kang murmured.

The two ladies rose and hand in hand wandered out of the room. Tea was set in the court and some cakes.

"Will you not stay and refresh yourself, Sister?" Madame Kang asked.

But Madame Wu shook her head. "If you will forgive the

116

discourtesy," she said, "I will go home. To-day may be the right time for me to speak to Fengmo."

She did not like to tell even Madame Kang that Fengmo might be disturbed because he had seen Ch'iuming before she had gone into his father's court. She said good-bye and left some money for a gift to the maid who had prepared tea, and Ying came from the servants' rooms where she had been gossiping, and so Madame Wu went home again.

The first person whom she saw, however, upon her return was not Fengmo, but the foreigner, Little Sister Hsia. Even as all the servants in all the houses of the city knew what went on in the Wu family house and the Kang family house, who were the two great families, so Madame Wu knew that Little Sister Hsia's cook also had heard and told the news.

Little Sister Hsia was just crossing the main court inside the gate when she saw Madame Wu. She stopped at once and cried out, "Oh, Madame Wu, I have just *heard*—it can't be true?"

"Come in," Madame Wu said kindly. "Is it not a fair day? The air is not often so clear at this season. We will sit out-doors, and Ying must bring us something to eat. It must be nearly noon." She guided Little Sister Hsia across the general court and into the one which was her own.

"Please sit down," she said. "I must go to my own rooms for a moment. But rest yourself. Enjoy the morning."

Smiling and making her graceful bows, Madame Wu with-drew into her own rooms. Ying followed her sourly.

"It must be we shall have rain, again," she muttered. "The devils are out."

"Hush," Madame Wu said. But she smiled as she sat down before the mirror. She smoothed a hair out of place, touched her cheeks with powder, and changed her ear-rings from plain gold ones to her jade flower ones. Then she washed and perfumed her hands and went outdoors again.

Little Sister Hsia's pale face was twisted with sympathy. She rose from her chair with the awkward swiftness which was her habit.

"Oh, good friend," she sighed, "what a trial has come on you! I never dreamed—Mr. Wu seemed so different from other men—I always thought——"

"I am very glad you have come this morning," Madame Wu said lightly, with her warm smile. "You can help me."

117

They were seated. Little Sister Hsia leaned forward in her intense way, her hands clenched together. "Anything," she murmured, "anything! Dear Madame Wu, sometimes the Lord punishes those whom he loves——"

Madame Wu opened her large eyes widely. "Do you wish to preach gospel this morning, Little Sister?" she inquired. "If you do, I will postpone what I was about to say."

"Only to comfort you," Little Sister Hsia said, "only to help you."

"But I am very well," Madame Wu said in surprise.

"I heard, I thought——" Little Sister Hsia faltered, much bewildered.

"You must not heed the gossip of servants," Madame Wu said gently. "They always wish to be bearers of some exciting news. Had they their way we shall all be ill to-day and dead to-morrow and risen again on the third day."

Little Sister Hsia looked sharply at Madame Wu. Was she making a joke? She decided not to be angry. "Then it is not true?" she asked.

"I do not know what is not true or true," Madame Wu returned. "But I can assure you that nothing happens in this house without my knowledge and my permission."

She took pity on the slight purplish blush that now spotted the pale foreign face at which she looked. "You are always kind," Madame Wu said gently. "Will you help me?"

Little Sister Hsia nodded. Her hands fell limply apart. A shade of disappointment hung about her pale lips and eyes.

Madame Wu touched her own pretty lips with her perfumed silk handkerchief. "I feel my third son needs more education," she said in her gentle voice, whose gentleness seemed always to put distances between her and the one to whom she spoke. "I have decided, therefore, to have him taught by a suitable foreign man to speak a foreign language and read foreign books. After all, what was enough for our ancestors is not to-day enough for us. The seas no longer divide the peoples, and Heaven is no more our own canopy. Can you tell me if there is a foreign man in the city whom I can invite to teach Fengmo?"

Little Sister Hsia was so taken aback by this request that had nothing to do with what she had heard that for a moment she could not speak at all.

"I hear that there is a foreign priest," Madame Wu went on. "Can you tell me about him?"

"Priest?" Little Sister Hsia murmured.

"So I hear," Madame Wu said.

Little Sister Hsia looked doubtful. "If it is the one I think you must mean," she said, "I don't think that you would want him for your son."

"Is he not learned?" Madame Wu inquired.

"What is the wisdom of man, dear friend?" Little Sister Hsia asked. "He is as good as an atheist!"

"Why do you say that?" Madame Wu asked.

"I cannot think he is a true believer," Little Sister Hsia said gravely.

"Perhaps he has his own religion," Madame Wu said.

"There is only one true religion," Little Sister Hsia said positively.

Madame Wu smiled. "Will you ask him to come and see me?" she asked.

She was astonished to see a flying dark blush sweep over the plain face before her.

"He is unmarried," Little Sister Hsia said. "I don't know what he would think if I were to visit him."

Madame Wu put out a kind hand and touched the bony fingers lying on Little Sister Hsia's lap. "None could suspect your virtue," she said.

The kindness melted the foreign woman's shyness. "Dear Madame Wu," she said, "I would do anything to help you."

The edge of intensity crept into her voice again, but Madame Wu put it off gracefully, disliking intensity above all things. "You are so good," she said. She clapped her hands, and Ying came in with the tray of tea and sweetmeats.

For half an hour Madame Wu busied herself with this. Then she took steps to help her guest to leave.

"Now," she said in her sweet way, "would you like to make a prayer before you go?"

"I'd love to," Little Sister Hsia said.

She closed her eyes and bowed her head, and her voice began its fervent address to someone unseen. Madame Wu sat in graceful silence while this went on. She did not close her eyes. Instead she watched Little Sister Hsia's face with forbearing comprehension. How empty was this soul, so alone, so far from home! She had come across the sea to do her good works. All knew of her, of her weekly meeting to teach sewing to beggar women. All knew that she lived poorly and gave away most of what she had. But how lonely the woman in this poor creature! A kind affection stirred in the depths of Madame Wu's heart. Little Sister Hsia was ignorant, of course, and one could not listen to her, but she was good and she was lonely.

When Little Sister Hsia opened her eyes she was astonished at the liquid warmth she saw in the great beautiful eyes of Madame Wu. For a moment she thought her prayer had been miraculously answered. Perhaps God had touched the heart of this heathen woman?

But Madame Wu rose and by that firm movement bade Little Sister Hsia farewell. "You will send the priest to me soon?" she asked, and made it a command in the asking.

Against her will Little Sister Hsia found herself promising that she would.

"How can I repay you?" Madame Wu said courteously. "At least, let me say this, Little Sister. In return for your kindness in arranging a teacher for my third son, please pray for me whenever you like." So she dismissed her visitor.

All day during this day Madame Wu had not forgotten what Ying had told her, that she had heard Rulan sobbing in the night. But Madame Wu had long ago learned that the affairs of a great household must be managed one by one and in order. This order was first in her own mind. She had tried to see Tsemo and heaven had prevented it. The time was not ripe, therefore. And as she had learned to do, while she pondered on large things, she acted on small ones.

She sent for the cook to bring in his monthly accounts, which had been due two days earlier but which he had withheld, feeling the confusion in the house. Madame Wu read these accounts and remarked on the high price of the fuel grass.

Now Ying always took care to be present when the accounts were presented, for she believed that her husband, although a better cook than any could find, was nevertheless not clever at anything else. When Madame Wu spoke of the fuel, she knew at once that some other servant had reported the matter, and she guessed that it was a certain middle-aged

120

woman servant who had once approached the cook with offers of love. But Ying's husband knew better than to look at another woman, and now the woman had turned sour and could not find enough fault with Ying and the cook.

When Madame Wu mentioned the fuel, Ying cried out to her husband, "You bone, I told you not to get it at the West Gate Market! Everything is more dear there."

"We should not buy any fuel at all as early as this," Madame Wu said. "The fuel from our own lands should be enough until the eighth month, when new grass can be cut."

"The steward has ploughed some of the grass lands," the cook replied.

Madame Wu knew it was not necessary to carry the matter further. She accepted his excuse since she had administered her rebuke, and she closed the books and gave them to him. Then she went to her money-box and brought out what was due on the past month and enough to use as cash for the next month. The family numbered something over sixty persons, including all mouths, and the sum was never small.

The manservant in charge of the clothing and repairs came next, and with him the two sewing women, and Madame Wu discussed with them the summer garments required for servants and family, the changes of bedding, and such matters. When these were finished, carpenters came in to estimate the costs of repairs to two leaking roofs, and the building of a new outhouse for storage.

To all such affairs Madame Wu gave her close and entire attention. It was her talent that whatever she did, it was with the whole of her mind, and for that time nothing else was. When one affair was settled, her mind went wholly to the next one. Thus during this day she accepted one task after the other. It was only when dusk came on and the household matters were finished that she acknowledged her own thoughts again. They centred on Fengmo.

"I have this day proceeded very far towards the decision of his life," she thought. She had not risen from the big chair by the library table, at which she had worked all day. While she was now more than ever firm in her decision that he should marry Linyi, nevertheless it was only just that she should talk with him and allow him some freedom first to rebel. She summoned Ying from the next room where she was preparing the bed for the night.

"Go and tell Fengmo to come here," she said. She hesitated while Ying waited.

"And when you have summoned my son," Madame Wu went on, "invite the Second Lady to appear at the family meal to-night."

Ying pursed her mouth and went away, and Madame Wu sat, her finger and thumb to her lip, while she waited. At this time Fengmo would be in his room, since it was about the hour for the evening meal. If Fengmo were in good humour with what she decided, she would eat to-night with the family instead of alone, as she had done during the last few days. It was time for her to come out and take her place among them again.

In a few minutes she heard Fengmo's step. She knew the step of each son. Liangmo's was slow and firm, Tsemo's quick and uneven, and Yenmo ran everywhere. But Fengmo walked with a rhythm, three steps always quicker than the fourth. He appeared at the door of the library, wearing his school uniform of dark-blue cloth. On his head was a visored cap of the same cloth, and on the cap was a band giving the name of his school, the National Reconstruction Middle School.

Madame Wu smiled at her son and beckoned to him to come in.

"What is the meaning of this National Reconstruction?" she inquired half playfully.

"It is only a name, Mother," Fengmo replied. He sat down on a side chair, took off his cap, and whirled it like a wheel between the fingers of his two hands.

"It means nothing to you?" Madame Wu inquired.

"Of course we all want national reconstruction," Fengmo replied.

"Without knowing what it means?" Madame Wu asked in the same half-playful manner.

Fengmo laughed. "At present I am having difficulty with algebra," he replied. "Perhaps when I have overcome that I will understand National Reconstruction better."

"Algebra," Madame Wu mused. "In India several such studies were first devised and then found their way to Europe."

Fengmo looked surprised. He never expected his mother to have any knowledge out of books, and Madame Wu knew this and enjoyed surprising him.

"You look pale," she said suddenly. "Are you taking your tonic of deers'-horn powder?"

"It tastes worse than rotten fish," Fengmo objected.

Madame Wu smiled her pretty smile. "Then don't take it," she said comfortably. "Why take what you dislike so much?"

"Thank you, Mother," Fengmo said, but he was again surprised.

Madame Wu leaned forward, and her hands fell clasped into her lap. "Fengmo," she said, "it is time we talked about your life."

"My life?" Fengmo looked up and stopped whirling the cap.

"Yes," Madame Wu repeated, "your life. Your father and I have already discussed it."

"Mother, don't think I will consent to your choosing a wife for me," Fengmo said hotly.

"Of course I would not," Madame Wu said quickly. "All that I can do is to bring certain names to you and ask you if you like any of them. Naturally I have considered your tastes, as well as the position of the family. I have put aside any thought of such a girl as the Chen family's second daughter, who has been brought up in old-fashioned ways."

"I would never have such a girl," Fengmo declared.

"Of course not. But there is another difficulty," Madame Wu said in her calm way. "The girls are also demanding much to-day. It is not as it was when I was a girl. I left all such things in my mother's hands, and my uncle's who took my dead father's place. But now the girls—the sort you would want, Fengmo—do not want a young man who cannot speak at least one foreign tongue."

"I study some English in school," Fengmo said haughtily.

"But you cannot speak it very well," Madame Wu replied. "I do not know that language myself, but certainly I hear you stammer and halt when you make those sounds. I do not blame you, but so it is."

"What girl will not have me?" Fengmo asked angrily.

Madame Wu rode to her goal upon this anger as a boat rides the surf to the shore. "Madame Kang's third daughter, Linyi," she said, and while she had seen no interest pass between them, Fengmo's present anger was enough. He was immediately interested.

123

"That girl!" he muttered. "She looks too proud. I hate her looks."

"She is really very handsome," Madame Wu retorted. "But that is not the important thing. I do not speak of her except as one of others. If Linyi, who knows our family and position, still objects to you, can we look higher?"

"You could send me away to a foreign school," Fengmo said eagerly.

"I will not do that," she replied in her pretty voice that was nevertheless as inexorable as sun and moon. "There will be war over the whole world in a few years from now. At such a time all my sons must be at home."

Fengmo looked at her astounded. "How can you tell such things, Mother?"

"I am not a fool, though all the world around me are fools," Madame Wu said quietly. "When certain steps are taken and none prevents them, then more steps are taken."

The boy was silent, his eyes fixed on his mother's face. They were large and black like hers, but they had not the depth of her eyes. He was still too young. But he did not speak, as though he were struggling to comprehend the things of which she spoke.

"I have heard there is a foreign priest here in the city,' she went on, "and he is a learned man. It is possible that for a sum he would teach you to speak other languages. For this are you willing? Foreign languages may serve you well some day. It is not of marriage only that I think. The times ahead are due for change."

Her voice, so clear, so musical, was nevertheless full of portent. Fengmo loved and feared his mother at the same time. To him she was always right, and the few times that he had disobeyed her she had not punished him, but he was always punished nevertheless. Slowly and hardly he had learned that what she said carried wisdom. But, being a boy, he demurred for a moment.

"A priest?" he repeated. "I do not believe in religions."

"I do not ask you to believe in religions," she said in reply. "It is not of that we speak."

"He would try to convert me," Fengmo said sullenly. "Little Sister Hsia is always trying to convert everybody in the house. Whenever she passes me she hands me a gospel paper."

124

"Do you need to yield to conversion?" Madame Wu asked. "Are you so weak? You must learn to take from a person that which is his best and ignore all else. Come, try the priest for a month, and if you wish then to stop his teaching, I will agree to it."

It was the secret of her power in this house that she never allowed her will to be felt as absolute. She gave time and the promise of an end, and then she used the time to shape events to her own end.

Fengmo began to whirl the cap slowly again between his hands. "A month then," he said. "Not more than a month if I do not like it."

"A month," Madame Wu agreed. She rose. "And now, my son, we will go to the night meal together. Your father will have begun without us."

In the Wu household men and women ate at separate tables. Thus at the threshold of the great dining-room Fengmo parted from his mother and went to one end, where his father and brothers and the men cousins were already seated, and Madame Wu walked with her usual grace to the tables where the women were seated. All rose at her approach. She saw at once that Ch'iuming had taken her place among them. The girl sat shyly apart from the others and held a small child on her knee. With this child still in her arms she rose and managed to shield her face with the child. But Madame Wu had taken a full look at her before she did this. The girl was grave, but that was natural in a strange household. It was enough that she was here.

"Please sit down," Madame Wu said courteously to all and to no one. She took her own place at the highest seat and picked up her chopsticks. Meng had been serving the others, and Madame Wu put her chopsticks down again. "Proceed for me, please, Meng," she said. "I have been busy all day with household matters, and I am a little weary."

She leaned back smiling, and in her usual way she gave a word to each of her daughters-in-law, and she spoke to Meng's little boy whom the nurse held. The child was fretting, and Madame Wu took her chopsticks and chose a bit of meat and gave it to him. Then she spoke directly to Ch'iuming.

"Second Lady," she said kindly, "you must eat what you like best. The fish is usually good."

Ch'iuming looked up and flushed a bright red. She rose and gave a little bow, the child still clutched in her arms. "Thank you, Elder Sister," she said in a faint voice. She sat down and did not speak again. When a servant put a bowl of rice before her she fed the child first.

But by this kind address Madame Wu told the whole house that Ch'iuming's place was set, and that the life of the family must now include this one added to it. All heard the few words, and a moment's silence followed them. Then servant spoke to servant and nurse to child to cover the silence.

Madame Wu accepted the food given her and began to eat in her delicate slow fashion. The little grandson, wooed by the gift of the meat, now clamoured suddenly to come and sit on her knee. Meng reproved him tenderly. "You with your face and hands all dirty!"

Madame Wu looked up as though she had been in a dream. "Is it me the child wants?" she asked.

"He is so dirty, Mother," Meng said.

"Certainly he is to come to me," Madame Wu said. She put out her hands and took the heavy child and set him on her knee. Then with her instinctive daintiness she took up a pair of clean chopsticks and found bits of meat in the central bowls and fed them to the child. She did not speak, but she smiled at each mouthful.

The child did not smile back. He sat as though in a dream of content, opening his little mouth and chewing each bit with silent pleasure. It was Madame Wu's usual effect on children. Without effort she made them feel content to be near her. And she took content from the grandchild. In him her duty to the house was complete, and in him, too, her secret loneliness in this house was assuaged. She did not know she was lonely, and had anyone told her that she was, she would have denied it, amazed at such misreading. But she was too lonely for anyone to reach her soul. Her soul had outstripped her life. It had gone out far beyond the four walls within which her body lived. It roamed the world, and reached into the past and climbed towards the future, and her many thoughts played about that constant voyaging. But now and again her soul came home to this house. It came back now. She was suddenly fully aware of this child and of his meaning. The generations marched on, hers ending, his beginning.

"Son of my son," she murmured and continued to put bits of meat into his small red mouth, opened for what she gave. When he was fed she gave him to his mother.

But before the others had finished she was finished, and she rose begging them to continue, and walked slowly out of the room. As she passed Mr. Wu and her sons they greeted her, half rising from their seats, and she smiled and inclined her head and went on her way.

That night again she slept the whole night through and did not wake.

·　　·　　·　　·

But to Ch'iuming the half-hour of Madame Wu's presence was her marriage ceremony. The night had left her confused. Had she pleased him or not? Mr. Wu had not spoken one word to her, and he had left her before dawn. She had slept after that until noon. No one had come near her all afternoon except a woman servant. Then she had been bidden by Ying, at evening, to join the family meal. She had hastened to make herself ready for this, and when the time came she had slipped into the dining-room late, and had quickly taken the child from his nurse. He had not cried. But children never cried with her. In the village she had cared for many babies of farm mothers. One by one the ladies who were now her relatives had greeted her, half carelessly, half shyly, and she had only bent her head a little in reply. Nor could she eat.

But after Madame Wu had left the room she suddenly felt ravenous and, turning herself somewhat so that she did not face the others, she ate two bowls of rice and meat as quickly as she could.

When the meal was over she stood waiting in deepening shyness while Meng and Rulan went away. But Meng in her gentle kindness stayed a moment to speak to her. "I will come to see you to-morrow, Second Lady," she said.

"I am not worthy," Ch'iuming replied faintly. She could not meet Meng's eyes, but she was comforted and happy. She lifted her eyes, and Meng saw the timid desolate heart.

"I will come and bring my child," she promised.

127

And Ch'iuming went out with the women and children, hiding herself among them from the men. But they looked at her, each in his own secret fashion.

That night Mr. Wu came early to the peony court, and she was not yet in bed. She was sewing upon her unfinished garments when she heard his step. She rose as he entered and turned her face away. He sat down while she stood, and he cleared his throat, put his hands on his knees, and looked at her.

"You," he began, not calling her by name, "you must not be afraid of me."

She could not answer. She clung to the garment she held with both hands and stood like stone before him.

"In this house," Mr. Wu began again, "there is everything to make you happy. My sons' mother is kind. There are young women, my sons' wives, and young cousins' wives, and many children. You look good-tempered, and certainly you are obliging. You will be very happy here."

Still she did not answer. Mr. Wu coughed and loosened his belt a little. He had eaten very heartily, and he felt somewhat breathless. But he had not finished what he wished to say.

"For me," he went on, "you have only a few duties. I like to sleep late. Do not wake me if I am here. In the night I like tea if I am wakeful, but not red tea. I am hot in blood, and cannot have two quilts even in winter. These and other things you will learn, doubtless."

The garment dropped from her hand. She looked at him and forgot her shyness. "Then—I am wanted?" She put the question to him out of her longing to find shelter somewhere under Heaven.

"Certainly," he said. "Have I not been telling you so?" He smiled, and his smooth handsome face lit from a sudden heat from within him. She saw it and understood it. But to-night she would not be afraid. It was a little price to pay, a very little price to pay a kind man, for a home at last.

⋆ 6 ⋆

LITTLE Sister Hsia was always acute to her duty, but Madame
Wu had not expected such promptness, for seven or eight
days later Ying came running in. Her little round eyes were
glittering with surprise.

"Lady, Lady!" she cried.

Madame Wu was walking among her orchids, and she
stopped in displeasure. "Ying!" she said firmly. "Close your
mouth. You look like a fish on a hook. Now tell me what is
the matter."

Ying obeyed her, but almost immediately she began again,
"The largest man—I ever did see—a foreigner! He says you
sent for him."

"I?" Madame Wu said blankly. Then she remembered.
"Perhaps I did," she said.

"Lady, you said nothing to me," Ying reproached her. "I
told the gateman by no means to let him in. We have never
had a foreign man in this house."

"I do not tell you everything," Madame Wu replied. "Let
him come in at once."

Ying retired, stupefied, and Madame Wu went on walking
among her orchids. Even in so short a time the plants had
revived after their transplanting. They would do well in
this shadowy court. She wondered if the new peonies were
doing as well. At this moment she heard a deep, resonant
voice from the round gate into the court.

"Madame!"

She had been expecting the voice but was not prepared
for the quality of its power. She looked up from the orchids
and saw a tall, wide-shouldered man in a long brown robe
which was tied about the waist by a rope. It was the priest.
His right hand clasped a cross that lay on his breast. She
knew that the cross was a Christian symbol, but she was not
interested in that. What interested her was the size and
strength of the hand which held it.

"I do not know how to address you," she said in her light

silvery voice, "otherwise I would return your greeting. Will you come in?"

The priest bent his great head and came through the gate into the court. Ying followed behind him, her face pale with fright.

"Come into my library if you please," Madame Wu said. She stood aside at the entrance for the priest to enter ahead of her. But he loosened his hand from the cross and made a slight gesture towards the door. "In my country," he said smiling, "it is the lady who enters first."

"Is it so?" she murmured. "But it is true that I had perhaps better lead the familiar way."

She went in and sat down in her accustomed seat and motioned towards the other chair across the table. Ying crept to the door and stood staring, half hidden. Madame Wu saw her. "Ying, come out," she commanded her. Then she turned to the priest with a slight smile. "This silly woman has never seen a man of your size, and she cannot keep from looking at you. Pray forgive her."

The priest replied with these curious words, "God gave me this immense body perhaps for the amusement of those who look at me. Well, laughter is a good thing." His great voice rumbled round the room.

"Heaven," Ying said faintly, looking up into the beams above her, "it is like thunder."

"Ying, go and fetch hot tea," Madame Wu commanded to calm her, and Ying scuttled away like a cat.

The priest sat motionless, his huge body filling the big carved chair. Yet he was lean to thinness, Madame Wu now saw. The cross on his breast was of gold. He was dark-skinned, and his large dark eyes lay very clear and sad in their deep sockets. His hair was neither short nor long, and it curled slightly. He wore a beard, and the hair of it was black and fine. In this dark beard his lips showed with unusual redness.

"How am I to address you?" Madame Wu inquired. "I forgot to ask Little Sister Hsia your name."

"I have no name of my own," the priest replied. "But I have been given the name of André. It is as good as another. Some call me Father André. I should prefer, Madame, that you called me Brother André."

Madame Wu neither accepted nor rejected this wish. She

did not pronounce the name or the title. Instead she asked another question. "And your religion?"

"Let us not speak to-day of my religion," Brother André replied.

Madame Wu smiled a little at this. "I thought all priests wanted to talk of their religion."

Brother André gave her a long, full look. In spite of the power in his eyes there was no boldness in this look, and Madame Wu was not startled by it. It was as impersonal as a lamp which a man holds up to show someone an unknown path. "I was told you wanted to speak to me, Madame," Brother André said.

"Ah, so I do," Madame Wu said. But she paused. She now perceived that Ying had scattered the news of a monster as she went to the kitchens. She heard whisperings and flutterings at the door. From where she sat she saw glimpses of children. She called in an amiable voice, "Come, children—come and see him!"

Immediately a flock of the children crowded about the door. They looked like flowers in the morning sunshine, and Madame Wu was proud of them.

"They want to look at you," she explained.

"Why not?" he replied, and turned himself towards them. They shrank back at this, but when he remained motionless and smiling they came near again.

"He does not eat little children, doubtless," Madame Wu said to them. "Indeed, perhaps he is like a Buddhist and eats only fruits and vegetables."

"That is true," Brother André said.

"How are you so big?" a child asked breathlessly. He was the son of a younger cousin in the Wu family.

"God made me so," Brother André replied.

"But I suppose your parents were also large," Madame Wu said.

"I do not now remember my parents," Brother André said gently.

"What is your country?" a lad inquired. He was old enough to go to school, and he knew about countries.

"I have no country," Brother André said. "Wherever I am is my home."

"You have been here for many years," Madame Wu said. "You speak our language perfectly."

"I speak many languages in order to be able to converse with all people," he replied.

"But you have lived long in our city?" she persisted. She was beginning to be exceedingly curious about this man.

"Only a year," he replied.

By now the children were bold, and they came quite close to him. "What is that on the chain around your neck?" one of them asked. He pointed his delicate golden little forefinger.

"That is my cross," Brother André said. He took up the heavy plain cross as he spoke and held it towards them.

"Shall I hold it?" the child asked.

"If you like," Brother André said.

"No," Madame Wu spoke sharply. "Do not touch it, child."

Brother André turned to her. "But Madame, it is harmless."

"He shall not touch it," she replied coldly.

Brother André let the cross drop upon his breast again and folded his big hands on his knees and kept silent.

Ying came in with the tea, pushing her path among the children. "Your mothers are calling you," she said loudly. "All your mothers are calling!"

"Return to your mothers," Madame Wu said without lifting her voice. Immediately the children turned and ran away.

Brother André looked at her with sudden appreciation in his deep eyes. "They do not fear you, but they obey you," he said.

"They are good children," she said, and was pleased with his understanding.

"You are also good," he said calmly. "But I am not sure you are happy."

These words, said so calmly, struck Madame Wu as sharply as though a hidden knife had pierced her without her knowing exactly where it had struck. She began at once to deny them. "I am, on the contrary, entirely happy. I have arranged my life exactly as I wish it. And I have sons——"

He lifted his deep and penetrating eyes, but he did not speak. Instead he listened attentively. It was the quality of this silent and absolute attention which made her falter. "That is," she went on, "I am entirely happy except that I feel the need of more knowledge of some sort. What sort I do not know myself."

"Perhaps it is not so much knowledge as more understanding of that which you already know," he said.

How did it come about that she was speaking to this stranger of herself? She considered this a moment, and then put aside her reply. "It was not for myself that I have invited you to come hither," she said. "It is for my third son. I wish him to speak a foreign language."

"Which language?" he inquired.

"Which is the best?" she asked.

"French is the most beautiful," he said, "and Italian is the most poetic, and Russian the most powerful, German the most solid. But more business is done in English than in any other."

"He had better study English then," Madame Wu said with decision. She lifted her eyes to his dark face. "What is your fee?"

"I take no fee," Brother André said quietly. "I have no use for money."

"A priest with no use for money?" Her smile held a fine irony.

"*I* have no use for money," Brother André repeated with emphasis upon himself.

"But you put me into a lower position if you compel me to take something for nothing," Madame Wu said. "Shall I not give money to your religion then—for good works?"

"No, religion is better without such gifts," Brother André replied. He considered a moment and then went on, "It may be that from time to time there will be things which ought to be done in this your own city—such, perhaps, as a place for foundlings to be housed. I have taken some of these foundlings myself until I could find good parents for them. When there are such things to be done I will come to you, Madame, and your help will be my reward."

"But these things in our own city are not for you," she said. "Is there nothing I can do for you?"

"This is to do for me, Madame," he replied. His voice tolled through the room, and she did not contradict it. Ying, who had withdrawn into the court, came and looked in and went away again when she saw them sitting there as they had been.

"When shall we begin the lessons?" Madame Wu asked. She felt unable to contradict this man.

"Now, if you like," he replied. "All times are alike to me."

"Will you come every evening?" she asked. "My son goes to the national school by day."

"As often as I am wanted," he replied.

She rose then and summoned Ying. "Tell Fengmo to come here." She stood on the threshold of the door, the garden on one hand, the library on the other. She had for a moment a strange sense of being between two worlds. She stepped into the court and left the priest sitting alone. She stood listening as if she expected him to call. But she heard nothing. On the encircling wall a nightingale alighted as it did every evening about this hour. Very slowly it sang four clear notes. Then it saw her and flew away. She was nearly sorry she had invited this foreigner to come here. What strange things he might teach in foreign words! She had been too quick. She walked to the door again and glanced in. Would he think it rude that she had left him alone? But when she looked in she saw his great head sunk on his breast and his eyes closed. He was asleep? No, his lips were moving. She drew back in a slight fear and was glad to see Fengmo approaching through the gate opposite where she stood.

"Fengmo!" she called.

She turned her head and saw the man's head lift, and the dark eyes opened and glowed.

"Fengmo, come here!" she called again.

"I come, Mother," Fengmo replied. He was there in an instant, very young and slight in comparison to the great priest. She was surprised to see how small he was, he who she had always thought was tall. She took his hand and led him into the library.

"This is my third son, Fengmo," she said to Brother André.

"Fengmo," the priest repeated. In courtesy he should have said Third Young Lord, but he simply repeated his name, Fengmo. "I am Brother André," he said. He sat down. "Sit down, Fengmo," he said. "I am commanded to teach you a foreign language which your mother has said must be English."

"But only the language," Madame Wu stipulated. Now

134

that the lessons were to begin she asked herself if indeed she had done wrong in giving the mind of her son to this man. For to teach a mind is to assume the power over it.

"Only the language," Brother André repeated. He caught the fear in Madame Wu's words and answered it at once. "You need not be afraid, Madame. I am an honourable man. Your son's mind will be sacred to me."

Madame Wu was confounded by this foreigner's comprehension. She had not expected such delicate instincts in so hairy a body. She had known no foreigner—except, of course, Little Sister Hsia, who was only a childish woman. She bowed slightly and went away into the garden again.

An hour later the priest appeared at the door of the library. He was talking to Fengmo in unknown syllables. He pronounced them clearly and slowly, and Fengmo listened as though in all the world he heard nothing else.

"Have you taught him so quickly?" Madame Wu asked. She was sitting in her bamboo chair under the trees, her hands folded in her lap.

"Madame, he does not understand them yet," Brother André replied. "But I teach by speaking only the language to be learned. In a few days he will be using these words himself." He turned to Fengmo. "To-morrow," he said, and bowing to Madame Wu, he strode through the gate with his long, unhurried steps.

With the passing of this huge priest everything took its proper shape and proportion again.

"Well, my son?" Madame Wu said.

But Fengmo seemed still dazed. "He taught me a great deal in this one hour."

"Speak for me the words he taught you," she urged him.

Fengmo opened his lips and repeated some sounds.

"What do they mean?" she asked.

Fengmo shook his head and continued to look dazed. "I do not know—he did not tell me."

"To-morrow he must tell you," she said with some sternness. "I will not have words said in this house which none of us can understand."

* * * * *

All through the great house the word went on wings of the big foreign priest, and Mr. Wu heard them too. It was about mid-afternoon of the next day when Madame Wu saw him coming towards her. She was matching some silks for the sewing woman, who was about to embroider new shoes for the children.

"Send this woman away," Mr. Wu said when he came near.

Madame Wu saw that he was annoyed. She pushed the silks together and said to the woman, "Come back in an hour or two."

The woman went away, and Mr. Wu sat down and took out his pipe and lit it. "I have heard that you have engaged a foreign tutor for Fengmo without telling me a word about it," he said.

"I should have told you, indeed," Madame Wu said gently. "It was a fault in me. But somehow I did not think you could want to be disturbed, and yet I felt it necessary that Fengmo have his eyes turned toward Linyi."

"Why?" Mr. Wu inquired.

She had long since learned that nothing is so useful at all times for a woman as the truth towards a man. She had not deceived Mr. Wu at any time, and she did not do so now. "Fengmo happened to see Ch'iuming the other day while she was here," she said. "I do not think anything lit between them, but Fengmo is at the moment in his youth when such a thing might happen with any woman young and pretty. Therefore I have fanned the flame from another direction. It would be awkward to have trouble in the house."

Mr. Wu was as usual confounded by the truth, and she saw his tell-tale sweat begin to dampen the roots of his hair. "I wish you would not imagine such things so easily," he said. "You are always pairing men off to women. You have a low opinion of all men. I feel it. I feel you have made even me into an old goat."

"If I have made you feel so, then I am a clumsy person, and I ought to beg your pardon," she said in her silvery voice. She sat with an ineffable grace that made her as remote from him as though she were not in the room. She perfectly understood this. Long ago she had learned that to seem to yield is always stronger than to show resistance, and to acknowledge a fault quickly is always to show an invincible rectitude.

But she saw he was still hurt, and secretly she did feel humiliated that she had indeed been so clumsy as to hurt him. "I wish you could see the way you look to-day," she said with her charming smile. "It seems to me I never saw you so handsome. You look ten years younger than you did a few days ago."

He flushed and broke into a laugh. "Do I, truthfully?" he asked.

He caught the tenderness in her eyes and leaned towards her across the table between them. "Ailien, there is still nobody like you," he exclaimed. "All women are tasteless after you. What I have done has been only because you insisted."

"I know that," she said, "and I thank you for it. All our life together you have only done what I wished. And now when I asked so much of you, you have done that too."

His eyes watered with feeling. "I have brought you a present," he said. He put his hand into his pocket and brought out a handful of tissue paper which he unwrapped. Inside were two hair ornaments, made in the shape of butterflies and flowers of jade and seed pearls and gold. "I saw these yesterday, and they made me think of you. But I am always thinking of you." He wiped his bedewed forehead. "Even in the night," he muttered, not looking at her.

She was very grave at this. "You must not think of me in the night," she said. "It is not fair to Ch'iuming. After all, her life is now entirely in you."

He continued to look unhappy.

"Is she not pleasant to you?" she asked in her pretty voice.

"Oh, she is pleasant," he said grudgingly. "But you—you are so far away from me these days. Are we to spend the rest of our lives as separately as this? You who have always lived in the core of my life——" His full underlip trembled.

Madame Wu was so moved that she rose involuntarily and went over to him. He seized her in his arms and pressed his face against her body. Something trembled inside her, and she grew alarmed, not of him but of herself. Was this moment's weakness to defeat all that she had done?

"You," he murmured, "pearls and jade—sandalwood and incense——"

She drew herself very gently from his clasp until only her hands were in his. "You will be happier than you have ever been," she promised him.

"Will you come back to me?" he demanded.

137

"In new ways," she promised. The moment was over, now that she could see his face. The lips with their lines of slight petulance were loosened. At the sight of them she felt her body turn to a shaft of cool marble. She withdrew even her hands.

"As for Fengmo," she said, "do not trouble yourself. As to the tutor, it seems Linyi wants him to speak English. She says he is too old-fashioned otherwise. He will be ready to marry Linyi in a month. See if he is not!"

"You plotter," Mr. Wu said, laughing. "You planner and plotter of men's lives!" He was restored to good humour again, and he rose and, laughing and shaking his head, he went away.

A few minutes later when Ying came in she found Madame Wu in one of her silences. When she saw Ying she lifted her head.

"Ying," she said, "take some of my own scented soap and tell Ch'iuming to use no other."

Ying stood still, shocked.

"Do not look at me like that," Madame Wu said. "There is still more you must do. Take her one of my sandalwood combs for her hair, and put my sandalwood dust among her undergarments."

"Whatever you say, Lady," Ying replied sourly.

It was at this moment that Madame Wu saw Mr. Wu's pipe. He had put it on a side table as he went out. She perceived instantly that he had left it on purpose as a sign that he would return. It was an old signal between man and woman, this leaving of a man's pipe.

She pointed towards it as Ying turned, and her pretty voice was sharp.

"Ying!" she called. "He forgot his pipe. Take it back to him."

Ying turned without a word and picked up the pipe and took it away.

.   .   .   .   .

When Madame Wu had finished matching the silks it was too dark to see the colours. She was about to have the candles lit when Fengmo came in from the twilight. He had taken off his school uniform and put on a long gown of cream silk brocaded in a pattern of the same colour. His short hair he had brushed back from his square forehead. Madame Wu when she had greeted him praised him for his looks.

"A robe looks better than those trousers," she said. She studied his brow as she spoke. It was a handsome brow, but one could not tell from it what was the quality of the brain it hid. Fengmo was only beginning to come into his manhood.

"Can you remember the words you learned last night?" she asked him, smiling. He had lit a foreign cigarette, of which he and Tsemo smoked many. The curl of rising smoke seemed somehow to suit him. He did not sit down but walked restlessly about the library, and he stopped and repeated the foreign words clearly.

"Can you understand them yet?" she asked.

He shook his head. "No, but to-night I shall ask him what they mean," he replied.

He paused to listen. "He comes now!" he exclaimed.

They heard the long, powerful footsteps of leather shoes upon stones. Then they saw Brother André at the door, escorted by the gateman, who fell back when he saw Madame Wu rise.

"Have you eaten?" Madame Wu asked in common greeting.

"I eat in the middle of the day only," Brother André said. He was smiling in a pleasant, almost shy fashion. Again as he stood there Madame Wu felt the whole room, Fengmo, even herself, shrink small in the presence of this huge man. But he seemed unconscious of his own size or of himself.

"Fengmo was repeating the foreign words you taught him last night, but we do not know what they mean," Madame Wu said as they sat down.

"I gave you words once spoken by a man of England," Brother André said. "That is, he was born in England, and he lived and died there. But his soul wandered everywhere."

He paused as though he were thinking, then he translated the words in a sort of chant:

> And not by eastern windows only
> When daylight comes, comes in the light.
> In front the sun climbs slow, how slowly!
> But westward, look, the land is bright!

To this Madame Wu and Fengmo listened, drinking in each word as though it were pure water.

"This is not religion?" Madame Wu asked doubtfully.

"It is poetry," Fengmo said.

"I teach you the first English words that were taught me," Brother André said, smiling at him. "And I did not understand them either at first, when I was a little boy in Italy."

"So this same sun lights the whole world," Madame Wu said musingly. She laughed. "You will smile at me, Brother André, but though I know better, my feeling has always been that the sun has belonged only to us."

"The sun belongs to us all," Brother André said, "and we reflect its light, one to another, east and west, rising and setting."

The four walls of the room seemed to fade; the walls of the courts where she had spent her whole life receded. She had a moment's clear vision. The world was full of lands and peoples under the same Heaven, and in the seven seas the same tides rose and fell.

She longed to stay and hear the next lesson which Brother André would give, but she knew that Fengmo would not feel at ease if she stayed. She rose. "Teach my son," she said, and went away.

*   *   *   *   *

"How does Linyi feel now that Fengmo is learning English?" Madame Wu asked Madame Kang. Her friend had come to see her late one evening, after the day's turmoil was past. Here was a symbol of the friendship between the two women, that a few times a year Madame Wu went to Madame Kang, but twice and thrice in seven days Madame Kang came to Madame Wu. To both this appeared only natural.

"I am surprised at my child," Madame Kang replied. "She says she will marry Fengmo if she likes him after she has talked with him several times, and after he has learned enough English to speak it. How shameless she is to want to see him! Yet I remember when I was a young girl I yielded to a mischievous maidservant who enticed me one New Year's Day when Mr. Kang came with his father to call at our house. I peeped through a latticed window and saw him. I was married and our first son born before I dared to tell him. And all that time the shame of it weighed on me like a sin."

Madame Wu laughed her little ripple of mirth. "Doubtless the damage was done, too, by that one look."

"I loved him all in one moment," Madame Kang said without any shame now.

"Ah, those moments," Madame Wu went on. "You see why it is wise to be ready for them. The hearts of the young are like fires ready to burn. Kindling and fuel are ready. Yet how can we arrange a meeting between our two, or several meetings?"

The two friends were sitting in the cool of the evening. On a table near them Ying had put a split watermelon. The yellow heart, dotted with glistening black seeds, was dewy and sweet. Madame Wu motioned to the portion at her friend's side.

"Eat a little melon," she said gently. "It will refresh you. You look tired to-night."

Madame Kang's plump face was embarrassed as she heard these kindly words. She took out a flowered silk handkerchief from her bosom and covered her face with it and began to sob behind it, not hiding her weeping, since they were alone.

"Now Meichen," Madam Wu said in much astonishment, "tell me why you weep."

She put out her hand and pulled the handkerchief from her friend's face. Madame Kang was now laughing and crying together. "I am so ashamed," she faltered, "I cannot tell you, Ailien. You must guess for yourself."

"You are not——" Madame Wu said severely.

"Yes, I am," Madame Kang said. Her little bright eyes, so merry, were now tragic too.

"You, at your age, and already with so many children!" Madame Wu exclaimed.

"I am one of those women who conceive when my man puts even his shoes by my bed," Madame Kang said.

Madame Wu could not reply. She was too kind to tell her friend what she thought or to blame her for not following her own example.

"The strange thing," Madame Kang said, twisting and folding the big handkerchief now spotted with tears, "is that I do not mind any of them so much as Linyi. Linyi is so critical of me. She is always telling me I am too fat, and that I should comb my hair differently, and that it is shameful I cannot read, and that the house is dirty, and that there are too many children. If Linyi stays with me and I have to tell her——"

"Linyi must come here quickly," Madame Wu said. In her heart she asked herself whether it was well to bring into her house a stubborn, wilful young girl who judged her own mother.

"You can teach her," Madame Kang said wistfully. "I think she is afraid of you. But she fears neither her father nor me." She laughed suddenly through her tears at the thought of her husband. "Poor man," she said, and wiped her eyes. "When I told him this morning he pulled his hair out in two handfuls and said, 'I ought to go and set up a business alone in another city.'"

Madam Wu did not answer this, and as though her friend found her silence cool she looked at her and said, half shrewdly, half sadly, "Perhaps you are lucky, Ailien, because you do not love your husband."

Madame Wu was pierced to the heart by these words. She was not accustomed to sharpness from this old friend. "Perhaps the difference is not in love, but in self-control," she replied. She picked up a slice of the frosty golden melon. "Or," she said, "perhaps only it is that I have never liked to be laughed at. You, after all, are stronger than I am, Meichen."

"Don't quarrel with me," Madame Kang pleaded. She put out her plump hand, and it fell hot upon Madame Wu's cool narrow one. "We have the same trouble, Ailien. All women have it, I think. You solve it one way, I another."

"But is yours a solution?" Madame Wu asked. She felt her true and steady love for her friend soften her heart as she spoke, and she wound her slender fingers round the thick kind hand she held.

"I could not bear—to do what you have done," Madame Kang replied. "Perhaps you are wise, but I cannot be wise if it means somebody between—my old man and me."

Who could have thought that at that moment Madame Wu's heart would be wrenched by an inexplicable pain? She was suddenly so lonely, though their two hands clasped, that she was terrified. She stood on top of a peak, surrounded by ice and cold, lost and solitary. She wanted to cry out, but her voice would not come from her throat. Twilight hid her. Madame Kang could not see the whiteness of her face and, engrossed as she was, she did not see the rigidity of Madame Wu's body through her tightening fright.

In the midst of this strange terror Madame Wu saw Brother André. The priest's huge, straight figure appeared upon her loneliness, and it was dispelled in the necessity of speaking to him.

"Brother André," she said gratefully, "come in. I will send for my son."

She loosed her hold on Madame Kang's fingers as she spoke, and rose. "Meichen, this is Fengmo's teacher," she said. "Brother André, this is my friend, who is a sister to me."

Brother André bowed without looking at Madame Kang, but his face was kind. He went on into the library. There in the light of a candle they saw him sit down and take a book from his bosom and begin reading.

"What a giant," Madame Kang exclaimed in a whisper. "Do you not fear him?"

"A good giant," Madame Wu replied. "Come, in a moment Fengmo will be here. We should not seem to be speaking of him. Shall we go inside?"

"I must go home," Madame Kang replied. "But before I go, shall Linyi speak with Fengmo or not?"

"I will ask him," Madame Wu said, "and if he wishes it I will bring him to your house first, and then one day you can come here and bring her. Twice should be enough for them to know their minds."

"You are always right," Madame Kang said and, pressing her friend's hands, she went away.

. . . . .

Madame Wu delayed Fengmo that night after his lesson. The two men had sat long over their books. Madame Wu had walked past the door, unseen in the darkness, and had looked in. Something in Fengmo's attentive look, something in Brother André's deep gravity, frightened her. Was this priest witching the soul out of the boy by the very power of his own large being?

She sat down suddenly faint on one of the bamboo seats and was glad of the darkness. "How one tries," she thought, "and how one fails! How could I imagine when I invited a priest to come and teach my son that this priest would be so full of his god that he glows and shines and draws all to him?"

She knew that Fengmo's soul was at that moment of awakening when, if a woman did not witch it, a god might. She did not want him to be a priest, and this for many reasons; but most of all because a priest's body is barren, and Heaven is against barrenness. When a god steals the soul out of a body, the body takes revenge and twists the soul and wrecks it and mars it. Body and soul are partners, and neither must desert the other. If twenty-five years from now, having begat sons and daughters, Fengmo should wish to turn priest, as many men living in temples had done, then let him serve his soul when his body has been served. But not now!

Should she enter and break the spell she saw being woven? She hesitated on the threshold, still unseen. Then she withdrew. She, the mother and only the mother, was not strong enough to withstand this great priest. To show himself independent of her, if for no other reason, Fengmo would turn against her. No, she must have a young woman, a gay girl, a lovely piece of flesh and blood, to help her. Linyi must come quickly.

When the lesson hour had passed she called out from the darkness, "Brother André, my thanks for teaching my son so well. Until to-morrow, my greetings!"

She rose and came forward with these greetings. Both men stopped as though shocked by her presence. Brother André bowed and went swiftly away, his long robes flying shadows behind him. But Madame Wu put her hand into Fengmo's elbow, and when he was about to follow she clung tightly to him.

"My son," she said, "stay with me a little while. I have a very strange thing to tell you."

She felt refusal stiffen in Fengmo's arm, and she lifted her hand. "Dear son, I am sometimes quite lonely. To-night is one of those times. Will you stay with me a little while?"

What son could refuse that voice? She had her hand on his arm again, pulling gently. "Come and sit down in this cool darkness," she said. "Will you let me speak and answer me nothing until I have finished?"

"If you wish, Mother," Fengmo said. But she could feel him wanting to leave her, longing to be free of her. Ah, she could read those signs!

144

"Fengmo," she said, and her voice was music coming out of the darkness. He could not see her. There was only the lovely voice pouring into his hearing. "I do not know how to tell you," she said. He heard a soft half-embarrassed laugh. "You are so grown now—a man. I suppose I must expect—— Well, certainly I must not be selfish. Linyi wants to talk with you. Such a thing I would have said was impossible when Liangmo was your age. I do not think Meng would have thought of asking it. But Linyi is very different from Meng, and you are very different from Liangmo."

The pretty voice poured all this into the night. It was difficult to believe that this was his mother's voice, so young, so shy, half laughing, broken with pauses.

"How do you know?" he asked brusquely.

"To-day her mother told me," she replied.

Madame Wu, leaning back in her chair, her face tilted up to the black soft sky, weighed and measured every tone of Fengmo's voice. She felt an excitement, as though she were pitting herself against a force stronger perhaps than her own. But she would win. She had Fengmo by the body, and body is stronger than soul in man.

"It is perhaps very wrong of me," she said half plaintively now to Fengmo's silence. "My first feeling is to say that if Linyi is so bold—I do not want her in the house."

These were the right words. Fengmo answered hotly out of the darkness. He leaned towards her. She could feel his fresh young breath against her face.

"Mother, you don't understand!"

"No?" She felt secure again at these familiar words of the young. So all sons say to all mothers.

"Many young men and women meet together these days," Fengmo declared. "It is not as it used to be when you were young, or even when Liangmo was married."

"Perhaps you are right," she sighed. "I want you to be happy—that is all. I do not want you to see Linyi if you would rather not. I can tell her mother it is not convenient. Then she will know you care nothing for Linyi."

"Of course I will see her," Fengmo said in a lordly way. "Why should I object?"

"Fengmo," she said in the same pleading voice, "do not lead Linyi to imagine things. There are many young women who would like to come into our house. Now that I think

145

of Linyi, I remember that I have always thought she was a trifle cross-eyed."

"If she is I will see it clearly," Fengmo declared.

"Then shall I tell her mother that in a few days you and I will——"

"Why you, Mother?" he asked very clearly.

"Fengmo!" she cried sharply. "I will not yield too far. How can you see the girl alone?"

"Certainly I shall see her alone," Fengmo said with some anger. "Must I be led by my mother like a small child?"

"What if I say you shall not go at all?" Madame Wu asked with vigour.

"Mother, do not say it," Fengmo said with equal vigour. "I do not want to disobey you."

Silence now fell between them. Madame Wu rose from her chair. "You insist, then, on going to see Linyi!"

"I will go," Fengmo said doggedly.

"Go, then," Madame Wu said, and swept past him and into her own room. There she found Ying waiting for her. Ying had heard the loud voices. "Lady, what——" she began.

But Madame Wu put up her hand. "Wait!" she whispered, "listen!"

They stood listening, Ying's mouth ajar. Madame Wu's eyes were shining, and her face was lit with laughter. They heard Fengmo's harsh and angry footsteps stride from the court. Madame Wu hugged herself and laughed aloud.

"Lady," Ying began again, "what is the matter?"

"Oh, nothing," Madame Wu said gaily. "I wanted him to do something, and he is going to do it—that is all!"

. . . . .

Fengmo did not come near her the next day, but the morning after Madame Kang came again. The two friends clasped hands quickly.

"Fengmo and Linyi have met," she said.

"How was the meeting?" Madame Wu asked smiling.

"I laughed and wept," Madame Kang replied, smiling back. "I sat far off, pretending not to be there. They wanted me gone and could not speak for wanting me gone. They were speechless, miserable together, and yet they could not keep from gazing at each other. I went away for only a few minutes, and when I came back again they were exactly as they had been. Neither had moved. They were only staring into each other's faces. Then he rose and went away, and they said to each other 'Until we meet again.' "

"Only those common words?" Madame Wu asked.

"But how they said them!" Madame Kang replied. "Ailien, you will laugh, but it made me go and find my old man just to sit near him."

"He thought you a simpleton, doubtless," Madame Wu said, still smiling.

"Oh, yes," Madame Kang said laughing, "and I didn't tell him anything, for I didn't want to stir him up again!"

"What damage could it do now?" Madame Wu asked mischievously.

"Ah, Ailien, don't laugh!" Madame Kang said sighing. "When I saw those two young things—so much happiness— such troubles ahead—one dares not tell the truth to the young!"

"Let the wedding be soon," Madame Wu said.

"The sooner the better," Madame Kang agreed. "It is wrong to light the fire under an empty pot."

Fengmo did not come near his mother that day nor any day. She did not see him until Brother André came again at night. She passed and repassed the door. Fengmo was asking him new words. He wanted to write a letter. She looked at Brother André's face. It was kind and patient but bewildered. He spelled the words out for Fengmo over and over again and wrote them down. Madame Wu heard the letters without comprehending them, strange sounds without meaning. But whether she understood them did not matter. Fengmo understood, and Linyi would understand. He was eager to write her a letter in English. Madame Wu laughed silently in the darkness. Then she felt shamed before Brother André for the ease of her victory. She went away and did not see him that night. Instead she went early to bed and to sleep.

7

On a pleasant day near the end of the ninth month Linyi came to the house, a bride. The season was a good one for marriages, for the harvest was ready to be cut and the rice was heavy in the ear. Summer had paused and autumn had not yet begun.

The two families came together in mutual joy for this second union between them. Liangmo and Meng were especially full of joy. Meng's little body was swelling with her child. She was hungry day and night, and her sickness had left her. She looked beautiful and ripe with happiness as she welcomed her sister. The two mothers talking together had decided to follow the children's wishes, and they did not have the old-fashioned long wedding which they had given to Liangmo and Meng. Three days' feasting was too long for these impatient two, Fengmo and Linyi. They wanted the swift marriage of the new times, a promise made before the elders and that was enough.

So it was done, and Madame Wu made amends to the townspeople, who were dismayed by the loss of the feasting, by hiring a restaurant for three days. This saved the trouble of crowds passing through the house.

"There are some good things about these new ways," Madame Kang said at the end of the marriage day. Again the men were in Mr. Wu's court and the women in Madame Wu's. Sweetmeats of the most delicate kinds were served to the women and heartier meats to the men. Fengmo and Linyi had withdrawn to their own court. Luckily an old cousin had died about a month before and left two rooms empty, and by Madame Wu's command these had been repaired and painted.

"Certainly we do not have broken furniture and filthy floors as we did after Liangmo's marriage," Madame Wu agreed.

She felt happy to-night, as she always did when some member of the household was settled. Her freedom grew yet more complete. For a week Fengmo by his own will had taken no lessons, and Brother André had not come. Madame Wu did not object. This was the hour of the flesh. She did not fear Brother André's power now. Whether he came any more or not was nothing to her. She had saved Fengmo for the family.

The court was lit with red-paper lanterns, and these drew the moths out of the darkness. Many of them were only small grey creatures, dusty wisps. But now and again a great moth would flutter forth with pale green-tailed wings, or wings of black and gold. Then all the women cried out, and none could rest until it was imprisoned and impaled upon the door by a pin where all could exclaim at its beauty while they sat in comfort and ate their sweetmeats. Old Lady especially enjoyed this sport and clapped her hands with pleasure.

One such moth had just been caught when Ch'iuming came into the court. Madame Wu saw her instantly, as she always did whenever she entered, and always she made no sign. The young woman had taken her place in the house day by day, in grave silence. None spoke of her, either good or ill, in Madame Wu's presence. But Madame Wu was conscious of her always. Sometimes at night when she woke she wondered—and put the wonder away.

Now as Ch'iuming came in she saw her. The girl looked thin and a little too pale, but prettier in her delicacy.

"I must inquire how she is," Madame Wu thought in unwilling self-reproach. "After the wedding is over I will send for her."

Again, as always she did, she put Ch'iuming aside and out of mind, and Ch'iuming made herself quietly busy pouring hot tea for the guests. She had taken part in the day but half hidden and quietly busy about the food or the children or some such thing. Now and again some would call to her, "Second Lady, rest yourself!" But Ch'iuming replied always with the same words, "I do only this one thing more."

Now, as they were all looking at the new moth, she, too, went to look at it. It was of a creamy yellow colour, like the yellow of the lemon called Buddha's Hand, and it had long black antennae. These quivered as it felt itself impaled. The wide wings fluttered and dark spots upon them showed green and gold for a moment. Then the moth was still.

"How quickly they die!" Ch'iuming said suddenly.

They all turned at the sound of her voice, and as though

149

she had surprised herself by speaking, she shrank back, smiling her half-painful, half-shy smile. She stood waiting until all were seated again. Then in silence she slipped behind the others and, coming to Madame Wu, she felt of her tea bowl.

"Your tea is cold," she said. "I will warm it."

"Thank you," Madame Wu said. She sat quite still while Ch'iuming leaned to perform the task. And as the girl leaned she smelled the fragrance of sandalwood, and as she smelled it she looked into the girl's face. A look of humility was there.

"May I have some talk with you to-night, Elder Sister?" she asked in a low voice.

"Assuredly you may," Madame Wu replied. She did not know how to answer otherwise, for how could she refuse? But she felt mirth go out of her. What new trouble cast its shadow on her? She sipped her tea and was silent until the guests were gone.

When they were gone Ch'iuming waited alone, except for Ying.

"Go away," Madame Wu told Ying, "and come back a little later."

She did not want to take Ch'iuming into the house. The air in the court was still and cool. The late purple orchids were blooming under the lanterns. Meng to-day had brought her the first seed-pods of lotus. The white flesh inside the pods was scentless and the taste bland.

She sat down after the guests were gone and took up one of the big soft pods. Ch'iuming stood half drooping, hesitating.

"Please seat yourself," Madame Wu said. "I have been thinking of these lotus seeds. While we talk we will eat them."

But Ch'iuming said, "I will not eat, I thank you."

"I will eat then and listen," Madame Wu replied. Her delicate hands tore the pod apart. These hands of Madame Wu's always looked as though they had no strength in them. But they had strength. The pith inside the pod was tough fibre, yet it gave way beneath her fingers and she plucked out of it one of the many seeds it hid. With her small sharp teeth, which were as sound to-day as they had been when they grew, she peeled the green skin from the white flesh.

"Let me peel them for you," Ch'iuming begged.

But Madame Wu felt a distaste for Ch'iuming's hands

against the meat she wanted in her own mouth. "Let me do this for myself," she said, and as though Ch'iuming read something beyond the words, she did not offer again.

And while Ch'iuming sat watching this tearing apart of the pod, and this peeling of the nuts within, and while she heard Madame Wu's teeth breaking the crisp meats, neither spoke. Then suddenly as though her hunger were assuaged, Madame Wu threw down the ruined seed-pod upon the stones.

"You are with child," she said abruptly. She used the common words of the common woman.

Ch'iuming looked up at her. "I have happiness in me," she acknowledged. She used the words which women in a great house use when an heir is expected.

Madame Wu did not correct herself nor did she correct Ch'iuming. She said in the same clear sharp voice, "You are very quick."

To this Ch'iuming replied nothing. She drooped her head and sat with her hands lying apart on her lap, the palms upward, the fingers listless.

"I suppose he is pleased," Madame Wu said in the same sharp way.

Ch'iuming looked at her with her large honest gaze. "He does not know," she said. "I have not told him."

"Strange," Madame Wu retorted. She was angry with Ch'iuming and amazed at her own anger. She had brought Ch'iuming into the house for a purpose, and the girl had fulfilled it. Why should she feel angry with her? But the anger lay coiled in her like a narrow green serpent, and it sprang up and its poison lay on her tongue. "Concubines," she said, "usually hasten to tell the men. Why are you different from other women?"

Ch'iuming's eyes filled with tears. By the light of the flowered lantern above her head Madame Wu could see the tears glisten.

"I wanted to tell you," Ch'iuming said in a low, half-broken voice. "I thought you would be pleased, but you are only angry. Now I would like to destroy myself."

These desperate words brought Madame Wu to her right mind. It was common enough for concubines in great houses to hang themselves or swallow their rings or eat raw opium, but this was always held a shame to the house. She was quick now, as ever she was, to guard the house. "You speak foolishly," she said. "Why should you destroy yourself when you have only done your duty?"

"I thought if you were glad that I could then be glad too," the girl continued in the same heart-broken voice. "I thought I could warm my hands at your fire. But now, at what fire shall I warm myself?"

Madame Wu began to be frightened. She had taken it for a matter of course that Ch'iuming was a common girl, country bred, who would welcome as a beast does the signs of its own fertility. The cow does not think of the sire, but of the calf. If ever she had thought at all of Ch'iuming's own life, she had comforted herself because, she thought, Ch'iuming would be rewarded with a child and with a child would be satisfied.

"What now?" she asked. "Are you not glad for your own sake? You will have a little toy to play with, someone to laugh at, a small thing of your own to tend. If it is a boy, you will rise in your place in the house. But I promise you that if it is a girl, you will suffer no reproaches from me. Male and female I have made welcome in my house. When my own daughter died before she could speak I wept as though a son were gone."

The girl did not answer this. Instead she fixed her sad eyes on Madame Wu and listened.

"You must not talk of destroying yourself," Madame Wu went on briskly. "Go back now and climb into your bed. Tell him, if he comes, that you have good news."

She spoke coldly to bring the girl back to her senses, but in her own heart she felt the chill of the mountain peak coming down on her again. She longed to be alone and she rose. But Ch'iuming sprang forward and clutched the hem of her robe.

"Let me stay here to-night," she begged. "Let me sleep here as I did when I first came. And you—you tell him for me. Beg him—beg him to leave me alone!"

Now Madame Wu was truly afraid. "You are losing your mind," she told Ch'iuming severely. "Remember who you are. You came to me without father and mother, a foundling, picked out of the street by a farmer's wife. You were widowed without having been wed. To-day you are second only to me in this family, the richest in the city, a house to which any family in the region longs to send its daughters. You are dressed in silk. Jade hangs in your ears and you wear gold rings. You may not return to my court. How could I explain it to the house? Go back at once to that court where you belong, for which you were purchased."

Ch'iuming let go the hem of Madame Wu's robe. She lifted herself to her feet and fell back step by step towards the gate. Madame Wu's hardness cracked suddenly at the sight of her desperate face.

"Go back, child," she said in her usual kind voice. "Do not be afraid. Young women are sometimes afraid and unwilling with the first child, although I had not expected it of you, who are country bred. Fall asleep early and do not wake if he comes in. I know that if he finds you unwilling to wake he will let you sleep. He is good enough, kind enough. Do I not know him? Why fear him? And I will do this for you— to-morrow I will tell him. That much I will do."

As though restored by this kindness, Ch'iuming whispered her thanks and slipped out of the court. Madame Wu put out the lanterns one by one until the court was dark. Wearily she went to her room, and Ying came and made her ready to sleep. She dared not ask her mistress anything when this lady wore the look on her face which she had to-night, a look so sad and so cold.

She drew the curtains about the silent figure and went into the noisy servants' courts. There the men and women and children were still eating what remained of the wedding feast, and Ying loved her food. She filled her bowl with many meats and she went and sat on a doorstep and ate with pleasure, listening as she ate to all the chatter of servants in the great house. She was above them all except for Peng Er, who was servant to the master. Peng Er sat eating too. His fat face was glistening with sweat. At his knee stood his youngest child, a small thing of some two or three years. Whenever he stopped for breath she opened her mouth and shrieked, and he held the bowl to her mouth and pushed food into it with his chopsticks.

"Peng Er!" a woman's loud laughing voice shouted out of the dusk. "Does the master sleep in the Peony Court every night?"

"I take tea there every morning," he shouted back.

"Ying!" The same loud mirthful voice shouted. "How is it in the Orchid Court?"

But Ying disdained to reply to this. She finished her bowl quickly and dipped cold water out of a jar, rinsed her mouth, and spat the water into the darkness whence the voice had come.

Men and women and children scattered at the sign. They were all afraid of Ying. In this house she sat too near the throne.

.　　　.　　　.　　　.　　　.

Madame Wu woke at dawn. She felt a load upon her, and under this load she struggled towards wakefulness. The night had not been a good one. She had slept and waked and slept again, never wholly forgetful. Living in the centre of the house, there were such nights when she felt the whole family as the heart feels the body. Now she remembered. It had been Fengmo's wedding night. Any wedding night was an anxious one. Were the two mated? Had the mating gone well or ill? She would not know until she saw them. Nor could she hasten to see them. Not until the matter took its own course and the day turned to the right hour could she know.

She sighed and then remembered the second weight. She had given a promise to Ch'iuming which she would like to have had back. Yet how could she take it back? Doubtless the girl had clung to it as a hope throughout the night. Then, as though she had not trouble enough, Ying came in when she saw her mistress awake.

"Old Lady is ill," Ying told her. "She says she feels she has eaten a cockroach in the feast yesterday, and it is crawling around in her belly. She feels it big as a mouse, sitting on her liver, and scratching her heart with its paws. Of course it can be no cockroach. My man, whatever his faults, would never be so careless as that."

"Heaven," Madame Wu murmured, "as if I had not enough without this!"

But she was dutiful above all else, and she hastened and Ying hastened, and in a few minutes she went into the court next hers where Old Lady lay high on her pillows. She turned dim sockets of eyes towards her daughter-in-law. "Do something for me quickly. I am about to die," she said in a weak voice.

Madame Wu was frightened when she saw the state in

which Old Lady was this morning. Yesterday she had been as lively as a mischievous child, boasting because she had won at mah-jong and eating anything at hand.

"Why was I not called earlier?" she asked Old Lady's maid.

"It is only in the last hour that our Old Lady has turned so green," the woman said to excuse herself.

"Has she vomited and drained?" Madame Wu inquired.

Old Lady piped up for herself, "I have vomited enough for three pregnancies, and all my bowels are in the night-pot. Fill me up again, daughter-in-law. I am all water inside—water and wind."

"Can you eat?" Madame Wu inquired.

"I must be filled somehow," Old Lady declared in a faint but valiant voice.

Thus encouraged, Madame Wu directed that thin rice soup be brought, and she herself grated fresh hot ginger root into it, and took up a spoon and fed the mixture to Old Lady.

Old Lady was always touching when she was ill. Her withered old mouth was as innocent and helpless as a baby's. Madame Wu looked into it with each spoonful. Not a tooth remained, and the gums were pink and clean. How many words had come from that pink tongue, now shrunk so small! Old Lady had always had a violent temper, and when she was angry she had hurled curses on anyone she saw. That tongue was her weapon. Old Gentleman had been afraid of it. But doubtless he had heard other words from her, too, and Mr. Wu, who had always been the core of Old Lady's life, had learned childish rhymes and laughter out of this same old mouth.

"I am better," Old Lady sighed at last. "I need only to be kept filled. At my age the body has no staying power. Life now is like a fire of grass. It burns only when it is fed."

"Sleep a little," Madame Wu said soothingly.

Old Lady's eyes opened very sharply at this. "Why do you keep telling me to sleep?" she demanded. "I shall soon sleep for ever."

Madame Wu was shocked to see tears well into Old Lady's eyes and dim their sharpness. Old Lady was crying! "Daughter, do you think there is any life after this one?" she muttered.

She put out a claw of a hand and clutched Madame Wu's hand. The old claw was hot and full of fever. Madame Wu, who had risen, sat down again. Old Lady all her life long had been nothing but a lusty body. She had been a woman, happy enough, dismissing from herself anything she could not understand. Rich, well clothed, powerful in this great house, what had she lacked? But since she had lived entirely in her flesh, now she was frightened when she saw the flesh wither. Where would she go when the body failed her?

"I hope there is a life beyond this one," Madame Wu said carefully. She might have deceived Old Lady as one deceives a child, but she could not do it. Old Lady was not a child. She was an old woman, about to die.

"Do you believe that I shall be born again in another body as the priests tell us in the temple?" Old Lady demanded.

Never had Old Lady talked of such things before. Madame Wu searched herself for honest answer. But who could penetrate the shades ahead? "I cannot tell, Mother," she said at last. "But I believe that life is never lost."

She did not say more. She did not say what she believed, that those who had lived entirely in the body would die with the body. She could imagine Brother André alive with no body, but not Old Lady.

Old Lady was already falling asleep in spite of all her will to stay awake. Her eyelids, wrinkled as an old bird's, fell over her eyes, and she began to breathe deeply. Her bony hand fell out of Madame Wu's soft one. Madame Wu went away, staying only to whisper to the servant, "She will recover this time. But try to keep rich foods out of her sight so that she will not crave them."

"Our Old Lady is wilful," the servant murmured to defend herself, "and I do not like to make her angry."

"Obey me," Madame Wu said sternly.

But as she approached Mr. Wu's court she was pleased with this one good thing out of evil, that Old Lady's illness gave her a reason to come here beyond the real one. She had sent Ying ahead to announce her. When she came to the gate of the court she found Ying waiting for her to tell her that Mr. Wu had gone out on some business and had only just returned. He sent word by Ying to beg her to sit down while he changed his outer garments.

So to wait she went into the familiar court where she had spent so many years of her life. The transplanted peonies were growing there most heartily. The blooms were over, the petals dropped, but the leaves were dark and thick. In the pool someone had planted lotus roots, and the great coral flowers lay open on the surface of the water. In the centre of each flower ripe stamens quivered, ready and covered with golden dust. Their fragrance drenched the air of the court, and Madame Wu took out her handkerchief and held it before her face. The scent was too heavy.

She passed through the court into the main room. The furniture was as she had left it, but certain things had been added. There were too many potted trees. Some framed foreign pictures were on the wall. Nothing was quite as clean as it used to be. She was displeased to see dust swept under chairs and into corners. She rose and went to the heavy carved doors, set with lattices, and now wide open. She looked behind one of these doors.

Mr. Wu came in, buttoning his grey silk jacket. "Is there something behind the door, Mother of my sons?" he asked in his hearty voice.

She looked at him and flushed faintly. "Dust," she said. "I must speak to the steward. The whole room needs cleaning."

Mr. Wu looked about it as though he saw the room for the first time. "Perhaps it does," he said. "It needs you," he said, after another moment. But he said it gaily and with a sort of teasing laughter. She grew grave and did not answer.

They seated themselves. She examined his face without seeming to do so. He looked well fed, and the curves of his mouth were cheerful again. This was what she wanted and what she had planned. Then why did she feel in herself a cruel desire to hurt him?

"Your mother is ill," she said abruptly. "Have you been to see her?"

He dropped his smile. "Alas, no," he said. "I should have gone the first thing this morning, but what with one thing and another——"

"She is very ill," she repeated.

"You don't mean——" he said.

"No, not this time," she said. "But the end is not too far off. Her soul is beginning to wonder what is to come next, and she asked me if I believed in another life after this one. Such questions mean that the body is beginning to die and the soul is afraid."

157

"What did you tell her?" he asked. His face turned suddenly solemn.

"I said I hope, but how can I know?" she answered.

He was inexplicably angry. "Now, how cruel you are!" he cried. "To an old soul how can you show your doubt?" He unbuttoned his jacket at his full throat and took his fan out of his collar at the back of his neck and began to fan himself with energy.

"What would you have said?" she asked him.

"I would have assured her," he cried. "I would have told her that nothing but happiness waits for her at the Yellow Springs. I would have said——"

"Perhaps you had better go and say it," she said. When she was angry she never raised her voice. Instead she poured into it molten silver. Now it flowed and flamed

But he thrust out his underlip. "I will tell her indeed," he retorted.

They sat in silence for a moment, each struggling for calm again. She sat perfectly still, her hands limp in her lap, her head drooping a little on her slender neck. He sat solidly motionless except for the fan in his hand which he moved constantly. Each wondered at being angry with the other, and neither knew why it was.

She was the first to speak. "I have another matter to mention." Her voice was still silvery.

"Speak on," he said.

She chose straight truth again. "Ch'iuming came to me last night and asked me to tell you that she is pregnant." Again she used the common word. She did not lift her head nor look at him, but continued to sit, motionless and graceful.

She heard the fan drop and brush against the silk of his garments. He was silent for so long that at last she looked up. He was staring at her, a clownish sheepish smile on his face, and his right hand was rubbing the crown of his head, rubbing round and round in a gesture she perfectly understood. It was a mixture of amusement, shame, and pleasure.

When he met her eyes he laughed aloud. "Poison me," he said. "Put bane into my rice—or ground gold into my wine. I am too shameless. But, Mother of my sons, I was only obedient to you—nothing else."

Against her will laughter came creeping up out of her belly. The corners of her mouth twitched, and her eyelids trembled. "Don't pretend you are not pleased," she said. "You know you are proud of yourself."

"Alas—I am too potent," he said.

Their laughter joined as it had so many times before in their life together, and across the bridge of laughter they met again. In that laughter she perceived something. She did not love him! Meichen had been right. She did not love him, had never loved him, and so how now could she hate him? It was as though the last chain fell from her soul. Time and again she had picked up those chains and put them on. But now no more. There was no need. She was wholly free of him.

"Listen to me," she said when their laughter was over. "You must be kind to her."

"I am always kind to everybody," he insisted.

"Please," she said, "be grave for a moment. It is her first child. Now do not plague her. Stay away from her for as long as she turns her face to the wall."

He wagged his head at her. "It may be that one concubine is not enough," he teased, and put the tip of his tongue out to touch his upper lip.

But he could not hurt her or harm her any more. She only smiled. "Now," she said, "you can go to your mother. And better than talking about her soul, tell her that you are to have another son."

. . . . .

But Old Lady was not even cheered by the news which her son brought to her. Madame Wu had scarcely reached her own court, she having stopped along her way to play with children, when Ying came running in to call her.

"Old Lady is worse," she cried. "Old Lady is frightened and is calling for you, Mistress! Our lord is there and he begs you to come."

Madame Wu turned herself instantly and hastened to Old Lady's bedside. There Mr. Wu sat stroking his mother's half-lifeless hand.

"She has made a wrong turn!" he exclaimed when he saw her. "My old mother has chosen a downward path!"

A flicker lighted Old Lady's glazed eyes, but she could not speak. Instead she opened her mouth and puckered up her face as though she were about to weep. But neither sound nor tears came as she gazed piteously at her daughter-in-law.

Madame Wu understood at once that Old Lady was now more afraid than ever. "Fetch some wine," she murmured to Ying, who had followed her. "We must warm her—she must feel her body. Fetch the Canton wine. Heat it quickly. And send the gateman to call the doctor."

Old Lady continued to look at Madame Wu, begging her for help, her face fixed in the piteous mask of weeping.

"Ying will fetch some hot wine," Madame Wu said in her sweet and soothing voice. "You will feel better and stronger. Do not be afraid, Mother. There is nothing to fear. Everything is as usual around you. The children are playing outdoors in the sunshine. The maids are sewing and tending the house. In the kitchens the cooks are making the evening meal. Life goes on as it has always gone, and as for ever it will. Our forefathers built this house, and we have carried on its years, and our children will come after us. Life goes on eternally, Mother."

Her singing, soothing voice sounded full and rich through the silent room. Old Lady heard it, and slowly the lines of her face softened and changed and the mask of weeping faded. Her lips quivered again and she began to breathe. While the mask had been fixed on her face her breathing had seemed to stop.

And soon Ying hurried in with the hot wine in a small jug with a long spout, and this spout Madame Wu held to Old Lady's parted lips and she let the wine drip into Old Lady's mouth. Once and twice and three times Old Lady swallowed. A faint pleasure came into her eyes. She swallowed again and muttered a few words.

"I can feel——"

Then a look of surprise and anger sprang out of her eyes. Even as she felt the hot wine in her belly her wilful heart stopped beating. She shuddered, the wine rushed up again and stained the quilt, and so Old Lady died.

"Oh, my mother!" Mr. Wu moaned, aghast.

"Take the jug," Madame Wu commanded Ying sharply. She leaned over and with the fine silk handkerchief she pulled from her sleeve she wiped Old Lady's lips and she lifted Old Lady's head with both her hands. But the head was limp, and she laid it down again on the pillow.

"Her soul is gone," she said.

"Oh, my mother!" Mr. Wu moaned again. He began to

weep openly and aloud, and she let him weep. There were certain things which must be done quickly for the dead. In a creature such as Old Lady had been, the seven spirits of the flesh could not be expected to leave the body at once. Old Lady must be exorcised and confined, lest these spirits loosed out of the flesh do harm in the house. Priests must be called. In her innermost heart Madame Wu did not believe in those priests nor in their gods. She stood looking down while Mr. Wu continued to fondle his mother's hand as he wept. She was surprised to find in herself the urgent wish to call Brother André here and give him the task of exorcising evil from the house. Yet this could scarcely satisfy the family. If even a year from now a child fell ill under this roof there would be blame because Old Lady's fleshly spirits had not been cared for. No, for the sake of the family, she must follow the old ways.

She turned to Ying. "Call the priests," she said. "Let the embalmers come in their time."

"I will attend to everything," Ying promised and went away.

"Come, Father of my sons," Madame Wu said. "Let us leave her for a little while. The maids will wash and dress her, and the priests are coming to exorcise her, and the embalmers will do their duty. You must come away."

He rose obediently, and they went out together. She walked along slowly by his side, and he continued to sob and to wipe his eyes with his sleeves. She sighed without weeping. It had been many years since she had wept, and now, it seemed, her eyes were dry. But when he heard her sigh he put out his hand and took hers, and thus hand in hand they walked to his court. There she sat down with him and let him talk to her of all he remembered about his mother, how she used to save him from his father's punishment, and how when his father compelled him to study his mother would steal into his room and bring him wine and sweet cakes and nuts, and how on holidays she took him to theatres, and when he was ill she called in jugglers and showmen to amuse him at his bedside, and when he had the toothache she gave him a whiff from an opium pipe.

"A good mother," he now said, "always gay and making me gay. She taught me to enjoy my life."

To all this, Madame Wu listened in silence, and she

persuaded him to eat and drink and then drink a little more. She despised drunkenness, but there were times when wine had its use to dull the edge of sorrow. So he drank the fine hot wine she ordered, and as he drank his talk grew thicker and he said the same thing over and over again until at last his head dropped on his breast.

Then she rose and on quiet feet went into the room which had once been hers. She peered under the satin curtains of the bed. There, rolled against the inner wall, she saw the back of a dark head, the outline of a slender shoulder.

"Ch'iuming," she called softly. "Are you sleeping?"

Ch'iuming turned, and Madame Wu saw her eyes staring out of the shadows.

"Ch'iuming, you need not sleep here to-night," Madame Wu said. "Our Old Lady is gone to the Yellow Springs, and he is drunk with wine and sorrow. Rise, child."

Ch'iuming came creeping out of the bed, silent, obedient. "Where shall I go?" she asked humbly.

Madame Wu hesitated. "I suppose you may go to my court," she said at last. "I myself shall not sleep to-night. I must watch over Old Lady."

"Oh, let me watch, too," Ch'iuming whispered. "I do not want to sleep."

"But you are young, and you ought not, for the sake of what is within you, to stay awake all night," Madame Wu replied.

"Let me be with you," Ch'iuming begged.

Madame Wu could not refuse. "Well, then let it be," she said.

So when she had seen Mr. Wu helped into his bed and had herself drawn the curtains about him, Madame Wu moved to take her place in the house this night. Those who had been sitting in watch now went to bed, but the servants did not sleep, nor the elder cousins. Old Lady was washed and dressed, and Madame Wu stood by to see that all was done as it should be, and Ch'iuming stood near, silent but ready to pick up this and hand her that. The girl had deft hands and quick eyes, and she read a wish before it was spoken. Yet Madame Wu saw clearly enough that Ch'iuming felt no sorrow. For her this was no death. Her face was grave but not sad, and she did not pretend to weep, as another might have done.

"Her heart is not yet here in this house," Madame Wu thought, watching her. "But when the child comes, he will tie it here."

So one generation now was fulfilled and passed from the house, and Madame Wu became the head within these compound walls as Mr. Wu was the head outside. Old Lady was not buried at once. When the geomancers were consulted they declared that a day in mid-autumn was the first fortunate day. Therefore, when the rites were finished and Old Lady slept within her sealed bed of cypress wood, the coffin was carried into the quiet family temple within the walls. No one, not even the children, felt that Old Lady was far away. Often in their play they ran to the temple and looked in.

"Great-grandmother!" they called softly. "Great-grandmother, do you hear us?"

Then they listened. Sometimes they heard nothing. But oftentimes, were the day gusty with wind, they told one another that they did hear Old Lady answer them from her coffin.

"What does she say?" Madame Wu once asked a small girl, the daughter of a first cousin.

The little child looked grave. "She says 'Little children, go and play—be happy.' But, Elder Mother, her voice sounds small and far away. Is she content in the coffin?"

"Quite content," Madame Wu assured her. "And now obey her—go and play—be happy, child."

.   .   .   .   .

After Old Lady was gone, for a time stillness seemed to come over the family. It was as though each generation, with her passing, knew itself further on in time and place. With her death life leaped ahead, and so all were nearer to the end. Mr. Wu when he had finished his first mourning and had taken off his garments of sackcloth was not quite what he had been. His full face looked older and more grave. Now sometimes he came to Madame Wu's court, and together they talked over the family of which they were the two heads. He worried himself because he fancied he had not been so good a son as he should have been. When they had discussed the crops and the evil taxes of overlords and government, and whether they should undertake an expense of one sort or another, and when they had talked over children and grand-children, then Mr. Wu would fall into brooding about his mother.

"You were good to her always," he said to Madame Wu. "But I forgot her much of the time."

Then to comfort him Madame Wu answered thus: "How can a man forget his mother? She gave you breath, and when you breathe it is to remember her. She gave you body, and when you eat and drink and sleep and however you use your body, it is to remember her. I do not ask of my sons that they come running always to me to cry, 'Ah, Mother, this,' and 'Ah, Mother, that.' I am rewarded enough when they live and are healthy and when they marry and are happy and when they have sons. My life is complete in them. So is it with our Old Lady. She lives in you and in your sons."

"Do you think so?" he said when he had listened, and he was always comforted so that he went away again and left her.

She, left alone, pondered on many things. Now more than ever her life was divided into two—that part which was lived in the house and that part which was lived inside herself. Sometimes one prevailed and sometimes the other. When the household was at peace she lived happily alone. When there was trouble of some sort she went into it and mended it as she could.

⋅ ⋅ ⋅

About the middle of that autumn she saw a little trouble begin in the house which she knew would swell big if she did not pinch it off, like an unruly gall bud on a young tree. Linyi and Fengmo began to quarrel. She saw their ill-temper one day by chance when she made her inspection of the house. For all her pert beauty Linyi was slatternly in her own court. At first Madame Wu had not wanted to speak of this, because Linyi was her friend's daughter and she knew that Madame Kang, with her great family, could not keep to constant neatness and cleanliness. It could only be expected that her daughters also might be less careful than Madame Wu was herself.

But Meng was Madame Kang's daughter too, and rather than reproach Linyi, Madame Wu went to the elder sister to take counsel with her.

164

She found Meng combing her long hair in the middle of
the morning. It was a soft grey morning, and the house lay
half asleep. Madame Wu did not reproach Meng that she
was only now combing her hair, but she thought that it
would perhaps aid the elder sister if she knew the younger
was reproached.

Meng hastily caught her hair in her hand when she saw
Madame Wu. "Is it you, Mother?" she called. "How ashamed
I am that I have not combed my hair! I will twist it up."

"No, child, do it properly," Madame Wu replied, and sat
down, and the maid went on combing Meng's long soft black
hair. Rulan and Linyi had short hair, but Meng kept her
hair old-fashioned.

"How many more days have you?" Madame Wu asked.

"Eleven, by the moon," Meng answered. "I hope, Mother,
that you will give me your counsel. You know I suffered
very much with the first one."

"When I had my children," the maid said cheerfully, "I
had them in the field where I was helping my man to
plough."

The maid was a woman from the Wu lands, and they had
known her always. Even now in summer she went back to
the land, and only when the harvests were reaped did she
return to the house to serve for the winter. This she did
because she was a widow and must be cared for, and yet she
loved the land and must go back to it once a year.

"You will not suffer so much with the second one,"
Madame Wu said to Meng. "But it cannot be expected that
women reared behind walls will bear their children so easily
as those who live freely."

"Will Linyi bear her children better than I do?" Meng
asked innocently.

"No, she will do no better," the woman said. "She is too
learned."

Madame Wu laughed. "That is scarcely true, good soul,"
she said. "I have perhaps as much learning as Linyi, but my
children came easily. But I have had much fortune in my
life."

"Ah, you are one of the ones that Heaven marks," the
woman agreed.

"Linyi says she wants no children," Meng said suddenly.
"Linyi says she wishes she had not married Fengmo."

165

Madame Wu looked up, startled. "Meng, be careful of your words!" she exclaimed.

"It is true, Mother," Meng said. She stamped her foot at the maid. "You pull my hair, dolt!" she cried.

"Blame your sister, who frightened me," the woman replied. "I never heard of a woman who did not want a child, except a concubine who was afraid her shape would be spoiled. But in this house even the concubine bears."

Madame Wu did not listen to this talk with servants. "Meng, I came here to speak of your sister's being a slattern and to ask you what I should say to her, but what you tell me is more grave than dust under a table. I should have inquired earlier into the marriage. But I have been busy with Old Lady's death affairs. Tell me how you know."

"Linyi told me herself," Meng said. Neither of the two ladies took thought of the woman servant. Indeed, what was there to be hidden? Whatever life brought about in this house was there for all to see and heed, and servants had their place here too.

"Say what Linyi told you," Madame Wu commanded.

"She says she hates a big house like this one," Meng said. "She says she wishes she had not married into it. She says Fengmo belongs to the family and not to her, and she belongs to the house against her will, too, and not to him. She wants to go out and set up a house alone."

Madame Wu could not comprehend what she heard. "Alone? But how would they be fed?"

"She says Fengmo could work and earn a salary if only he knew more English."

"She wants him to know more English?"

"So that he could get some money for the two of them to live alone," Meng replied.

"But no one disturbs them here," Madame Wu declared. She felt outraged that under her roof there should come out this spot of dark rebellion.

"Well, she means the family ways," Meng said. "The feast days and the death days and the birthdays and the duties of daughters-in-law and the servants who take over the children and all such things. She says Fengmo thinks of the family before he thinks of her."

"So he should," Madame Wu declared, "and so should she. Is she a prostitute that she does not belong to this house?"

Meng kept silent, seeing that Madame Wu did not like what she heard. The woman, too, knew that the matter was too deep for a servant to speak about. She finished her young mistress's hair, put in two pearl ornaments, and cleaned the hair out of the comb and wound it round her finger and went outside and blew it off.

Madame Wu and Meng were alone. "Have you such thoughts as these, too?" Madame Wu asked severely of this round, pretty creature.

Meng laughed. "Mother, I am too lazy," she said frankly. "I like living in this house. It is kept clean and ordered without my two hands. And I am glad when a servant takes my child if he cries, and I am happy all day. But then I never went to school, and I do not care if I read books or not, and my son's father tells me everything I ought to know, and what more do I want to know than what he wants me to know?"

"Liangmo is good to you?" Madame Wu asked.

Meng's soft cheeks turned very pink. "He is good to me in everything," she said. "There was never so good a man. Thank you, Mother."

"Is Fengmo not good to Linyi?" Madame Wu asked.

Meng hesitated. "Who can tell which is the hand that slaps first when two take up a quarrel?" she asked. "But I think it is Rulan's fault. She is always with Linyi. She and Linyi talk together about their husbands, and each adds the faults of the other's husband to her own."

Madame Wu remembered Rulan's sobbing on that night now long past. "Is Rulan also discontented?" she now asked.

Meng shrugged her shoulders. "Linyi is my sister," she replied, after hesitating for a second or two. "I have no talk with Rulan."

"You do not like Rulan!" Madame Wu exclaimed. It seemed to her that she was pursuing her way through a maze and sinking deeply into something which she had not suspected in her house. How monstrous it was for these to quarrel who should be the next after herself and Mr. Wu!

"I do not like Rulan," Meng said without change or hint of hatred in her voice.

"Must women always quarrel?" Madame Wu said severely.

Meng shrugged her shoulders again. "Not liking somebody is not to quarrel with them," she said. "I do not like Rulan because she is always behaving as though she were right and others wrong. And she behaves so to Tsemo, too, Mother, and I wonder you have not seen it. I have told Liangmo he should tell you, but he always says he does not want you to be troubled. But Old Lady knew—she used to slap Rulan."

"Slap Rulan!" Madame Wu cried. "Why was I never told?"

"Tsemo would not let Rulan tell," Meng said. She was now beginning to enjoy all this telling. "Rulan is too learned," she went on. "She is more learned than Linyi, and so Linyi listens to her. She is always talking about things women should not know."

"What things?" Madame Wu inquired.

"Constitutional and national reconstruction and unequal treaties and all those things," Meng said.

"You seem to know about them," Madame Wu said with a hint of a smile.

"Liangmo knows, but I do not," Meng said.

"Do you not want to know what Liangmo knows?" Madame Wu asked.

"There are too many other things for us to talk about together," Meng replied.

"What things?" Madame Wu asked again.

But Meng did not answer this with words. Instead she dimpled her cheeks with a smile and looked away.

And Madame Wu pressed her no more. She rose after a little while and went back to her court with this new knowledge in her of fresh turmoil in the house. But some sort of weariness fell upon her that day. She felt as one does who must run a race without food. These young, these men and women whose lives were dependent upon her, she was not strong enough for them. Her wisdom was too ancient for them—the wisdom of the unchanging human path from birth to death. She thought of Brother André. He had a wisdom that went far beyond these walls. She would call Fengmo and suggest to him that he begin again his studies. Then when Brother André came she could share with him the troubles of these young who leaned upon her.

She sent Ying to call Fengmo to her, and he came at once, having nothing to do and happening at that moment to be at home. There was a look about him that Madame Wu did not like. Had he not been properly wed, she would have said

he was dissolute. He looked sullen and dissatisfied and yet
satiated and overfed.

"Fengmo, my son," she said in her pleasant voice, "I have
been too busy all these days since your grandmother left us.
I have not asked how things have gone with you. I have seen
you and Linyi in your places in the family, but I have not
considered you alone. Now, son, talk to your mother."

"There is nothing to talk about, Mother," Fengmo said
carelessly.

"You and Linyi," she said coaxing him.

"We are well enough," he said.

She looked at him in silence. He was a tall young man,
spare in the waist, fine in the wrists and the ankles. He was
lightly made but exceedingly strong. His face was square, his
mouth full and easily sullen.

She smiled. "How much you look as you did when you
were a baby," she said suddenly. "It is strange how little
men change after they are born, while women change so
much. Sometimes when I look at each of you, it seems to me
that you are just as you were when you were first put into my
arms!"

"Mother, why are we born?" he asked.

She had asked this question of herself often enough, but
when her son asked it she was alarmed. "Is it not the duty of
each generation to bring the next into being?" she replied.

"But why?" he persisted. "Why should any of us exist?"

"Can we cease to be, now that we are made?" she replied.

"But if I exist only to bring forth another like myself, and
he but to bring forth another like us two, then of what use is
this to me?" he went on. He did not look at her. His thin
young hands were loosely clasped in front of him. "There is
a me," he said slowly, "that has nothing to do with you,
Mother, and nothing to do with the child to come from me."

She was frightened. Such questions and such feelings she
herself had, but she had not dreamed to find them in a son.

"Alas!" she cried. "I have been a bad mother to you. Your
father never had such thoughts. I have poured some poison
into you."

"But I have always had these thoughts," he said.

"You never told me before," she cried.

"I thought they would pass from me," he replied. "Yet I
continue to think them."

She grew very grave. "I hope it does not mean that you and Linyi do not go well together," she said.

He frowned. "I do not know what Linyi wants. She is restless."

"You are with her too much," she declared. "It is not well for husband and wife to be continually together. I see that she does not come and sit among the women as Meng does. She stays inside your court. Naturally she grows weary there, idle, restless——"

"Perhaps," he said, as if he did not care.

She continued to look at him anxiously.

"Fengmo, let us invite Brother André here again. While you were with him it seemed to me you were happy."

"I might not be now," he replied listlessly.

"Come," she said firmly. She had learned long ago that listlessness must be met with firmness. "I will invite him."

He did not answer.

"Fengmo," she began again, "if you and Linyi wish to go out of this house I will not forbid it. I desire the happiness of my sons. You are right to ask why you should only be a link in the chain of the generations. I have other sons. If you wish to go out, speak and tell me so."

"I do not know what I want," he said again in the same listless fashion.

"Do you hate Linyi?" she asked. "This can only be that you are entirely unhappy. How long have you been married to her? Only three little months. She is not pregnant and you are listless. What does this mean, Fengmo?"

"Mother, you cannot measure us by such things," he declared.

But she was too shrewd. "By this alone I will not measure you," she said, "but I know that if man and woman are not well mated in the body first, there is no other mating. If the body is mated, then other mating will come, or if it does not the two can still live as one. But the body is the foundation of the house the two build. Soul and mind, and whatever else, is the roof, the decoration, whatever one adds to a fine house. But all this fails without the foundation."

Fengmo looked at her. "How does it happen my father has a concubine?"

She would not accept this rudeness. "There is a time for

170

everything," she said severely, "and one time passes into another."

He knew that he had overstepped the boundaries of a son, and he rubbed his short-cut hair and passed his hands down over his cheeks.

"Well, let Brother André come," he said at last. He thought again a while and then he said, "He will be my only teacher. I shall stop going to the national school."

"Let it be so, my son," she said.

171

8

IN this way Brother André came again into the house of Wu. He made no mention of the time since he had been here, nor of anything that had happened since. Fengmo came in the evening for his lesson and went away again. But when Brother André was passing through the court after the lesson Madame Wu called to him gently. She was sitting in her accustomed place where she always sat in the evening until the autumn grew too cold. It was cold to-night, but because she was reluctant to let the summer escape her she held fast to a night or two longer. Ying had complained against her for sitting outdoors, and now in the library a brazier of coals burned ready to cure the chill which Ying declared was ready to fall upon her.

"Good Brother André," Madame Wu called.

Brother André's tall figure stopped. He turned his head and saw her.

"Did you call me, Madame?" he asked.

"Yes." She rose as she spoke. "If you have some time, please spare it to me to talk for a little while about this third son of mine. I am not pleased with him."

Brother André inclined his great head.

"Bring tea, Ying," Madame Wu told her, "and stay to mend the coals." She remembered that Brother André was a priest and she wished to spare him uneasiness at being alone with a woman.

If he was uneasy he did not show it. He sat down when she motioned him to a chair and waited. His deep eyes were fixed on her face, but she knew that he did not think of her. The eyes might have been looking down out of heaven upon her.

"Why is Fengmo unhappy?" she asked him directly.

"He is too idle," Brother André replied simply.

"Idle?" Madame Wu repeated. "But he has his duties. Every New Year's Day I assign duties to each son and to each daughter-in-law. This year my eldest son is responsible for the oversight, under me, of the lands. And Tsemo must look to the buying and selling, and Fengmo is learning about the grain shops where we market our grains in the city. Since he has left school he is busy at this for several hours every day."

"Still he is idle," Brother André said. "Fengmo has an unusual mind and a searching spirit. He learns quickly. You bade me teach him English. But with all he learns of the English he takes in something more. To-day I found he had forgotten nothing. The knowledge I gave him months ago has rooted in him and has sent up tendrils like a vine, searching into the air for something upon which to climb and flower and fruit. Fengmo will always be idle, although you fill every hour of the day, until he has found the thing which uses his mind and his spirit."

Madame Wu listened to this. "You are trying to persuade me to let you teach him your religion," she said shrewdly.

"You do not know what my religion is," Brother André answered.

"I do know," she said. "Little Sister Hsia has read me often out of your sacred books, and she has explained to me your foreign ways of praying and all such things."

"My religion is not hers, nor hers mine," this strange man replied.

"Explain me yours," she commanded him.

"I will not explain it, for I cannot," he said. "Little Sister Hsia can read you out of a book and speak to you a way of praying, but these are not my ways. I read many books, I have no set ways of prayer."

"Then where is your way of religion?" she demanded.

"In bread and in water," he replied, "in sleeping and in walking, in cleaning my house and making my garden, in feeding the lost children I find and take under my roof, in coming to teach your son, in sitting by those who are ill, and in helping those who must die, that they may die in peace."

"I wish I had called you when our Old Lady died," she said suddenly. "I had a strange wish to call you. But I was afraid the family would still want the temple priests."

"I would not have kept your priests away," Brother André said. "I never forbid anyone who can bring comfort anywhere. We all need comfort."

"Do you also?" she asked curiously.

"Certainly I also," he said.

"But you are so solitary!" she exclaimed. "You have no one of your blood."

"Everyone is of my blood," Brother André said, "and there is no difference between one blood and another."

"Is your blood like mine?" Madame Wu exclaimed.

"There is no difference," he replied. "All human blood is of the same stuff."

"Why are you only a priest?" she asked. This she knew to be rude, and so she made haste to be pardoned. "You must forgive me. I am too curious. I know that a priest is never to be asked why he became a priest. But I feel that you have committed no crime and that you need no sanctuary."

"Do not ask my pardon," Brother André replied. "Indeed, I scarcely know how I became a priest, unless it is because I was first an astronomer."

"You know the stars?" she asked in great surprise.

"Madame, no one knows the stars," he replied. "But I study their rise and fall, their coming and their going across the heavens."

"Do you still do this?" she inquired. She was ashamed of her curiosity concerning him, and yet she could not keep herself from it.

"Madame, when my day's work is done, unless the night is cloudy, I do so," he replied. His manner was so frank, so calm, that it piqued her. He answered her questions because she put them and because he had nothing to hide, but also as if he had no concern with her.

"You are very lonely," she said abruptly. "All day you work among the poor and at night among the stars."

"It is true," he agreed calmly.

"Have you never wanted a home and wife and children?" she asked.

"Madame, I once did love a woman," he replied, "and we were to be married. Then I entered into loneliness, and I no longer loved her nor needed her."

"This was very unjust to her, I think," Madame Wu said with dignity.

"Yes, it was," he agreed, "and I felt it so, but I could only tell her the truth. Then I became a priest in order to follow my loneliness."

"But your faith?" she inquired.

He looked at her with his full dark gaze. "My faith? It is

in space and in emptiness, in sun and stars, clouds and wind."

"Is there no God there?" she inquired.

"There is," he said. "But I have not seen His face."

"Then how can you believe in Him?" she asked.

"He is also in that which is around me," Brother André replied. His grave voice spoke the large, simple words. "He is in the air and the water, in life and death, in mankind."

"But your foundlings," she urged. "If you love your loneliness and need no one, why have you taken these chance children?"

He looked down at his huge work-worn hands. "These hands, too, must live and be happy," he said, as though they were separate creatures and did not belong to him. "The flesh, too, must be employed if it is to let the soul be free."

Madame Wu stared at him with ever-rising curiosity. "Are there other men like you?" she asked.

"No man is quite like any other one," Brother André said. His sun-browned face took on a warm, almost smiling look, as though a light came on within him. "But your son, Madame, young Fengmo, I think he could become like me. Perhaps he will become like me."

"I forbid it!" Madame Wu said imperiously.

"Ah!" Brother André said, and now he smiled. His lit, mysterious eyes glowed on her for an instant and then he said good-bye.

And she sat gazing up into the handful of stars above her court. Twice Ying came out to scold her.

"Leave me," Madame Wu told her. "I have things to think about."

"Can you not think in your bed instead of in this chill night air?" Ying complained.

When Madame Wu did not reply she went and fetched a fur robe and wrapped it about her knees. Still Madame Wu did not move. She leaned back in her chair, gazing at the stars. The walls of the court cut a square out of heaven as they did out of the earth, but up and down, beneath and above, her thoughts went deep and rose high.

In the earth beneath this house human roots ran down— the unseen, the unknown roots of all who had lived here of the Wu family. Here they had been born and here they died. The foundations were unshaken. And yet even before them there had been others. Old Gentleman had told her what he had heard from his own father, who had been told it by his father, that when the Wu house was founded, the hands that dug the earth out had placed the stones not upon earth but upon rubble and cracked porcelains and potsherds and fragments of tile. "No house can reach to the bottom of our earth," Old Gentleman had told her. "City upon city, our ancestors have built five cities one upon another. Man has built upon man, and others will build upon us."

In the thousands of years to come the Wu house would take its place to make the foundations for still other houses, and other eyes would look upon these stars. She comprehended the loneliness of Brother André, and yet she understood why he was content in it. She trembled upon the edge of this loneliness herself as she gazed up at the stars.

"Madame!" Ying cried out from the house in despair.

But Madame Wu did not hear her voice.

Ying grew frightened at last. She tiptoed near and looked down into Madame Wu's face. It was pure and cold and fixed. Her great dark eyes continued to gaze into the sky. In the dimness of the court, lit only by the shaft of candle-light from the library, her face looked almost translucent in its creamy whiteness.

"Alas, her soul is fled!" Ying murmured and then clapped her hands to her mouth. She backed away in terror at what she saw and tiptoed across the court.

Madame Wu heard her dimly, without caring or knowing why Ying was afraid. She was free from these walls. They did not, as she had thought, reach up to the sky and cut out a square among the stars. Instead, when she had surmounted them she saw the whole earth lying before her, the seven seas and the countries and the peoples of whom she had heard only in books, the two poles of the earth and their unmelting ice and snow, the tropics and their earthly life.

"From the stars," she thought, "doubtless all things are seen."

For the first time in her life she longed to rise out of these four walls and travel everywhere upon the earth to see everything and to know all.

"But there would still be the stars," she thought. "How can one reach the stars?"

She thought of Old Lady, now dissolved into free soul and

176

coffin-bound dust. But Old Lady's soul was hovering about this house.

"As soon as I am free," Madame Wu thought, "I shall leave this house. I shall go straight up until I know what stuff the stars are."

Thus dreaming, Madame Wu forgot that Ying had crossed the court and gone away, and now she did not see her come back with all three sons. Liangmo and Tsemo and Fengmo came together and stood gazing at their mother. Liangmo spoke first.

"Mother!" He made his voice gentle, for he feared that her soul had left her body, and when this happens the soul must be wooed and coaxed and not frightened, lest it never return. For the body is the cage and the soul is the bird, and once the door is left open and the bird goes forth free, why should it return to the cage? It must be tempted and deceived.

"Dear Mother," Liangmo said gently, "your children are here—your children wait for you——"

But Madame Wu was in a trance. She heard no voice.

Her sons looked at one another in terror.

"Call our father," Liangmo commanded Tsemo.

Tsemo made haste to obey, and in a few minutes, while the others waited in silence lest the runaway soul escape yet farther, Mr. Wu hurried into the court. Behind him, unnoticed, came Ch'iuming.

"How did this come about?" he demanded of Ying.

"The foreign priest left her so," Ying replied.

They looked at one another in renewed fear.

"Mother of my sons!" Mr. Wu called gently. His large face was paper-coloured.

Madame Wu did not answer.

"Ailien!" he called. He did not dare to touch her. Her hand hung from her wrists like limp white flowers.

But Ch'iuming said not a word. She knelt at Madame Wu's feet and slipped off the narrow satin shoes and the white silk stockings and began to chafe the bare feet. They were cold, and she put them against her bosom. "You will wake her too quickly," Mr. Wu urged.

"No, for she is not afraid of me," Ch'iuming said. She knelt, looking up at them, father and sons, in this house where Heaven had thrust her.

"She is afraid of no one," Mr. Wu said with dignity.

"She is not afraid of me because she does not care for me," Ch'iuming said strangely, and looked down on the narrow bare feet she held.

At this moment Madame Wu brought down her eyes from the stars and saw her three sons. "You three?" she said. "What do you want?"

Ch'iuming quickly put on her stockings and shoes again. Madame Wu seemed not to see her. But she saw Mr. Wu.

"Why are you here?" she asked in a cold and distant voice. All could see that her soul was unwilling to return to them.

"Mother, I think Meng is about to bear her child," Liangmo said quickly.

"Mother," Tsemo called, "I wish you would teach Rulan how to make honey cakes."

"Mother," Fengmo said in a low voice, "to-day I told you a lie."

One by one they called her back. Mr. Wu took his turn.

"Mother of my sons, the house needs you. And have you forgotten that it is time to allot the seed wheat for the land?"

So at last she returned. "You," she murmured, "will you never be done with your troubles?"

"No," said Liangmo, "never!"

She was fumbling with the robe about her knees, and now she rose and let it drop. She had come down from the stars and was here in the house again. She looked about her, dazed.

"Where is Ying? I am tired—I must sleep. To-morrow— to-morrow."

The men fell back and let Ying lead her into her room. Only Ch'iuming slipped off into the darkness. But the men stayed in Madame Wu's sitting-room in silence, looking at one another, listening until Ying came out and told them, "She is safe now—she has fallen asleep."

They went away then. "Can you explain this, Father?" Liangmo asked Mr. Wu as they went out of the court. "Her soul has never left this house before, has it?"

"I do not know what has come over her," Mr. Wu grumbled. "Ever since her fortieth birthday she has been too strange."

But Fengmo shook his head. "No one of you understands our mother as I do. I know how she feels. She feels that she

178

has wings and has never been allowed to fly—that is how she feels."

His father and Liangmo and Tsemo only looked at him as though he were out of his mind, and the next moment they bade one another a grave good night.

. . . . .

Madame Wu woke the next morning with great dread of what had happened to her the night before. Nothing in her life had been as sweet as those moments of whole freedom when her soul had left her body behind. She knew that this freedom could become drink to the soul, a liquor which it could no more resist than a drunkard his wine. For while her soul had been wandering among the stars she had neglected all else, and the burdens of this great house had dropped from her. She had cast them off and left them behind her as purely as a nun escapes the travail of womanhood, as surely as a priest escapes the burden of manhood. She felt angry with Brother André this morning because he had tempted her to such freedom, and she was afraid of herself because she had yielded. When she woke guilt was as heavy on her as though she had given herself to a secret lover.

She rose immediately and with severity to herself. She called Ying to account sharply for several small faults. She pointed to dust swept behind a big chair which was seldom moved and to a cobweb which hung from a polished beam. After her meal she took accounts with the cook and directed him concerning the foods for many days ahead. "Now that winter is not too far away," she said, "it is time you ceased to give us melon soups and cucumbers and such cooling things. It is time to brown pork and to stir-fry beef and beans and to put meat in the vegetables."

He opened his little eyes widely at this. "Where have you been eating, Lady, that you have not seen that I have already begun to do these things? After these years, do I need to be told of the seasons?"

He was surprised by Madame Wu's sharpness since, being so excellent a cook, he had his place in the house sure, and he was impudent when he liked, which was often, for he had the hot temper of all good cooks. But Madame Wu did not lessen her sharpness. "Go away," she said. "Do not tell me what you do and do not do."

179

She took no time for herself this day. No sooner was one gone than another came. She had not calmed herself from the cook when she saw Mr. Wu entering her court at a time earlier than he usually rose.

"Come in, Father of my sons," she said. "I have been taking accounts with the cook. Sometimes I think we should change him. He grows too loose in the tongue."

"But he is the only cook who makes crabs as I like them," Mr. Wu said in alarm. "You know how I searched in seven and eight cities before I found him, and then I married him to your maid to secure him."

"Ying is impudent too," Madame Wu said.

This was such unusual talk from her that Mr. Wu was more than a little disturbed. He sat down and drew out his pipe from his sleeve and filled it and lit it. "Now, Mother of my sons," he said, "you do not feel well this morning. Your eyes are shadowy."

"I am well," Madame Wu insisted.

Mr. Wu took two puffs and put down his pipe. "Ailien," he said in a low voice, first looking right and left to see that no one heard him, "you do very wrong to separate yourself from me. Truly, male and female have no health apart from each other. It is not only a matter of offspring. It is a matter of balance. Come, see yourself as you are. You are not toothless, your hair is still as black as it ever was, your flesh is firm, your blood quick. Have you forgotten how well we——"

"Cease there," she said firmly. "You know I am not a changeable woman. I have arranged my life. Have you discontent in you that you come here and speak to me so?"

"Indeed I would welcome you," he said frankly, "for I love you better than any other and must until I die, but I am not thinking of myself."

"You need not think of me," she insisted.

"I must think of you," he declared. For a moment he had the monstrous thought that perhaps she had by some strange twist of nature become attached, through the soul, to the foreign priest. But he was ashamed to put forth this thought to her. He knew her fastidiousness in all matters. Aside from his priesthood the man was foreign. Even when Mr. Wu was young and impatient he knew that it was better for him if he held his impatience and bathed himself and sweetened his breath and his body before he came near her. But foreigners

180

were rank from the bone because of the coarseness of their flesh, the profuseness of their sweat, and the thickness of their woolly hair. He put his monstrous thought aside, lest with her magic instinct she divine it and accuse him.

He had recourse, therefore, to the one thing which he knew would always command her attention. He put on peevishness and complained that he himself did not feel well.

"Ah, you are right. I am old, too," he sighed. "My belly rumbles, I wake up two and three times in the night. In the morning I am tired."

But she was still cruel. "Eat only a little broth for supper —and sleep alone for a few nights."

He gave up then and sat with his underlip thrust out, and she tapped her foot on the stone floor and sighed. Then she rose to pour tea for him. He saw her thin fingers tremble as she held the lid of the pot, but he said nothing. He drank tea, and she drank also from a bowl she poured for herself, and then he rose and went away. He had not reached the door when she called to him in that clear pure voice of hers which was as hard as silver, "You have forgotten your pipe yet again!"

He turned and his face was crimson. "Truly, I did forget it," he said.

But she stood there on the threshold and pointed at it as though it were a filthy thing, and he went back like a beaten boy and snatched it up, and then he strode past her, his lips pursed and his cheeks red. For a moment she stood looking after him, and in her breast there was a spot which ached as though a blow had fallen there.

But before she could heed it, who then should come in but Little Sister Hsia? Of all mornings it seemed to Madame Wu that this was the last one on which this poor pale woman was welcome, but what could she do except to invite her to come in and sit down?

"I have not seen you for so long," Little Sister Hsia said in her rapid, broken way. Madame Wu had learned to understand her meaning without understanding the words, for Little Sister Hsia controlled neither breath nor tongue. The sounds tumbled out, dull where they should have been sharp, and sharp where they should have been dull, and the rise and fall of her voice had nothing to do with the words.

"Have you been ill, Little Sister?" Madame Wu inquired.

"No," Little Sister replied, "but somehow—the last time—I felt perhaps I intruded."

"Can you intrude?" Madame Wu murmured politely.

"You are so kind," Little Sister said. In her innocence she accepted the politeness. "To-day I have come for something so special. Dear Madame, please, I have a plan and if you approve——"

"What is this plan?" she inquired.

"You know that priest?" Little Sister inquired.

"My son's tutor," Madame Wu murmured.

"He has a foundling home," Little Sister said. "I have long felt that a woman should have some oversight of the girls there. He has only an old servant. But they should be taught, Madame. Do you not think so? I was wondering if you would ask him—that is, perhaps, I would like with your approval to offer my services as a teacher."

"Why do you not ask him yourself?" Madame Wu inquired.

"You must know," Little Sister Hsia said earnestly. "His religion is not mine."

"How many religions have the foreigners?" Madame Wu inquired. "I am always hearing of a new one."

"There is only one true God," Little Sister Hsia said solemnly.

"Do you believe in this God?" Madame Wu asked.

Little Sister Hsia opened her pale blue eyes. She lifted her hand and brushed a lock of pale yellow hair from her cheek. "Why else do you think I left my home and my country to come to this strange land?"

"Is ours a strange land?" Madame Wu asked in some surprise."

"To me it is strange," Little Sister Hsia said.

"Did your God tell you to come?" Madame Wu asked again.

"He did," Little Sister Hsia replied.

"Did you hear His voice?" Madame Wu asked.

Little Sister Hsia blushed. She placed her long pale hands upon her breast.

"I felt it—I heard it here," she said.

Madame Wu gazed at her. "But did your parents never try to betroth you?" she asked.

Little Sister Hsia clasped her bosom more closely. "In my

country parents do not arrange marriages. Men and women marry for love."

"Did you ever love?" Madame Wu asked in her calm voice.

Little Sister Hsia's hands dropped into her grey cotton lap. "Of course," she said simply.

"But you did not wed?" Madame Wu asked.

"In my country," Little Sister Hsia said painfully, "the man must ask the woman."

Now Madame Wu was silent. She could easily have asked the next question, but she was too kind to do so. She knew that no man had asked Little Sister Hsia to marry him.

Little Sister Hsia lifted her eyes again bravely, although they were misted. "God had other plans for me," she said. Her voice was bright.

Madame Wu smiled kindly at her and said, "Do I not know you well!"

She took up her tiny silver-bound pipe and lit it and smoked two puffs and put it down again. "Here in my country," she said, "we do not leave so important a matter as marriage to men and women or God. Marriage is like food and drink and shelter. It must be arranged for, or some will have too much and others will starve. In my house I plan meals for all, even for the servants. Each has the right to his share. Some foods, of course, are liked better than others. But if I left foods to their choice, the children would eat nothing but sweets. My sons' father would eat nothing but crabs and fats. Some of the servants are greedy and would eat too much and leave nothing to the more timid ones, who would hunger. To each servant I allot a certain quantity, to each member of the family I allot a certain quality. Thus all are fed under my care."

Little Sister Hsia's fingers were knotting themselves. "I do not know how we came to talk about all this," she said. "I came here to ask you something—really, I've forgotten what it was now."

"You have forgotten because it was not what was really in your mind," Madame Wu said kindly. "I will answer you. No, Little Sister Hsia, you must leave Brother André alone. I assure you he is like a great high rock, hard because it is high. You must not beat yourself against that cliff. You will be wounded, your flesh will be torn, your heart will bleed, and your brains will be spilled like curds, but he will not know it. Occupy yourself with your own God—I advise it."

Little Sister Hsia was now pale to the lips. "I don't know what you mean," she stammered. "Sometimes I think you are a very wicked woman. You think thoughts—you put thoughts into me—I don't have such thoughts——"

"Do not be ashamed of your thoughts," Madame Wu said kindly. "They are good thoughts, for you are a good woman; but you are very lonely. You do not want to be lonely. But you must be lonely. It is your doom. Life has not provided for you. Yours is the strange cruel country. Not even your parents provided for you when life did not. Little Sister Hsia, I would myself arrange a marriage for you were it possible. But there is no man of your kind here."

Little Sister Hsia listened to her. Now her mouth opened and shut, she gasped, and suddenly she burst into tears of anger. "You are hateful!" she cried to Madame Wu. "You—you—I'm not like that—you're all alike, you Chinese—just thinking of such—awful things."

Madame Wu was deeply astonished. "Little Sister," she said, "I speak of life, the life of man, the life of woman, I pity you, I would help you if I could——"

"I don't want your help," Little Sister Hsia sobbed. "I want only to serve God."

"Poor soul," Madame Wu murmured, "then go and serve your God."

She rose and with a tender hand she took Little Sister's hand and led her to the door and bade her farewell. She resolved never to see her again. Serenely she sat down, her eyes still full of brooding pity, when Ying came running in.

"The First Young Lord, his wife is beginning travail," she cried.

"Ah," Madame Wu said, "send for her own mother. Meanwhile I will go to her at once." She rose and went into her bedroom and washed her hands thoroughly and changed her silk coat for one of clean blue linen. Then, perfuming her hands and cheeks, she went into Liangmo's court.

She welcomed the news. Nothing was so exciting in a house as the birth of a child. She had not enjoyed the act of birth for herself, and yet each time she had given birth she had felt purged and renewed. She had no fears to-day for Meng. Meng was young and healthy and made for children.

It was the day of women, as all days of birth are. The main room of her eldest son's court was full of excited women servants and female cousins and relatives. Even the children were excited and laughing as they tried to help carry pails of water and pots of tea. The great house was crowded enough and yet all welcomed the coming of another child. Moreover, since Meng was the wife of the eldest son, there was added dignity to this birth.

"Another son would be best," an elderly cousin was saying when Madame Wu entered the court. "Then if something happens to the first one, here is the second. A house with sons is always secure."

At this moment Madame Wu entered and all rose. The highest seat had been kept for her, and she took it. Murmured greetings came from the suddenly silenced room. Rulan as the second daughter-in-law rose and poured tea. Even she was silent.

"Ah, Rulan," Madame Wu said.

She looked with a sharp, swift gaze at the girl. Pale—she was looking pale. She never saw Rulan without remembering that once in the night she had wept aloud. Then Madame Wu saw Linyi sitting somewhat apart. She was cracking dried watermelon seeds between her teeth and blowing the shells on the floor. Madame Wu restrained a rebuke. In a few minutes Madame Kang would be here, and it was better not to disturb Linyi. The girl stood when she saw Madame Wu's eyes on her.

"Ah, Linyi," Madame Wu said.

Then she took up the affair of the birth. "How are matters?" she inquired of the midwife who had come running out of the bedroom when she heard the commotion of Madame Wu's arrival.

"All is well," the stout woman replied. She was a loud, coarse, hearty soul who performed her task everywhere, but who welcomed a birth in a rich house because her gifts would be rich, too, especially if she delivered the child whole and alive and if it were a boy.

"It is surely a boy," she said. Her broad face beamed. "Our First Son's Lady carried him high."

But Meng's voice raised in sudden screams now was clearly heard, and the midwife ran out of the room. In less than half an hour Madame Kang came hurrying in. She herself was already shapeless, although she had put on loose robes. Silence fell as she crossed the threshold. Curiosity and pity made the silence. She felt it and covered her shame with words.

"Sisters!" she exclaimed. "Here you all are. How good you are to care for my child!"

Then she spoke to Madame Wu. "And you, Eldest Sister, how is she?"

"I have waited for your coming," Madame Wu said. "Let us go in together."

Together they went into the room where Meng lay upon a narrow couch. Sweat poured down her cheeks and wet her long hair. The two ladies went to her, one on either side, and held her hands.

"Mother," Meng gasped, "Mother—it's worse than last time."

"Truly it is not," Madame Kang comforted her. "It will be much quicker."

"Do not talk!" Madame Wu commanded them both. "Now is the time for effort."

To Madame Wu's cool thin hand, to Madame Kang's plump warm one, Meng clung. She longed to lean her head on her mother's breast and weep, but she did not dare because it would not have been dutiful to her husband's mother. The reek of hot blood filled the room. The midwife was suddenly very busy.

"He comes, the little lord of life!" she cried. "I see his crown."

Meng shuddered and screamed and twisted the two hands she held. Neither flinched. She bent her head and bit her own hand that her mother held, and Madame Kang seized her hand and put it tightly against her bosom.

"Why wound yourself?" she exclaimed.

But Meng flung herself straight and made her body an arch of pain. She opened her mouth wide and put out a great groan that rose into a final scream. Madame Kang dropped her hand, pushed the midwife aside, and put out both hands and caught the child.

"Another boy," she said reverently. As though he heard her, the child who had drawn in his breath now let it out with a yell.

Madame Wu smiled down into the small wrinkled, furious

186

face. "Are you angry that you are born?" she asked the child in a tender teasing. "Hear him, Meng, he is blaming us all." But Meng did not answer. She was released from pain and, her eyes closed, she lay like a flower beaten upon the earth after rain.

. . . . .

That night Madame Wu and Madame Kang sat together. All was well in the house. The child was sound. The young mother slept. In mutual content the two friends now sat. Madame Wu, to spare her friend pain, had not spoken all day of Madame Kang's own shamefully swelling body. While they sat and talked of family matters and many small things and wove these in with memories of their youth, a long shadow fell across the open door. It was Brother André coming to give Fengmo his lesson as usual.

"The foreign priest?" Madame Kang asked.

"He comes here still to teach Fengmo," Madame Wu said. It seemed very long to her since last night when her soul had climbed out of the walls of the house. Now to-night it was fast again, caught and tied afresh by this new child born to-day. This was another mouth, another mind for which she was responsible.

"I do no more understand a priest or nun than I understand a foreign language," Madame Kang said.

Madame Wu smiled at her. "You," she said, "you——"

Madame Kang laughed roguishly and patted her full belly. "When I am alone," she confessed, "I am happy. I am glad to have one more child."

In Madame Kang's rosy face so far from youth Madame Wu saw to her amazement something of the same divine content which she had seen last night on Brother André's face. This friendship had been always upon the level of their common womanhood. Madame Wu knew that her friend had never so much as learned to read. Indeed, Madame Kang would have thought it a waste of time to read when she could bear a child.

"Meichen," Madame Wu said, half smiling, half tender, "you are insatiable. You are not willing to leave children to the young women. You are as good as bearing your own grandchild. Will you never leave off?"

187

"Alas," Madame Kang sighed with mock shame, "I find such pleasure in it!"

"Do you truly never wish for anything else than what your life is?" Madame Wu asked curiously.

"Never," Madame Kang replied. "If I could just keep on bearing a child every year—of what use am I if I cease bearing this fruit."

The thin and graceful shadow of Fengmo crossed the threshold. Madame Wu glanced at its passing.

"Fengmo is come for his lesson," she said.

Both ladies watched his slanting shadow move away.

"Linyi——" They both began and stopped, each waiting for the other.

"Go on," Madame Kang said.

"No, you are her mother, you proceed," Madame Wu insisted.

"No, I will not," Madame Kang said.

"Well, then," Madame Wu said after an instant, "I will proceed. Fengmo is not happy with your daughter, Meichen. It is a pity you did not teach her how to make him happy."

"Fengmo!" Madame Kang exclaimed. Madame Wu was surprised at the tone of her voice. "Fengmo not happy!" Madame Kang repeated with some scorn. "Ailien, let me tell you, it is Linyi who is not happy!"

"Meichen," Madame Wu said in her most silvery voice, "recall yourself."

"Yes," Madame Kang declared, "you think you have taught Fengmo well. But Linyi is not happy with him. In a marriage there must be two. Can there be hand-clapping with only one hand? You have not taught Fengmo his part in marriage."

"I?" Madame Wu said sharply.

"Yes," Madame Kang said. "Liangmo is like his father. He is a man by instinct, and so Meng is happy with him. But Fengmo is like you."

"That is to say, he demands something a little above the common," Madame Wu said bitterly.

Madame Kang wagged her head. "Then let him find it outside," she said. "Let him take up his book learning and let him find a work to soak up his discontent. It has nothing to do with Linyi."

"Meichen, you affront me!" Madame Wu exclaimed.

"Linyi had better come home for a while," Madame Kang

replied. "You and Fengmo, you can study your books and do without her until you see her value."

Madame Wu saw this friendship, deeply dear, tremble and crack. "Meichen, do we quarrel?" she exclaimed.

Madame Kang replied with passion, "I have been a good friend to you always, and I have never judged you even though I saw you thinking thoughts above a woman. But I have always known that you were too wise, too clever for happiness. I told your sons' father so——"

"Have you two talked of me?" Madame Wu asked. Her voice was too quiet.

"Only for your sake," Madame Kang replied. She rose as she spoke and gathered her loose robes about her and walked sturdily away from Madame Wu.

Late that night when Madame Wu was in her bed Ying said, "Do you know that Madame Kang took your third son's wife home with her to-night, Lady?"

"I know," Madame Wu said.

She closed her eyes as though for sleep. But she did not sleep. She had not believed that Madame Kang would reach into this house and take back her daughter, as though Linyi still belonged to her. She lay still, and she could scarcely sleep for anger all that night.

Had Madame Wu been a lesser woman she would merely have been angry with her friend and sure of herself, but she was not such a woman. She blamed herself for carelessness in her own behaviour. She had always known that her friendship with Madame Kang was of house and family, earth and clay. Why had she not been content with this instead of opening a door which frightened her friend? Every soul is frightened when it is forced beyond its level. Now out of her carelessness the rift between Fengmo and Linyi was widened. For surely it is very grave when a young wife is taken out of her husband's house and home again to the childhood shelter. Fengmo must go and bring her back. She sent for Fengmo.

He came in looking pale but quiet.

"Son," she said, "I have sent for you to confess my own fault. Linyi's mother and I quarrelled. Like stupid women, each of us declared for her own child, and she took her daughter home again. I have to tell you this so that you will know it was not Linyi's fault. Now we must invite her to come back to us."

189

To her horror Fengmo shook his head. "I will not invite her, Mother," he declared. "Let it be as it is. Linyi and I are not suited."

"How can you say that?" Madame Wu asked. Her heart was beating so quickly that she could feel it throb against the thick satin of her coat. The morning was cold, and she had put on a lined garment. "Any man and any woman, with intelligence, can suit each other. Marriage is a family matter, Fengmo. It is a discipline. One may not consider oneself only."

"Mother, I know that is what you have been taught," Fengmo replied. "And it is what you have taught us. Were I your only son I might in duty accept it. But I have two brothers ahead of me. Mother, let me go free."

Madame Wu leaned forward in her chair, her hands clasped together. "Fengmo," she said, "tell me what happened between you and Linyi. I am your mother."

"Nothing," Fengmo said doggedly.

But Madame Wu took this literally. "Nothing," she repeated aghast. "You mean you two went into the same bed and nothing happened?"

"Oh, Mother," Fengmo groaned. "Why do you think that is the only thing which can happen between men and women?"

"But it is the first thing," Madame Wu insisted.

Fengmo set his lips together. "Very well, then, Mother," he said. "It was the first thing. Then you see, Mother, I expected something more."

"What did you expect?" she asked.

He flung out his big thin hands. "Some kind of talk, some kind of understanding, companionship—something after the introduction. I mean, after you are through with the body, what then?"

"But at your age you are never through with the body," Madame Wu said. She began to see that she had not understood Fengmo. She had taken it for granted that all men were only males. She had once laughed at a foreign story she had read, an ancient story of Greece, of a woman who had fallen in love with a man not her husband because his breath was sweet. For this woman had known only her husband and had thought a foul breath was a part of man and that all men had such breath in them. Now she perceived she was as silly as this woman to consider that all men were alike. She herself had given birth to a man who was more than a male. This so astonished her that for some time she sat looking at her son.

But Fengmo seemed unaware of her thoughtful eyes. He sat, his body bent, his elbows on his parted knees, his hands hanging clasped between.

"I feel I cannot command you to do anything," she said at last in a low voice. "I see now that I have violated your being."

He looked up and she saw tears in his eyes.

"What do you call freedom?" she inquired. "Tell me and I will give it to you."

"I should like to go away out of this house," he said.

These words wrenched her heart. But she only asked next, "Where would you like to go?"

"Brother André said he would help me to cross the sea," Fengmo said.

"If Brother André had never come into this house," she said, pricked with self-reproach, "would you have thought of this?"

"I would have thought of it," he replied, "but I would not have known how to do it. Brother André has shown me the way."

To this she said nothing. She sat mute and thoughtful. Then she sighed, "Very well, my son," she said at last. "Go free."

9

In less than a month after this, on a day when the first light
snow fell, Fengmo went away. All the household stood at the
gate to see him go. The street that went past the gate ended
at the river, and the menfolk, and with them only Madame
Wu, walked with him to the water's edge. Hands helped him
with his baggage and hands helped him over the side of the
rocking row-boat that was to carry him to a small steam
launch that would take him to a river steamer. The river
steamer would take him to the ocean and the great ship that
lay waiting. Above the whitened ground a soft grey sky
brooded. The boat pushed off, and snowflakes melted on the
boatman's oars. A score of farewells followed Fengmo.
Madame Wu did not call after him. She stood, a small straight
figure wrapped in fur, and watched this son of hers cast off
from the shores of his home. She was frightened and sad, but
she comforted herself by these words, "He is free."

And wrapping her coat about her, she returned to her
own walls.

With Fengmo's going Brother André would have ceased to
come, but Madame Wu invited him to continue his lessons,
taking Linyi as pupil instead of Fengmo.

"When my son returns from foreign countries," she said to
Brother André, in her cool, graceful fashion, "I would like his
wife to know something of what he knows."

Now Fengmo's marriage had been patched together in this
fashion: One day Madame Wu went to the Kang house and
talked with Linyi very gently in her mother's presence. She
told Linyi that Fengmo was going away, and she herself
invited her to return in order that if possible before Fengmo
went away he might leave her with child.

"I do this, not only for the sake of our house," Madame Wu
said to Linyi, "but also for your own sake, lest you be un-
fulfilled."

She had studied Linyi's face as she spoke—a selfish, pretty
face, she thought. Good mothers always had selfish daughters.
Meichen was too good. She made her children too happy.

192

They thought of home as heaven and their mother as earth.

"It is not well for a young woman to be left empty when her husband goes away," she continued.

To this Madame Kang had heartily agreed. Since her quarrel with her friend she had repented her anger. Linyi had aided her in this. For, while the girl had come home with all her mother's pity, Madame Kang began after some days to see Linyi as a wilful young woman. She was no longer a girl, but a married wife. Yet she behaved as she had when she was a girl in a rich house. She rose late and dawdled about the courts and did not so much as pick up her handkerchief when it fell from her pocket, but she called for a maid to come and hand it to her. In small ways Madame Kang now began to reproach Linyi and to think that perhaps Fengmo had had something to complain about. When she heard that Fengmo was going away she, too, was eager for Linyi to return to him.

"You do not belong to this house any more," she told the girl more than once. "You belong to the Wu house."

"How can I make that slender, naughty girl become a woman and a wife?" Madame Wu now asked herself secretly. "And not only for my house but for her own happiness?"

So Brother André had come into her mind again. She saw his great patient frame, his dark kind face. But could he teach a young wife?

"You must go into your husband's house this very day," Madame Kang declared. And as eagerly as she had once taken Linyi back, she now sent her forth again. Linyi went in silence. She was not stupid, and clearly enough she felt the change in her own mother. She knew that she had been put out of her heaven and earth. Her heart smarted, and silently she went back into Fengmo's court. He had been exceedingly busy preparing for his going. But since he knew he was to be freed he was gay and careless to her. It did not now matter greatly whether she were here or not, since he was leaving the house.

"I have come back," she had said to him.

He did not say he was glad, she did not ask if he were. Neither expected the other's love. She helped him with new docility to fold his garments, and she dusted his books. At night they slept together. He took her and she yielded, partly for duty's sake to the house, partly because they were young and hungry. In the morning they had parted still without speech. For decency's sake she did not go outside the court.

"Until we meet!" he had said.

"Heaven give you safe journeying," she had replied, and stood leaning against the door to watch him while he went. Some faint uncertainty shook her heart from its middle place in her breast, but she was not ready to see any fault in herself.

"I am still sleepy," she thought, and yawned widely, and without hiding her red mouth she returned to the big bed and rolled into the silk quilts and slept like a little chrysalis.

From this sleep Madame Wu awakened her as soon as Fengmo was gone. "Come, Linyi," she said, "you have slept enough. Now you must wake and begin your education."

"My education?" Linyi faltered.

"You will learn cooking and embroidery in the morning," Madame Wu said. "Elder Cousin will teach you. Then for an hour before the noon meal you will come to me, and I will teach you the classics. In the afternoon Brother André will teach you foreign languages. In the evening you will help the maids to put the children to bed. You must learn how to care for children."

Linyi looked up out of the quilt. Her big eyes were startled, and her soft hair was all awry. "Now?" she asked.

"Now, at once," Madame Wu said firmly. She held a thin bamboo cane in her hand, and she tapped this on the floor. "Wash yourself," she said. "Brush your hair. Then come to me."

She went back to her own courts, her mouth set too grimly for its own beauty. "I do this for Fengmo," she thought. "Then when this is done I can think again about my own freedom."

But because she did not trust Linyi she stayed by her that afternoon when Brother André came. Linyi must not be idle. Then, too, for the sake of honour she herself must supervise the hours this foreign priest was with her own daughter-in-law in her son's absence. She knew that Brother André was a soul, but who else but her would believe the big body was only a husk?

In this way every day she sat in the highest seat in the library, her dragon-headed cane, which she carried now that Old Lady was dead, between her hands. She listened to everything Brother André taught Linyi. But while the girl plodded unwillingly along the hard part of learning,

Madame Wu's mind flew ahead and wandered into a hundred bypaths of wonder.

Thus she came to know how the earth and the seas are gathered into a great ball swinging among the stars and planets, and she understood the paths of sun and moon, the passage of winds and clouds. But these were as nothing to her wonder when she came to understand the tongues of man. For she liked to do this: she chose a word, such a word as life, or death, as love, hatred, food, air, water, hunger, sleep, house, flower, tree, grass, bird, and she learned this word through all the languages which Brother André knew. These languages were the voices of mankind. She learned everything with the excuse of helping Linyi to learn.

And as she learned, all the things which had occupied her life came to have meaning. In the past she had sometimes wondered why she should spend herself in the continued round of birth and death and birth again. Within these four walls, as man begot and woman conceived in order that the house of Wu might not perish, sometimes she had asked herself what it mattered if one house died. In a year when too many girls were born, in a year when an idiot was dropped too early from a womb, she had often been disheartened. Especially in the years when she had only looked forward to her fortieth birthday had she refused to answer the questioning of her own soul. Little Sister Hsia on one of those days had chanced to be there.

"May I read you from the blessed book, Madame?" Little Sister had asked.

Madame Wu had been weary to the bone that day, for in addition to all else she had known that she was pregnant again. But she was always too courteous to refuse a guest. "If it is your pleasure, read," she had replied.

Then Little Sister Hsia had taken out her sacred book, and she had read aloud in her broken childish fashion words like these:

"What is man that thou art mindful of him and the son of man that thou rememberest him? For the days of man are as grass——"

"Stop!" Madame Wu had cried.

Her voice had burst out of her, and so unusual was this that Little Sister Hsia had stared at her.

"Are these words to comfort a soul?" Madame Wu had

demanded. "Are these the words of a god? Rather, I say, of a devil! If I should listen to these words, Little Sister, I would hang myself. Read me no more from your book, lest I cannot live."

But she had brooded over the words, and she remembered them now. Yes, it was true. Man's flesh was as grass. When her child had been born dead she had remembered the words as she held the small, still body in her arms. But to-day, as she listened to the voices of mankind crying out in different tongues but always the same words, she felt in herself a new wonder.

"Do all men also cry out a word for God?" she asked Brother André.

"All men," he replied gravely, and then he rolled out sonorous syllables that struck upon her ears like drums. "God—God—God—God——" in twenty tongues, and all the tongues of man.

"From all over the earth we cry out to Old Heaven," she said musingly, and the drums echoed in her soul.

On such nights she could not sleep. In silence she allowed Ying to prepare her, and she climbed into the high redwood platform of the bed. Behind the silk curtains she gave herself up to her soul and meditated on the meaning of all she had learned. Brother André came to be for her a well, wide and deep, a well of learning and knowledge. In the night she thought of scores of questions to which she wanted answers. Sometimes when her memory grew burdened with their number she rose from her bed and lit her candle. And she took up her camel-hair brush and brushed down the questions upon a sheet of paper in her fine script. The next afternoon when Brother André came she read them to him one by one and listened carefully to all he said.

Now, his manner of answering questions was exceedingly simple, but this was because he was so learned. He did not need, as lesser men do, to talk over and above the pith of the matter. Instead, he knew how, as Taoists of old knew, to put into a handful of words the essence of the essence of truth. He stripped the leaves away, and he plucked the fruit and cracked the husk and peeled the inner shell and split the flesh and took out the seed and divided it, and there was the kernel, pure and clean.

And Madame Wu's mind was so whetted at this time of

her life, so bladelike and piercing, that she took this kernel and from it comprehended all. Young Linyi sat between the two, her eyes wide, as these few words were said and heard, and it was plain that for her it was all far above her and beyond her. Her mind still slept in youth.

But Brother André marvelled at Madame Wu. "You have lived behind these walls all your life," he said one day, "and yet when I speak as heretofore I have spoken only to one or two of my few brother scholars, you know what I mean."

To this she replied, "You have told me of the magic glass which makes small things large. A fragment of dust, you told me, could be made as large as a desert, and if the fragment were comprehended, the desert was known. This house is the fragment of dust, and from it I comprehend all. Inside these four walls is the whole of life." She caught sight of Linyi's hostile young face.

"Are you saying we are dust, Mother?" she asked.

"No, child," Madame Wu replied. "I am saying that you are all of life.

Over the young head her eyes met Brother André's. "Teach this child," she said.

"Mother, I am not a child," Linyi pouted.

But Madame Wu smiled. That afternoon when Brother André was putting his books together, she asked, "Dare I ask you to take me, too, as your pupil?" she asked humbly.

"I am honoured by the wish," he replied in his grave way.

"Then for an hour, perhaps, after you have taught Linyi?"

He inclined his head. Thereafter each evening for an hour he answered Madame Wu's questions. Scrupulous in spite of her age, Madame Wu bade Ying sit on the seat nearest the door while she and Brother André talked.

.   .   .   .   .   .

"Madame, I must ask you a question. If it makes you angry I beg you to send me away," Ying said one morning.

"Why should I be angry at you now after the years you have spoken as you liked?" Madame Wu asked.

She put down the book she was reading, but she kept her thumb in the pages, ready to read again when Ying had finished.

"I cannot please you in what I am about to say," Ying began. "But while you have been wandering around the earth

197

with this big priest, the household has been at sevens and eights with disorder. The wet nurse to your eldest son's wife's second son is losing her milk. The child grows thin. At night there is quarrelling in your second son's court. His wife's maid says there is no pregnancy there yet. And the Second Lady and our master—well, Madame, I will not presume. But I say it is wrong for a lady like you to withdraw herself into books as you do. It is not all evil that our ancestors taught us that women ought not to read and write."

This Ying said as though she had committed it to heart. Madame Wu listened, the old half smile on her face. But her thumb slipped out of the book, and she closed it and put it on the table. "Thank you, good soul," she said.

She rose and went into her bedroom. The morning was cool, and she put on a fur coat before she went out. In the court the orchids were drying with frost and the leaves were sinking into the loam of the earth. But the sprays of berries on the Indian bamboo were growing scarlet and heavy. A blackbird sat perched on a rock, eating them, and Ying ran at him to frighten him away as she followed. Now that her mistress had been so patient under rebuke, Ying felt guilty of impudence, and she tried to make amends with her usual chatter. Madame Wu listened to it without answering. It occurred to her as she went through Old Lady's empty court that it would be well if Liangmo brought his family here to live, near her, so that she could more easily watch over the children. Then she could move Tsemo and Rulan into Liangmo's present court, and the larger space might add peace to them.

The day was fair. She moved through the clear sunshine in a well-being which she herself did not understand. These four walls round this piece of earth were full of human troubles, but she felt herself able to meet them and even to cure them, because she was no longer a part of them. By her separation from Mr. Wu, in the flesh, she had cut all cords that had entangled her. She mused on this strong secret bond of body to body, which when it was cut, freed not only body but soul. And her soul followed the paths that were now opened over all the earth. Thus she stepped into Liangmo's court as a goddess might have come, to minister and not to share.

But the wail of the child crying struck her ear with painful sharpness. She forgot everything and hurried into the house. There Meng sat, and there, too, sat the young wet nurse holding the hungry child to her empty breast. Tears ran down her pale cheeks. The child sucked and turned his head away again to scream with anger when no milk came.

"What now?" Madame Wu asked. "How has your milk dried?"

The young woman laid the little boy in Meng's arms while she wept.

"Have you given her crab soup with poached eggs?" Madame Wu inquired of Meng.

"We have tried everything," Meng replied. "I thought it was nothing at first, a cold she had, or that she had over-eaten, and we mixed rice flour into gruel for the child for a meal or two. But this has gone on for two days, and the child is not fed. His flesh is slipping from his bones."

The older child's wet nurse now came in. "I have offered my milk," she said, "but it is too old for this child. He vomits it up." She looked pleased with herself as she spoke. "I have never lost my milk, Elder Lady, so how can I know what should be done?"

"Go away," Madame Wu ordered her, seeing her vanity and knowing that she was a woman greedy for gifts.

The young wet nurse went on crying, and Madame Wu sat down and folded her hands on her dragon-headed cane and looked at her.

"Your milk has dried because you are sad," she said. "What is your trouble?"

At first the young woman would not answer. She wiped her eyes on her sleeves, and looked down, and when the tears came welling out she wiped them away again.

"It is strange you have water enough for your own tears and not for milk for my son," Meng said distractedly.

"Hush," Madame Wu said. "She is a human being. Speak, good soul."

Thus encouraged, the young woman faltered in a voice so small as scarcely could be heard, "I have not seen my own child. I do not know how she does—I have been here nearly a month. Next week is the full month birthday of this child, and I do not know how my own little one does."

At this Meng looked exceedingly angry. She pursed her red mouth and opened her black eyes wide. "How can you think of your child and let your milk dry up?" she exclaimed.

"Hush," Madame Wu said again. "Let her child be brought here."

"To be nursed with mine?" Meng cried.

"To save your son," Madame Wu replied.

The young nurse fell on her knees before Madame Wu. "Oh, Elder Lady," she gasped, "you are not cruel—they told me you were cruel——"

"Who said I was cruel?" Madame Wu asked.

"The steward—on the lands—he said I must not disobey you—that no one dared to disobey you. I did not want to come here, Lady. I have my own little house, my man works on your land, we have our child—a girl, it is true, but our first child. I was so proud of her. I had such a lot of milk. The steward said I must come or he would drive my man away from the land we have rented."

"He had no command from me to speak so," Madame Wu said. "I told him only to find a wet nurse."

"In the villages he makes us all feel afraid of you," the young woman went on. "On the lands we all fear you through him, Elder Sister."

Madame Wu was not a little confounded by these words, but she did not want this servant woman to know her confusion. In a great household those who command must not put themselves at the mercy of those who obey. She inclined her head and said gently, "I will send word to-day that your child is to be brought here. She may sleep near you, but not in the same room with my grandson."

"You save a life," the woman said, and fell on her knees and knocked her forehead on the tiles before Madame Wu.

But the child was wailing again, and the woman rose from her knees and took him back. The tears dried on her cheeks, and she held the little boy to her breast. He snatched the nipple again and began to suck, and milk began to flow.

"You held back your milk," Meng cried. "You refused to let it come down."

But the woman looked up at her in timid wonder. She was a plain-faced farm woman. "I did not, Lady," she said. "I do not know where my milk went nor why now it has come back, except that when our Elder Lady said my little girl could come I felt loosened inside my heart, and so the milk came down."

But Meng was still angry. "You common soul, you are too stupid!"

Madame Wu rose. "Since your son's life depends upon her, it is perhaps better for you not to be angry, my daughter," she said. "And you, woman, when your child comes, do not forget your duty is to my grandson."

The young woman looked up humbly at Madame Wu. "I will not forget, Elder Lady," she said in a low voice. "I will always feed him first."

Something in her look and in her voice stayed Madame Wu's steps. Underneath the quiet she felt something sullen and strong. But she did not ask what it was. She had never inquired too far into the troubles of those beyond her own family, lest she be somehow entangled in them. So now she spoke to Meng.

"I will give our Old Lady's courts to my eldest son and you. Then I can be near my grandsons."

Meng did not look pleased, and Madame Wu hardened her purpose. "I will send servants to help you move to-day," she said, and without waiting for Meng to speak she went on to find her son Tsemo.

At this hour Tsemo should have been away from the house and at his business, which was to supervise the markets where they sold their produce. But he was still here. Madame Wu saw him in his court rinsing his mouth as though he had only just eaten.

She entered, and he spat hastily and put aside the cup he held.

"You are early, Mother," he said.

"I am going my rounds," she said. "I stopped to say that I shall give Liangmo's court to you because I give him Old Lady's rooms in order that my grandsons can be near me."

"I will tell Rulan," Tsemo said.

At the name she thought she saw a slight cold shade on his face, and she spoke straightly as her habit was when she saw trouble. "I am told that Rulan cries in the night."

"Who told you?" he asked shortly.

"The servants," she replied, "and it is a shameful thing when the troubles of the family become the talk of servants."

"You were right, Mother," he said. "I should not have married this woman."

"Has love ended between you already?" Madame Wu inquired.

But to this he would not say no or yes. He walked about the tiny court, ten steps this way, sixteen steps that. "We have nothing to say to each other without its leading to quarrelling," he replied at last.

"How is it that she is not with child?" Madame Wu asked. "Quarrelling always comes between men and women when there is no child."

"How can I tell?" he replied, and shrugged his shoulders. "She does not conceive. It is assuredly not my fault."

"There can be no conception where there is quarrelling," Madame Wu told him. "Hearts in a roil dry the body's juices and poison the blood. Between man and woman the stream of life forces must be kept clear." She looked at this handsome son. "It is always easy for men and women to quarrel," she went on. "Their natural difference is so great that unless they unite to create the new generation, they fly apart from each other like water and oil. A wife without child is a creature against nature, and she rebels against Heaven and earth, and the man is nothing to her. You must be patient with her until she conceives. Once that comes you will find her a new woman."

"Am I nothing to Rulan?" he asked arrogantly.

"She loves you too well," Madame Wu replied, "and that is why she hates you. Her love comes to no fruit. She is teased by it. She has no defence from you, no refuge. She has no place to hide from you and be herself."

She could see he was deeply hurt by what she said. "You shall take a journey somewhere," she went on. "Then when you come back be gentle, not arrogant. Do not remind her that she is older than you or that she sought you first."

"How do you know she sought me?" he asked. He stopped his pacing to stare at her. "How do you know everything?" he said, half laughing, half rueful.

"I can see with my eyes," she replied. She rested her round chin on her hands folded over the dragon-head of her cane. "She fears you and she hates her fears, and she loves you and she dreads her love. Yes, go away and leave her with me. There is an order between men and women, and you and Rulan have proceeded out of order. Look at Meng—with her all things proceed as Heaven ordains, and what harmony there is in her house! Her sons come one by one, and Liangmo is content with her. Neither of them loves the other too much, and together they create their new generation."

"Meng is old-fashioned," Tsemo said impatiently. "Also she is a little stupid. At least Rulan is not stupid."

"It is not necessary for a woman to be stupid or not stupid," Madame Wu replied with patience. "Such things are all in proportion. Man and woman in marriage must be in proportion to each other and so I chose Meng for Liangmo. He is wiser than she, but she is wise enough so that she understands what he says. In your marriage you are too equal and so you contend."

"You are wiser than my father," Tsemo said. He threw her a look so hard and bright that she was disturbed by it.

"Ah, I learned my wisdom," she said quickly. "I am wise enough so that there was never any trouble between your father and me. That is why I sent Ch'iuming into his courts so that he could continue to be happy as he grew old."

"And you?" Tsemo probed her cruelly.

"I also continue to be happy," she said tranquilly.

Now Rulan came out of the house, as though she could no longer pretend she did not hear all that was being said in the small court outside her window. Madame Wu knew well enough that she had heard all, but in courtesy she carried on the pretence. "I was telling Tsemo that if you please, my daughter, you may move into Liangmo's larger court, since I moved them into the court next to mine, where I can watch over my grandsons better."

"We thank you, Mother," Rulan said. But no thanks showed in voice or look. She was carelessly dressed in an ugly robe of grey and green squares laid next to each other, and she looked older than she was.

"As soon as Tsemo goes away," Madame Wu thought, "I will teach her not to look so ugly." She continued to sit and look thoughtfully at her daughter-in-law, and Tsemo, following this gaze, found new fault with his wife.

"I hate that robe," he said violently.

"Buy me another," she said insolently, tossing back her short hair.

Madame Wu rose at once. She would not sit and see the two quarrel lest she be compelled to strive for peace between them. But she could not keep back entirely her displeasure.

"Tsemo is going away for a while," she told Rulan. "I have given my permission. Be peaceful for these few days until he goes. Busy yourself with moving your goods to-morrow into your new court."

"If Tsemo goes, I go," Rulan said.

She stood very straight in the ugly robe, her hands clenched at her side. Madame Wu stood as straight, her hands on her cane.

"You do not go," she said distinctly. "You will stay here with me. You have much to learn, and I will teach you."

Again she did not wait for a daughter-in-law to answer. She turned and went out of the court, and not once did she look back.

"Ah, my sons' wives," she thought, "how troublesome they are to me! Would that I had early taken little girls into my house and reared them to be sons' wives and bent them to fit our need! To bring strangers into the house to bear our grandsons is to bring in trouble"

She found herself longing for evening and for peace, when, with Brother André for guide, she could leave body behind and sally forth, soul bare, into the world.

.   .   .   .   .   .

In the court she had left, Rulan looked at her young husband with surly, suffering eyes. "You want to go away and leave me," she muttered.

"It was wholly my mother's idea," Tsemo said lightly. He threw back his head and smoothed his long forelock. She saw those pale hands of his and felt the pull at her heart for which she now hated herself.

"I shall run away," she said in the same sullen voice.

He laughed. "Not with me—I would not dare to come home again."

"You are afraid of your mother!" she cried.

"I am, indeed," he agreed.

This easy agreement was his trick against her. Time and again he yielded the point and left her nothing to grasp for her weapon.

"I would rather have no sons than have them afraid of me," she declared.

"Well, you have no sons," he said in his tranquil voice.

Her heart broke at the ancient taunt. Try as she could she

could not free herself from its power. "Tsemo, do you really hate me?" she whispered. She came nearer to him as she spoke, and he looked down into her face.

"Why will you tear at me and wound me and give me no peace?" he said between his teeth.

"Peace from me!" she cried.

"No, only peace," he said, "simple peace."

"Peace so you can forget me!" she said passionately.

"I know that is why you will have me angry at you," he retorted. He laughed sourly. "You make me angry so that you can force my mind toward you for that, at least."

He had plucked truth out of her, truth she hid even from herself. Yes, when he had ceased to think of her day and night, when he grew careless after their marriage, she had forced anger on him to draw him back to her. She wanted suffering from him—pain, even, rather than nothing.

She saw him turn his head away from her, and the sight was dreadful to her. "I must save myself from him," she thought. "I must rid myself somehow of love. It is too bitter for me."

It was strange that at this moment when she longed to be free of him she thought of Madame Wu. All impulse as she was, she ran past him and through the courts, and did not stop until she found her sitting in her library smoking her little pipe.

"Mother!" she cried. "Let me go free too!"

Madame Wu heard this cry like an echo of her own soul. But she did not reveal her consternation. She put down the pipe on the table and gazed at her tall daughter-in-law. "Calm yourself," she said. "Sit down and smooth the hair out of your eyes. While I think of it, let me tell you never to wear that robe again. You ought always to wear gay colours. They will lighten your darkness. Now, how can I let you go free?"

"I want to go out of this house—away from Tsemo," Rulan said. She did not sit down in obedience to Madame Wu's motioning hand. She stood, having heard nothing of what Madame Wu had said to her, and the two women looked at each other.

"I told you Tsemo is going away," Madame Wu said. "Of him you will be free."

"I want to be free of him for ever," Rulan cried. "I ought

never to have married. I hate what I feel for him. I am a slave to it. He has me as he wants me, not as I want to be."

"Is he to blame for this?" Madame Wu asked.

"Let me go away," Rulan repeated.

Madame Wu unwillingly began again to like this strange, angry girl. "Where will you go?" she asked. "What is there for a woman outside her husband's house? Even if I free you from this house, can you be free? A woman without a husband— she becomes despised of all. Through man and child only is she made free."

Rulan looked down at her with horror. "Tell me how to free myself," she whispered.

Madame Wu felt a great welling pity for her. "Alas, my child," she said gently, "I cannot tell you, for I do not know."

"Have you never loved anybody?" the girl urged.

Madame Wu looked down and did not answer. She began to feel that Tsemo had somehow wronged this girl. But how could he know what she meant? He had been only himself, and could he help it if this was not enough for the girl? She began to perceive that she had been fortunate in not allowing herself to love Mr. Wu too well. At one time there had been some danger of it, when she was very young. But her own fastidiousness had been her guard. Rulan was not fastidious.

"If you had a child," she said at last, "you might be free of him. At least you divide your love. The child demands much, and you are compelled to give it. Or it might be, if you have no child, that you could undertake study, or painting, or some such thing. You must divide yourself, my child. You have allowed all your powers to flow in the deep narrow river. Now dig yourself canals and rivulets and drain off your love here and there."

"Forced labour," Rulan said bitterly.

"If need be," Madame Wu said gently. "But it is your only way to peace. You will surely die otherwise. For he will hate you, I promise you. He is trembling on the verge of hatred now. Therefore have I commanded him to go away from you for a while."

Rulan wet her pale lips. "Are all men like him?" she whispered.

"Men are as like one another as minnows," Madame Wu said in her pretty silvery voice. "It is when women discover it that they are free."

206

"Then why do I love only Tsemo?" Rulan inquired shrewdly.

"Some trick of his looks," Madame Wu said in the same pretty voice, "the way his eyebrows move, the turn of his mouth, the set of his shoulders in his coat, his hands——"

"How do you know?" Rulan whispered aghast.

Madame Wu laughed. "Heaven sets a hundred snares to carry on our kind," she replied. She could not be angry at this girl. What was she but a poor trapped creature? Now that she saw how pitiably well Rulan loved Tsemo, she forgave her everything.

She put out her narrow hand and pulled Rulan's hands apart and patted them one after the other. "No more unhappiness," she said coaxingly. "I do not like anyone to be unhappy under our roof. See, I spend my life trying to make you all happy. What do you want, child, to make you happy here?"

Rulan could not but yield to the beautiful coaxing face, the kind and melodious voice. She allowed herself to be pulled along until she stood like a child at Madame Wu's knees. "Let him go," Madame Wu said in her soothing way. "Do not weep when he goes. Help him to pack his boxes, and bid him good-bye gaily, however your heart weeps. Sleep heartily at night and do not wake. Let him be sleepless, child, not you."

"But if I am sleepless without him?" Rulan asked naïvely.

Madame Wu laughed aloud, relishing this frankness. "Get up and take a walk in your court," she said. "The night air is very cold now, and when you are cold your warm bed will put you to sleep, even though you lie down alone."

The two women looked steadily into each other's eyes. Madame Wu discerned the young hot soul, trembling with distress, and all the fountains of her pity broke open. Some loyalty deeper than that to the Wu family reached out and poured its waters of balm upon this soul, who was also a woman.

"You are free when you gain back yourself," Madame Wu said. "You can be as free within these walls as you could be in the whole world. And how could you be free if, however far you wander, you still carry inside yourself the constant thought of him? See where you belong in the stream of life. Let it flow through you, cool and strong. Do not dam it with your two hands, lest he break the dam and so escape you. Let him go free, and you will be free."

"I cannot live without love from him," Rulan faltered.

"Then hang yourself to-night," Madame Wu said calmly, "for I promise you he will not love you unless you let him first go free. Love only lives in freedom."

"I could be a slave if he loved me," Rulan said.

"You are not the slave!" Madame Wu exclaimed. "You are striving to be the master through your love. He feels it, he will not have it so. He must be free of you because you love him too much. Oh, foolish woman, how can I make you see how to be happy?"

Then Rulan fell at her knees. "I do see," she sobbed. "I know what you mean—and—I am afraid to do it!"

But Madame Wu would not let her weep. "Get up—get up," she said, and she stood and lifted Rulan and made her rise and stand on her feet. "If you are afraid," she said sternly, "then I am finished with you. Never come back to me. I have no time for you. Yes, I will let you go out of the house for ever."

Looking down at this exquisite, indomitable, slender creature. Rulan felt her restless bitter heart grow still in her bosom. This solitary cool woman appeared now to be the only happy woman she had ever known. Her own mother had been fretful and discontented, and her sisters quarrelsome and restless, as all Shanghai women are restless. But this Madame Wu was as still and deep as a pool in a mountain stream.

"I will obey you, Our Mother," she said humbly.

When she had gone Madame Wu reflected with quiet astonishment at herself that she had sent two sons out of her house because of two young women, neither of whom she loved, and that upon herself she had taken this double burden.

"I, who myself crave my freedom!" she exclaimed.

And, stupefied at her own contradiction, she gave herself over to Ying's hands to be made ready for bed.

.   .   .   .   .   .

"I cannot explain myself," Madame Wu said to Brother André the next day. She had told him of Tsemo's going.

"Is explanation necessary?" Brother André asked with one of his smiles.

She had often observed this smile. It began in the thicket of his eyebrows and beard like light beginning to glow in a wood. The immensity of this man's head, his whole size and bulk and hairiness, would once have terrified her. Now she was used to it.

"What are you thinking about?" he inquired in a strange and half-shy fashion.

"You often say we are all kin on this earth," she replied, "and yet how can you explain your own appearance?"

"What do you find so strange in me?" he asked, still in the half-shy voice.

"You are too big," she said calmly, "and too hairy."

"You cannot explain yourself—perhaps you can explain me?" Brother André retorted.

The lights in the wood were very bright now. She saw glimmers of white teeth in the darkness of his beard and points of laughter in the dark eyes.

"I have read that foreigners are hairy because they are nearer the animals," she observed.

"Perhaps," he replied. He opened his great mouth and let out a roar of laughter. . . . In the depths of the night, when he lay alone on his bamboo pallet, he had thanked God that he had not met Madame Wu when she was a young girl. "I would not have answered for my soul, O God," he said grimly through the darkness. But now he was master of his huge body and was only amused by her.

"In that case," he now said to Madame Wu, "would it not be true that, having made me first, God improved upon his original design in making you?"

Now she laughed too, and the deep roar and the delicate silvery laughter mingled together. Out in the court a bondmaid was washing Madame Wu's fine undergarments while Ying sat beside her to tell her what to do. Ying caught the bondmaid's upward wondering look.

"Do not rub soap upon silk, you beggar's bone!" Ying cried, "and keep your eyes on your work." But she wondered too how that dark tall priest could make Madame, her mistress, laugh so heartily. She did not hide from herself her own wonder.

For it was true that in spite of her troubles in the house

Madame Wu was coming to some sort of secret exquisite bloom. She met each day with relish and joy. Her only impatience was with the tasks of the house, and yet she controlled her own impatience and did each task with firm self-discipline. But Ying, who knew every breath of change in her mistress, knew, too, that she had no interest any more in the house.

She dared not think for one moment that this priest had an evil bond with Madame Wu. The lady was too rigorous for that. Besides, she was cooler than ever, more silvery, more clear in her look, more composed—and yet more gay. Ying watched her closely on one or two days when Brother André had been prevented from coming and had sent messages to tell her so, and Madame Wu was altogether indifferent. She sat as happily alone in her library as though her teacher were there. How could these things be explained?

The bondmaid snickered. "The Wu family also," she whispered. "Have you heard?"

"Heard what?" Ying asked indignantly. "I do not listen to cats yowling."

"I suppose you know that while our mistress sits learning of a priest, our master is going to flower houses?"

"He is not," Ying declared.

She sat on a low bamboo stool, and she leaned over and slapped the maid on the cheek and her hand left a red mark. The girl's eyes blazed. Then she turned her other cheek.

"Slap me again," she said, "for it is true he goes and with old Kang, the two of them. What can you expect?"

Now Ying pretended that she had heard nothing, but the truth was she had heard a whisper of this before, although so great was the fear that all other servants had of her that they hushed themselves when she came into a room. "That old Kang," she now thought to herself, "he is the mischief maker," and she thought gloomily on the nature of all men, and how she would not put anything beyond even her own cook.

In the long quiet room Madame Wu had forgotten her own house. She sat gazing at Brother André's brown, rugged face, and he, entranced by her gaze, taught this soul as he had never taught another. It was so pellucid a soul, so wise and yet so young. She had lived in this house and had learned so much through her own living that she was ripe with understanding. Her mind was a crystal cup, the workmanship complete, the cup only waiting to be filled.

How could he help telling her everything he knew? Into the beautiful crystal vessel he poured all the learning that he had until now kept for his own possession, because until now none had cared to share it with him. He told her the history of the world, the rise of peoples and their fall, the birth of new nations. He told her of the discovery of electricity and of radium; he explained to her the waves of the air which carry man's words and his music round the world.

"Have you the instrument for catching these words and this music?" she inquired to-day.

"I have," he said. "I made such an instrument myself."

"Will you bring it to me?" she asked eagerly.

He hesitated. "Alas, it is fixed with many wires into the walls. Can you—would you come to my poor house and see it?" he asked in return.

She pondered this. How could she go to a foreigner's house, even though accompanied? She felt suddenly shy. "Perhaps," she said, and turned her head away.

"Do not be disturbed," he said. "There is nothing in me to disturb you. The man in me is dead. God killed him."

With these strange words he went away, and she was comforted as she always was after he had gone. He put much into her mind. She sat thinking, half smiling, smoking her little pipe, her mind wandering over the world of which he told her.

"I wonder if I shall ever go beyond this city," she mused in her heart. "I wonder if I shall ever sail on those ships and fly on those wings."

For the first time she felt sorrowful at the shortness of life. Forty years only, at the most, could be left to her. What could she do in forty years? She had spent forty years already and had not stirred from her own doors.

"What do I know even about my own city?" she mused. "And here is our nation, set in the midst of these seas and mountains." Thus the enchantment of the world took hold of Madame Wu.

Day upon day she came and went among her family, smiling and unseeing. They gathered at meals, and she sat in her accustomed place among them and saw none of them while she looked at all.

Upon this Ying broke rudely one day when she was cleaning her mistress's jewels. The day was in midwinter, and Madame Wu had set some lilies into a dish of pebbles on the table, and the sunlight chanced at that moment to fall through the latticed windows upon lilies and jewels.

"See how alike they are, the jewels and the flowers, the pearls, the emeralds, the topaz, and the yellow and white and green of these flowers," Madame Wu exclaimed.

Ying looked up from a bracelet in her hands. "Lady, you are so quick to see such things, and it is strange you do not see what is happening in your house," she said.

"What do I not see?" Madame Wu asked half-guiltily. She thought of her two daughters-in-law.

"Our lord," Ying said.

"What of him?" Madame Wu asked quickly.

"Flower houses," Ying said shortly.

"He would not!" Madame Wu said.

"He does," Ying insisted. "Not that it is a great thing, since many men do it, but what if he brings something into the house which should not be here?"

Madame Wu thought deeply for a moment. "Ask our Second Lady to come here," she said.

Ying rose, looking the bearer of important messages, and went away, and Madame Wu took up her jewels and began to look at them. Every piece except the bracelets which her mother had given her at her wedding spoke of Mr. Wu. These jade ear-rings he had given her the morning after their wedding night to signify his pleasure in her. These emerald rings he had brought from a foreign shop in Shanghai, and she had never seen emeralds before. This diamond bird he had brought another time from Hong Kong, and she had not seen diamonds. The rubies he had brought from a distant province, and the jade hair ornaments from Yunnan. There were small bits which had caught her own fancy when jewellers came to the house at her command. She had never bought much for herself. Two moth hairpins made of silver filigree and pale jade made her remember the night when the women had caught moths and impaled them on the door. She sat turning a pin over and over in her hand. It was filigree from Canton, very fine and quivering with delicacy. The antennae were hair-fine silver wires tipped with pin points of jade, and they trembled as though the moth were alive.

At this moment Ch'iuming came in. She was heavy with child now, and her face had changed. Her eyes were larger and her mouth more red.

Madame Wu held out the moth pins. "I will give these to you," she said. "I use them no more."

Ch'iuming put out her hand and took the pins and examined them silently. "They are too fine for me," she said. "I would not know how to wear them."

"Nevertheless keep them," Madame Wu said. She turned over the jewels in the box with her forefinger. She had the wish to give Ch'iuming everything which Mr. Wu had given, but this she knew she must not. Then she saw two flowers made of rubies and pearls. The jewels were round and not polished too finely. "These too," she said. "Take them. They will look well in your ears. I suppose he gives you jewels."

"No," Ch'iuming said slowly. "But I do not want jewels."

Madame Wu took her little pipe and filled it and puffed it twice and laid it down again. A soft morsel of ash fell out on the table, and Ch'iuming leaned forward and brushed it into her hand.

"Now," Madame Wu said, "does he go to flower houses?"

Ch'iuming's face flushed red. "I hear he does," she said simply. "But he does not tell me."

"Can you not see for yourself?" Madame Wu inquired. "What is the measure of his feeling for you?"

Ch'iuming looked down. "It is too much for me, whatever it is," she said. "Because I cannot love him."

These words she said with sad firmness. Madame Wu heard them, and then to her amazement felt a great pity for Mr. Wu.

"Between you and me," she said, "we have dealt him evil, I with my age, you with your youth. Have you tried to love him?"

Ch'iuming lifted her dark, honest eyes. "Oh, yes, I have," she said simply. "Is it not my duty?"

"It is your duty, indeed," Madame Wu retorted.

"So I know it to be," Ch'iuming said. Then she added with the same humble sadness, "I obey him in everything. That at least I do."

"Does he know you do not love him?" Madame Wu asked next.

"Yes, for he asked me and I told him," Ch'iuming said.

"Ah, alas, that you should not!" Madame Wu exclaimed. "What would happen if all women spoke so truthfully to men?"

"I am stupid," Ch'iuming said.

"So he goes to flower houses," Madame Wu mused. Then she sighed heavily. "Well, there is no end to trouble between man and woman. When is the child to be born?"

"Next month," Ch'iuming said.

"Are you glad?" Madame Wu asked her abruptly.

Ch'iuming, whenever she did not speak, fell always into the same pose, her hands clasped loosely on her lap, her eyes downcast, her shoulders drooping. When she was spoken to her hands tightened and she lifted her eyelids.

"It will give me something of my own in this house," she said, and looked down again.

It seemed to Madame Wu that there was nothing more to be learned from her. "Go back," she said. "I will speak to him and see where his heart is."

Ch'iuming rose with her patient, simple air and bowed and went away. In a moment she came back again and held out her hand. The jewels shone on her brown palm. "I forgot to thank you for these," she said.

"Do not thank me," Madame Wu replied. "Wear them and that will be my thanks."

"I do thank you, Elder Sister," Ch'iuming said, and again she was gone.

That day Madame Wu sent her excuses to Brother André, and in the late evening before the night meal she sent Ying to Mr. Wu to announce her coming. He received this message and himself came to her immediately.

"Let me come to you, Mother of my sons," he said courteously.

She was surprised to see that he was thinner and less ruddy than he had been, and she blamed herself again. She rose and greeted him, and they sat down, and the more she looked at him the more her own anxiety grew. He did not look well. His eyes, always so bright and roving, were now dull, and his full lips were pale.

"You look ill," she said. "Are you ill?"

"Not at all," he replied.

"But you are not well," she insisted.

"Well enough," he replied.

"The Second Lady?" she inquired.

He put up his hand. "She does her best for me."

"But she is not good enough for you."

Mr. Wu looked embarrassed. "I tell you, Mother of my sons, it is difficult for a young woman. You see, I am not so young."

She decided to seize the truth by the neck. "But I hear you visit flower houses," she said.

He shrugged and did not look a whit ashamed. "I go with old Kang sometimes, yes," he admitted. "You see, it is easier simply to buy women without expecting them to love. Well, there is no pretence. The difficult thing is this pretence. I never pretended with you, Ailien, I did so love you. Now with this second one—I cannot either love or not love——" He continued to rub his head and looked dazed. "It is better simply to go to a flower house."

"But next month your child is to be born," she reminded him.

"Yes, well," he rubbed his head again in the puzzled fashion. "The strange thing is, I do not feel it is mine. After all, you and I, we have the four boys."

"It seems to me then that this Ch'iuming is no use in the house," she said after a little time.

He rubbed his head again. "Well, no, perhaps she is not," he agreed.

"I think you have not treated her well," she said severely.

He looked apologetic. "I am very kind to her."

"You have given her no gifts," she declared.

He looked surprised. "That is true, I have forgotten. I forget her continually."

Madame Wu was impatient. "Tell me, what is it you want of a woman?"

He looked somewhat embarrassed. "What woman?" he asked.

"Any woman," she said.

Mr. Wu felt her impatience and, being anxious always to please her, he put his mind on the matter.

"Well," he said, "I——" He felt he had begun badly and so he began again. "It is not so much what I want of a woman. It is what I—want. That is to say, I like to laugh—you know that. I like to hear something interesting—you used to tell me many interesting things. And you know I used to laugh at many things you told me. Well, all that——" He tailed off with this vagueness.

"I cannot go on amusing you for ever," she said sharply.

"No, of course not," he agreed readily. "So, you see, I go to the flower houses."

"What happens there?" Madame Wu asked. She was surprised to feel curiosity in herself.

"Nothing much," he said. "We usually have something to eat and drink. We gamble while the girls play lutes or something."

"Girls?" she repeated. "How many are there?"

"Five—six—whoever is free," he said. "Kang and I—— Well, we are kind-hearted and they usually——" His voice tailed off once more.

"And then?" she inquired.

He began again with some effort. "Well, then, you see, the evening goes very quickly. The girls are full of stories and tricks." He was unconsciously smiling.

"And do you stay all night?" she inquired.

"Not usually," he said evasively.

She studied his bland face. There were lines in it, and she did not like them. The youthfulness which she had thought so permanent was fading. She sighed and felt her impatience increase.

"Would you like to bring one of these flower girls into the house?" she asked abruptly. "I would not approve it, but I ask your will."

He looked surprised. "Why should I?" he asked.

"You really go there just to play," she declared.

"Perhaps," he agreed.

"How childish you are!"

"I am not as clever as you, Ailien," he said with humility. "I could never read books. And now there is not much I need to do. Liangmo manages everything. Even with Tsemo and Fengmo gone, he can manage. I am not much needed." He paused, and then he said with the humility which somehow she could not endure, "If there is anything you think I should do, I will do it. I want to do anything I should do."

She had nothing to say. It was true that there was nothing for which he was needed. He sat there, handsome and kind and willing and childlike, and she had no heart to reproach him.

When they parted she saw with sadness that he was cheerful again because they had talked together. She knew that as long as she lived she could not be free from him. Through her body he had entered into her soul, too. It was not enough that she had never loved him. Love had nothing to do with responsibility.

"Oh, Heaven," Madame Wu cried in a sort of strange agony, "am I to be responsible for ever for him?"

She felt the wings of her soul, poised and widespread, now droop and falter earthward again.

10

But Mr. Wu went direct from Madame Wu to the flower house to which she had objected. He had first followed Mr. Kang there somewhat against his will and certainly against his conscience. Then he had dealt with both and had come off the victor. His will had yielded entirely so that now he looked forward to his innocent visits there, and his conscience was reduced to confusion and temporary silence.

Ch'iuming he did not understand. She was not as wise as Madame Wu, whom he steadfastly adored as a priest might adore the Kwanyin whom he daily served. Ch'iuming was neither goddess nor woman. When he treated her as a goddess she was bewildered. Besides, she was not quite a goddess. When he treated her as a woman, he felt he shocked her, and then he was confused and could proceed no further. Matters had come to such a pass between them that he did not know how to treat her, and so he left her alone.

The experience had made him more than ever adore Madame Wu, who had been able, as he now perceived, to be alternately goddess and woman, but never the two at the same time. But, since she resolutely refused to return to being a woman, and was apparently to be continually a goddess, he had been reduced to finding a woman elsewhere.

This he had found in the person of a small round rollicking girl in the House of Peony Flowers on the Street of the Blind Lute Player. The house was an old one, outwardly a tea-house, but also a gambling place and a brothel. The girls were always clean and young and cheerful. Mr. Kang assured him that he had for years been a client there and had never found any other sort of girl in it. Moreover, the place made a policy of not being grasping. If a man wished only to look at a girl while he ate and drank, it was possible not to be committed further. If he wished her only as a companion for a guest, that too could be. Indeed, to purchase more took some arrangement, for there was always a waiting list of clients. But it had not been hard for Mr. Wu to ascend this list at once, thanks to his position as the head of a great family.

Now he entered the gaily decorated hall with an air of a familiar and was greeted on all sides. The proprietor called to his assistant in a loud voice.

"Tell Jasmine that Mr. Wu is here."

Mr. Wu proceeded amiably to an inner room and was at once served with tea and then in a few minutes with wine and a bowl of small dumplings by way of light refreshments. He ate these, and before he was half through, Jasmine came into the room.

She had been perfuming her long black hair when she was called, and now she came in with it in two coils over her ears. Since she was named Jasmine, she used the same flower scent and made the most of it, so that the scent became her own, and she had usually one or two of those flowers tucked into the coils of her hair. Her face was powdered almost a pure white, and her lips were red and her eyes round and very dark. She was plump and her lips were always smiling. She came running in on her little feet and perched on the arm of Mr. Wu's chair and rubbed her scented cheek against his.

He pretended not to notice her, and she pouted. "I am hungry," she whimpered. He dipped his porcelain spoon into the dumpling soup and fed it to her gravely, and she leaned forward like a child to receive it. Between them in silence they finished the food, and he pushed his chair from the table and she slipped to his knee.

"What have you been doing to-day?" Mr. Wu inquired.

She examined her scarlet finger nails. "Oh—waiting for you—that is all I do."

"I cannot be here all the time," Mr. Wu said. "I have business. I am a man of affairs. I have the shops and the markets and the lands all to superintend. They can do nothing without me."

"You work too hard," she complained. "It seems to me your sons ought to help you."

"Oh, my sons," he grumbled, "they think only of themselves and their own families. Two of them have actually gone away, and the eldest one—— Well, he tries, but I cannot trust everything to him."

He enjoyed the pressure of her round little body against his shoulder. He liked the jasmine scent of her hair. Even her breath was scented. He remembered Madame Wu's question. Did he want to bring her into the house? Left to himself, certainly it would be a pleasure, but he could not persuade himself to add to the house of his ancestors a flower girl. The shade of his father forbade it.

As though she knew his thoughts, Jasmine nestled closer and slipped her arm about his neck. "I wish I could come and live with you," she said. "I would be very good. I would not trouble any of the great ladies. I would stay by myself all the time until you came."

"No, no," he said hastily. "I don't want you there. I like to come out of the house and visit you here. If you were to come to the house, you would become a part of it, and I would have nowhere to go for my own pleasure. A man must be himself somewhere."

She was quite ready for this. She had an old mother who had been a flower girl in her youth, and had taught her to take care of herself. "A concubine, if possible," old Lotus had said, "but if not that, then a house of your own."

"Couldn't you buy a little house for me, Mr. Wu?" she asked. "I would never let any man come in but you, and I would wait for you all day and all night. Then you could be yourself whenever you liked."

Mr. Wu had already considered this possibility. He did not like the assurance with which his name was now called out when he came to this house of flowers. He was, after all, the head of the house of Wu and a man higher than any among the gentry of the city.

But Madame Wu kept the family accounts, and how was he to ask her for so large a sum as it would require to take a house for Jasmine? "You see, my small flower," he said tenderly, "my sons' mother is a wonderful woman. She keeps the accounts. What would I tell her if I wanted to take a house for you?"

"Couldn't you sell a piece of your land and not tell her?" Jasmine asked. She sat up and looked at him pleadingly. She had a childish little voice that went straight into his heart.

"I have never deceived her," Mr. Wu said, troubled.

"Does she know about me?" Jasmine asked in astonishment.

"Approximately," Mr. Wu replied.

"What is approximately?" Jasmine asked.

"It means somewhat."

220

"How can she know somewhat?" Jasmine asked again. "Either she knows or she doesn't know."

"Let us then say she knows," Mr. Wu replied. "It is always safer to say that she knows than that she doesn't."

Jasmine tried again. She hid her face on his shoulder. "I am afraid I have happiness in me," she whispered. "That is why I want the house. I can't have a child here."

Mr. Wu was alarmed. He took her from his knee and set her on her feet, and she stood there before him, her hands over her face. "Now," he said sternly, "there were others before me. You were no virgin, young as you are."

She took her hands from her face. The powder was undisturbed. "But my amah can prove to you that there have been none since you came, and this is within the last three months. You came before that."

She turned away and wiped her eyes with the edges of her sleeves. "Never mind." Her childish voice was sad. "It is my fate. Girls like me—sometimes it happens in spite of ourselves. Especially when we really love a man. That is my mistake."

Had she insisted, had she demanded, he would have risen and gone away perhaps never to return. But his heart was soft.

"Now," he said, "whether it is my fault or not, you know there are ways of purging yourself. Here is something to help you."

He put his hand in his purse, but she would not take the money he held out to her. She pushed his hand away with her two little ones. "No, please," she said. "I will bear the child, I want to bear him."

"You must not," Mr. Wu insisted.

They were interrupted at this moment by loud cries from the outer room. "Mr. Wu, Mr. Wu!" the proprietor was shouting. The door burst open. Mr. Wu saw his own servant, Peng Er.

"Master, Master!" Peng Er cried. "You are wanted at home. The Second Lady has hanged herself from the old pomegranate tree!"

"My mother!" Mr. Wu muttered. He leaped to his feet and strode away, leaving Jasmine in the middle of the floor looking after him and frowning with anger.

The commotion of his own home rose over the walls of the

compound and met him on the street. Priests had been called, and they were beating their gongs and crying for the lost soul of Ch'iuming. He ran through the open gate where no one stood to watch and hastened into the Peony Court. There the priests were, and there the whole household had gathered to wail and to weep and to call Ch'iuming's name. He pushed through them, and in the midst of them upon the flags of the court she lay. Madame Wu knelt beside her and held her head on her arm. But Ch'iuming's pale face hung over Madame Wu's arm as though she was wholly lifeless.

"Is she dead?" Mr. Wu shouted.

"We can find no life in her," Madame Wu replied. "I have sent for the foreign priest. If we have all these priests, why not him?"

At this very moment Brother André appeared, and the crowd divided before him like a sea before a wind. The other priests were silent in jealousy. In the centre of this silence Brother André fell to his knees and thrust a needle into Ch'iuming's arm and held it there.

"I do not ask what you do," Madame Wu said to him. "I know whatever it is, it is wise."

"A stimulant," Brother André said. "But it may be too late." He put the needle away so quickly that no one saw it except Mr. and Mrs. Wu.

But it was not too late. Ch'iuming's lips quivered. While they watched, her eyelids fluttered. Madame Wu sighed. "Ah, she is alive. Then the child is alive."

"But why did she hang herself?" Mr. Wu exclaimed.

"Let us not ask until she can tell us," Madame Wu replied. "But announce to the priests her soul has returned. Pay them well, Father of my sons. Let them think they were successful so that they will go away and we can have peace."

Mr. Wu obeyed her and called out to the priests and led them away to the outer court. The women of the family remained, the elder cousins to commend the priests, and Meng and Rulan and Linyi to gaze quietly down into the face of Ch'iuming, whom they scarcely knew even while she was here in their own house. She was of their generation and yet linked to the older ones, and they could not be free with her, and so they had forgotten her.

But by this act she had brought herself nearer to them. She was unhappy, she did not want to belong to the elders. In each young woman's heart an interest arose in Ch'iuming, and this interest was mingled with pity in Meng's heart, with curiosity in Linyi's, and with revolt in Rulan's. Each determined in her own way to know Ch'iuming and why she had done this thing.

Yet there was no time for any of these feelings, for as Ch'iuming came to herself it became clear that her child was to be born too early. She must be carried in to her bed and the midwife sent for. These things were done, and Brother André was about to go away when Ch'iuming spoke.

"Did I see the foreign priest?" she whispered.

"He is about to go away," Madame Wu said. She stood by the bed of fecundity while the women servants made Ch'iuming ready for the birth.

"Tell him to come here—only for a moment," Ch'iuming begged.

Madame Wu was surprised. She did not know that Ch'iuming knew the tall foreigner. But since the girl was still so near death she did not dare deny her. She went herself and stayed Brother André as he was about to leave. "She asks for you," she said. "For a moment come in."

So Brother André turned, and he stooped his head and went in through the low doorway into the room where Ch'iuming lay in the huge bed. Mr. Wu stayed behind. He was suddenly stiff with embarrassment. To what a pass had he brought the household! He did not doubt that Ch'iuming had hung herself because of Jasmine. In her silent way she had protested with her life.

When Brother André leaned over the bedside Ch'iuming spoke, but in so faint a voice he could not hear her. He leaned closer over her, and these were the words he then heard:

"If a girl is born I give it to you when I die—— It is only a foundling."

"How can a foundling be born in this house?" he inquired gently.

"But I am only a foundling," she said, "and this is the child of a foundling."

With that she closed her eyes and gave herself up to pain. He went away with a grave face and told no one what she had said, and so low was her voice that no one else had heard her words.

Late that night a girl was born to Ch'iuming, a creature so small that Madame Wu took her and wrapped her in cotton fleece and put her into her bosom to keep her alive. Then she went quickly into her own courts, leaving Ch'iuming to the midwife and to Ying, and in her own room she put the child into her bed and lay down beside her to keep her warmed. A woman servant came in to see what was needed.

"Heat bricks and bring them here," Madame Wu said. "This child is a bud that must be carefully opened."

"Oh, Mistress," the woman said, "why not let her die? A girl—and what can she grow into but a sickly thing to make trouble in the house?"

"Obey me," Madame Wu said.

The woman went muttering away, and Madame Wu looked at the little creature. She was still breathing.

.   .   .

Two days later Brother André told Madame Wu of Ch'iuming's strange request. The child had not died. She could not suckle, being too young, but she had swallowed a few drops of mother's milk put into her mouth with a spoon. Ch'iuming's milk had come, although she was too weak to speak. Even when Madame Wu told her that the child was alive she had not answered.

"Certainly the child is not a foundling," Madame Wu said to Brother André, with dignity. "She has been born into our house."

"I knew you would say that," he replied, "and you are right. But why does this young mother say she is a foundling?"

"She was, until she came here," Madame Wu replied. She hesitated, and then to her own wonder she found herself telling Brother André what she had never told him, how it was she who had brought Ch'iuming into this house.

Brother André listened, his eyes downcast, his great hands clasped on his knees. She never saw those hands without wondering why they were so calloused. Now she asked suddenly, "Why are your hands so calloused?"

He was accustomed to her changes. "Because I till the land for the children's food," he said. He did not move his hands from under her gaze.

She went on with her story, her eyes on his hands.

"I suppose since you are a priest you cannot understand

either man or woman," she said when her whole story was told.

"Being priest, I can understand both man and woman," he said.

"Then tell me what I have done that is wrong." She lifted her eyes from his hands to his face and wondered that out of all the world she had chosen to open her entire heart to a foreigner who had been born in some country across the sea whose waters and winds she would never know.

He answered her: "You have not considered that man is not entirely flesh, and that even such a man as your husband must be in communion with God. You have treated him with contempt."

"I?" she exclaimed. "But I have thought of nothing but his welfare."

"You have considered only the filling of his stomach and the softness of his bed," Brother André said plainly. "And even worse than this, you have bought a young woman as you would buy a pound of pork. But a woman, any woman, is more than that, and of all women you should know it. You have been guilty of three sins."

"Guilty?" she repeated.

"You have despised your husband, you have held in contempt a sister woman, and you have considered yourself unique and above all women. These sins have disturbed your house. Without knowing why, your sons have been restless and their wives unhappy, and in spite of your plans no one is happy. What has been your purpose, Madame?"

Confronted by his clear, calm eyes, she trembled. "Only to be free," she faltered. "I thought, if I did my duty to everyone I could be free."

"What do you mean by freedom?" he inquired.

"Very little," she said humbly. "Simply to be mistress of my own person and my own time."

"You ask a great deal for yourself," he replied. "You ask everything."

She felt nearer to tears than she had felt in many years. He had shattered the calm core of her being, her sense of rightness in herself, and she was frightened. If in this house she, upon whom all had so long depended, had been wrong and was wrong, then what would happen to them all?

"What shall I do?" she asked in a small voice.

"Forget your own self," he said.

"But all these years," she urged, "I have so carefully fulfilled my duty."

"Always with the thought of your own freedom in your mind," he said.

She could not deny it. She sat motionless, her hands folded on the pearl-grey satin of her robe. "Direct me," she said at last.

"Instead of your own freedom, think how you can free others," he said gently.

She lifted her head.

"From yourself," he said still gently.

She had never been a religious woman, and now she looked at him in some doubt. "Are you speaking out of your foreign religion? If so, I cannot understand it."

"I am not speaking out of a foreign religion," he said.

"Do you want me to be a nun?" she exclaimed.

"I do not want you to be anything," he replied tranquilly.

He rose to his great height, smiled down at her according to his habit, and went away without farewell. This, which in another would have seemed rudeness, simply gave to Madame Wu the feeling that there was no break between this time they had spent together and the next time, whenever that would be.

She did not move for a long moment. Upon the grey tiled floor the pattern of the latticed windows was fixed in a lacework of shadows and sunshine. The air was still and cool, but the room was not cold. A great brazier of coals stood in front of the table set against the centre of the inner wall, and out of the coals, smothered with ashes, colourless quivering rays of heat shone in the air. Nothing, she reflected, was as easy as she had thought. Freedom was not a matter of arrangement. She had seen freedom hanging like a peach upon a tree. She had nurtured the tree, and when it bore she had seized upon the fruit and found it green.

She sighed, and then she heard Ch'iuming's little child cry in the next room, and she went to it and took it into her arms and carried it into the room and sat down by the brazier. Whether it was the warmth or whether it was the feeling of support of her arms, some comfort came into the child, and she ceased crying and lay looking up into Madame Wu's face.

"I do not love this child," Madame Wu thought. "Perhaps I have never loved any child. Perhaps that is my trouble, that I have never been able to love anyone."

But it was like her that without love she held the child carefully, and when Ying came in and took her she superintended her feeding again and was even pleased that the child ate her food heartily.

Watching this, she said to Ying, "Give me back the child and I will take her to her mother. She will live, this small woman, and she will hold her mother to life."

So a little later she carried the child in her own arms through the sunshine and into her old courts and into the room where Ch'iuming lay on the big bed whose curtains were still hung with the symbols of fecundity. Ch'iuming lay with her eyes closed and her lips pressed together. She was intensely pale. Upon the silk coverlid, her hands lay open and relaxed. These hands had changed in the past months. When she came they had been rough and strong with work, but now they were thin and white.

"Here is your child," Madame Wu said gently. "She has eaten so well that she is strong enough to come and lie on your arm."

When Ch'iuming did not move, Madame Wu lifted her arm and put the child into its circle and covered it with the quilt. Ch'iuming's arms tightened. She opened her eyes. "You must forgive me that I did not repay you with a son," she said humbly.

"Do I not know that sons and daughters alike come from Heaven?" Madame Wu replied. "Besides, in these days, daughters, too, are good."

Then she remembered what Brother André said, and she went on quickly, "You must not feel that you have a duty to me. You have none."

Ch'iuming looked surprised at this. "But why else am I here?" she asked.

Madame Wu sat down on the edge of the bed. "It has been shown me that I did you a great wrong, my sister. It is true that you were brought here as I might have bought a pound of pork. How could I dare so to behave toward a human being? I see now that I had no thought for your soul. What can I do to make amends?"

She said this in her pretty voice, neither lifting nor deepening it, and Ch'iuming's face grew frightened. "But where shall I go?" she stammered.

Madame Wu saw that Ch'iuming had altogether failed to understand her, and that she thought that she was being told courteously, in the way of the rich and the great, that she was useless and not wanted.

"I do not want you to go anywhere," Madame Wu said. "I am only saying that I have done wrong to you. Let me put it thus: If you had your own way, if there were no one to consider, what would you do with yourself?"

"How can there be no one to consider?" Ch'iuming asked, perplexed. "There is our lord and there is you. And beyond you two honourable ones, there is the whole family."

"Why did you ask the foreign priest to take your child if you died?" Madame Wu asked.

"I did not want to trouble you with a girl," Ch'iuming said.

"Why did you try to die before your destiny day?" Madame Wu asked again.

"Because Ying told me she saw from my shape that I would give birth to a girl, and so I said, in my heart, we will both go together and be no trouble to anybody."

"Death can be a trouble as well as life," Madame Wu said.

"Not mine," Ch'iuming replied innocently, "for I am of no worth to anyone."

To this Madame Wu had no answer. She rose, feeling for the moment entirely helpless. "Give up these thoughts," she exclaimed. "Should you die it would be a great trouble to bring up this child, and you know that I have never been one of those who think a female child can be allowed to die."

"You are good," Ch'iuming said, and she closed her eyes again. The tears crept out from under her eyelids. This Madame Wu saw, but she saw also that Ch'iuming's arm now held the child very tightly, and so she took it for a good sign and went away.

When she was crossing the courtyard she met Mr. Wu coming in from the street. They came face to face without expecting it, and she perceived instantly that he had been doing something which she would not approve, for his face flushed and a light sweat broke out on his forehead.

"Mother of my sons!" he exclaimed.

"I have just been in to see our Second Lady," she said amiably. "We must think about her case. She tried to die because she feared the child would be a girl, and that the two of them would be a burden in the house."

"How foolish!" he exclaimed. "As if we were common people, who consider one mouth more or less!"

"I will turn back with you," Madame Wu said. "I have need of your wisdom." They went back together and came into the large square room where they had spent so many hours in their common life. Beyond them was the bedroom where Ch'iuming lay with her child on her arm, but there was no danger of their being overhead. Above them the roof rose into high beamed spaces and swallowed any human voice.

"Now we have this life in our house," Madame Wu said, "what shall we do with her, and the one she has brought? For I see that she is not to your heart. Yet here she is. I must apologize to you."

Mr. Wu looked uncomfortable. He had put on one fur robe too many this morning, and the day had turned milder than the morning, and he went easily hot in any discomfort, even in winter.

"I feel ashamed that I—after your thoughtfulness——" he stammered. "Well, she is good enough. But you know how it is. Goodness is excellent in a woman. But——"

"I was very selfish," she said simply. She sat in her usual pose with her hands folded on her lap. She did not look at him. Instead she gazed thoughtfully at the shadows on the floor. They were now of the winter bamboo which stood about the sunlit open door, and the arrowy leaves danced in the wind. She thought of Brother André, and suddenly she understood what he had meant. She could never be free until she had offered herself up utterly, and this she could only do by taking upon herself the thing which she most hated.

"I see my wrong," she said, without lifting her eyes. "Let it all be as you wish. We will send Ch'iuming away if you like. And I will return. We will forget, you and I, these last months."

She waited for his welcoming cry, but it did not come. When the silence grew sharp she looked up and saw his ruddy face now streaming with sweat. He laughed with misery when he saw her looking at him and snatched open his collar, and pulled out his silk handkerchief and wiped his face.

"Had I known," he gasped, "had I dreamed——"

An ice-cold pressure crept into her heart. He did not want her. What she had heard was true. He had found someone else for himself.

"Tell me about her," she said gently.

Halting and stammering, with grunts of embarrassed laughter, he told her that he wondered if he should not now put Jasmine into a separate house. She was young, she was childish.

"I do not want to add to your cares under this roof," he said.

She opened her long and lovely eyes. "Can it add to my cares if you are happy?" she asked in her most silvery voice. "Let her come and live under your own roof. Why should your house be divided?"

He rose and went over to her and took her hand. It lay in his plump palm, cool and limp. "You are a good woman," he said solemnly. "It is not given to every man to have what he wants and at the same time to live in peace under his own roof."

She smiled and took her hand away.

But long after they had parted she was amazed at the coldness in the pleasure she had felt. For her to choose a woman to take her place was one thing. To have him choose a woman was quite another. She marvelled at the tangle that life could make between a man and a woman. She had thought herself free of him because she did not love him. But she was not free of him if when she knew his love had ceased she could feel this wounded pride. Brother André had been right. She thought always and only of herself.

· · · ·

"How shall I be rid of myself?" she asked Brother André.

"Think only of others," he replied.

"Does that mean I am always to yield to others?" she asked.

"If not to yield means that you are thinking of yourself, you must yield," he said.

"My sons' father wants to bring another woman into the house," she said. "Am I to yield to that?"

"It was your sin that brought the first woman here," he said.

She was angry at this in her fashion. A gust of sharp temper flew like a sudden small whirlwind out of her heart.

"Now you speak like a priest," she said maliciously. "You

230

can have no understanding of what it is to be compelled to yield your body to a man year after year, without your will." She felt in herself a strange desire to make him share her unhappiness, and she went on, sparing him nothing. "To give one's delicate body to indelicate hands, to see lust grow hot and feel one's own flesh grow cold—to feel the heart grow faint and the mind sick, and yet to be compelled, for the sake of peace in the house."

His face was pure and unchanged. "There are many ways in which the body may be offered up a sacrifice for the soul," he said.

She sighed. "Shall I allow this second woman to come in?"

"Is it not better to have her under this roof with your consent than under another without?" he replied.

"I never thought a foreign priest would give me such advice," she said with new malice.

She opened her book without further talk, and under his direction she studied the poetry of the Hebrew Psalms. She was deeply moved as the hour went on by what she discerned they were. Here the human heart cried out after that which it could worship. And what was worship except trust and hope that life and death had meaning because they were created and planned by heaven?

"Is our Heaven your God, and is your God our Heaven?" she inquired.

"They are one and the same," he replied.

"But Little Sister Hsia told me they are not," she retorted. "She always told us to believe on the one true God, and not in our Heaven. She declared them not the same."

"In a temple there are always a few foolish ones," he said gently. "There is only one true God. He has many names."

"Then anywhere upon the round earth, by whatever seas, those who believe in any God believe in the One?" she asked.

"And so are brothers," he said, agreeing.

"And if I do not believe in any?" she inquired wilfully.

"God is patient," he said. "God waits. Is there not eternity?"

She felt a strange warm current pass through him and through her. But it did not begin in him, and it did not end in her. They seemed only to transmit it, from the ends of the earth to the ends of the earth.

"Heaven is patient," she repeated. "Heaven waits."

Upon these words they parted. Brother André tied his books into a worn black handkerchief and put them under his arm. She stood at the door of the library watching him as he walked across the court. His great form was beginning to stoop, as though his grizzled head were a burden upon the vast shoulders. Or, she told herself, perhaps it was because more and more he walked with his eyes fixed upon the path just ahead of him. Seldom did he lift his head to see what lay at the end of the road.

She turned and went back into the library as her habit was when the lessons were over. She sat sometimes for as much as an hour to fix in her mind the things which Brother André had taught her, to read again what they had read together, to look at the pictures he had left, to consider the words he had spoken.

But this day she had scarcely sat an hour when she heard loud voices shouting in the outer courtyards, and she lifted her head to listen. Whatever it was, Ying would bring her the message of it. In less than the framing of her thought she saw Ying come running into her court. She was wailing and crying and she threw her apron over her face and wept.

Madame Wu rose at once, and the book she had been holding dropped to the floor. Something very evil had come about. She thought of Liangmo, her eldest son. But this morning he had left the house as usual. She thought of Mr. Wu. Then Ying was on the threshold. She pulled the apron from her face and cried out, "Alas—the foreign priest!"

"What of him?" Madame Wu asked sharply. "He left here but a few moments ago."

"He has been struck down in the street," Ying cried. "His skull is cracked open!"

"Struck down?" Madame Wu's voice was an echo.

"It is those young men." Ying sobbed. "The Green Band— the evil ones! They were robbing the moneylender's shop, and the priest saw the moneylender crying and cursing Heaven, and he stopped to save him and the young men came out and beat him over the head too."

Madame Wu had scarcely heard the name of the Green Band. But she knew that those were young ruffians who roamed the country roads and the city streets. The land steward had always on the bills an item, "For fee to the Green Band."

"Where is Brother André?" she exclaimed.

"They have carried him into his own house and he lies on his bed, but the gatekeeper is here and says he asks for you," Ying said.

"I must go," Madame Wu said. "Help me with my robe."

"I will order the bearers," Ying cried.

"No, there is no time," Madame Wu said. "I will take a rickshaw at the gate."

All the house knew a few minutes later that Madame Wu had for the first time in her life gone to a place which was strange to her, the house of the foreign priest. She sat erect in the rickshaw, and behind the runner's back she said, "I will pay you double if you double your usual speed."

"Triple me and I will triple my speed," he cried over his shoulder.

Far behind her Ying came in a second rickshaw, but for once Madame Wu did not think of what people might say. She had the one thing in her mind, that she must somehow reach his side in time to hear his voice speak once more and give her direction for the rest of her life.

So she stepped out at the plain unpainted wooden gate set in the midst of a brick wall and without looking at anything she went within. An old woman waited, weeping.

"Where is our elder brother?" she asked.

The old woman turned and led her into a low brick house, through an open door, across a court filled with crowding, sobbing children, into a room.

There upon a narrow bamboo bed Brother André lay. Ragged men and women from the streets were standing about him. They parted to let Madame Wu come to his bedside and, as though he felt her presence, he opened his eyes. His head was rudely bandaged in a coarse white towel, and the blood was running from under it down his cheek and soaking the pillow under his head.

"I am here," she said. "Tell me what I must do."

For a long moment he could not speak. He was dying. She could see the emptiness at the bottom of his dark eyes, and then she saw his will gather there in light. His lips parted, his breast rose in a great breath as he gazed at her.

"Feed my lambs," he said distinctly.

Then she saw death come. The breath ceased, the eyelids flickered, the will withdrew. His great body shuddered, and he flung out his hands so that they hung over the sides of the bed and struck upon the cold brick floor. She stooped and picked up his right hand, and a ragged man stepped forward and took up his left, and they stood holding these two hands. She stared across the body into the man's eyes. He was nothing, nobody, a servant, a beggar. He looked at her timidly and put down Brother André's hand gently on the stilled breast, and she laid the right one over it. The children came running into the room and swarmed about the bed that was now a bier, all crying and calling, "Father—father!" She saw that they were all girls, the eldest not more than fifteen, and the older ones were carrying little ones who could not walk. They leaned on Brother André and felt him with their little hands, and stroked his beard, and they took the edges of their coats and wiped the blood from his face, and they kept on crying.

"Who are you?" she asked in a strange quiet voice.

"We are his lambs," they cried in a disorderly chorus.

"Strays," the ragged man said. "He picked the little ones up from outside the city wall where they are thrown. The big ones are runaway slaves. He took in anybody."

She wanted to weep alone and for herself because he was dead. But the children were flinging themselves upon him, their arms wrapping him.

"Oh, he's cold," a little girl sobbed. The tears were shining on her cheeks. She held his hand to her wet cheek. "His hand is so cold."

Madame Wu stood immobile in the midst of this strange family. Then it occurred to her that she did not yet know all that had happened.

"Who brought him to his bed?" she asked in a low voice.

The ragged man beat his breast. "It was I. I saw him fall. Everyone on the street was frightened. The Green Robbers ran when they saw him dying. The moneylender put up his shutters and went into his house. But I am only a beggar, and what have I to fear? This foreign priest often gave me a little money, especially in winter. And sometimes he brought me home into this house at night and I slept here until morning, and he gave me food."

"You carried him here!" she said.

"These brother beggars and I," he said. She saw half a dozen ragged fellows. "He is too big for one or two to carry."

She looked down on Brother André's peaceful face. She had come, hoping for a few words for herself. Instead he had said, "Feed my lambs." Here were all these children. She looked at them, and they looked back at her. With the quick instinct of children they watched her, transferring their hopefulness from Brother André's silent figure to her motionless but living frame.

"What shall I do with you?" she said uncertainly.

"Lady, what did our father tell you to do?" a thin little girl asked anxiously. She held a fat cheerful baby in her arms.

Madame Wu could only answer the truth. "He said I was to feed you," she said.

The children looked at one another. The thin little girl shifted the baby to the other arm. "Have you enough food for us all?" she asked gravely.

"Yes," Madame Wu said.

Still she continued to stand, looking at the little girls.

"There are twenty of us," the little thin girl said. "I am fifteen years old—at sixteen he provides for us."

"Provides for you?" Madame Wu repeated.

The old woman had come in now. "At sixteen he finds them homes and good husbands," she said.

They were speaking as if the big quiet figure on the bed was still alive.

Madame Wu looked at Brother André. His eyes were closed, and his hands were folded on his breast.

"Come away from this room," she said abruptly. "All of you! Leave him in peace."

They went out obediently, beggars and children and the old woman, and only she was left. At the door Ying stood stiffly. "Go away, Ying," Madame Wu said.

"I will stand outside the door," Ying replied.

Madame Wu closed the door. What she was doing would cause gossip. Why should a lady wish to be alone with a foreign priest even when he was dead? She did not care. He was neither foreign nor a priest to her now. He was the only being she had ever met whom she worshipped. Old Gentleman had taught her much. But Old Gentleman had feared many things. Brother André feared no one. He feared neither life nor death. She had never thought of him as a man when he was alive, but now that he was dead she saw him as a man lying dead. In his youth he must have been extremely beautiful. His great body lying outstretched before her had the proportions of majesty. His skin was pale and in death was growing translucently clear.

Suddenly she recognized him. "You whom I love!" she murmured in profound astonishment.

This recognition she made, and in the instant she accepted it she felt her whole being change. Although she did not move, her body tingled, her blood stung her heart, and her brain was clear. Her whole frame grew light and strong. She lifted her head and looked about the room. The four walls stood, but she felt free and whole. Upon his bier the body lay as it had since he died, but now looking down upon it she knew that he had escaped it. She was sceptic to the soul. Not in years had she entered a temple or burned incense before a god. Her father had cleansed her of the superstition common to women, and Old Gentleman had finished the work. She did not now believe in an unseen God, but she knew certainly that this man continued.

"André." She said his name to him in a low clear voice, and never again would she call him brother. "You live in me. I will do my utmost to preserve your life."

The moment she had said these words peace welled up in her being. It was so profound, so quieting, so contenting, that for the first time in her life she knew that never before had she known what peace was. Standing motionless in the bare room before his shell, she felt happy.

Nor was this happiness a trance. It was an energy which began to work in her mind and in her body. There were certain things which she must do that now became perfectly plain to her. His dead body must be buried, not with priests and prayers. His few possessions must be disposed of, and this she herself would do. Then simply she would continue to do whatever he had been doing.

She went tranquilly from the room and into the other room where Ying and the old woman, the beggars and the children were waiting. She sat down on one of the wooden chairs.

"Now as to his funeral," she said. "Did he leave any directions?"

They looked at one another. The children were awed and said nothing. The old woman sobbed and wiped her eyes with her apron. "Certainly he never thought of dying!" she exclaimed. "Nor did we think of such a thing as his death."

"Does he have relatives anywhere?" Madame Wu asked. "If so, I suppose we should send his body to them."

No one knew of relatives. He had simply come here an unknown number of years ago and had never gone away again.

"Did he get letters?" Madame Wu asked.

"When he did, he never read them," the old woman said. "He let them lie about unopened, and I took them after a while and sewed them into the children's shoe soles."

"And did he never write letters?" Madame Wu went on.

"Never," the old woman said.

"And you," she said to the beggar, "did he never speak to you?"

"Never of any who belonged to him," the leader replied. "We spoke only of people in the city and the country round about who needed help in some fashion."

Madame Wu considered this. André belonged wholly to her. There was no other. She would buy a plain black coffin. As for the land, she would bury him in her own land. She thought of a favourite spot upon a certain hill-side that circled some of the rice fields. There a gingko-tree grew, very old, and she always rested in its shade when she went out to watch the spring planting.

She rose. "I will go this afternoon and see that the grave is dug."

The children and the old woman looked at her anxiously as she rose, and she understood their anxiety. What, they were all thinking, was to become of them?"

"This house," she said, looking about the bare rooms, "does it belong to him?"

The old woman shook her head. "It is a rented house," she said, "and we got it very cheap because it is haunted. Nobody else wants to live in it because it is inhabited by weasels, who carry the spirits of evil ones. But evil spirits feared him, and here we have lived safely for very little cost."

"He owns nothing?" she asked.

"Nothing except two changes of garments. One he wore and one I washed. He has a few books and his cross. Once he had a very pretty image nailed to a wooden cross, and he hung it on the wall of his room above his bed. But it fell down one night and broke, and he never got another. He had a rosary, but one of the children played with it and the string broke, and he never put it together again. Some of the beads rolled away and were lost, and he said that he did not need it any more."

Madame Wu was looking about the room as the old woman talked.

"What is in that black box?" she asked, and pointed her middle finger.

The old woman looked. "That is a magic voice box," she said. "He used to listen to the voices in the night."

Madame Wu remembered that he had told her of it. She approached the box and put her ear against it and heard nothing.

"It speaks for no one else," the old woman explained.

"Ah, then we will bury it with him," Madame Wu said.

"There is one more thing he possesses, and it is magic too," the old woman said hesitatingly. "He told us never to touch it."

"Where is it?" Madame Wu asked.

The old woman crawled under the bed and drew out a long wooden box. She opened it, and there lay an instrument like a pipe.

"He held it to his right eye whenever the night was clear, and he looked into Heaven," she said.

Madame Wu knew at once that this was his means of gazing at stars. "I will take that with me," she decided. "And now bring his books to me," she said, "and let his garments and the cross be buried with him. As for this house, let it be returned to the owner. Tell him I say it is exorcised and clear now of evil. He can rent it again at a good price."

All the children clustered about the old woman and listened in breathless silence and fear. Their home was gone. They had nothing left.

Madame Wu smiled down on them. She understood with a tenderness wholly new to her what they were thinking.

"As for you, all of you, and you too, Old Sister, you are to come to my own house and live."

A great sigh went over the children. They were safe. With the ease and confidence of childhood they accepted their new safety and immediately became excited.

"When—when—" they began to clamour.

"I think you should stay here with him until to-morrow," she said. "Then we will all go to the grave together. But you

238

will not come back here. You will come home with me."

"Good heart," the old woman sobbed, "kind good heart! He knows—be sure he knows!"

Madame Wu smiled without answering this. "Have you rice enough for their meals?" she asked. "They will need food to-day and to-morrow morning. Their noon meal they will have in my house."

"He always kept a day's food in the house," the old woman sobbed. "At least one day's food we always have."

"Then to-morrow I will come back," Madame Wu said.

She let the children press against her for a moment, knowing that they were accustomed to cluster about him and feel his bodily presence, and so they needed the same reassurance from her. Then she said gently, "Until to-morrow, my little ones," and she left the house where his body lay dead and went out, a different creature from the woman she had been when she came in.

She went back to her own court and sat long alone with her changed self. She accepted André's death. If he had lived there would most certainly have come the moment when she would have discovered that she loved him. There could then have been only one of two choices for her. She must have made excuses never to see him again, or she must have yielded up her soul to him and told him her love. This she knew would have parted them.

She sat awake and alone for hours that night, refusing to allow Ying to come in and put her to bed. She did not want to lie in a bed. She wanted to sit, alive, alert, alone, searching out the whole of her new knowledge. She loved a man, a foreigner, a stranger, a man who had never once put out his hand to touch hers, whose touch would have been unthinkable. She smiled into the darkness after a long time. The house was dark and silent about her, but beside her a candle burned, and her heart was speaking aloud.

"Had I put out my hand to you," she said, "would you have been afraid of me?"

But she knew André was afraid of no one. There was that God of his. It occurred to Madame Wu that men's gods were enemies to women. She felt jealousy for the first time in her life.

"We have no gods of our own," she reflected.

But for women true gods were impossible. She pondered on

239

the women she knew who worshipped gods. Little Sister Hsia was continually talking of her god. But then, Little Sister Hsia had nothing else to talk about, neither husband nor children, neither friends nor family. In this emptiness she had gone out and found for herself God. No, the only true test of women was whether, having all else, as men did, they rejected all and went and found a god. The women whom she knew best and had known best in her whole life, not one of them had truly sought God. Not one, that is, in the way that André had done, when as a young man he had put aside the woman he loved and the wealth he might have had and the fame from his learning, and had simply given his life to God.

She paused in her musing to consider for a moment the woman whom André had loved in his youth and had put aside, loving loneliness better. Young she must have been and beautiful doubtless. She felt more jealousy, not that André had loved the woman, but because this unknown and long-forgotten woman should have looked upon André when he was young and not yet a priest.

"I should have liked to have seen him when he was a young giant," Madame Wu thought. She sat at perfect peace, in complete stillness, her hands folded one upon the other, and her rings gleaming softly on her fingers. Yes, André as a young man must have been a good sight for a woman. He was handsome even in his middle age, but young he must have been himself a god. Then she felt sorry for that woman whom he had rejected. Now she was married doubtless and perhaps she had many children, for women do not die because a man will not have them, but somewhere in her heart she still thought of André, with love or with hate. If she were a woman of little heart she would hate him, or if she were of great heart she had not blamed him and so she loved him still. Or perhaps she thought of him no more. It might be perhaps she was simply tired and past any feeling, as women can grow to be when their hearts and bodies have been too much used. It was the weakness of a woman that heart and body were knit together, warp and woof, and when the body was too much used the heart, too, became worn, unless it had love, such as she now felt towards André. Death had relieved her of his body. Had he lived they might have lost their souls in the snare of the flesh. She was surprised to feel at this moment a sudden rich flush of blood into her vitals.

"I am a woman in spite of everything," she thought with some amusement. Even the thought of André's great body could cause this enrichment in her being. How dangerous to peace had he been before her in the flesh! She felt an impulse of gratitude towards those robbers of the Green Band who had removed such danger. Then, noticing through the door how exquisite the moonlight was upon her orchids, under the bamboos, she was contrite. It was cruel to be glad that André's eyes were closed.

"It is not that I am glad you are dead," she explained to him. "It is simply that you and I are both spared a great misery and so we can keep our great joy. Doubtless you know I love you."

As she murmured these words she was conscious of his perfect understanding. Nothing less could have given her so instant a sense of complete comfort and cheerfulness. She knew that for André to have violated his priesthood would have caused him as much pain as her own were she to violate the duty she had to her family. They would have preached renunciation to each other, but in order to practise this, it would have been necessary for them never to meet. Now no renunciation was necessary. She could think of him as much as she liked and without danger.

"But of course I am changed," she thought. She sat, still outwardly motionless, but wondering how she was changed. She did not know. She would have to discover herself. Her heart was changed. "I am a stranger now to myself," she thought with some astonishment. "I do not know how I shall act or how I shall feel."

For an hour after this discovery she sat in the same motionless pose. "I have no knowledge of how I shall act," she thought. "The springs of my being are different. I shall no longer live out of duty but out of love." This was her discovery of herself through love.

Again she felt the strange enrichment flow through her whole being, followed by serene content.

It was at this moment she thought of the instrument for stars. She had ordered it to be brought with her, and now it was in the library. She went and lifted it out of its box with difficulty, for it was heavy, and she set it up on three folding legs she found also in the box. Then she peered through it at heaven outside the door.

She expected instantly to see the shapes of stars and the moon in its path. To her disappointment, although the night was clear, she saw nothing. This way and that she tried, but Heaven was sealed to her, and with a sigh she put the instrument away again. She had not the knowledge for it. "It belongs only to him," she thought. "I will bury it with him, together with the box of voices from the night."

Upon this decision she went to her bed and slept.

The funeral was like none that had ever taken place before in this city. Madame Wu could not let it be like a family burial. But she gave it honour as the funeral of her son's tutor. The children were dressed in white cloth, unhemmed, and the beggars who had carried Brother André into his house demanded mourning for themselves. Madame Wu wore no outer mourning.

Now, after some thought, before the funeral she had asked whether the few other foreigners in the city should not be told of the death. Little Sister Hsia should know, perhaps, and certainly the foreign doctor should know.

Madame Wu had never seen this foreign doctor and did not want to see him now. She had heard that such doctors went always with knives in their hands, ready to cut any who were ill. Sometimes they were clever in cutting off tumours and excrescences, but often they killed people, and there was no redress against a foreign doctor as there was against one of their own who killed instead of healing. For this reason few of the people in the city went near the foreign doctor unless they were already sure of death.

She sent a message by a manservant to the few foreigners in the city, and the man came back saying that he was told that Brother André was a stranger to them, not being of their religion, and they would not come.

The end of it was that the funeral was as Madame Wu planned it. It took place not the next day as she had first thought, because no coffin was found big enough and one had to be made. Working night and day, the coffin maker finished it in two nights and the day between; and then early in the morning before the city was astir Madame Wu in her sedan chair headed the procession, which came on foot behind her and André in his coffin. She herself had seen to the lifting of his great body into the coffin.

She stood while men lifted André into the coffin, and herself put in the voice box and the instrument for stars before the lid was nailed down. She had carried the instrument here again to his house that it might be buried with him. Thus she stood, and she did not delay by sign or word the fitting of the heavy lid. She saw him sleeping, and she yearned over him and said nothing, and then the lid went down and she saw him no more.

Neither did she weep. Why should she reveal herself through weeping? She heard the nails pounded into the wood and saw the ropes tied to great poles. Twenty men were hired to lift the mighty casket, and they carried it out into the streets, and through the city gate to the western hill, and now she led the way and others followed, and under the gingko-tree the hill was ready to receive him.

None spoke while the coffin was lowered into the cave made for it. The children cried and the old woman wailed, but Madame Wu stood motionless and silent, and the earth was filled into the cave and the mound made.

In her heart for a moment was a hard, dry knot of pain that she would see him no more except as he lived for ever in her memory.

When all was done, Madame Wu led the procession home again, and she led the children into her own gates, and from that day they were homeless no more.

243

II

NEXT morning as she looked about the familiar room she knew that the world was exactly as it had been every other morning. Yet, instead of waking to weariness and a longing not to begin the day, she was aware of fresh energy in herself. The energy flowed from a source in her which she had never had before. What she had felt for her husband in her youth had certainly been a kind of love. It was impossible not to have loved Mr. Wu when he was young. He had been too handsome, too healthy, too good-natured not to have won her half-provoked affection and blood-longing. But that love had nothing to do with herself. It was as instinctive as the reflex of a muscle. The heart indeed was nothing but the central muscle in the body.

This she knew. She had once watched her old grandfather take into his hands the still-living heart of a dead tiger, in the days when to eat a tiger heart was to absorb its strength. She remembered the scene as sharply as though it were now before her eyes. She was a little girl of eight, perhaps nine. The hillmen had trapped the tiger and brought it snarling into the courtyard, caught in rope nets. They had all run out into the wintry sunshine to see the golden spotted beast, and at the sight of them it had opened its wide red mouth and had hissed at them in hopeless enmity. The women had shrieked, but she had stood still, staring into its wild yellow eyes. As though it felt its power over her, the tiger had closed its jaws and stared back at her. She had taken one blind step forward when her grandfather shouted. A hillman leaped and plunged his dagger into the tiger's heart. The knife ripped through the fur, and the beast sank back. The hillman lifted out the heart whole and still beating, and held it before her grandfather's eyes.

But what she felt in herself now for André had nothing to do with the beating heart. This love, quiet and strong, was sunlight at noon. She was warmed and strengthened by it, and made certain of herself. She had only to act out of the warmth and light, and what she did would be right. Love permeated her brain as well as her body. André was not dead. He was living, and he was with her because she loved him. The reticence of the body was gone. It was unnecessary. She who all her life had been sceptic to the bone, who had smiled at priests and temple mummery, who had looked up to the sky and seen no gods, to whom the spirits of nature were only childish imaginations, she now was sure that André was alive and with her.

"I loved him when he came and went in these courts, but I did not know it," she thought. "I had to see his body dead before I knew how I loved him."

And, then being a woman, she asked herself if he had loved her. At this question of returned love she felt her first loneliness.

"Since I cannot hear his voice I shall never know," she thought. She turned her head towards the court and missed the tread of his feet upon the stones. Then, as she listened, hearing nothing but the twitter of small birds in the bamboos, she saw his face appear slowly against the dark curtain of her memory. His eyes were warm upon her, his bearded lips smiled, and the half-merry sagacity which was his usual look came before her so vividly that she smiled back at him. She could not hear his voice, but she felt suddenly assured that André did love her. Behind the walls of his priesthood, which kept him separated from her while he was alive, he had loved her. Now he was no longer priest, and the walls were gone. There was no reason why she should not summon him at any moment, no reason why he should not enter her mind without waiting for summons. His body was dead, and hers had become the means through which they could live together.

It occurred to her that now she might have a new wisdom which alone she had never had.

"How stupid I have been," she reflected, gazing up into the blue curtains of her bed. "The men and women in my house, how confused they are by what I have done!"

What she had done so selfishly was to try to free herself from them all by withdrawing herself. She had wanted them to be happy, each in his own fashion, but she had not wanted to be troubled with making them happy, nor had she been able to tell them how to be happy. Food and clothing she had provided, discipline and order she had maintained, and yet the whole house was in a turmoil and nobody was happy.

She had been angry with them because they were not happy. This she now saw was completely foolish.

At this moment Ying came into the room, looking very discontented. "Do you not get up this morning, Lady?" she asked. Her voice was querulous.

"It is a rainy day," Madame Wu said, smiling.

"How do you know, Lady?" Ying inquired sourly. "You have not even drawn your curtains."

"I know by your voice," Madame Wu replied, "and there are clouds upon your face."

"I never thought I should have to see a flower-house girl in our house," Ying retorted, "nor the sons of the house out wandering over the earth and a concubine cast aside and still having to be fed."

"So the girl Jasmine is come?" Madame Wu said.

"She is in the back court waiting," Ying replied. She busied herself about her mistress's toilet table while she went on talking. "They asked me what to do with her. I don't know what to do with her." Ying's underlip thrust itself out. "The girl says she's expected. I told her I did not expect her."

Madame Wu got up out of bed and thrust her narrow feet into flower-embroidered slippers. "Did she come alone?" she asked.

"A snag-toothed old woman came with her and then went away in a hurry. Oh, she's on our hands," Ying said very sourly.

Madame Wu did not speak. She proceeded to her bath, and then she put on her silver-grey brocaded satin robe over soft white silk undergarments. Ying dressed her hair carefully, her underlip still sullen.

"Fetch my breakfast," Madame Wu commanded. She sat down a few moments later and ate it with appetite. She felt a new hunger even for food, and was amused. Had she not heard that love destroyed the appetite? Then she remembered that it was only unrequited love that did so.

"André loves me," she thought in triumph.

In less than half an hour she rose to go to the back court to see the girl Jasmine.

"Shall I not bring her here, Lady?" Ying inquired. "It will give her big thoughts if you go to her."

"No," Madame Wu said calmly, "I will go to her." She wished as few persons as possible now to enter her own court.

Here let the spirit of André dwell undisturbed, she told herself. Then on the threshold of the moon gate she felt her feet cling, as though hands held them to the marble. A new thought came into her mind.

"But André never held himself back from anyone," she thought. "He would have met this girl freely to discern what he could do for her. His spirit here will help me."

She turned to Ying. "You may bring her after all," she said.

So while Ying went she sat down. Anyone looking in through the gate would have seen her sitting, a slender, silvery figure, her head bent, a smile upon her almond-pale face. But no one passed, and in a few moments Ying returned, marching ahead of a rosy, plump, short young girl.

Thus Madame Wu looked up and saw Jasmine. She was at the same instant aware that this was the sort of woman whom she naturally most disliked, a robust and earthly creature, coarse and passionate. She averted her eyes and felt her soul stagger between yesterday and to-day. Her dainty flesh shivered.

She felt her protest cut off, stilled by André. There his face was again, dark upon the curtain of her memory. Gazing at his face she began to ask the girl questions in a soft and gentle voice. Ying fell back a few paces and stood listening and staring. This was not at all Madame Wu's usual silvery clear voice. There was no hardness in it. Yet it was not the voice in which Madame Wu habitually spoke to children. It was something new, this voice.

"Tell me why you want to come here to live," Madame Wu asked.

Jasmine looked down at the stones under her feet. She wished she had put on her blue cotton jacket and trousers instead of her green satin ones.

"I want to settle myself before the child is born," she said.

"Is there to be a child?" Madame Wu asked.

Jasmine lifted her head for one quick look at her. "Yes!" she said loudly.

"There is no child," Madame Wu replied.

Jasmine lifted her head again, opened her lips to protest, and stared into Madame Wu's eyes. They were fixed upon her with piercing light, and she burst into tears.

"So there is no child," Madame Wu repeated.

"Lady, we don't have to keep her!" Ying cried.

Madame Wu put up her long narrow hand. "This is for me to decide," she said. "Please go away, Ying."

"And leave you with this rotten egg?" Ying demanded.

"You may stand just outside the moon gate," Madame Wu said.

She waited for Ying to go, and then she motioned the girl to sit down on a porcelain garden seat. Jasmine sat down, rubbing her eyes with her knuckles and drawing her sobs back into her throat. Madame Wu began to speak.

"You know," she said to Jasmine, "it is a very grave thing to enter a man's house, especially when there is a large and honourable family such as ours. You can come into it and ruin all happiness here. Or you can come in and add happiness by your presence. All this depends on your true heart. If you come for rice and shelter I beg you to tell me. I will promise you these. You may have them freely without having to buy them here with your body."

Jasmine looked shrewdly at Madame Wu. "Who gives a woman something for nothing?" she asked.

Madame Wu marvelled at herself. Had this happened a month ago she would have despised the girl's coarseness. But now she understood it.

"You have never had food or shelter freely," she murmured. "It is hard for you to believe me."

"I believe nobody," Jasmine said. She pulled a bright red silk handkerchief out of her bosom. One end of it was fastened to a button, but she twisted the other about her fingers.

"Then you do come here for shelter," Madame Wu said.

Jasmine shook her head. "I don't say so," she declared. She lifted her thick eyelids, and a sly look came into her round black eyes. "Other men have promised me shelter," she said.

"But you come here for something," Madame Wu persisted. "Is it because there is honour belonging to our family, even though you live in our back court?"

Jasmine's face was suddenly scarlet under its powder. "I like the old head——" she muttered in the jargon of the street.

Madame Wu knew she spoke of Mr. Wu, but she did not reprove her. Truth was stealing new-born out of the girl's heart.

"He is much older than you, child," Madame Wu said.

"I like old men," the girl said, trembling.

"Why do you tremble?" Madame Wu asked. "You need not tremble before me."

"I have never known anyone who was noble," the girl said, frightened. "He is very noble."

"What do you mean by noble?" Madame Wu asked. She would never have used the word noble for Mr. Wu. Impetuous, impatient, wilful, stupid, good-natured sometimes, selfish always—these were all possible words for him, but not noble.

"I mean—noble," Jasmine said. She lifted her arm. "This bracelet," she said. "It is solid gold. A young man would have given me a brass one with a coat of gold and sworn it was true. It would have lasted until he left me. But no, the old one gave me solid gold." She bit it and showed the toothmarks to Madame Wu. "See?"

"Yes, it is gold," Madame Wu agreed.

"He is so patient," the girl went on eagerly. "When I don't feel well, he notices it—he doesn't press me. Young men don't care. They take what they want. But this old one always asks me how I feel."

"Does he indeed," Madame Wu replied. This was not the Mr. Wu she had known.

The girl sat down again and twisted the bracelet about her arm. "If I have no child——" she began.

"A child is not important," Madame Wu said.

Jasmine looked at her cornerwise while Madame Wu went on. "The important thing is, will you add happiness to this house or take it away?"

Jasmine lifted her head eagerly. "I will bring happiness, I promise you, Lady——"

"To-morrow I will decide," Madame Wu said. She rose as she spoke, and Ying hurried into the court and led the girl away.

When she was gone Madame Wu walked straight along a path of new sunlight that now fell across the stones into the doorway. The light dazed her, but her feet were warmed by it. "I did well," she thought in some wonder at herself. "How did I know to do so well?"

And then she understood herself. If Jasmine really loved Mr. Wu, that love, too, must be allowed. Did Mr. Wu also love Jasmine? If so, then real happiness would be added to

249

the house. All the unhappiness in homes came because there was not love.

"When I have rested," she said to Ying, who came in dusting her hands, "I will go to the courts of my sons' father."

"Do, Lady," Ying said. She looked more cheerful. "Perhaps you can persuade him to wisdom. We have already too many women in this house."

"Are you to stay?" she had asked Jasmine while she led her away.

"I don't know," Jasmine had faltered. "She said she'd tell me to-morrow."

"Our Lady always makes up her mind quickly," Ying said. She did not finish what she thought, that if her mistress did not say "yes" to-day, it would be "no" to-morrow. She had put the girl outside the back gate and had drawn the iron bar.

"I go, Lady, and let him know," she now said. The sparkle had come back into her impudent eyes. Madame Wu saw it, understood, and smiled.

. . . . .

Madame Wu woke to her usual full consciousness, her heart serene. All her life she had struggled for calmness and serenity. She had made herself a prisoner inside the confines of her will, imposed upon her body. Thus her will had commanded her body to behave in certain ways at certain times, regardless of its repulsions and desires. She felt now that she need never again compel herself to anything.

"André," she said to herself, "it is strange, is it not, that you had to die before I knew you?"

"Not strange," the answering thought came into her mind. "There was my big body between us. You had to look at a face and at features with which I really had nothing to do. They were simply given me haphazard by my ancestors, who actually were strangers to me. Even though I was willing to realize them as strangers and leave them, still I was held in their flesh. Now I am wholly myself."

"André," she said to him within her, "should I still call you brother, perhaps?"

"It is no longer necessary to qualify our relationship." So he answered in her heart.

Madame Wu lay straight and exquisite in her bed. She was frightened by this conversation which was taking place entirely in her own mind. Sceptic that she was, she would have laughed at any supernatural appearance even of the one she loved. But there had been no appearance and no sound. The austere room was exactly as it had been when she closed her eyes to sleep. Simply within her brain she heard André's voice answering her questions. It was perhaps no more than an obsession caused by his death and by her discovery that she loved him. To have comprehended within a handful of seconds that she loved a man who had just died was enough to shake Heaven and earth. It was not surprising that the brain doubled upon itself in its confusion. She recalled that André had told her how thought was driven along the cells which composed the brain stuff. Her recognition of him, crashing into those cells, must doubtless have disturbed all the previous thought lines of her life.

"I do not know what I shall be from now on," she thought.

She listened for the answering voice. Instead she suddenly remembered how he looked when he smiled. She saw light welling up through the deep darkness of his eyes, and she smiled back at him.

Ying came into the room, looking alarmed. "The front court is full of the beggar children," she said fretfully. "And the prostitute is sitting in the entrance hall again. She says you sent for her."

Madame Wu laughed. "I feel I could eat a roll of wheat bread this morning," she remarked.

Ying stared at her. "You look changed, Lady. Your skin is rosy as a child's. You are not feverish?"

She came to the side of the huge bed and took Madame Wu's little hand and held it to her cheek.

"No fever," Madame Wu said. "Nothing but health."

She withdrew her hand gently and threw back the silken quilt. Then, rising, she allowed Ying to wash and dress her. But she refused the grey silk robe Ying had put out for her. Instead she chose one of an old-rose colour which the day before her fortieth birthday she had laid aside, thinking she would never wear such hues again.

To-day it was becoming to her as it had never been. The last time she had worn it she had thought it made her paleness sallow. But this morning it lent her colour.

"It was wrong of me to have put it away," she thought as she looked at herself in the mirror. Her natural vanity stirred.

"A pity he never saw me in this," she thought. She smiled at herself in the glass. She glanced at Ying, to see whether any of this had been seen. But Ying was folding the grey robe, sleeve to sleeve.

Madame Wu walked into the library. In common sense to-day she should have felt her life tangled with unsolved problems. Twenty children waited in the court, the young prostitute sat in the entrance hall, and Mr. Wu was more than ever a responsibility. There were the new-born girl and her mother, Ch'iuming, and her own sons and their wives. But she had none of her usual shrinking from human beings. She now realized that for the first time in her life she disliked no one. All her life she had struggled against her dislike of human beings. None had been wholly to her taste. Thus her mother she had disliked because of her ignorance and superstitions. Her father she had loved, or would have said she had, but she had disliked him, too, because his heart was far away and she could never come near him. And though Mr. Wu had been a handsome young man when she married him there were secrets of his person which she disliked. Even when she had shared his passion she had been aware of shapes and odours, and she had felt violation in his touch even while she allowed it. Old Gentleman had been dear to her, but she was so delicately made that she could not forget what she disliked while she found what she liked. His heart was good, his intelligence clear, but his teeth were broken and his breath came foul.

"If André had been alive when I found I loved him I wonder if I could have——"

Before she could frame the thought, another came to answer. "You see how wise is death! It removes the body of a man and lets free his spirit."

"But if I were younger," she reminded him, "could I have been satisfied only with your spirit?"

She looked down at the smooth grey tiles of the floor. Would it have been possible, when she was young, to have loved a foreign man? For of course André was a foreign man, a man from another country and of another blood. She tried to imagine him young and ardent as a man is ardent, and all her blood rose in strange anger.

"Don't!" This cry burst into her mind.

"No, I will not," she promised.

Ying came in with her breakfast and placed it upon the table in neat rows of dishes. Madame Wu took up her chopsticks.

"Have the children in the court been fed?" she asked.

"Certainly not, Lady," Ying said sternly. "No orders have been given for so much food."

"Then I give orders now," Madame Wu said gently. "Let rice be cooked at once, and bread brought and tea made for their noon meal."

"It is lucky it is not raining," Ying said. "We should be put to it if we had to take such people under our roof."

"There is room here for all," Madame Wu said.

She was amazed to see Ying begin to cry and, with her blue coat to her eyes, run sobbing out of the room. "You are changed—you are changed," she cried.

But at noon she had great buckets of rice set in the court, and when Madame Wu went there it was to see the little girls eating happily and feeding the younger ones by pushing rice into their open mouths. The old woman who had been their caretaker rose, her cheeks full of rice, and cried out to the children that they must greet Madame Wu as their mother.

"Now that your father has gone, I am your mother," Madame Wu said, smiling. The orphan children looked at her with love, and suddenly for the first time in her life Madame Wu felt the true pangs of birth in her being. She felt her being divided and merge again with another nature far larger than her own. These children were André's and hers.

"All are my children," she said, wondering that the words could be hers. At the sound of her voice the children rushed to her to embrace her, to touch her, to lean against her. She looked down at them and saw their small lacks and defects as well as their beauty. But she felt no dislike.

"Your father did the best he could for you," she said smiling, "but you need a mother too." She touched a sore red scar on a child's cheek. "Does it still hurt?" she asked.

"A little," the child replied.

"And how did you come by it?" Madame Wu asked.

The child hung her head. "My mistress held the end of her cigarette against me there——"

"Oh, why?" Madame Wu asked.

"I was her slave—and I couldn't move fast enough——" the child replied.

She put her hand into Madame Wu's. "Will you give me a name?" she begged. "He was going to give me a name and then died too soon. All the others have names."

"They shall tell me their names, and then I shall know what to name you," Madame Wu replied.

One by one they repeated their names, and each name was a word spoken from André.

Pity; Faith; Humility; Grace; Truth; Mercy; Light; Song; Star; Moonbeam; Sunbeam; Dawn; Joy; Clarity—such were the names he had given the older ones. The younger ones he had called playful names. Kitten and Snowbird and Rose-petal and Acorn, Silver and Gold. "Because he said silver and gold had he none," these two small creatures proclaimed, "until we came."

They all laughed at such nonsense. "He did make us laugh every day," Gold said. She was a round little creature, and she clutched Silver by the hand.

"Are you sisters?" Madame Wu asked, smiling.

"We are all sisters," twenty voices cried.

"Of course," Madame Wu agreed. "I am stupid."

The scarred child pressed her close. "And my name?" she asked.

Madame Wu looked down into the tender face. The child was exquisite, a bud of a child, full of beauty to come. The name rose in Madame Wu's mind. "I will call you Love," she said.

"I am Love," the child repeated.

By now the court was fringed with silent onlookers. The servants in the house had made one excuse and another to pass this way to stop and stare, but the children of the household and the lesser relatives made no pretence of errands. They stood gaping at this new Madame Wu. At last Jasmine, who had grown weary of waiting in the entrance hall, rose and came to the court herself, and behind her came her servant. Jasmine had braced herself to be very strong and to demand her rights as one who had within herself hope of a son for the house.

But instead of the stern, proud lady whom she had expected to see, this morning she saw a gentle, beautiful woman, laughing in the midst of beggar children. Madame Wu looked up at the bustle behind the pillars of the veranda, and their eyes met.

254

"You see I have many children," Madame Wu said, smiling, "but I have not forgotten you. When I have planned where they are to sleep and play I will talk with you."

She turned to the relatives. None of them were sons or sons' wives. They were only old cousins and poor nephews who, having no shelter elsewhere, had returned to the ancestral house to find a corner here and a bed there.

"Where shall we house my children?" she asked gaily.

"Our Sister," an old widow answered, "if you are doing good deeds, let them be housed in the family temple."

Madame Wu had been without any anxiety whatever, but she simply had not known where to put these children. Now she accepted the widow's words at once. "How wise you are," she said gratefully. "No home could be better than our temple. There are courts to play in, and the pool and the fountain. The family gods will have something to do now."

She led the way as she spoke, and the children ran after her in the sunlight, and the old woman hobbled after them. In the very back of the Wu courts there was a large old temple, built by one of the women ancestors two hundred years before. She had desired to become a nun after her husband died, and yet she did not wish to leave her home to live in a public temple. So she had built here within the shelter of the house walls a beautiful temple where she lived with the gods until she died nearly one hundred years old. Since then a priest had been appointed to care for the temple, none being allowed to serve who were under fifty years of age because of the many young women in the house.

Madame Wu, although sceptic, had nevertheless allowed the priest to continue and had maintained the temple, paying for the gilding of the gods once every ten years and once a year allowing a sum for incense. Such of the family as wished could worship here, and it was considered a benefit that women need not go to outside temples to worship and be perhaps exposed to lewd priests.

To this temple she now led the children. She paused for one moment on the wide stone threshold. Two gate gods loomed above her, one black, one white.

"But will these gods offend André?" she asked herself. "His religion had no gods like these."

She seemed to hear his mighty laughter, echoing among the painted beams high above the heads of the gods.

She smiled in reply and, holding by the hand the child she had named Love, she stepped over the high wooden doorsteps and into the temple. The air was fragrant with incense and lilies. Incense burned before the gods, and lilies bloomed in the court. The old priest, hearing footsteps, came running in from his kitchen. He had been burning grass for cooking of his meal, and his face and hands were sooty.

He stared at the crowd of children and at Madame Wu. "I am bringing gifts," she said. "Tell him your names, children."

One by one they called their names in their soft gay voices.

"And this one," Madame Wu ended, "is Love. They are all gifts for the temple."

Now, the old priest had heard of what had happened. He took it that Madame Wu wished to do good deeds before Heaven and so he could not forbid it, however difficult it might be for him. He bowed and clasped his sooty hands and fell back against one god after another as he retreated before Madame Wu, who swept on into the temple, assigning rooms where until now only gods had stood silently gazing into the courts of the Wu family.

"This room is for the little ones," she said, "because the Goddess of Mercy is here, and she will watch over you for me during the night. This room is for the big ones, because there is space for everybody, and you must help to keep it very clean."

Then she felt the child Love cling to her. "Let me come with you," she begged Madame Wu. "I will wash your clothes and serve your food. I can do everything."

Madame Wu's heart turned into warm flame. But she was just. She knew that André would not have showed favour to one above another. She shook her head. "You must stay and help the others," she said. "That is what your father would have wished." Then she knew it was not all justice. She wanted no one with her to share her life with him.

"Where shall we sleep, Our Mother?" the children asked of Madame Wu.

"By night there will be beds," she said. "But first you must play all day long."

And seeing them happy she left them with the gods.

Jasmine pursed her red mouth and looked hard at the corner of her brightly flowered silk handkerchief. One corner of it was fastened to the glass button on her left shoulder, and it hung from this like a scarf. With the handkerchief she concealed her face, or she played with it when she wished not to look at the one to whom she was talking.

"It is hard for me to speak," she said to Madame Wu.

"Surely there is not much to say," Madame Wu replied.

"There is a great deal to say," Jasmine said pertly. "If I have no child now, I will have." She placed her hands on her belly.

Madame Wu looked at her with interest. "You ought to be able to bear a very fat fine child," she said. "You look strong."

Jasmine was taken aback. "But what will my position be in the house?" she demanded.

"What position do you want?" Madame Wu asked.

"I ought to be the third wife," Jasmine said sharply. It was strange that so young and pretty a creature could be so sharp. But her round bright eyes, her straight small nose, her pink cheeks and little full mouth all grew sharp and bright together.

"Why not?" Madame Wu said amiably.

"You don't mind?" Jasmine asked these words in a whisper. The sharpness went out of her face, and the lines of it softened.

"Why should I mind?" Madame Wu asked simply.

"You mean I can live here—in this great house—and be called Third Lady—and when my child——"

"I would not want any child of our house to be illegitimate," Madame Wu said. "That would be unworthy of our name. You are the vessel that receives the seed. You are to be honoured."

Jasmine stared at her with rounding black eyes and then began to cry in loud coarse sobs. "I thought you would hate me," she gasped. "I made myself ready for your anger. Now I don't know what to do."

"There is nothing you need to do," Madame Wu said calmly. "I will have a maid lead you to your rooms. They are small, you know, only two, and they are to the left of my lord's court. His Second Lady lives to the right. You need not meet. I will myself go now and tell my lord you are coming."

She hesitated, and then said with a delicate frankness, "You will find him very just. If he leaves his silver pipe upon your table it is his message. If he goes away with it in his hand do not be angry. That is my own request in return for shelter. Bring no anger into our house."

She looked at the stolid old woman who had sat beside Jasmine all this time without a word. "And this one, is she your mother?"

The woman opened her mouth to speak, but Jasmine spoke first. "She belongs to the house from where I come."

"Let her go back to it, then," Madame Wu said. She put her hand into her bosom and took out silver and put it on the table. It shone there so largely that the woman could only get up and bow again and again.

But all was interrupted by Jasmine, who fell on her knees before Madame Wu and knocked her head on the floor. "They told me you were just, but now I know you are kind!"

Madame Wu's cheeks flushed upward from her neck. "Had you come another day I might have been only angry," she said honestly. "But to-day is different from all days before it."

She rose, not lifting the girl to her feet, and walked quickly out of the room.

"I am a wicked woman," she told herself. "I do not care how many women come into these courts. My own heart is full."

She paused, waiting for some answer to this. But there was no answer, unless the complete peace within her heart was answer. "Had I discovered you while you lived," she said, "would there have been silence between us?"

Still he did not answer and she smiled at his silence. Even as a spirit he was shy of love. The habits of his life held. The silence broke a moment later. As she stepped into the main court she saw three men standing there. They were decent-looking, well-dressed men, and they turned their backs as she came in and pretended not to see her, as though she were a young woman. It was a pleasant compliment, but she put it aside.

"I am Madame Wu," she said. "Is there anything you want here?"

They turned sidewise at this, and the eldest man, in great courtesy, answered still without looking at her.

"It is Madame Wu whom we seek," he said. "We are come to ask if the dead should not be somehow avenged. That

Green Band is a danger to our whole town, but never before have they killed a man. It is true he was only a foreigner and a priest, but if they begin killing foreigners and priests to-day, they will be killing us to-morrow. Ought not the town to demand justice on behalf of the stranger? If so, will Madame Wu make the accusation?"

There was a stir of protest in her mind. She saw André's eyes, fiercely refusing vengeance, and she spoke instantly. "Certainly he would want no vengeance done for him," she said. "He talked often of forgiving those who do not know what they do. But who are these robbers?"

"The worthless young men of the town, the adventurers, the ones who want to rise not through honest work, but through making others afraid of them," the elder replied indignantly.

"Are there many such men?" she asked with wonder.

The men laughed but without noise, in respect to her. "There are many in these days," one said.

"And why should there be?" she asked.

"The times are bad." One of the other men spoke. He was a small withered man whose face was wrinkled but whose hair was still black. She stood there in the strong sunlight in her rose-coloured robe, and there was admiration in the man's eyes. But she was far beyond seeing it. She was wholly safe from any man's admiration.

"What makes the times bad?" she asked. She knew well enough the times, but she asked.

"Lady, you have lived behind these high walls," the eldest man spoke again. "You cannot know in what a turmoil the world is. The turmoil begins in the wickedness of foreign countries, where war continually threatens. None of us can escape. This turmoil makes the young everywhere restless. They ask themselves why they should submit to ancient ways which must soon change. They have no new ways to offer, and so, rejecting the old and delaying the new, they live without law."

She looked at the men. Doubtful though she might be of all else, of André's mind she was sure.

"He will take no vengeance," she said.

They bowed and went away. But she was troubled after they were gone. She walked on to find Mr. Wu, that she might see how his spirits were this day, and as she went she pondered what the men had said. Should she have sent her sons forth into these troubled times?

"Were I alone," she thought, "I might be afraid."

But she was not alone. With this comfort she remembered that she had said she would announce Jasmine's coming to Mr. Wu, and she went at once.

．　　　．　　　．　　　．　　　．

She entered the moon gate and saw Mr. Wu poking into the earth of the peony terrace with the brass end of his long bamboo pipe. He wore a lined robe of dark-blue satin, and he had put on his velvet shoes padded with silk. He was thinner than he had been. In his youth he had been full fleshed, and in his middle age nothing less than fat. Now, without his being slender, the inner fat was beginning to melt away, and his smooth brown skin was loosening.

"Are you well, Father of my sons?" she asked courteously.

"Very well, Mother of my sons," he replied, and went on prodding the earth.

"You will ruin your pipe," she remarked.

"I am testing the roots of the peonies to see if they are firm," he replied. "There has been so much rain that I fear their rotting."

"These terraces are well drained," she said. "I had the tiles laid, you remember, the year Tsemo was born. We raised the height of the walls so that I could see the orchids from my bed."

"You remember everything," he said. "Shall we sit outdoors or inside? Better perhaps inside? The winds are insidious. They curl about the ground and chill one's feet."

She was amazed to perceive that she did not feel at all strange with Mr. Wu. Certainly she could not possibly have explained to him how she felt concerning André. He would have held her beside herself—a foreigner? A priest? A dead man?

She followed Mr. Wu into the main room, where the sunlight lay in a great square upon the tiles beside the open door. She felt towards him exactly as she always had. At this thought pity for Mr. Wu stirred her vitals. It was a piteous thing for him that she had not been able to love him. She had deprived this man of the fullness of life. Nothing that she had given him, neither her body nor her sons, could be reward enough for her unloving heart. Her only excuse was that she and Mr. Wu had been given to each other, without the will of either, and she had done the best she could. But had she chosen him of her own free will, she could not have forgiven herself. Nothing could recompense a man for the lack of love in the woman who was his wife.

"Therefore somehow I must now give him love," she thought.

"I have just spoken to the girl Jasmine," she said calmly. She seated herself to the left of the table against the centre wall of the room, and he took his usual seat at the right. So they had been wont to sit together through the evenings of their marriage, while they talked of the affairs in this house which belonged to them both.

Mr. Wu busied himself with his pipe. She saw with her peculiar discernment that he was afraid of her. In other days this knowledge would have amused her. She had not disliked the fear that others had for her, accepting it as the due of her superiority. But now she was sad to see the furtive turning of his eyes and the slight tremble of his plump hands. Where there was fear, no love could be. André had never feared her, nor did she fear him. She understood, with a strange pang that held no pain, that Mr. Wu had never really loved her, either, else he would not now be afraid of her.

"Tell me how you feel toward this girl," she said to Mr. Wu.

At the gentleness of her voice he looked at her across the table, and she caught in his eyes a sort of shyness that she had never known was in him. "I know how this girl appears to you," he said. "Of course she is inferior in every way. I can see that also. But I feel very sorry for her. What opportunity has she had, after all? The story of her life is a sad one, poor child!"

"Tell me the story of her life," Madame Wu said gently.

The great house was so still that only the two of them might have been in it. The walls were thick, and court led to court. In this wide room the heavy tables and chairs stood as they had stood for centuries, and they two human beings were only two in the long chain of men and women who had lived under the huge beams upholding the vast roof. But something new was here now. The order of the old life was broken.

"Yes, certainly she is nothing unusual, this girl Jasmine," Mr. Wu went on apologetically.

"If she has won your love," Madame Wu said with her strange new gentleness, "then she is unusual."

Mr. Wu looked startled. "Are you feeling well, Mother of my sons?" he inquired. "Your voice sounds weaker than I remembered."

"I never felt stronger in my life," Madame Wu replied. "Tell me more about this girl whom you love."

Mr. Wu hesitated. "I am not sure I love her," he said. "That is, I do not feel toward her at all as I have ever felt toward you. I have no respect for her as I have for you. I do not admire her. She has no learning. I would not ask her advice about anything."

He felt more at ease when he saw Madame Wu's face warmer than usual, and her eyes encouraging. She was not at all angry. "Your common sense is superb," he said. "Shall I go on?"

"Please do, Father of my sons. Tell me how she affects you. Then perhaps I can help you to know whether you truly love her."

"Why are you interested?" he asked.

"Put it that I feel I did you wrong in arranging for Ch'iuming coming," she said.

"You meant well," he said courteously.

"I acted selfishly," she said, more gently still.

It was the first time she had ever acknowledged herself wrong in anything she did, and he was much moved.

"There remains no one like you," he told her with some of his old impetuosity. "I still say that had it not been for your fortieth birthday I would not have known there was another woman in the world."

She smiled again. "Alas, for women the choice is only between this fortieth birthday—or death." Had she loved him, she would have chosen death rather than Jasmine in this house.

"Do not mention death," he said, still courteously. "Well, you ask me how this girl affects me. You know—she makes me feel strong. Yes, that is the effect she has on me."

"Strong?" Madame Wu repeated.

"She is so little, so ignorant, so weak," Mr. Wu said. A thick, soft smile crept about his lips. "No one has ever taken proper care of her. Really, she is a child. She has had no shelter. No one has ever truly understood her. She seems simple and ordinary, but there are qualities in her heart. She is not, you understand, a creature of high intelligence. But she has deep emotions. She needs constant guidance."

Madame Wu listened to this with amazement. Never in her life had she heard Mr. Wu speak of anything except his own needs and desires.

"You really love her!" she exclaimed.

There was admiration in her voice, and Mr. Wu responded to it proudly and modestly. "If what I have told you is love, then I do love her," he replied.

They had never been so near to each other as they now were. She had not known that he had this heart in him. He was made new, too. This perception filled her with astonishment. It was not a wonder that a man like André should have wakened love in her. But that this Jasmine, this common, rosy little street girl, this creature of ignorance and earthy innocence, should have roused in Mr. Wu something of the same energy was a miracle.

"You do not mind?" Mr. Wu said. His face, turned towards her, was tender and pleading.

"I rejoice," she said quickly.

They rose at the same instant and met in the middle of the sunlight upon the floor. Her warmth rushed out to him, and his replied. He seized her hands, and for that swift moment they were one, his eyes looking into hers. She longed to tell him why she rejoiced, and why they were so near. She longed for him to know that she understood this miracle in him that was love, whether it came through a great man or through a girl from a brothel. Priest or prostitute, the miracle was the same. It had reached her, hidden in her secret courts, and it had reached him in a flower house and had changed them both. But she knew that she could never make him understand the miracle. She must only help to make it complete for him.

"There is no woman on earth like you," he said.

"Perhaps there is not," she agreed, and gently she withdrew her hands from his.

It was at this moment that Ying came upon them. According to her usual habit she had first peeped round the corner of the door to see what they were doing. She was amazed and

263

then delighted to see them holding hands. Surely this meant reconciliation and that the girl from the brothel would be sent away! She stepped back and coughed, and then appeared again with her urgent message.

"Lady, a man has come running at the gate to say that Madame Kang is in labour and it goes badly with her and Mr. Kang asks your immediate presence as her sister-friend."

Madame Wu rose at once from her chair, to which she had returned at the cough. "Oh, Heaven," she murmured, "is it so! Did the man say what the trouble is?"

"The child refuses to be born," Ying said dolefully. "It will not leave the womb."

"I must go at once," Madame Wu exclaimed. She made haste to the door and there stopped for an instant to speak again to Mr. Wu. "And you, Father of my sons, let down your heart and be at ease. The young girl shall come quietly into your court. I will myself silence all tongues. I ask only one thing—that Ch'iuming be allowed to leave."

"Indeed, I am quite willing for her to remain," Mr. Wu said kindly. "She is very good, and where would she now go if you send her away?"

"I shall not send her away," Madame Wu replied. "When I return I will decide her life. For the present, let her move into my own court." She turned to Ying. "You hear what I say, Ying. Let it be so."

Ying by now was standing flat against the wall, clinging with her nails to the bricks. "Is the whore to stay?" she wailed.

"She is now not that," Madame Wu replied with sternness. "She is the choice of my lord."

With these words she made haste away, and within a very few minutes she was seated in her sedan chair, lifted upon the shoulders of the bearers, and carried through the streets.

"We borrow your light—we borrow your light——" the bearers chanted while they strode along, and the crowd parted before the urgency of their cry.

12

THE House of Kang was all in turmoil. This Madame Wu heard and saw the moment her sedan was lowered in the outer court. The young slave girls and the bondmaids were running everywhere, crying and reproving one another, and men servants stood silent and distraught. When the head steward saw Madame Wu he ran forward and, bowing, he begged her to come at once to the inner court. She followed him, and at the sight of her the confusion grew quiet. All eyes were fixed on her with fresh hope. Her wisdom was known, and her deep affection for the mistress of the house was trusted.

"She reads many books," one woman whispered to another. Out of these books, they hoped, she might know what to do.

In the main room of the inner court Mr. Kang sat weeping. Madame Wu had seen him often through many years, but never had she spoken a word to him nor heard his voice directed to her. They had bowed across rooms to each other, and at the weddings of Meng and Linyi they had bowed as outer relatives do. But she knew him only through her friend, his wife.

Yet this meant she knew him very well. She knew what he liked to eat, how he liked duck seasoned with wine and garlic, and that he did not like limed eggs, and that he could eat seven pork-stuffed rolls at a meal, and that it took two catties of wine to make him drunk, and that when he was drunk he only went to sleep and was never fierce. She knew that he was proud of the number of his children, but that if any of them cried in his presence he sent it away. She knew that he left his slippers at his wife's bedside every night, and when he did not it meant he was at a flower house, and so his wife cried half the night through, and this made him angry. She knew that he had a black mole over his heart, which was a sign of long life, and she knew he suffered from wind in his bowels, and she knew that when storms blew from the north, bringing sand from the deserts, his eyelids itched, and she knew that his cheeks broke into a red rash when he ate crabs, but still he ate crabs. That is, Madame Wu knew everything about this man who sat with his fat hands on his knees weeping because his wife was dying. But of her he knew nothing except what all the town knew, that she had chosen a concubine for her husband when she was forty years old.

He rose when he saw her come in, and the round tears ran down his yellow cheeks. "She is—is——" he began.

"I know," Madame Wu said, looking away from him. Again she would have marvelled at her friend, that she could love this man, except now she knew how strange love could be. She moved quickly to the satin curtains that hung between this room and the bedroom. "I will go in at once, if you will allow me," she said.

"Go in—go in—save her life," he blubbered.

She went in quickly to Madame Kang's bedroom. The smell of wasted blood was hot in the air. A lighted oil lamp flickered in the cavern of the great bed where she lay, and over her body an old woman bent. Two servant women hovered near, one at her foot and one at her head. Madame Wu brushed away the one at her head and looked down into the deathlike face of her friend.

"Meichen," she said softly.

Slowly Madame Kang opened her eyes. "You," she whispered, "you've come——" Her face wrinkled piteously. "I'm dying——"

Madame Wu held her friend's wrist between her fingers. The pulse was very faint indeed, and she did not answer this.

"Stop pulling at the child," she commanded the midwife.

The old woman looked up. "But it is a boy!" she cried.

"Leave us alone," Madame Wu commanded. "Go out, all of you." She straightened her slender figure.

All the women stared at her. "Do you take responsibility?" the old midwife cried, and pursed her lips.

"I take responsibility," Madame Wu said.

She stood waiting while they went out. Then in the stillness she leaned again over her friend. "Meichen, do you hear me?" she asked clearly.

Madame Kang's eyes had closed, but now with great effort she opened them. She did not speak, but Madame Wu saw consciousness in their depths.

She went on: "You will lie here quietly while I go and fetch some broth for you to drink. You will drink it and you

266

will rest. Then you will feel strong again. When you are strong I will help you give birth to the child. Between us it will be easy."

The eyelids flickered and closed. The faintest of smiles touched Madame Kang's lips. Madame Wu covered her warmly and went into the other room. The midwife had gone away angry, but the servant women were there, pouring tea for Mr. Kang, fanning him, begging him to rest himself. They turned as she came in, but she did not speak to them. She spoke to Mr. Kang.

"I need your help," she told him.

"Will she live?" he cried at her.

"If you help me," she replied.

"Anything, anything!"

"Hush." She stopped his babbling.

Then she commanded a servant, "Bring me a bowl of the best soup you have ready."

"Cow's-flesh broth we have ready and chicken broth and special fish soup."

"The fish soup," she decided, "and put into it two spoonfuls of red sugar. Have it hot."

She turned again to Mr. Kang.

"You are to bring it in—not one of the maids."

"But I——" he sputtered. "I assure you I am clumsy."

"You will bring it in," she repeated.

She went back again into the shadowy room, and once more she took Madame Kang's wrist between her fingers. The pulse was as it had been, but not weaker. She stood waiting, and soon she heard Mr. Kang's heavy footsteps tiptoeing into the room. In his two hands he held the jar of hot soup.

"We will put the soup into the teapot," she decided. Swiftly she emptied the tea into a brass spittoon and, taking the jar from him, she poured the soup into the teapot.

Then she turned again to the bed.

"Meichen," she said, "you have only to swallow." She tested the heat of the soup in her own mouth, and then she put the spout of the teapot to Madame Kang's lips and allowed the soup to trickle into her mouth. Madame Kang did not open her eyes, but she swallowed again and again as many as five or six times.

"Now rest," Madame Wu commanded.

She did not speak to Mr. Kang. No, she kept him there

standing, watching. She set the teapot on the table, and she turned back her satin sleeves and tied round her waist a towel that was hanging on a chair. He watched her, his eyes staring in horror.

"I ought not to be present," he whispered.

But she motioned him to come nearer, and in deep horror he obeyed her. He had begotten many children, but never had he seen what his begetting did. In carelessness and pleasure had he begotten.

Madame Wu turned back the covers, and she leaned over her friend.

"Meichen," she said clearly, "give yourself no trouble. Allow your body to rest. I will work for you."

But in spite of her words, the moment she touched the sore flesh, Madame Kang groaned. Mr. Kang slapped his hands to his mouth and turned his head away.

"Hold her hands," Madame Wu said to him. "Give her your strength."

He could not disobey her. Her great eyes were fixed on him with stern power. He stepped forward and took his wife's hands. And this, this alone, could have made Madame Kang open her eyes. She, feeling her hands in those she knew so well, opened her eyes.

"You," she gasped, "you—Father of my sons!"

At this moment of recognition Madame Wu slipped her strong narrow hands round the child, and Madame Kang screamed.

Mr. Kang burst into sweat. He groaned and clenched his hands round his wife's. "If you will only live now," he muttered through his teeth, "I swear, I swear——"

"Swear—nothing," she gasped. "I am glad—your child."

"Children are nothing to me beside you," he shouted. "If you die I will hang myself." The sweat ran down his face.

"Then you do—love me?" Her voice was so faint, it came in such breaths, that for a moment Madame Wu was afraid of what she had undertaken.

"Heart of my heart," Mr. Kang was crying. "Don't die—don't die——"

"I won't die," Madame Kang said aloud.

At this moment Madame Wu moved the child out of her body. A gush of blood flowed, but Madame Wu staunched it with handfuls of cotton that the midwife had put by the bed.

Mr. Kang still clutched his wife's hands. "Is it over?" he mumbled.

"All over," Madame Wu said.

"The child?" Madame Kang whispered.

Madame Wu wrapped the small torn body in the towel she took from her waist. "The child is dead," she said quietly, "but you two do not need this child."

"Certainly not," Mr. Kang babbled. "Meichen, I beg you —no more children. Never, never, I promise you——"

"Hush," Madame Wu said sternly. "Make no promises you cannot keep." She felt the teapot and it was still hot. She put the spout to her friend's lips. "Drink," she said. "You have promised to live."

Madame Kang drank. Her eyes were closed again, but the pulse in her wrist, when Madame Wu felt it, was stronger by the least possible strength.

Madame Wu motioned to Mr. Kang to loose his wife's hands. "She must sleep," she directed. "I will sit here beside her. Do you take the child away for burial."

She took the burden of the dead child and put it into Mr. Kang's arms, and he held it.

"Let this child be the proof of what you have told her," Madame Wu said. "Remember for ever his weight in your arms. Remember that he died to save the life of his mother —for you."

"I will remember," Mr. Kang promised. "I promise you I will remember."

"Make no promises you cannot keep," Madame Wu said again.

Through the day she sat there and through the night that followed. Servants brought her food and hot tea, but she allowed them to come only to the door. Mr. Kang came in to thank her and to look at his wife while she slept. For Madame Kang slept, not opening her eyes even when she drank hot broth. Into this broth Madame Wu put the herbs which thicken the blood so that it will not flow, and she put in the dust of certain moulds which prevent poisoning. These things she knew from her ancient books, and they were not common knowledge.

Meng and Linyi had come back to their mother, but even them she would not allow to enter this room. She let in only so much air through the window as she needed for her own breathing and for her friend's, for the wind was cool and she did not want a brazier brought, lest charcoal fumes foul the air.

Under her silken quilts Madame Kang slept, washed and clean and fed every hour or two with the medicines and the broth, and hour by hour she returned again to life.

On the morning of the second day, when Madame Wu was certain of the pulse in her friend's wrists, she left the room at last. Outside the door Mr. Kang still sat waiting alone. He had not washed himself, nor had he eaten or slept, and all pretence and courtesy and falsity had left him. He was tired and frightened and worn down to his true being. Madame Wu saw this and took pity on him and sat down in another chair.

"I owe her life to you," Mr. Kang said, hanging his head.

"Her life must not be put into this danger again," Madame Wu said gently.

"I promise——" Mr. Kang began, but Madame Wu put up her hand.

"Can you keep that promise when she is well again?" she asked. "And if you can, how will you keep it? Have I brought her back to life only to be sad and sorrowful because you run hither and thither to flower houses? Will it be any comfort to her that you spare her children only to sow wild seed elsewhere? It is unfortunate that she loves you so much, unless you also love her."

"I do love her," Mr. Kang protested.

"But how much?" Madame Wu pressed him. "Enough to make her life good?"

He stared at her, and she gazed back at him, her eyes very great and dark. "Better that she dies if she is to be always sorrowful," she said calmly.

"I will not make her sorrowful," he said.

His look faltered, he pulled his lip with his two fingers. "I didn't know——" he began. "I never thought—she never told me——"

"What?" Madame Wu asked. She knew, but for the good of his soul she forced him to say on.

"I never knew about life," he mumbled. "How hard it comes—it costs too much."

"Too much," she agreed. "But she has loved you more than it cost."

"Has she suffered like this each time?" he asked.

"Like what?" she pressed him again.

"Near to death——"

"Birth for any woman is always near to death," she replied. "Now for her it has become either birth or death. You must take your choice. You can no longer have both."

He put his hand over his eyes. "I choose her life," he muttered, "always—always——"

She rose silently while he hid his eyes and went out of the room. She would never perhaps see him again. In their life men and women remained apart from each other, and she might never come into his presence. It was not necessary. This coarse, simple man was now terrified by love, his own love for his wife.

So Madame Wu went home, very tired and not a little sickened by all she had seen and done. To step again into her own court, clean and still, was to bathe her soul. Here André had been with her, here he had walked and talked. Could the communion she felt with him now have anything in common with the crude heart of Mr. Kang and his love for his wife?

She went into the library and warmth wrapped her about. Ying had lit the brazier, and the heat from it shimmered above the coals. At the far window sunlight poured through the lattices.

Had she not known the warmth of love in her own heart, she could not by any means have saved Meichen's life. The horror of the flesh would have overwhelmed her, the smell of blood, the stench of death, the ugliness of Mr. Kang's fat, weeping face, the disgust of his thick body, the sordidness of his mind. But she knew that love had lifted her out of herself.

Ying came in, scolding. "You," she cried, "Lady, Lady—look at your coat—why, there's blood on it—and you're so pale——"

She looked down at herself and saw blood on her satin garment. She who was so fastidious now only murmured, "I forgot myself."

* * * * *

It must not be thought that Madame Wu understood fully the change that had taken place in her being. She felt, indeed, that she did not know from one moment to the next

271

where her path lay. She had no plan. But she felt that she was walking along a path of light. While she kept her feet in that path all would be well with her. Should she step into the shadows on either side of the path she would be lost. And the light that lit this path was her love for André. Did she need to know what step must next be taken, she had only to think of him and then she knew.

Thus the next day when Ying brought her the little girl to whom Ch'iuming had given birth she felt a great tenderness for the child. Through this child she had knit Ch'iuming, a stranger, into the house of Wu. Whereas before she had felt this child a new burden, and the whole matter of Ch'iuming nothing but a perplexity, now she felt that there was no burden and no perplexity. She must deal with both mother and child as André would have her do.

"Where is Ch'iuming?" she asked Ying.

"She busies herself about the kitchen and the gardens," Ying said.

"Is she happy?" Madame Wu asked.

"That one cannot be happy," Ying replied. "We ought to send her away. It is bad luck to have a sad face everywhere. It curdles the milk in the breasts of the wet nurses and it makes the children fretful."

"Let Ch'iuming come here to me," Madame Wu said.

This was the next morning after she had been to Madame Kang's. As soon as she had risen she had sent a messenger to ask how her friend did, and good news had come back. Madame Kang had slept well through the night, the blood in her wounds had clotted without fresh flow, and this morning she had eaten a bowl of rice gruel mixed with red sugar. Now she slept again.

The day was still and grey. Yesterday's sunshine was gone, and the smell of mist from the river was in the air. Madame Wu sniffed it delicately into her nostrils.

Near her in a basket bed the little girl lay playing with her hands. She lost them every now and then, and a look of surprise came over her tiny face. Then she saw them again as she waved them, and she stared at them and lost them again. Watching this play, Madame Wu laughed gently.

"How small are our beginnings," she thought. "So I once lay in a cradle—and André also." She tried to imagine André a child, a little child, and she wondered about his mother.

Doubtless the mother knew from the first what her son was, a man who blessed others through his life.

Out of the grey and silent morning Ch'iuming came slipping between the great doors that were closed against the coldness. Madame Wu looked up as she came in. The girl looked a part of the morning mist, all grey and still and cold. Her pale face was closed, and her lips were pale and her eyelids pale and heavy over her dark eyes.

"Look at this child of yours," Madame Wu said. "She is making me laugh because she loses her hands and finds them and loses them again."

Ch'iuming came and stood beside the cradle and looked down, and Madame Wu saw she did not love the child. She was alien to her.

Had it been another day, another time, Madame Wu would have refused to speak of it, or she would have turned her head away, declaring to herself that it was not her affair whether this ignorant girl loved the child. But now she asked, "Can it be you do not love your own child?"

"I cannot feel her mine," Ch'iuming answered.

"Yet you gave birth to her," Madame Wu said.

"It was against my will," Ch'iuming said.

The two women were silent, and each watched the unknowing child. In other days Madame Wu would have reproached the mother for not loving the child, but love was teaching her while she sat silent.

Once, André had told her, there had been a child born of a young mother and an unkown father, and there had been such a radiance about that child that men and women still worshipped him as a god because he was born of love.

"And why was the father unknown?" she had asked.

"Because the mother never spoke his name," André had replied.

"Who cared for and fed them?" she had asked.

"A good man, named Joseph, who worshipped them both and asked nothing for himself."

"And what became of the radiant child?" she had asked.

"He died a young man, but other men have never forgotten him," André had replied.

Remembering what he had said, she felt herself illumined. Why did Ch'iuming not love this child, except that she did not love the father, Mr. Wu? And how did she know she did not love Mr Wu except that she knew one whom she did love?

"Whom do you love?" she asked Ch'iuming suddenly.

She was not surprised to see the young woman's face flush a bright red. Even her small ears grew red.

"I love no one," she said, and lied so plainly that Madame Wu laughed.

"Now how can I believe you?" she said. "Your cheeks and your very ears tell the truth. Are you afraid to let your lips speak it too? You do not love this child—that means you do not love the father. Well, let that be. Love cannot be forced, love cannot be coaxed and teased. It comes out of Heaven, unasked and unsought. Shall I blame you for that? I know my wrong that I did. But when I brought you here I myself did not understand love. I thought men and women could be mated like male and female in the beasts. Now I know that men and women hate each other when they are mated only as beasts. For we are not beasts. We can unite ourselves without a touch of the hands, or a look of the eyes. We can love even when the flesh is dead. It is not the flesh that binds us together."

This was such strange talk, so monstrous from Madame Wu, whose words were always plain and practical that Ch'iuming could only look at her as though she looked at a ghost. But Madame Wu assuredly was no ghost. Her eyes were bright and her whole frame vigorous in spite of its delicacy. She had a new life of some sort, Ch'iuming could see.

"Come," Madame Wu said, "tell me the name in your heart."

"I die of shame," Ch'iuming said. She folded the edge of her coat between her thumb and finger.

"I will not let you die of shame," Madame Wu said kindly.

Thus persuaded, and with much hesitating and doubtfulness, Ch'iuming spoke a few words at a time. "You gave me—as concubine to the old one—but——" Here she stopped.

"But there is someone else to whom you would rather have been given." Madame Wu helped her so far, and Ch'iuming nodded.

"Is he in this house?" Madame Wu asked.

Ch'iuming nodded again.

"Is he one of my sons?" Madame Wu asked.

This time Ch'iuming looked up at her and began to weep.

274

"It is Fengmo," Madame Wu said and knew it was, and Ch'iuming went on weeping.

What a tangle was here, what a confusion between men and women, Madame Wu told herself. This was all the fruit of her own stupidity, without love!

"Do not weep any more," she said to Ch'iuming. "This is all my sin, and I must make amends somehow. But it is not clear to me yet what must be done."

At this Ch'iuming fell on her knees and put her head on her hands on the floor. "I said I should die of shame," she murmured. "Let me die. There is no use for a creature like me."

"There is use for every creature," Madame Wu replied, and lifted Ch'iuming up. "I am glad you told me," she went on. "It is well for me to know. Now I beg you, wait patiently here in this house. Light will be given me, and I shall know what I ought to do for you. In the meantime, help me to care for the foundlings that I have taken. It will be of great use to me if you will care for them for me. They are here, and I have not enough time to look after them."

At the mention of them Ch'iuming wiped her eyes. "I will tend the foundlings, Lady," she said. "Why not? They are sisters of mine." She stooped and lifted her child out of the cradle. "I will take this child with me—she is a foundling too —orphan, I suppose, since her mother cannot love her, poor toad."

Madame Wu did not answer. Where happiness could be found for Ch'iuming she did not know. Time must discover it.

.   .

From the central courts of the house Madame Wu considered the family as the days passed into weeks and months.

"Were I evil," she thought one day, "I could be likened to a spider weaving my web around all these in our house."

A bird sang in the bamboos. She heard its unfamiliar voice and knew what it was. Twice a year the brown bulbul from India passed this way. Its voice was tuneful but harsh. It marked the coming of spring, and that was all.

She mused on. "And how do I know that I am not evil? How do I know that what I consider good is truly good?"

As was her habit she put this question to her memory of André.

One day, she remembered very well, they had been sitting here in the library where she now sat, he on one side of the great carved table and she on the other, not opposite so that they had to look into each other's faces, but with the table between and both facing the open doors into the court. It was a day as fine as this, the air exceedingly clear, and the sunshine so strong that the colours in the stones that floored the court, usually grey, showed tints of blue and rose and veins of silver. Her orchids were blooming a dark purple. In the pool the goldfish darted and flung themselves against the sunbeams slanting into the water.

André had been telling her an ancient legend of the fall of man into evil. It came about, he said, by the hand of a woman, Eve, who gave man forbidden fruit.

"And how was this woman to know that the fruit was forbidden?" Madame Wu had inquired.

"An evil spirit, in the shape of a serpent, whispered it to her," André had said.

"Why to her instead of to the man?" she had next inquired.

"Because he knew that her mind and her heart were fixed not upon the man, but upon the pursuance of life," he had replied. "The man's mind and heart were fixed upon himself. He was happy enough, dreaming that he possessed the woman and the garden. Why should he be tempted further? He had all. But the woman could always be tempted by the thought of a better garden, a larger space, more to possess, because she knew that out of her body would come many more beings, and for them she plotted and planned. The woman thought not of herself, but of the many whom she would create. For their sake she was tempted. For their sake she will always be tempted."

She had looked at him. How well she remembered the profound and sad wisdom in his dark eyes! "How is it you know women so well?" she had asked.

"Because I live alone," he had replied. "Early I freed myself."

"And why did you free yourself?" she asked. "Why did you remove yourself from the stream of life? Do we not all belong in it? Can it be right for any to free himself from it?"

For the only time in the months she had known him she

had seen him in doubt. "You have put the one question which I have never been able to answer," he had replied. "I freed myself first out of vanity. Yes, that I know and acknowledge. When I was like other men, about to marry and beget children, I thought myself loved by a woman. But God gave me a sight into human beings too quick for my own happiness. I saw her like Eve, planning for other human beings whom she was to create—with some small help from me, of course, but which nevertheless she would make in her own body. And I saw my small part, so brief a satisfaction of the flesh, and all my life then spent in digging and delving, like Adam, in order that our garden might be bigger and the fruits more rich. So I asked myself if it was I she loved, and the answer was, perhaps—but only for the moment, because she needed to be served. So I said to myself, 'Shall I not rather serve God, who asks nothing of me except that I do justly and walk humbly before him?' On that day I became a priest."

"And have you been happy?" she had asked him with a little malice.

"I have possessed myself," he had replied. . . .

Now, alone in the library where nowadays she always sat because his presence was there too, she pondered upon the man and the woman. The woman Eve, she considered, must not be blamed because into her had been put the endless desire to carry on life. The man left to himself would never go further than himself. He had made the woman a part of himself, for his own use and pleasure. But she, in all her ignorance and innocence, used him in her endless creation of more life. Both were tools, but only the woman knew she was a tool and gave herself up to life.

"Here," she told André, "is the difference between man and woman, even between you and me."

The air came in mild and soft as she sat alone, and no wind blew. A small blue-tailed lizard came out from the crevice between the brick wall and the stone floor, and lay basking in a bar of sunlight. She sat so still it thought her part of the room, and in its meagre way it made merry, turning its flat head this way and that and frisking its bright tail. Its eyes were shining and empty. She did not move. It was good luck to have small harmless animals about a house. They felt the house eternal and made their home in it.

She mused on, motionless while the lizard played. Such, then, was the unhappiness that lay between men and women. Man believed in his own individual meaning, but woman knew that she meant nothing for herself, except as she fulfilled her place in creating more life. And because men loved women as part of themselves, and women never loved men except as part of what must be created, this was the struggle that made man for ever dissatisfied. He could not possess the woman because she was already possessed by a force larger than his own desire.

Had she not created even him? Perhaps for that he never forgave her, but hated her and fought her secretly, and dominated her and oppressed her and kept her locked in houses and her feet bound and her waist tied, and forbade her wages and skills and learning, and widowed her when he was dead, and burned her sometimes to ashes, pretending that it was her faithfulness that did it.

Madame Wu laughed aloud at man and the lizard rushed into hiding.

Once, when André had sat in the chair across from hers, she had said to him, "Is man all man and is woman all woman? If so, they can never come together, since he lives for his own being and she lives for universal life, and these are opposite."

André had answered gravely enough, "God gave us each a residue for our own; that is, a part simply human, and neither male nor female. It is called the soul. It is unchanging and unchangeable. It can comprehend also the brain and its functions."

"But a woman's brain is not the same as a man's?" she had asked.

"It is the same only when it is freed from the needs of the flesh," André had replied. "Thus a woman may use her brain only for her female duties, and a man may use his only in pursuing woman for himself. But the brain is a tool, and it may be put to any use that the creature wishes. That I cut cabbages with a fine knife is not to say that I cannot use that knife to carve an image of the Son of Man. If the Son of Man is in my heart, and within the vision of my soul's sight, then I will use my tool, the brain, to make him clear."

"The soul, then, is a residue neither male nor female," she had repeated.

"It is so," André had replied.

"And what is the soul in its stuff?" she had pressed him on.

"It is that which we do not inherit from any other creature," he had said. "It is that which gave me my own self, which shapes me a little different from all those who came before me, however like to them I am. It is that which is given to me for my own, a gift from God."

"And if I do not believe in God?" she had inquired.

"It does not matter whether you believe or not," he had answered. "You can see for yourself that you are like no other in this world, and not only you, but the humblest and the least beautiful creature also has this precious residue. If you have it, you know it exists. It is enough to know that. Belief in its giver can wait. God is not unreasonable. He knows that for belief we like to see with the eyes and hear with the ears, that we like to hold within our hands. So does the child also know only what its five senses can tell it. But other senses there are, and these develop as the being grows, and when they are fully developed we trust them as once we trusted only our senses."

Remembering these words of his, she looked across the table. The chair was empty, and she heard no voice. But his face was as clear to her with its grave smile, his voice as deep as ever she had seen or heard.

"I only begin to understand," she murmured. "But I do begin. And with my soul I thee love."

Was it not possible that there could be love and friendship between souls?

"It is possible," she told him.

.   .   .   .   .

Now Madame Wu was a practical woman, and what she learned, she put to use. Within this house, which was her world, there were two disordered beings—that is, two who were not in right relation to the house and therefore to the universe. These two were Rulan and Linyi.

Without haste, and allowing many days to pass, she nevertheless approached the day when she chose in her own mind to speak with them. and first she would speak with Rulan, who was the elder.

It had been many months since Tsemo and Fengmo had left the home. Letters came to Madame Wu regularly, for the two were good sons. These letters were addressed to their father and to her, and after she had read them first and pondered over them, she sent them to Mr. Wu. After he had read them he sent them to Liangmo, who more and more was taking over all the duties of the lands and shops, in preparation for the day when he would be the head of the family, and he read them and then put them in the family records.

From these letters Madame Wu had discerned clearly that her two sons were growing in opposite ways. Fengmo had wished to go abroad to study. She had given her permission and had sent the money which he required. There was some haste, he said, for the ocean roads were closing because of approaching war, and were he not to be caught, he must set sail without taking the long inland journey back to his home.

Had he been an only son Madame Wu would never have allowed this, but since she had so many sons she did not press him to return before he went. He had set sail on a late winter day, he had crossed the seas in safety, and his letters now bore a strange postmark and stamp. These were American, but for this Madame Wu cared nothing. All outer countries were equally interesting and even alike to her, if they lay beyond the four seas. Fengmo pursued the studies which André had begun. Madame Wu was relieved to see that they had nothing to do with priesthood and religions. They had nothing to do with gods, and everything to do with men.

But Tsemo had not asked to cross the waters. Instead, he had gone to the capital and there had found a good place through his family's wealth and influence. This did not amaze either Mr. Wu or Madame Wu herself, for however large her mind was, still it seemed only natural to her that everywhere the family should be known. Then Tsemo wrote the real reason why he had been so fortunate. Were there to come the war which threatened, the government would retreat inland, and there it would depend very much on the highest citizens and their families, of whom in their province the Wu family was the greatest and most ancient. Tsemo was given much preference, therefore, and had to endure jealousy and envy and some malice from others who were put aside. But he was young and hard and drove his own way for himself.

Madame Wu could not discover from his letters what he

was. Fengmo she understood better. In his own way he was opening his mind and heart even as she had done. He was growing into a man and, more than that, his own residue, as André had called it, was growing also. But Tsemo seemed possessed. What possessed him she did not know.

The matter of Tsemo was hastened by the sudden news of attack by the East Ocean people that year on the coast. Madame Wu heard this, and she sent for newspapers, which she never read usually, to discover what had taken place. What she read was common enough in the history of the country. So other attacks had been made in many previous centuries by other peoples, and the nation had always stood. It would stand now, and she was not troubled. It was not likely that enemies would pierce the hundreds of miles inland to this province where the house of Wu had stood so long. But she was grateful to the past generations in the family that they had not yielded, as so many had, to new times, and so had not pressed towards the sea to build new houses on the coast. The Wu family had built upon its ancestral lands and had remained there. To-day they were safe. True, this enemy attacked also from the air. Yet there were no great cities near here, and it was not likely that the ignorant East Ocean people would know the name of one family above another. Madame Wu felt safe in her own house.

But the attack forced a swift change, nevertheless. The government was moved inland, and Tsemo came with it. He wrote one day in the next early autumn that he would come home for ten or twelve days.

With this letter Madame Wu knew she must not delay the matter of Rulan. She sent for the young woman by Ying as messenger.

Now it is not to be supposed that in all these months Madame Wu had not seen her daughter-in-law. She had seen Rulan often. At the table she had seen her among the others, and at the usual festivals of spring and winter Rulan was there, always quiet and sober in her dress. There were also times when Madame Wu had wished some writing done for the records of the family and for the harvests, and she had called upon Rulan for this, because of them all Rulan brushed the clearest letters. She had been kind to her young daughter-in-law at all times, and once she had even said, "It is well enough to have one daughter-in-law who is learned."

To this Rulan had replied with only a few necessary words of thanks.

But at no time had Madame Wu drawn the girl out of her place in the family. Now, with Tsemo's last letter in her hands, she knew the time had come.

Rulan walked quietly through the courts. She no longer wore the hard leather shoes which she had brought with her from Shanghai. Instead she wore velvet ones, cloth-soled. Madame Wu did not hear her footsteps, and when the tall shadow fell across the floor she looked up in surprise.

"Daughter, how softly you walk!" she exclaimed after greetings.

"I put aside my leather shoes, Mother," Rulan replied. She sat down, not sidewise, but squarely on her chair, which was against a side wall and so was lower than the one Madame Wu used. They sat in the sitting-room, not in the library.

Madame Wu did not at once approach what was in her mind to say. Instead she said courteously, "It has been in my thoughts these several weeks to ask about your family in Shanghai. When the enemy attacked, did they escape?"

"My father took the household to Hong Kong," Rulan replied.

"Ah, a long way," Madame Wu said kindly.

"But not long enough," Rulan said with some energy. "I have told my father so."

"You believe that the enemy will dare to attack so far?" Madame Wu inquired. She could not but be impressed with the girl's quickness.

"It will be a long war," Rulan replied.

"Indeed!" Madame Wu remarked.

"Yes," Rulan went on, "for it has been long in preparation."

"Explain this to me, if you please," Madame Wu said. The girl's certainty amused her.

So Rulan explained: "Mother, the East Ocean people have long been afraid, centuries afraid. And of what? Of foreign attack. They have seen one country after another attacked and possessed. Out of the West have the conquerors come. Even when Genghis Khan came and conquered our nation, the East Ocean people began to be afraid. Then men came out of Portugal and Spain, out of Holland and France, and took countries for themselves. And England took India, and we have been all but taken, too, again and again, by these greedy Westerners. 'Why,' thus the East Ocean people reason, 'should we be spared?' So out of fear they have set out to seize lands and peoples for their own, and we are their nearest neighbour."

This was monstrous talk for a young woman, and Madame Wu was amazed by it. Even André had not said these things.

"Where did you get all this knowledge?" Madame Wu asked.

"Tsemo writes me every week," Rulan said.

Madame Wu felt her heart loosen with relief. She smiled. "You two," she said, "are you good friends again?"

Rulan's cheeks grew red. By nature she was pale, except for her crimson lips, and the flush was plain enough, but she did not turn her head away.

"We agree wonderfully when we are not together," she said. "As soon as he comes we will quarrel again—I know it. I have told him so. We both know it."

"But if you know it," Madame Wu said with laughter, "can you not guard against it? Which of you begins it first—you or he?" In spite of her amusement she was pleased that the girl did not try to hide anything.

"Neither of us knows," Rulan said. "We have sworn to each other this time, in our letters, that whoever begins, the other will speak to stop it. But I have no faith in our ability. I know Tsemo's temper. It comes up like thunder in the summer. Without reason it is there, and when he is angry, then I am angry." She paused and frowned. She searched herself, and Madame Wu gave her time. She went on, "There is something in me which he hates. Now that is true. He says there is nothing, but there is. When we are parted he does not feel it. When we come together it is there. If I knew what it was I would take a knife and cut it out of myself."

"Perhaps it is not something which is there, but something which is not there," Madame Wu said gently.

Rulan lifted her head. Her eyes, which were her beauty, looked startled. "That I never thought of," she said. Then she was downcast again. "But that will make it very hard. It would be easier to take something out of myself that I have than to put something in which I have not."

"This need not be true," Madame Wu told her. "It depends

283

altogether on your love for Tsemo. If you think of your marriage as something only for your two selves, well, then you must always quarrel unless you can determine to stay apart from each other."

"You mean——" Rulan said and could not finish. In the female part of her being she was very shy.

"I do mean that," Madame Wu said. She went on speaking out of a wisdom which she knew came to her from her own knowledge of love. Now she knew that between men and women there is no duty. There is only love—or no love.

She reached for her silver pipe and began to fill it slowly. She did not look at her daughter-in-law for a while. Instead she gazed into her court, where the orchids were yellow at this season. The bamboos fluttered their leaves like tassels in the slight wind. It was the sort of day that she and André had loved best because of its peace.

"In the first place you must know that neither of you owes anything to the other," she began at last.

Rulan interrupted her with surprise. "Mother, this is the strangest thing I ever did hear said from a mother-in-law to her son's wife."

"I have learned it only recently," Madame Wu said. She smiled with secret mischief. "Credit me, child, that I am still learning!"

She was pulling Rulan by the heart. The girl had come prepared for her mother-in-law's anger and humbled to receive it. Now hope moved in her. It was not anger that she was to receive, but wisdom. She leaned forward like a tall lily waiting for rain.

"Trouble between men and women always arises from the belief that there is some duty between them," Madame Wu went on. "But once having given up that belief, the way becomes clear. Each has a duty only to himself. And how to himself? Only to fulfill himself. If one is wholly fulfilled, the other is fulfilled also."

She paused, lit her pipe, smoked two puffs, and blew out the ash. Then she went on, "And why is this true? Because, in the words of sages, 'The husband is not dear for the husband's sake but for the self's sake, and the wife is not dear to him for her sake, but for his own sake.' It is when the one is happy that the other is happy, and it is the only happiness possible for both."

Rulan sat motionless, listening.

Madame Wu went on, "As for procreation, it is a duty not to him nor to you. It is your common duty to our kind. Where you have made your mistake is that you have confused the bearing of children with your love for Tsemo. And by your confusion you have confused Tsemo. That is why he is so easily angry with you."

"Mother," Rulan begged her, "speak on to me. You are coming into the heart."

"You and Tsemo departed from the usual tradition," Madame Wu said plainly. "You chose each other because you loved each other. This is dangerous because the chances of what may be called happiness are much lessened thereby. You and Tsemo thought only of yourselves, not of your children, not of your family, not of your duty to carry on your kind. You thought only of yourselves, as two beings separate from all others. But you are not separate, except in a small part of yourselves. Now you are trying to force all your lives into that small part of yourselves. The begetting, conceiving, and bearing of your children, the living together in all ways of eating and sleeping and dressing and coming in and going out—all you are trying to force into that small separate place. But it will not contain so much. It is crowded, and you are choking each other at your sources. You are too close. You will hate each other because that part of you which is you, yourselves—your residue—your soul—has no space left in which to breath and to grow."

Now she looked at Rulan. The girl's whole being was listening.

"Separate yourself, my child," she said. "Let him separate himself. Accept as a matter of course, as a duty to our kind, that you will bear children. They are not his children nor yours. They are the children of the race. Bear them as naturally as you breathe and eat and sleep and perform all your other functions as a physical creature. Begetting and conceiving have nothing to do with your souls. Do not test the measure of his love for you by the way in which he expresses his body's heat. He is not thinking of you at those times. He is thinking of himself. Think you also of yourself. Does one man's passion differ from another's? It does not. And no more does one woman bear children differently from another. In such things we are all alike. Do not imagine

285

that in this he or you is different from the commonest man and woman." She paused, and a strange feeling of exhaustion came over her.

"You make me feel that marriage is nothing," Rulan said in a low voice. "I might as well have been married to anyone as to Tsemo."

Energy returned to Madame Wu. "I have not finished," she said. "In one sense you are right. Any healthy young woman can marry any healthy young man and both can fulfil their duty to life. For this reason it is well that our old traditions be maintained. Older persons can certainly choose better for the race than the young ones can for themselves. Consider Liangmo and Meng—they are happy. But certainly they have not absolute happiness, as you and Tsemo demand. They accept the bearing of children as their whole life. Liangmo has no other ambition than to be a good husband and father. Neither of them asks more. For this it is best that the elders choose the two who are to marry, if the two are like Liangmo and Meng."

"But we are not like them," Rulan said with some heat.

"You are not," Madame Wu agreed. "You wish friendship and companionship between your two individual selves. Ah, you ask very much of marriage, my child. Marriage was not designed for this extra burden."

"What should we have done? Lived without marriage?" Rulan inquired without meaning rudeness.

"Perhaps—perhaps." Madame Wu was surprised to hear herself say. "But that, too, is difficult, since you are man and woman, and the body demands its own life."

She paused, searching for words which were never in her before, and she found them. "You and Tsemo are very lucky. You love each other in all ways. Then love each other, my child! Life is too short for such love. Love one another and do not waste one hour in anger. Divide your love from your passion and let there be no confusion between the two. Some day, when the division is clear and established by habit, when your children are born and growing and your bodies are old, and passion gone, as, mercifully, it does go, you will know the best love of all."

She was suddenly intensely lonely for André, and the knowledge that never again would she look upon his living face pierced her with an agony she had not yet felt. She closed her eyes and endured the pain. Then after a while she felt Rulan take her hand and press it to her cheeks. She felt one warm cheek and then the other. But still she did not open her eyes.

"And in secret the woman has to lead," she said. "In secret the woman always has to lead, and she must, because life rests upon her, and upon her alone. I warn you, my son will be of no help to you in making your marriage happy."

When she opened her eyes again the room was empty. Rulan had gone.

· · · · ·

That night when Ying undressed her for bed Madame Wu spoke, after silence so long and deep that Ying had not dared to break it with her usual chatter. "Ying!"

"Yes, Mistress?" Ying looked into the mirror over Madame Wu's head. She was brushing the long black silken hair that was only now beginning to show a few feathers of white at the temples.

"I have a task for you."

"Yes, Mistress?"

"In less than a month my second son will come home."

"I know that, Mistress. We all know it."

"This is the task. Every night when you have finished with me you are to go to my second son's wife and do for her what you used to do for me."

Ying smiled into the mirror, but Madame Wu did not smile back. She went on, not meeting Ying's eyes, "You are to forget nothing that I used to do—the fragrant bath, the scenting of the seven orifices, the smoothing with oil, the perfume in the hair."

"I know, Lady." Ying's voice was warm and intimate. Then she stayed the brush. "What if she forbids me?" she asked. "That one cares nothing for her beauty."

"She will not forbid you," Madame Wu said. "She needs help, poor child, as all women need it. And she knows it now."

"Yes, Mistress," Ying said.

13

TSEMO came home on the fifth day of the ninth moon month. The news of his coming was brought by electric letter to the city and by foot-messenger to the house of Wu, and Mr. Wu himself took the letter to Madame Wu. He did not often enter her courts now for any cause, and when she saw him she knew that it had to do with one of the sons. He held out the sheet of paper.

"Our second son comes home," he said with his wide smile.

She took the letter and read it and turned it over and over in her hands. It was the first time she had ever seen an electric letter. She knew, because once André had explained it, that the paper itself was not blown over the wires as she had imagined it. Not even words were spoken. Symbols were beaten upon a machine, and by these the messages were carried.

"The drums of savages, beaten in the jungle," she had remarked.

"Much that man does is only the refinement of savagery," he had replied.

She recalled these words as she mused over the electric letter. "We must prepare a welcoming feast," she said aloud.

"I shall invite all my friends," Mr. Wu declared.

She proceeded to plan. "We ought also to give a secondary feast for the shop clerks and the farm workers."

"Everything—everything," he declared in his large, lordly manner.

She looked at him from under her half-veiled eyes. He had returned to his old self. Jasmine had done him good. He was reassured of his own worth. His failure with herself, for in his own way he had been mortified that she had rejected him, and his failure with Ch'iuming had done him harm. He was the sort of man who had constantly to feel himself successful with his women. How well she knew, who had for so many years made his success her duty! But Ch'iuming was young and ignorant, and she had not understood these things, and Jasmine was, in the midst of all her falsity, sincere enough

288

in this business by which she earned her rice and roof. Madame Wu felt her secret heart grow light, and also cool and scornful. She felt somewhat ashamed of such malice, although once she would have accepted it as her share of human nature.

"I am not a woman without sin," she had once told Andre. "That is, if I am to accept your measure of sin—the secret thought, the hidden wish. Outer rectitude I can attain, but who can control the heart?"

"A few can also do it," he had replied. "You are one of those few."

She knew that if she were to continue near him she must attain the heights where he lived. He would not come down to her.

So now she spoke patiently with Mr. Wu, who was the father of her sons. "Let everything be as you wish."

He leaned forward, his hands on his fat knees, smiling. He lowered his voice to speak to her in confidence. "It may be you do not know that Tsemo is my favourite son. For that reason I have always been disturbed that his wife is an angry woman. Tsemo should have married someone soft and reasonable."

Madame Wu could not conceal all her barbs. "You mistake Tsemo somewhat," she said. In her own ears she heard her voice too silvery sharp. "He is intelligent. Rulan is also intelligent. I find I think better of her as time goes on."

Mr. Wu looked alarmed, as he always did at the mention of intelligence, and hastily he withdrew. "Well, well," he said, in his usual voice, "I dare say you are right. Then will you arrange matters or shall I?"

"I will order what is to be within the house, and you shall invite the guests and decide the wines," she said.

They bowed and parted, and she knew as he went away that what had been between them was only of the flesh. He was repulsive to her. Yet had they not fulfilled the very duty of which she had spoken to Rulan? They had carried on the family through their generation, they had fulfilled the instincts of their race, and they had freed themselves from each other when this was done. Now she knew that, even as André had discovered for her the residue of her individual self, Jasmine had done the same for Mr. Wu. No ties had been broken, the house continued as before, and their position in it was the same. She felt the wisdom of bringing Jasmine under the roof, this roof wide enough for all of the least of the house of Wu. The supreme sin of giving birth to a nameless and illegitimate child would not be theirs. Jasmine's children would have their place in the human order.

She felt peace upon her as she proceeded to the day's duty. She had no time to-day for herself. She sent for cook and steward and head-waiter, she sent for the cleaning maids and the seamstresses. The children's clothes must be inspected, and those who needed new garments must have them made. Yenmo, her youngest son, must come in from the country.

"It is time," she told the land steward, "that my fourth son return to the home. Affairs are now clear in the family."

The steward laughed. "Madame, this son will be the one to manage the land after you. Our eldest young lord does well in the shops, but the little fourth lord is made for the land."

Madame Wu had not seen her fourth son in many months, and now she felt some wonder in her about him. During the years of change from child to man all males were the same, she had always said. They needed only to be fed, to be taught the same things, to live much in the open air, to be kept away from gambling places and brothels and family dissensions. For this reason she had sent Yenmo into the country to live with country cousins and farmers. Now he must come back and let her take his measure.

"Prepare the two small rooms in my eldest son's east court," she commanded Ying. "They are full of boxes and waste now, and used by no one. Let them be furnished for Yenmo. They shall be his until he marries."

Properly Yenmo should have been placed near his father, but that she would not allow. Neither did she want him too near herself, this hearty lusty growing youth. But Liangmo and Meng would be kind to him, and the children would enjoy him.

Thus everything was prepared. Last of all did Madame Wu herself inspect Rulan. It was the very day of the return. Tsemo would come sometime after midday, but none could tell when, for he must come by boat. It was a pity that the motor-car could not be sent for him, but the road was too narrow and the farmers cried to Heaven if its great wheels ran on their soil. It remained therefore in the special room by the gate where it was kept, a thing for wonder and amazement to all who saw it, but of little real use. Yet Mr. Wu would have felt himself very backward and old-fashioned had he not bought it, and it was comfort even to Tsemo to say carelessly in company, "My father's foreign car——"

So Rulan stood before Madame Wu, very docile and even shy. She had put on a new robe of a clear dark red, and this firm colour suited her pale skin and red mouth. Madame Wu approved its close cut, its length, and did not mention the shortness of the sleeves, since Rulan had beautiful arms and hands. She bade Ying open her jewel box and from it she selected a thick gold ring set with rubies. This ring she put on the middle finger of Rulan's right hand, and Rulan lifted her hand to admire it. "I dislike rings usually, Mother," she said, "but this one I like."

"It suits you," Madame Wu replied, "and what suits a woman makes her beautiful."

Rulan had washed her hair freshly, but she had not oiled it, and it lay on her shoulders as soft as unwound silk. Ying had cut its edge even and smooth. It was a very new fashion for young women to let their hair go unbound, and Madame Wu did not like it. She would have complained had Meng copied it. But to-day she saw that the softness set off Rulan's face, and again she did not speak against it. Whatever made a woman more beautiful was to be accepted.

"Open your mouth," she commanded Rulan. The girl opened her mouth, and Madame Wu peered into it. It was red and clean as a child's and the teeth were white and sound. From this mouth came a sweet, fresh breath.

She lifted the girl's skirts and examined the inner garments. All were clean as snow, all scented, and prettily embroidered.

She lifted the girl's hands and smelled the palms. They were scented, and her hair was scented, and from her body came the delicate scent which once she herself had used.

"You will do well enough, my child," Madame Wu said kindly. "I find no fault with your body. I cannot examine your heart and your mind—these you must examine for me. The body comes first, but the residue is what lasts."

"I have forgotten nothing you told me," Rulan said solemnly.

Now Tsemo was expected any time within four or five

hours, but who could know that while all this was going on in the house of the Wu family he was approaching by sky and not by water? Thus, instead of coming to the land by the river, he came down out of the sky and touched earth just outside the low wall on the south side of the town. When his superior officer in the capital had heard of his return home, the weight of the Wu family in that province was such that he had sent him with a government plane and pilot.

The pilot was concerned when he dropped his passenger upon a field, with no one near to meet him. But Tsemo laughed at him.

"This is my home town," he said. "I can find my own way."

So the pilot took off again into the sky, and Tsemo walked calmly homeward, everybody staring and greeting him as he went and asking him how he came, and goggling and silenced by wonder when he said, "I came by empty air."

Children and idlers ran ahead to tell them at the house of Wu that the Second Lord was coming, but Tsemo walked in such long, strong steps that he was very close behind. Thus Madame Wu and Rulan had barely heard the gateman's wife, who had run in to gasp out her news, when Tsemo himself was at her heels. By right he should have gone first to his father, but be sure Liangmo had written him who was in his father's courts, and he had no mind to see a strange woman before he saw his mother. Therefore he went first to Madame Wu and was confounded to see with her Rulan, his own wife.

It was an awkward moment, for by old tradition he should not greet his wife before his mother. To his surprise Rulan helped him. She fell back gracefully and gave him time and space.

"My son, you have come at last." This was Madame Wu's greeting.

She put out her hands and felt of his arms and his shoulders as mothers do. "You are thinner than you were but sounder," she said. "Harder and healthier," she added, looking at his ruddy face.

"I am well," he said, "but very busy—indeed, busy half to death. And you, Mother, look well—better than when I went away."

This and more passed between them, and still Rulan stood waiting, and Tsemo wondered very much at this patience. It was not like her to be patient. To his further surprise his mother now stepped back and put out her hand and took Rulan's and drew her forward.

"She has been very good," Madame Wu said. "She has been obedient, and she has tried hard and done well."

Nothing could have pleased Tsemo so much as this commendation of his wife by his mother. Like all sons of strong mothers he needed her praise of what he had done. She had never praised Rulan before, and it had been one of the causes of his anger against Rulan that his mother had not praised her. This Madame Wu now understood. She saw the pleasure in his handsome face, in his free smile, in his brightening eyes. He spoke a few words to Rulan, cool as such words should be in the presence of the older generation.

"Ah—you are well?"

"Thank you, I am well—and you?"

These were the few words they spoke with their lips, but their eyes said more. For Rulan lifted her eyes to his, and he saw her more nearly beautiful than he had ever seen her, the red cloth of her gown close fitting about her neck and lending depth to her golden pallor.

He withdrew his eyes and turned to his mother, stammering and blushing. "Mother, thank you very much for taking time to teach her—for taking time to—to—to——"

Madame Wu understood and answered him. "My son, at last I will say, 'You have chosen well.' "

She saw tears come into Rulan's eyes, and a tenderness she had never known before filled her being. How helpless were the young and in spite of all their bravery, how needy of the old to approve them!

"Be tender to the young, they did not ask to be born," André had once said to her. She remembered it well, for on that day she had been angry with Fengmo because he came late.

"Nor did I ask to be born," she had retorted.

He had looked at her with that large deep gaze of his. "Ah, because you have suffered is the one reason why you should never make others suffer," he had said. "Only the small and the mean retaliate for pain. You, Madame, are too high for it."

She had accepted this in silence, swallowing anger. He had gone on, escaping from her into the universe. "And of what meaning is suffering," he had mused, "if it does not teach us, who are the strong, to prevent it for others? We are shown what it is, we taste the bitterness, in order to stir us to the will to cast it out of the world. Else this earth itself is hell."

Now, remembering his words, she felt an immeasurable longing to make these two happy in her house. She took Rulan's hand and Tsemo's hand and clasped them together.

"Your duty to me is done, my son," she said. "Take her to your own courts and spend your next half-hour with her alone. It will be time enough then to go and greet your father."

She watched them go away, hand still in hand, and sat down, smiled, and smoked her silver pipe awhile.

·   ·   ·   ·   ·

For the next ten days the house was a turmoil of feasting. Every relative near and far wished to see Tsemo and talk with him and ask his opinion concerning the new war and the removal of the seat of government inland and what he thought the price of rice would be as a consequence of the disturbances, and whether the foreign white people would fight with the East Ocean dwarfs or against them. No one thought of defeat by the enemy. The only question was whether there should be the open resistance of arms or the secret resistance of time. Tsemo, being young, was for open resistance. Mr. Wu, knowing nothing of such things, followed his mind.

But Madame Wu, sitting among the family, listening, smoking her little pipe, saying nothing except to direct a child to be taken out to make water, or to be put to bed to sleep, or bidding a servant be quiet in filling the tea bowls, or some such thing, knew that for herself she believed that only by secret resistance of time could they overcome this enemy as they had overcome all others. In her own mind she did not favour foreign peoples to come in to help them. Who in this world helped another not of his blood without asking much in return? It was beyond justice to give without getting, outside the family.

But she kept silence. Here she was only a woman, although the most respected under the roof. Long ago in that freedom which she had known only with André, they had argued human nature.

"You believe in God and I believe in justice," she had declared. "You struggle towards one and I toward the other."

"They are the same," he had declared.

To-day, sitting among her family, she felt deeply lonely. Here André had never come and could not come.

"Those foreigners," she said suddenly to Tsemo, "if they come here on our soil can we drive them out again?"

"We can only think of the present, day by day," he declared.

"That is not the way of our people," she replied. "We have always thought in hundreds of years."

"In hundreds of years," he replied, "we can drive them all out."

"In this residue of the individual creature," she had once asked André, "are there colour and tradition and nationality and enmity?"

"No," he had replied. "There are only stages of development. At all levels you will find souls from among all peoples."

"Then why," she had asked, "is there war among people and among nations?"

"Wars," he had replied, "come between those of the lowest levels. In any nation observe how few actually join in war, how unwillingly they fight, with how little heart! It is the undeveloped who love war."

She pondered these things while Tsemo talked briskly of regiments and tanks and bombing planes and all these things which for her had no meaning. At last she forgot herself and yawned so loudly that everyone turned to look at her, and she laughed.

"You must forgive me," she said. "I am getting old, and the youthful pastimes of war do not interest me." She rose, and Ying hastened to her side and, nodding and smiling her farewells, she returned to her own courts.

On the eleventh day Tsemo went away. The airplane returned for him, and this time a great conclave of people from the house and the town gathered to see him fly up. Madame Wu was not one of these. All that he had said during these ten days had fatigued her very much. She felt that it was only folly for a young man to spend his life at these matters of war and death. There was no value here, either for the family or for himself. Life was the triumphant force, and the answer to enemy and to death was life and more life. But when she said this he was impatient with her. "Mother," he cried, "you do not understand."

At this universal cry of youth she had smiled and returned to silence. She bade him good-bye sweetly and coolly, received his thanks, and let him go. She was not sorry to see him gone again. His talk had made the whole house restless, and especially it had made his younger brother afraid. Yenmo had come back, brown and fat as a peasant boy, and taller by inches than when he had gone away. She had not spoken to him beyond the ordinary greetings, preferring to wait until the turmoil was over and she could discover him in quiet. But she saw he was afraid.

So she sat alone in her court, and there Rulan came to her after Tsemo was gone. She came in and knelt at Madame Wu's side and put her head on the elder lady's knees. Madame Wu felt a warm wetness creep through the satin of her robe.

"What are these tears?" she asked gently. "They feel warm."

"We were happy," Rulan whispered.

"Then they are good tears," Madame Wu said. She stroked the girl's head softly and said no more, and after a while Rulan rose, wiped her eyes, smiled, and went away.

.   .   .

If life were known one moment ahead, how could it be endured? The house which had been filled with feasting and pleasure was plunged in the same hour into blackest mourning. Who can know what happened in the clouds? In less than half an hour after Tsemo had climbed towards the early rising sun on that day, the steward came hot foot into the gates and behind him followed all the tenants and farmers of the Wu lands, wailing and tearing their garments and the women loosening their hair. Such noise filled the courts that even Madame Wu heard it. She had just gone into the library to be alone awhile, after Rulan left her, and she heard sobbing and shouting of her name. Instantly she knew what had happened.

She rose and went out of the room and met them at the gate of her court. Mr. Wu was first, the tears streaming down his cheeks. Even Jasmine was there behind others, and the orphan children and the old woman and every servant and follower and neighbour from the street were crowding into the gates left open.

"Our son——" Mr. Wu began, and could not go on.

The steward took up his words. "We saw fire come whirling down out of the sky above the farthest field," he told Madame Wu. "We ran to see what it was. Alas, Madame, a few wires, a foreign engine, some broken pieces of what we do not know—that is all. No body remains."

These words fell upon her heart. But she knew them already.

"There is nothing left even to bury," Mr. Wu muttered. He looked at her bewildered. "How can what was alive and our son, only an hour ago, now be nothing?"

She grieved for him, but first she thought of Rulan. "It is of his young wife we must think now," she reminded Mr. Wu.

"Yes, yes," all agreed. "It may be she has happiness. What a mercy they had ten nights together! If there is a child you will be comforted, Madame, sir——"

Mr. Wu's tears dried in this new hope. "Go to her," he commanded Madame Wu. "Comfort her—we leave her with you."

So Madame Wu went alone to the court where Tsemo had so lately lived with his young wife, and slowly the crowd disappeared. Mr. Wu returned to his own court with Jasmine and shut the gate, and the steward bade the workers return to the land. As for him, he said, he would wait until he had his orders from Madame Wu. He sat down in the gatehouse to wait until such a time as she sent for him.

The children went back to the temple, and there the old priest lit incense and muttered prayers for the dead son.

"In these days," he told the ancient gods, "affairs happen too quickly for us. There is no time to pray for the dying. They live, and they live no more, and it is all we know. Seek for his soul, O you who live in heavenly spaces! Find him among the many and lead him to the ones who will know him and comfort him. And when he is born again, grant that he may be born once more into this family, where he belongs."

So prayed the old priest.

In the court where she had been so happy Rulan sat crouched on the floor beside Madame Wu, her forehead pressed against Madame Wu's hand, which she held. Both were silent. What was there to say? These two women were knit together in love and sorrow. Madame Wu longed to tell Rulan of herself, and how she had looked on André, dead. But she could not tell it, now or ever. Rulan's sorrow was worse than hers. She had buried André's body, and of Tsemo there was nothing left. The winds had taken his fresh ashes and scattered them over the land. The winds had buried him where they would. And what else of Tsemo was left? She, the mother, had the memory of his birth and his babyhood, his boyhood, his young manhood. She had the memory of his voice, arguing, declaring, of his face ardent, confident, handsome; and now she had the knowledge of his death. What had been between her and the son was altogether of the flesh, and it was no more except in the memory of her own flesh.

But for Rulan what was left? Had they, in these ten days, gone beyond the flesh? Did the young wife now hold fast what the mother had not?

It was too soon to ask. She sat silent and motionless, and the warmth from her being flowed into the girl who crouched beside her.

It was Rulan who first moved, who stood, who wiped her face and ceased weeping. "I shall thank you for ever, Our Mother," she said, "for in these ten days we did not quarrel once."

"Are you able now to be alone?" Madame Wu asked. She admired the girl very much, she felt her love grow exceedingly strong.

"I am able," Rulan said. "When I have been alone awhile, Mother, I will come and tell you what I must ask for myself."

"My doors are always open for you," Madame Wu replied. She rose, accepting the help of Rulan's hand. It was hot but strong, and the fingers did not quiver. "Night and day," Madame Wu said, "my doors are open for you."

"I shall not forget," Rulan said.

Madame Wu, walking away, heard the door of Tsemo's court close behind her. She halted and half turned. The girl was not going to shut herself up for some damage? No, she decided, this would not be Rulan's way. She would sit alone and lie alone and sleepless on her bed and alone she would

298

come to life again, somehow. Had Tsemo lived, Madame Wu told herself, they would have quarrelled again and again. The grace of the ten days could not have held. They were too equal, and they loved each other too fiercely. Each wished to subdue the other, and neither could allow freedom. But now they would live for ever in peace.

"In peace!" she murmured. It was the sweetest word upon the human tongue.

. . . . . .

Even though there was no dead body over which to mourn, nevertheless mourning went on for the needful number of days in the house of Wu. A coffin was brought and prepared, and into it were put Tsemo's possessions which he had loved best, and it was closed and sealed. The day of the burial was decided upon by the soothsayers of the town with all that was necessary for grief, and on that day the funeral took place. Tsemo's coffin was buried in the family graveyard on the ancestral lands, and his tablet was set up in the ancestral hall, among those who had died for the hundred years before him.

While this was being done Madame Wu allowed grief everywhere to go on unchecked. She mourned, also, and in her mourning she accepted the help of her friend Madame Kang. There had been little and less going to and fro between the houses. Madame Wu had been aware of it throughout the months, but she had not been inclined to mend it. Her own inner concern, her constant remembering of André, had weaned her away from her friend. Moreover, she still thought of that birth night with repulsion.

But the loss of a son is too grave for any breach, and the two ladies came together again, though never closely, and Mr. Kang himself came to the funeral. Had there not been the death, Madame Kang could not have entered the house with such goodwill. But she put aside all else and came with her old hearty way to Madame Wu's court, crying aloud as she came.

"Our children grew up together," she exclaimed, "and I feel as though a son of my own were gone."

Madame Wu knew this was true, and she welcomed her friend, and they sat together in the old way for a while, and Madame Kang insisted on wearing mourning in the funeral procession.

Nevertheless, Madame Wu knew that this friendship had passed. She had entered too deeply into the private life of her friend. Madame Kang could never quite forgive her for this, in spite of gratitude. This gratitude she spoke out freely.

"Had you not come that night, my sister, I would have died. My life is yours."

But there was shyness in her look even when she spoke, and Madame Wu knew that, while she was thankful to be living, yet she was unthankful that her friend had been there at the hour of her greatest weakness. There was a little jealousy somewhere in Madame Kang towards Madame Wu, and Madame Wu knew this. She did not blame her friend, but inwardly she withdrew from her. She perfectly understood that, although Madame Kang sincerely grieved because Tsemo was dead, she did not altogether grieve that the Wu house had lost a son. In such sorrow she could be somewhat superior to her friend. Once Madame Wu would have been angry, but now no more. She comprehended the weakness of Madame Kang and gave her no blame.

"Are we to tolerate the stupidity and malice of the small?" she had asked André long ago.

"Yes, because to destroy them would be to destroy ourselves," he had replied. "None of us is so much better or wiser than any other that he can destroy a single creature without destroying something in himself."

"How shall we endure them, then?" she had asked. She remembered with a pang of the heart a child once born to a servant in the house who had been put out of life with her own consent. The child was a girl, deformed and imbecile. She had been told of the birth by Ying, and then Ying had lifted her hand, with the thumb outstretched, and Madame Wu had nodded.

"No one of us can afford to take the life of the least one," André had replied.

She had not had the courage then to tell him of the child. Now, sitting in her sedan, in the procession of her son's funeral, she wished she had told André. The burden of the dead child lay on her at this moment when she had lost her son. She felt a dart of superstition that somehow the early evil had brought the later one. Then she dismissed superstition. She believed in no such causes. Beyond the soul itself, all was chance. In the soul alone was there cause and effect.

300

What was the effect of the child's death upon her? None, she concluded, since at that time she had not understood what she did. Now, understanding, she would not hate her old friend, however small she was in mind.

"Neither can I be compelled to love her any more," she thought with some rebellion.

This rebellion reminded her of André again, and of a passage between them. He had been reading some words from his holy book.

"Love thy neighbour as thyself," he read slowly.

"Love!" she had exclaimed. "The word is too strong."

She had always been exceedingly critical of his holy book, jealous, perhaps, because he read it so much and depended upon it for wisdom. But he had agreed with her. She saw the sudden lifting of his mighty head.

"You are right," he had said. "Love is not the word. No one can love his neighbour. Say, rather, 'Know thy neighbour as thyself.' That is, comprehend his hardships and understand his position, deal with his faults as gently as with your own. Do not judge him where you do not judge yourself. Madame, this is the meaning of the word *love*." He had gone on reading in his immense deep soft voice, whose sound was for ever in her hearing.

The day of this funeral was too fair for young death. The water in ponds was clear and the sunlight was warm and many birds sang. Through the glass window of her sedan Madame Wu saw it all and was made more sad. She thought of Rulan, whose sedan was behind hers, and she looked through the back pane of glass to see if she looked out too. But the curtain was drawn over Rulan's window, and her mind went back to her dead son. And how had it been for him to meet death in the sky, among the clouds? Did he know whom he met? She felt herself in Tsemo, rejoicing in the swiftness and the freedom above the earth. Then the machine had failed. He had trusted too much in machines.

She had said anxiously before he left her, "Can you be safe with only that foreign machine to hold you up?"

He had laughed at her ignorance. "Mother, they are magic!"

So he had cried at her, but the magic had failed. He had been given perhaps a few seconds in which to compress all that was his life. She saw his terror and his rage and then his end. Against the sky's infinity his body hurtled to the earth. She bowed her head and covered her eyes with her hand.

The funeral went on its usual way. There had been many funerals in the family, and she must endure one more, even of her own son. On a day last summer Old Lady's coffin had been taken out of the temple where it waited and had been brought here, too, to the family lands. A marble stone had been set up, smaller than Old Gentleman's but like it. A space lay on Old Gentleman's left for Mr. Wu, and beside that space another for herself, and beyond that space for Liangmo and Meng. Still beyond that was now dug the pit for Tsemo's empty coffin, and it was lowered to the bottom, the white cock killed and its blood spilled out, and the paper utensils burned. A paper airplane had been made, and it too was burned to ashes. When all was done the grave was covered and under the top of it, shaped from a great clod of turf, white paper streamers were fastened. The funeral was over, and the family returned and left the hired mourners wailing behind them.

.   .   .   .

Alone in her room in the night Madame Wu pondered her sorrow. She had not wished to be with anyone when they came home. Mr. Wu would, she knew, immediately seek diversion. Rulan must suffer until she was healed. But Madame Wu lay in her bed and thought of her second son and of his empty place in the house of Wu and of all the sons that would have come from his body and now would never be born. These she mourned for. She sorrowed deeply for all the empty places in the generations. When a young man dies many die with him. She cursed the dangerous machines of foreigners and all wars and ways which take the lives of young men. She blamed herself that she had not kept all sons in this house to live out their lives.

Against the dark curtain of her mind she saw André's great shape. They had been once arguing the matter of Fengmo's learning. "Teach my third son," she had told André, "but teach him nothing that will divide his heart from us."

"Madame!" André had exclaimed. "If you imprison your son he will most surely escape you, and the more you hold him the farther from you he will go."

"You were wrong." she now told the remembered face, so

302

clear against the blackness of her hidden brain. "I did not imprison him, and he has gone the farthest of them all."

The morning woke her early as it always did, and the day was as clear as the one before. She got up restless. Yesterday the countryside had been so beautiful in the midst of her sorrow that she longed to reach beyond the walls. But what excuse had she to leave the house of mourning? She moved about her rooms, not wanting to leave and not wanting to stay. The house was silent, and all slept late after the weariness of yesterday. Ying came in late, pale and without her chatter, and her eyelids were red. She did her duty, and Madame Wu sent her away again and went into her library and took down her books.

The air came in through the open windows with such sweetness that she felt it upon her skin like fragrant oil.

It was mid-morning when she was roused by footsteps, and she looked up and saw Yenmo, her fourth son, in the court.

He greeted her sturdily, in a half-rude fashion, but she did not correct him, knowing that he had learned his ways from peasants.

"Come in, my son," she said kindly.

She took him by the hand and felt in her soft palm his young rough hand. He was as tall as she was now, to her amazement.

"You grow very fast," she said in mock complaint.

He was not like any of her other sons. His words were not ready nor his smile. But she saw his eyes were calm, and that he was not shy. It was simply that he felt no necessity to please anyone. She dropped his hand, and he stood before her, dressed in a blue cotton robe, and on his feet were heavy cloth-soled shoes.

"Mother," he said, "I want to go back to the farm. I will not live here."

He looked so strong and fresh, his eyes were so round and black, his cropped hair so stiff, his teeth so white, that she wanted to laugh at him.

"How far have you read in books?" she asked.

"I am in fifth year of the New Readers, and I have read the Book of Changes," he said.

It was well enough for his years. "But ought you now not to go beyond the village school?" she inquired.

"I hate books," he said immediately.

"Hate books!" she repeated. "Ah, you are going to be like your father."

He turned red and stared down at his feet. "No, Mother, I am not," he declared. "I shall be like nobody. And if I am not to go back to the land, then I will run away."

He looked up at her and down again, and in spite of sadness she laughed. "Have I ever told a son of mine he could not do what he wished?" she asked.

"These walls are so high," the boy complained.

"They are very high," she agreed.

"I want to go now," Yenmo said.

"I will go with you," she said.

He looked doubtful at this. "Where will you sleep?" he asked.

"Oh, I shall return to-night," she declared. "But it will be well for me to go and see the land, and see for myself where you stay and talk with your teacher, and then my heart will rest about you."

So he went to get his clothes ready, and she ordered her sedan and refused to take even Ying with her.

"In the country no one can harm me," she said when Ying opened her eyes wide.

They set out together, she in her sedan and Yenmo on a grey pony which was his pet, and so they went through the streets, and everybody knew who they were and where they went, and fell back in respect before them as gentry.

As soon as they had passed beyond the city walls Madame Wu felt the wide calm spirit of the countryside descend upon her, and slowly her restlessness left her. She put aside all else this day, and she watched the strong firm body of her fourth son astride his pony and cantering before her. The boy rode well, though without grace. He sat as hard in his saddle as though he were part of the beast, rising and falling with the pony's steps. But he was fearless, and twirled his horsehair whip in his hand and sang as he went. Plainly he was happy, and she made up her mind that he should have what made him happy. She was thankful that for this son, as for Liangmo, happiness lay within the family's boundaries.

So that day she spent in the main village, eating her noon meal in the steward's house and listening to all those who came to call upon her. Some came with thanks and some with complaints, and she received them all. It was a good day. Her spirits were refreshed by the simplicity of the people. They were honest and shrewd and did not hide their thoughts. Mothers brought their children to see her, and she praised their health and good looks. She inspected the lands near the village and looked at the seed set aside for various crops. She peered down the well and agreed that it was too shallow and needed to be dug out again, and she counted the jars of ordure that were for the fertilizing of the cabbage fields. She went to the school and spoke to the old scholar who was the teacher and startled him and pleased him by her presence. She laughed when he tried to praise Yenmo's faithfulness, and she told him that she knew her son did not love books. She inspected the room where Yenmo slept in the steward's house, a comfortable earth-walled space with a wide bed and clean covers. Then before the sun sank too far she said good-bye to him and entered her sedan again.

Now when she was alone she did what she had long wanted to do. On the hill-side she saw the great gingko-tree under which André was buried. If she stopped without explanation, the news would be strange in the countryside and in the city and the house, for everyone told of her comings and goings, and nothing that went on in the Wu family could remain unknown. So she said boldly to the bearers, "Take me to the grave of the foreign priest who was teacher to my son. I will pay my respects to him, since he is here with none to mourn him, and I pass so near."

They carried her there without wonder, for they admired this courtesy, and she came down from her sedan at some distance from the grave so that she might be alone. Alone she walked along a narrow path between the fields and mounted the low hill and came into the shadow of the gingko-tree. The evening wind waved its small fanlike leaves and they dappled the shadows of the setting sun upon the grass. She knelt before the grave and bowed her head to the earth three times while at a distance the bearers watched. Then she sat down on the bank of earth encircling the grave and closed her eyes and let him come to her mind. He came in all his old swift-ness, his robes flying about his feet, the winds blowing his beard. His eyes were living and alight.

"That beard," she murmured half playfully. "It hid your

face from me. I never saw your chin and your mouth for myself."

But then he had always hidden his body. The brown cassock hid the broad lines of his huge frame, and his big shapeless cloth shoes hid his feet.

"Those feet of yours," she murmured, smiling. "How the children laugh at them!"

It was true. Sometimes when she went to visit the foundlings in the evening, for she tried to go very often, they would tell her how huge the soles had to be made for his shoes. They measured off space with their little hands.

"Like this—like this," they told her, laughing.

The old woman had cut the soles and the sides from scraps and rags and found the whole cloth to cover them. "The hard stitching I did," she had told Madame Wu.

"But we all helped," the children reminded her.

"All put in stitches," the old woman had agreed. "Even the very small ones pushed the needle through once or twice while I held the cloth."

So she sat a while and thought of him and then she went home again, and she felt her heart big with thankfulness. In her lifetime it had been granted to her to know, and even to love, one creature wholly good.

.   .   .   .   .

A few days later a craftsman came from a shop in the town and brought something which he had made. Upon a small piece of alabaster he had painted a portrait of André,

Madame Wu gazed upon it, half frightened. "Why have you brought it to me?" she demanded. She could not believe that her innermost life was known to others, and yet she knew the strange wisdom of the unlettered.

"I made it out of goodwill for that man," the craftsman said innocently. "Once when we had trouble in the house and I lost my business, he fed us and cared for us until we were able to care for ourselves. I made this picture of him then, so that I might never forget his face. But yesterday my children's mother said, 'Ought we not to put this in the temple of the Wu House, where the foundlings now live, so that they may remember him as their father?' For this reason I bring it."

She let her heart down. It was not to her he brought the

306

gift. She set the alabaster on the table. The man had made a carved wooden stand to hold it, and there the picture of André was. The man had caught his look, even though he had put in something not quite his, the eyes turned up a little at the corners, the hands were a trifle too fine, and the frame was too slender. But it was André, nevertheless.

"What shall I pay your for it?" Madame Wu asked.

"It is a gift," the man said. "I cannot sell it."

"I will receive it, then, for the children," she said.

So she did, and the man went away. She kept the painting for a day with her, and then she took it at evening to the temple. The children were eating their night meal, and their table was set before the gods who guarded the gates. She paused at the door and admired the sight. High red candles flamed in the candlesticks beneath the gods, and the incense on the altar curled its length upward in a scented cloud. Out of the light and the smoke among the rafters the great gods of painted clay looked down upon the children at their feet.

By now the children were used to their home. At first they had feared the gods, but now they forgot them. They ate and chattered, and the old woman and the old priest served them, and the older ones helped the younger ones. When they saw Madame Wu they made a clamour, and she stood smiling and receiving their welcome. Here was a strange thing, that she had often shrunk from the touch of her own children when they were small, and she had sometimes disliked even their hands upon her. But these children she never put away from her. They were not of her flesh nor of André's, but they were his by the choice of his spirit, and when she was with them she was with him. Whether she would ever add one to their number she did not know. Perhaps she would, but perhaps she never would.

Now she held the portrait high so they could see it. "I have a gift for you," she told them. They parted for her to walk, and she went and set the alabaster picture on the table below the gods and in front of the great pewter incense urn. So André stood, and he looked out at them, and the children looked at him. At first all was silence, for they wanted only to see him. Then they began to speak in sighs and murmurs and ripples of laughter. "Ah, it is our father. Ah, it is he——"

So they stood, gazing and longing, and she said gently,

"There he will be always with you, and you can look at his face every day and at night before you sleep."

Then she showed them what was on the other side. The craftsman had carved four words into the stone and had painted the lines black. These were the words: "One Honourable Foreign Heart".

When she had showed them she set the picture in place again, and from that day on it stood in that place.

Now after she had gone back to her own courts it occurred to her that she had not seen Ch'iuming in the temple. She mentioned this to Ying that night. "I gave our Second Lady permission to live in the temple with her child, and yet I did not see her."

To which Ying replied, "She does live there, Lady, but she goes often to sit with your second daughter-in-law. They have become friends and are like sisters, and they comfort each other, for since the coming of that third prostitute our Second Lady is as good as a widow. Our lord never leaves his pipe on her table."

To this Madame Wu did not reply. She held her peace and pondered while Ying rubbed oils into her flesh after her bath. In a great house it was always true that those whose hearts were alike found one another and knit themselves together in a bond of their own making. If Ch'iuming could comfort Rulan, let it be so. It might be that Rulan, too, would be led to work for the temple children and find comfort in them. True it was the children should be educated somehow. André would want them taught to read and write, and they must learn sewing and cooking and be made ready for the ordinary life of men and women anywhere in the world. Madame Wu went to sleep that night making plans for these children and ready to set up a school for them under her own roof. But she was one who did nothing in haste. Whatever she did was planned and clear, and she let days pass.

★ 14 ★

In the next year after this there came again an electric letter across the sea from her third son, Fengmo. Mr. Wu received it and he sent it to her by the hand of a servant, not coming to her himself. It was a strange letter. She read it in all possible ways and still could not understand it. He announced his coming, and that was all. If winds and waves did not prevent progress, he would be home within the month at soonest and within two months at longest. But the allotted years had not passed, and he did not say why he came home early.

The more Madame Wu read the few words, the more unsettled she became. She wished very much now for the presence of André, for this one son she had shared with him. "If you could only look down on him," she murmured, "and then tell me why he comes home so suddenly, and whether he has done something wrong——"

But when she closed her eyes and looked for André's face against darkness she saw him only grave. He was silent, and nothing came up out of memory to give him voice.

Neither did she wish to talk with Mr. Wu about this son, and neither did she wish to talk with Rulan, and least of all with Ch'iuming. Yet the more she considered the whole matter, the more she felt perplexed and uneasy, and at last she feared Fengmo's return very much, lest it bring fresh trouble. It occurred to her now that of all persons she ought perhaps to speak with Madame Kang, who was the mother of Linyi.

The distance between these two had continued until now the path between their house would have grown in weeds had it been countryside. Even when Madame Wu had made up her mind to call upon Madame Kang she felt reluctance which she could not explain. She sat down with herself to discover what was still wrong. Why should she feel so far from her old friend, whose smallness she did not blame? The cause had its roots in their great difference from each other, and this difference she found upon reflection was that

Madame Kang loved her husband exceedingly, even as she loved André, and these two loves, though as separate and unlike as Heaven and earth, were nevertheless of the same nature. That is, each of the two women knew what it meant to love another better than herself. But for Madame Wu the disgust for her friend lay in that Madame Kang loved her careless, fat old man more than herself. To use love in this coarse way belittled high and splendid devotion. Yet in honesty she could not but discern the truth, that Madame Kang felt as she felt, and the difference was not in degree or in quality but in level. Madame Kang loved her old man as high as she could love, and was not ashamed.

"Yet old Kang ought not to live and breathe under the same Heaven with André," Madame Wu thought with indignation.

She sat in the library, thinking these thoughts on a clear morning, and after she had thought a while she laughed aloud softly at herself. Why should she be angry at love? It descended as the sunshine did and the rain, upon just and unjust alike, upon rich and poor, upon the ignorant and the learned, and did this make her angry?

The laughter welled up in her heart. She closed her eyes and saw André laughing with her, and she sat watching his face until she could see it no more. Then she opened her eyes, cleansed and strengthened, and Ying fetched her outer robe and made her ready, and sent a messenger ahead to announce the visit, and so she went to Madame Kang.

The house of Kang was unchanged in its disorder, and the staring children were more than ever in their number. Every son's wife and concubine had added a child or two since Madame Wu had last entered these gates, and all were unmannerly and all as happy as ever. A cheerful bondmaid led her to the court where Madame Kang sat all day in a rattan easy chair, under a willow-tree by a small pool. The easy chair had yielded itself to Madame Kang's increasing flesh until now its woven sides had taken on the curves of her body. She sat down in the morning, and unless it rained she did not get up until night.

Around her children played and cried and drank from the breasts of their wet nurses, and the maids sewed and washed vegetables and rice in the pool, and her daughters-in-law gossiped, and neighbour women stopped by to tell the news and vendors came in to show their wares, and ladies came from other great houses to play mah-jong all day. Here Madame Kang sat when Madame Wu was brought in and she shouted her welcome and her excuses for not rising to her feet.

"I put on such pounds that when night comes I swear I am heavier on my feet than I was in the morning," she cried.

All in the court laughed at her, and a laugh from inside showed that Mr. Kang had heard her too, but he did not come out. Being a man, he could only sit near by and listen and watch from his distance while he pretended to read or sleep.

Now Madame Wu saw that in the midst of all this company she could not say what she wished about Fengmo and Linyi. But without haste she sat down in her courteous fashion on a chair which some maid or other came and set near Madame Kang. Madame Kang knew very well that Madame Wu had come with a purpose, and so she waved her fat hands and shouted that all were to go away and leave them alone. So after much shouting and scampering and confusion, during which Madame Kang sat with her hands on her knees directing everybody loudly, the two ladies were alone.

Now Madame Wu took out Fengmo's electric letter and showed it to her old friend. But Madame Kang laughed and waved it away. "The few characters I ever knew I have forgotten," she said cheerfully. "I have never needed them, and why do I need them now with you here, Aileen?"

If there was any distance between them Madame Kang's manner ignored it, and she behaved as though she had seen her friend daily and yesterday too.

Madame Wu smiled. It was impossible not to smile at this woman, however she might feel disgust for her. So she read aloud Fengmo's words, "I return home immediately."

"Does he say nothing more than that?" Madame Kang asked, staring at the letter.

"Only so much," Madame Wu replied. She folded the letter small again and put it in her bosom. She lifted the tea bowl on the table at her side, saw the cup was dirty, and put it down again.

"Clearly something has happened," she said. "He planned to be away five years."

311

"He is ill!" Madame Kang exclaimed.

"It may be," Madame Wu said, "and yet in such case I feel he would have told us."

"You think he has committed some sin?" Madame Kang exclaimed again.

"I cannot think that," Madame Wu said. Indeed, after André's long teaching she could not believe that there was grave fault in Fengmo. "It is about Linyi that I have come to see you," she went on. "I blame myself that I have not continued her lessons since her tutor died."

She turned her head away while she said these words, for she knew that Madame Kang was exceedingly quick to see behind words when it came to matters between men and women.

"Linyi does not mind that," Madame Kang said heartily. "She dared not tell you, Aileen, but she hated those lessons, and she disliked the priest. She says he was always talking his religion."

"But he never taught her his religion," Madame Wu said with indignation. "I forbade his teaching Fengmo, and certainly he would not have taught Linyi. He understood my feelings."

"It was not about gods that he spoke," Madame Kang yielded thus far. "But he kept telling her how she should think and how she ought to feel towards her husband and towards you and towards all with whom she met and with whom she lived under the roof."

"That was not religion," Madame Wu said.

"She was made uncomfortable just the same," Madame Kang said. "She said it made it hard for her to eat and sleep."

"Ah, a good teacher does stir the soul," Madame Wu said quietly.

"If Fengmo has grown like that foreign priest," Madame Kang said, yawning, "it will go hard between them."

She stared about the court, and Madame Wu saw that she wanted something.

"Are you in need, Meichen?" she inquired courteously.

"At this time I usually sup a bowl of rice and beans stewed together with chicken broth," Madame Kang said. "I feel empty."

One by one all who had been sent away were now drifting

back into the courts. First the children ran in to play and no child in Madame Kang's house was ever forbidden for long what it wanted. Then wet nurses ran after the children, and when they picked them up the children screamed, and Madame Kang called out, "Let them be, then!"

The maids came back and the gruel was brought, and Madame Wu refused to share it, and Madame Kang supped it down loudly and let this child and that one drink from the side of the bowl, after she had blown it cool for them.

Madame Wu rose to go away again. She told herself that it might be her last visit to the house and perhaps she would never see her old friend again. They had parted already, long ago.

Nevertheless, she had learned something from her visit, and she was not sorry she had come. André had taught Linyi her duty, and she would discover what he taught her.

. . . .

All else Madame Wu now put aside in this expected coming of Fengmo. The temple children must wait for their school, and she would let Rulan and Ch'iuming wait. Her first duty was to prepare Linyi for her husband.

This she could do easily enough, for it was within her right to ask that her daughter-in-law come and visit her. In so great a house as this it was often that Madame Wu did not speak to one certain member for many days at a time, and so it had been with Linyi. She saw the girl almost daily at the main family meal, and she saw her at festivals and on days of honouring the ancestral tablets, and on all such family occasions. But she had no reason to ask for Linyi's presence. The girl had lived in the house, been waited upon by the servants, had visited her sister, and idled her time away, except for the few duties which Madame Wu assigned on the written scroll for the arrangement of the household at the beginning of each season. Thus Madame Wu had marked for Linyi such duties as feeding the goldfish, placing flowers in the main hall, airing and sunning Fengmo's fur garments and satin robes, and the supervision of the court where she lived, while Fengmo was away, with an old woman servant she had brought from home. Once or twice the girl had been ill, and Meng had tended her and had sent word to Madame Wu when she was well, and that was all that Madame Wu knew.

Now she must know much more. She did not deceive herself that it was all purely for her son's sake. She wanted herself to hear from Linyi what André had taught her. She wanted to hear his very words, as well as to know how they had taken root in this young woman's heart.

So Linyi came in, dressed and painted and powdered, and the ends of her hair were curled. Madame Wu welcomed her with her usual smile and the gesture of her hand which invited her to sit down and be at ease. She looked at Linyi from head to foot before she spoke. The young woman was very pretty, and she knew it and did not fear Madame Wu's gaze. Madame Wu smiled at the bold, innocent eyes. Were they not innocent? Yes, but they were also mischievous and idle and careless and gay.

"I smile when I think how times change," Madame Wu said. "When I was a young girl I would have wept to see the ends of my hair curled. To be straight and smooth and black —that was then considered beauty for the hair. But now curls are beautiful, are they? Meng must be glad, since her hair curls itself. But I believe Meng wishes it did not."

Linyi laughed and showed small white teeth, and a red tongue. "I think Fengmo will be used to curly hair," she said in her fresh high voice. "All foreign women have curly hair."

"Ah," Madame Wu said. She looked suddenly grave. "Tell me why you have always been so fond of what is foreign."

"Not of everything foreign," Linyi said, pouting. "I was never fond of that hairy old priest."

"But he was not old," Madame Wu said in a low voice.

"To me he was old," Linyi said. "And hairy—ah, how I hate hairy men!"

Madame Wu felt this talk was unbecoming to them both. She considered how to begin otherwise. "But he taught you very well," she suggested. "I believe what he taught you was full of goodness and I should like you to recall it for me, if you please."

When she said these words, "if you please", it was in such a tone of voice that Linyi knew she must obey, and it was not whether she pleased. She frowned and drew down her long narrow brows and twisted one end of her black hair about her finger.

"I haven't tried to remember," she said, "but he was always

314

saying that Fengmo was born to do a great work, and that my
part in it was to make him as happy as I could so that he
could work better."

"How are you to make him happy?" Madame Wu
inquired.

"He said I must find out the stream of Fengmo's life,"
Linyi said unwillingly, "and he told me I must clear away
the straw and the sticks and things which hinder the flow,
and I must do all I can to let the water rise to its level. The
priest said I mustn't be like a rock thrown into the
clear stream and dividing it. I must not divide Fengmo's
life."

Yes, Madame Wu thought, these could be André's words.
Knowing the mind of the girl, he would use such simple
words and pictures. "Go on, my child," she said gently.
"These are good words."

Linyi went on. She dropped the curl and her eyes were
pensive as she talked. "And he said I must read books about
what Fengmo did, and I must understand his thoughts. He
said Fengmo would be lonely all his life if I did not follow
closely behind him. Fengmo needs me, he said."

She returned her eyes to Madame Wu's face. "But I am
not sure if Fengmo knows he needs me," she said.

Madame Wu met the childlike gaze. "Do you love him?"
she asked.

It was an amazing question for a lady to ask her son's wife.
Who besides Madame Wu would have cared? Tears filled
Linyi's eyes. "I could love him," she whispered, "if he loved
me."

"Does he not love you?" Madame Wu asked.

Linyi shook her head so hard that the tears fell out of her
eyes and lay in drops on the pale blue satin of her robe.

"No," she whispered, "Fengmo does not love me."

With these words she bent her head on her two hands and
wept. Madame Wu waited. She knew that nothing was so
good for woman's troubles as tears. How often had she not
longed to weep and could not!

She waited until Linyi's sobs grew softer and then silent,
before she spoke. "Ah," she said, "Fengmo does not love anybody. That is his lack. We must heal it. I will help you,
my child."

Her words were few enough and simple, but such was the

confidence that everyone in this house felt in Madame Wu that Linyi took away her hands from her face and smiled with wet lashes.

"Thank you, Our Mother," she said. "Thank you and thank you."

. . . . .

The day of Fengmo's return was before winter but after the last heat of autumn. The harvests were gathered and stored. The Wu house, the town which depended on them for wisdom and government, the villages where those who worked on the lands and lived as their forefathers had lived, all were roots of peace in the nation where to the east war was raging. Elsewhere houses were destroyed and families driven out and scattered and the lands laid waste. But here in the inland the house of Wu went on.

Madame Wu waited for her son's coming, and Fengmo's first words to her, after greeting, were of this peace. He looked about the rooms where all was the same, as though he could not believe them so.

"Nothing is changed!" he exclaimed.

"Why should we change?" Madame Wu replied.

And yet even as she spoke she knew she did not speak the truth. There was the great change in herself, the inner change which daily found expression in all she said and did and in the way she governed those who looked to her for advice and shelter and care. But she did not choose to speak of these things.

"You are changed, my son," she said instead.

She sat in state in the library, dressed in her robe of silver-grey brocaded satin. She had made up her mind to receive Fengmo here in the great room where they had so often sat with André. She would not speak of André, but memory would speak. So after the festivities at the gate, after the fire-crackers and the noise were over and the crowd gone, and only the feast was to come, that night she had sent word to Fengmo that she waited for him.

He sat down without her bidding. He had changed his foreign garments, which he wore when he arrived, and had put on his own robes. He had even taken off his foreign shoes, and he wore his own of black velvet. No one had spoken to him of Tsemo, for it is not lucky to speak of the dead to one

316

living and just returned. But Fengmo spoke now himself of his brother.

"I miss my second brother," he said.

Madame Wu wiped her eyes delicately. While Tsemo was alive she had not much missed him, but now she missed him very much and thought of him often. She knew that what she missed was not what she had known, but what she had never known. She reproached herself very much that she had allowed a son to grow up in her house and had never really discovered him. She had known him only as a son, hers because she had made his flesh, but not because she had become acquainted with his being.

"What graces he had I did not know, and now can never know," she had often thought to herself.

"How is my second sister-in-law?" Fengmo asked next.

"Rulan is silent," Madame Wu said. "When I have time I shall discover a way for her to live. She is too young to become like a nun."

"She will not marry again, surely?" Fengmo asked.

"If she will I will help her," Madame Wu said.

This astonished Fengmo a good deal. He would not have imagined that his mother could put a woman above the family.

Seeing his surprise, Madame Wu continued in her soft way, "I have learned as I have grown older," she said. "If the springs within are not clear, then life is not good. And I have learned that there is a debt due to every soul, and this is the right to its own true happiness."

"That is what Brother André used to say," Fengmo said suddenly. Mother and son, by these words they felt themselves drawn together, as though by some power or presence they did not see.

"Mother, do you remember Brother André?" Fengmo asked her.

Madame Wu hesitated. How much should she say, tell how much? Her old diffidence fell on her. No, the silence between the generations must not be wholly broken. Life itself had created the difference, and time had hung the veil. It was not for her to change the eternal. She and André were on one side and Fengmo was on the other.

"I do remember him." That was all she said.

But if Fengmo felt himself separated he did not show it.

317

"Mother, he changed me very much," he said in a low voice. He gazed at André's empty chair. "He made me understand true happiness. He showed me my own soul. And that is why I have come home."

She did not speak. She heard a quiver in her son's voice and she knew that even her answer would be too much for him. She smiled her lovely smile, she folded her hands on her lap, she waited, inviting him by her readiness to listen.

"No one will understand why I came home suddenly," he began. "They will ask and I cannot tell them. I do not know how to tell them. But I want to tell you, Mother. It was you who brought Brother André into this house."

She had so profound a surety of André's presence, though perhaps only through her memory, that she dared not speak. No, André was here not because she remembered him but because she loved him.

"Mother!" Fengmo cried her name. He lifted his head and forced himself to speak quickly, to push the words and have them said. "I came home because I learned to love a foreign woman over there, and she loved me and we parted from each other."

Had Madame Wu been her old self she would have cried out her indignation. Now she said gently, "What sorrow, my son!"

Yes, she knew what sorrow.

"You understand!" Fengmo exclaimed with the amazement of youth at age.

He had grown very much. He was taller by inches, thin and straight as Old Gentleman had been, Madame Wu now saw. Indeed, she perceived what she had never seen before, that Fengmo was not at all like his father, but he was very like his grandfather. The same sternness sat on his features, the same gravity shone in his eyes. He was handsome, but grave. Liangmo's placid good looks and Tsemo's bold beauty were not here. Fengmo looked like a young scholar.

"I learn as I grow older," Madame Wu said.

"Ah, Mother," Fengmo breathed in a sigh. "I wondered if there would be anyone in this house who could understand." Now that he could trust her, the story poured out of him. "She was one of the students, like me. Men and women study together over there. She was lit with wonder and curiosity.

318

She sought me out, not boldly, you know, Mother, but because she said she had never seen anyone like me. She asked me hundreds of questions about us, about our country and our home, and I found myself telling her everything, even about myself. And she told me of her life. We knew each other so well—so quickly."

"And at last you had to tell her about Linyi," Madame Wu said gently.

Shadow fell between him and the sun. His shoulders drooped, he turned his face away. "I had to tell her," he said simply, "and then I had to come home."

"To put the sea between you," Madame Wu said in the same voice.

"To put everything between us," he agreed.

She sat in the calm stillness so usual to her. André had nurtured her son's soul and had made it exceedingly tender and quick towards good. She yearned over him, she longed for him to be happy, and yet this son was not like other men. He could not find happiness in women nor in his own body. When she had asked André to be his teacher she had asked blindly, seeing only a shallow step ahead. She had touched a lock, half turned the key, but a wide gate had opened under her hand, and her son had gone through to that new world.

Had he come home again? Had he closed the gate behind him and turned the key and made fast the lock once more?

"And now," she said, "and now, my son, what will you do?"

"I have come home," he said. "I shall never go away again. I shall make my life here somehow."

They sat in silence, the long silence of two understanding each other.

"You must help Linyi, my son," she said.

"I know that," he said. "I have thought very much of her. I owe her very much."

"You must find a way to need her," Madame Wu went on. "You must ask for her help in any small thing you have to do. Ask her to care for your things and sort your books and fetch your tea. Do nothing for yourself, my son, that she can do, so that she may be busy and never know anything else."

"I will," he promised.

319

And so they sat, and would have sat another long space, so comforting were they, mother and son, to each other, except that Ch'iuming chose this moment to come and make a request of Madame Wu which had long been in her mind to make.

All these months that she had been living with Rulan, Ch'iuming had listened to the young widow's sorrowing talk about her love for her dead husband. And the more she listened to Rulan the more Ch'iuming found her thoughts turning to Fengmo, and the more she knew that she must leave the house and take her child and go away. Yet where could she go?

One night, when Rulan had not been able to sleep and when they had talked long of the things which are deepest in women's hearts, Ch'iuming broke her own vow of silence and told Rulan of her love for Fengmo.

"I am wicked," she told Rulan. "I allow myself to think of him."

Rulan had listened to her with burning attention. She threw back her hair from her shoulders. "Oh, I wish you and I could get out of this house," she cried. "Here we are all locked behind these high walls. The family preys upon itself. We love where we should not and we hate where we should not. We are all too near to one another while we hate and we love."

"Are we not safe behind these walls?" Ch'iuming asked. She was always a little timid before Rulan, admiring while she feared her boldness.

"We are not safe from one another," Rulan had retorted.

It was at this moment that the same thought had come to them both. Eyes stared into eyes.

"Why should we stay?" Rulan had asked.

"How dare we go?" Ch'iuming had asked.

And then they had begun to plot. Ch'iuming would ask first to be allowed to live in the ancestral village. To her old village she could not return, for it would appear that the Wu family had sent her out, and this even Madame Wu would never allow. But she would ask to go and live in a Wu village, and then when Madame Wu demurred that a young woman should not live in a farmer's village she would ask for Rulan. And when Rulan had to speak for herself she would say that

320

she wanted to begin a school for young children in the village as a good work for her widowhood. Everyone knew that widows should make good works. This conclusion they had reached after much talk, for Rulan wanted to go immediately and speak out for herself. But Ch'iuming pointed out the discourtesy of this, for how could Madame Wu, if she was unwilling, be put to the difficulty of refusing her daughter-in-law to her face? It was better for Ch'iuming to go first and take the brunt of refusal if it must come. Then there need be no difference between Madame Wu and her daughter-in-law.

This Rulan cried out against as being old-fashioned, but Ch'iuming declared it to be only decency, and so it was settled.

Now Ch'iuming knew well enough where Fengmo was, but she had decided in her own mind that she would approach Madame Wu in his presence and would greet him only in Madame Wu's presence, and never would she speak to him otherwise. So she dressed her child in a clean red dress and washed the little creature's hands and face and painted a red spot between her brows and braided her hair and tied the ends with new red yarn, and with the child, who was now a very fair fat little girl, she appeared unannounced.

Thus Madame Wu looked to the door and saw Ch'iuming. It was late afternoon, for Fengmo had come home in the morning. The sun had left the court, but it was filled with mellow light, and in this Ch'iuming stood, her child in her arms. She looked almost beautiful, and Madame Wu saw this to her dismay. Ch'iuming's love, secret and unrequited though it was, had made her soft and alive. She looked quickly at her son to know what he saw. But he saw now nothing. Ch'iuming greeted Fengmo carefully.

"Ah, our Third Sir, you have come home," she said.

Fengmo answered as simply, "Yes, yes. Are you well?"

"I am well." Ch'iuming replied.

She looked at him once and then did not look at him again. Instead she said to Madame Wu, "Our Lady, may I ask a favour even now, and not be held too coarse for disturbing you?"

Madame Wu knew that Ch'iuming must have a purpose in coming at this time, and so she inclined her head. "Sit down and let the heavy child stand on her own feet," she said.

So Ch'iuming, blushing very much, did as she was told. She asked for the favour, and Madame Wu listened.

"Very good," she said, "very good."

She comprehended at once the purpose that Ch'iuming had in coming here at this time. Ch'iuming wished to make clear to Madame Wu that she wanted to retire from this house now that Fengmo had come home, and to disturb nothing in the family. Madame Wu was grateful for such goodness.

When Madame Wu's permission was given, Ch'iuming then asked for Rulan also. "Since the family mourning is over, and since her own mourning can never cease, she wishes to ease her sorrow by good works," Ch'iuming said. "She wishes to make a school for the children of the farmers."

At this Fengmo, who had been staring down at the floor, looked up astonished. "That," he declared, "is what I have come home to do."

Here was confusion! Ch'iuming was aghast and Madame Wu confounded.

"You said nothing of this, my son!" she exclaimed with silvery sharpness.

"I had not reached the point," Fengmo declared. "After what happened it became necessary to consider what work I could do."

Madame Wu held up one narrow hand. "Wait," she commanded him. She turned to Ch'iuming. "Have you any other request?" she asked kindly.

"None," Ch'iuming replied.

"Then you have my permission to go, you and Rulan also," Madame Wu said. "I will call the steward in a few days and bid him find suitable houses for living and school, and you shall go when you like after that. But you will need special furniture, better than what is usually in a farm-house, as well as other goods. Decide what you need, and I will tell Ying to prepare it. You will need two maids with you and a cook. The head cook can send one of the undercooks with you."

At this Fengmo spoke again. "If they live in the village they should not live too far above the others there, or they will be lonely."

Ch'iuming threw him a soft, quick look and did not speak. She was surprised that he could know this, who all his life had lived in a rich house. How did he know what common people felt? Then she put the question away. It was not for her ever to ask a question about him.

She rose and lifted up her child and thanked Madame Wu and went away. Rulan waited for her, and as soon as she heard the permission she and Ch'iuming began to plan their new lives with more joy than could have been possible to them even yesterday.

In the room which Ch'iuming had left, Madame Wu spoke to her son. "Explain your heart to me," she commanded him.

He rose and walked restlessly to the open door and stood looking out. The quietness of coming night was in the walled space. Here the seasons came, even as they did over the whole world.

"It is necessary for me to devote myself," he said. "So much Brother André taught me. If I am not to devote myself to one thing, it must be to another. After I left here I cast about for devotion. Religion is not for me, Mother. I am no priest. As far as a man can go, Brother André taught me, but not beyond."

"Good, my son," Madame Wu said, and waited.

He sat down again. "The way was shown me entirely by accident," Fengmo went on. He drew out of his pockets some foreign tobacco and a short foreign pipe and filled it and began to smoke. Madame Wu had not seen these before, but she would not allow her curiosity to interrupt him.

"There was in the city where I lived over there a laundry man of our own race," Fengmo told her. "I took my clothes to him every few days to be washed."

Madame Wu looked surprised. "Did he wash clothes for others?" she asked.

"For many," Fengmo replied. "It was his trade."

"Do you tell me he even washed the clothes of the foreigners?" Madame Wu inquired next with some indignation.

Fengmo laughed. "Somebody has to wash clothes," he said.

But Madame Wu did not laugh. "Certainly our people ought not to wash the soiled garments of foreigners," she said. She was displeased and forgot what Fengmo was about to say.

He tried to soothe her. "Well—well——" he said. Then he

323

went on, "The man was not from our province but from the south. One day when I went to fetch my clothes——"

"You fetched your own clothes!" Madame Wu repeated. "Had you no servant?"

"No, Mother, over there none of us had servants."

She restrained her curiosity again. "I see it is a very strange country and you must tell me more of it later. Go on, my son," she commanded him.

"I went to fetch my clothes, and the man brought me a letter from his home," Fengmo went on. "Mother, he had been away from his home for twenty years, and he could not read the letters that came to him. Nor could he write. So I read and wrote his letters for him, and he told me that in his village none read or wrote, and they had to go to the city to find a scholar. I had never understood the pity of this until I came to know him. He was a good man, Mother, not stupid but very intelligent. 'If I could only read and write for myself,' he would say, 'but I am like one blind.' I went back to my room and I looked out of the window and saw the great buildings of the college and the thousands of students coming and going, learning many things, and the one poor old man could not read his letters from home. Then I remembered that this is true in our villages too. None of our own people can read and write, who live on our land."

"Why should they?" Madame Wu inquired. "They do not come and go. They only till the fields."

"But Mother, Mother!" Fengmo exclaimed, "to know how to read is to light a lamp in the mind, to release the soul from prison, to open a gate to the universe."

The words fell upon Madame Wu's ears and lashed her heart. "Ah," she said, "those are the words of him who taught you."

"I have not forgotten them," Fengmo said.

How could she forbid Fengmo after this, and how could she tell him why he must not live outside his own house?

"Rulan will be just the one to help me," he said eagerly. "I had not thought of her before. And Linyi shall help me too, and we will forget ourselves."

He was on his feet again. "You know, Mother, if I succeed here in our own villages, it might be a thing that would spread everywhere. How great a good that would be——"

She saw his thin young face light with something of the

light that had burned eternally in André's eyes. She would not put it out.

"My son, do what seems good to you." So she answered him.

* * * * *

Madame Wu lay awake in her bed as now she did very often. This neither displeased nor alarmed her. The young must sleep, for they have work to do and long life ahead. But the old need not sleep. The body, knowing that eternal rest is not far off, may lie awake while it can.

It seemed to her, as she lay awake, that the house was alive in the night as it was not in the day. She let her mind's vision roam over the many courts. Elderly cousins lived in the distant and outer courts, and younger second and third cousins, here not to stay, but only because for the moment they had no other shelter, and these wide roofs could cover them, too, for a while. From the courts where Jasmine lived with Mr. Wu she turned her eyes quickly. Well, she knew what life it was. She had no judgment for it, only weariness. The old man's body lived on, fed and solaced, and the young woman grew fat and lazy and was ready for sleep, day as well as night. Jasmine was no trouble in the courts. She was barren. No child was conceived, and Madame Wu was content to have it so. Jasmine's was wild blood, and it was well to keep it in her own veins. She did her duty by Mr. Wu and, having had her pleasure in years before, she was glad to please the old man who now gave her jewels and silks and dainties of every kind to eat, and laughed at her and fondled her. All her life Jasmine had been a wayside flower and subject to any wind that passed. Now her happiness was to know that behind these high walls no wind could touch her. Even though the old man were to die, she would live on, her place secure in his house. There was nothing more for her to fear as long as she lived.

As for Mr. Wu, what his mother had begun in his youth, his young concubine now finished. Whatever Madame Wu had fostered in him had faded away, like a light dimmed because it fed on no fuel. He grew gross and heavy, eating too much and drinking often but always with Jasmine. He went no more to flower houses, for Jasmine gave him all her arts. Even his old need for the companionship of his friends left him, and seldom did he go to tea-houses to hear the news and discuss the town's gossip. Jasmine gave him both, and she had all from the servants. There in the court where they lived so closely together that almost they lived alone, they were ribald and gay and drunken and happy, two pieces of meat and bone, and content so to be. The name of Mr. Wu was seldom heard now even in his own house. In malice a servant whispered it to another, and that was all.

With her divining mind Madame Wu knew all of this, and she went no more to the court that had once been her home. Never once did Jasmine come to her court. The two lived as far apart as ever they had lived before Jasmine had come.

Pondering upon this, Madame Wu asked herself, as she lay between her silken quilts, if she had failed in her marriage. Was there anything she should have done that she had not? She put the question to André, but for once there was no answer ready in her memory. Instead she saw the face of Old Gentleman against the velvet black of her brain. It was as clear as it had ever been, neither older nor younger. His face had always been thin, the golden skin drawn smooth over the fine bones beneath. His skull must even now be a thing of beauty as he lay in his grave, its lines cleaned and polished by time.

"I fear I have not done well by your son, my father," she said sadly, within her own self.

She felt, as she gazed at the kind, good old face, that perhaps if she had not separated herself from Mr. Wu on her fortieth birthday, he might not have sunk to what he was now. But out of her youthful memories Old Gentleman spoke to her.

She remembered well the day. They had been reading together, for he had sent for her, and she found him with his finger in a book. He had pointed to the lines when she came in and she had read:

"To lift a soul above its natural level is a dangerous act. Souls, like springs, have their natural sources, and to force them beyond is against nature and therefore a dangerous act. For when the soul is forced, it seeks its own level again and disintegrates, being torn between upper and lower levels, and this is also dangerous. True wisdom it is to weigh and judge the measure of a soul and let it live where it belongs."

Her eyes and Old Gentleman's had met as they met now across the many years since he had been in this house.

"Had I not separated myself," she mused—and could imagine no further. What she had done was inevitable. Her being she had subdued to duty for how many years, and for how many years had her soul waited, growing slowly, it is true through the performance of duty, but growing in bondage and waiting to be freed.

Strange that now in the middle of the night while the house lay silent she thought with anxiety of Liangmo, her eldest son. Why should she be anxious for him, who of all her sons was the most content? Him, too, she must discover when she could.

And in Fengmo's court she did not pause. Fengmo was a man. He had disciplined himself as only a full-grown man could do. He had not yielded up his soul. Upon this comfort her mind drifted towards sleep, like an empty boat upon a moonlit sea.

.   .   .

"Now my English books," Fengmo commanded.

Linyi ran to fetch them out of the box. There were two armfuls of them. "How many you have!" she exclaimed.

"Only my best ones," he said carelessly. "I have boxes yet to come."

He knelt by the bookshelves against the wall and fitted in the books as she brought them. Outwardly calm, his face constantly smiling, inwardly he was deep in turmoil and pain. He felt now that he could never sleep again, and he was feverish to settle his things, to put all his possessions into their places, to put his travelling bags out of sight, not to be used again.

"Must you put everything away to-night?" Linyi asked.

"I must," he replied. "I want to know that I have come home to stay."

She was happy to have these words said, and too young to dream why it was he said them without looking at her. Indeed, when he said them he saw a face very different from hers. He saw Margaret's face, blue eyes, brown hair, and the skin so white and smooth that he would never forget the touch of it. Would he ever be sorry that he had done what he did that day in the forest across the sea? For he had forced himself to let her go as soon as he had taken her in his arms.

"I can't go on," he had said.

327

She had not spoken. She had stood, her blue eyes fixed on him. There was something strange and wonderful about blue eyes. They could not hide what was behind them. Black eyes were curtains drawn down, but blue eyes were open windows.

"I am married," he had told her bluntly. "My wife waits for me at home."

She knew something about Chinese marriages. "Was she your own choice or did your family arrange it?"

He had waited a long time to answer. They sat down under the pine-tree. He had hugged his knees in his arms and hid his forehead on his hunched knees, thinking, feeling for the truth. It would have been easy, and partly true, to say, "I did not choose her." But when he prepared to say these words Brother André came into his mind.

"To lie is a sin," Brother André had taught him simply, "but it is not a sin against God so much as a sin against yourself. Anything built upon the foundation of a lie crumbles. The lie deceives no one so much as the one who tells it."

He had not dared to lie to her, lest some final day the structure of their love crumble between their hands, and their love be buried in reproach.

"I was not forced to marry," he said. "Let us say—I chose."

She had sat motionless after that, listening to him, while he tried to explain to her what marriage meant in his family.

"With us marriage is a duty not to love or to ourselves, but to our place in the generations. I know that my mother has never loved my father, but she has done her duty to the family. She has been a good wife and mother. But when she was forty years old she retired from wifehood and chose another for my father. This grieved us, and yet we all knew the justice of it. Now she is free to pursue her own happiness, still within the house, and around her we all stand to support her and do her honour. I have my duty, too, in the family."

He knew in some strange distant fashion that he was wounding Margaret to the soul.

"I want to marry for love," she said.

Had he been free, not only of Linyi but of all the generations of Wu in the centuries gone and all the generations of Wu yet to come, he would have said to her, "Then let us marry each other. I will send Linyi away."

But he was not free. The hands of his ancestors were fastened on him, and the hands of his sons and grandsons not yet born beckoned to him. He owed her further honesty.

"I know myself," he went on. He lifted his eyes not to hers but to the landscape before them, to the river, its ships and harbour, and to the span of a great bridge between the banks.

"I know that I am made, not only by Heaven, but also by my family whose roots are in legend, and I cannot live for myself alone. My body was given to me—it does not belong to me. Something in me is my own, that is true, and that something—call it soul if you wish—is my own possession and I can give it to you because I love you. But if I were to give my body, which is not mine, I should be robbing the generations."

"You are wrong—you are wrong!" she had cried. "Love and marriage can be the same."

"Sometimes," he admitted, "but only by the accident of Heaven. Sometimes even among my own people a man, lifting the bridal veil from his unknown wife's face on their wedding night, beholds the one among all whom he would have chosen, had he been free to choose. But it is the accident of Heaven."

"Here we always marry for love," she had insisted proudly.

He had been aware of distance growing between them. "No, you do not," he had answered. He would tell the truth though it killed them both. "You marry as we do, to preserve your species, but you deceive yourselves and call it love. You demand the personal fulfilment, even though you deceive yourselves. You worship the idea of love. But we are the truthful ones. We believe that all must marry, men and women alike. That is our common duty to life. If love comes, it is added grace from Heaven. But love is not necessary for life."

"It is to me," she had said in a low voice.

He had gone on, not answering this, "Content is necessary, but content comes when duty is done and fulfilled—not the personal expectations of love, but the expectations of family and children, home and one's place in the generations."

He was speaking out of his deepest being, and as he spoke he felt that Brother André approved. He knew that this approval was not because of what he said, but because he spoke from the truth of his being.

How long had that silence been that fell between them! He did not break it. He had allowed it to grow and swell, an ocean in depth and distance.

She broke it by putting out her hand. "Then it's good-bye for us, isn't it?"

He had held her hand for a long moment, and put his other hand over hers. "It is good-bye," he had agreed, and had let her go.

The last book was put away, the last garment folded. He took the bags and set them into the passageway where a servant would find them in the morning. Then he went back into their bedroom. Linyi stood in the middle of the floor, uncertain and waiting. He went to her without hesitation and gripped her shoulders in his hands.

"You are going to help me," he said. "I have a work to do here on my own earth, and I need you. It is impossible for me to do my work alone. You must promise to help me with all you have in you."

The fierceness in his eyes half frightened her. But she found the fright delightful. She wanted to be afraid of him. She needed his command.

"I will help you," she whispered, "I will do anything you tell me to do."

. . . . .

Fengmo was like a fire in the house. Everything was fanned to feed the flame. He rose before dawn and ate by candlelight and by earliest day was riding his horse across the fields on narrow paths to the village he had chosen for his first school. Young and old must learn, he decreed. He planned schools for children and schools for men and women and old people.

Be sure there was much complaint among the old who had never troubled about books and who saw no need now to read. "When we have only a few years left us, must we trouble ourselves to know what other men have written?" Thus they complained. "Have we not our own thoughts?" they cried. "Have we not learned a little wisdom, too, after all these years? Our own wisdom is enough for us."

But Fengmo was too young to grant this, and at last the

330

older farmers came to Madame Wu to beg her to command her son to forbear, and Madame Wu received them. She was scrupulous always to receive courteously those beneath her. Superiors she had none, and her equals she could deny; but lesser folk never. So she received them in state in the main hall of the house, and she sent for Mr. Wu to come and take his usual place to the right of the central table while she sat on the left, so that the house should be honourably presented to the land folk. Mr. Wu came in with dignity. He wore robes of wine-coloured satin under a black velvet sleeveless jacket, all new because he was grown too fat for his old ones. Madame Wu was amazed at his fatness, for some time had passed since she had seen him except sitting at the table, and now less and less often did he appear even at the family table. He would die earlier than need be, she thought, looking at his jowls, and then she thought again that it was better to die happy, even though earlier, than to die less happy, even though later. She held her peace, therefore, and gave no warning.

When the two elders were seated the farmers came in dressed in their blue cotton garments and with new straw sandals on their feet. They brought small packages of cakes wrapped in heavy brown paper and tied with straw string, and under the string they had put pieces of red paper for good luck. These they presented and Mr. Wu received them, protesting properly that they need not show so much courtesy.

Then, standing humble before the gentry, the farmers made known their difficulty. Madame Wu listened and so did Mr. Wu, though with less interest. Mr. Wu agreed heartily with the farmers. "These brothers are entirely right," he announced. "My son is behaving like a fool, and I shall command him to return at once to my house and leave you in peace."

But Madame Wu knew all sides of the matter, and she had no intention of allowing Mr. Wu to act in ignorance. So she first agreed with him and then disagreed with him mildly. Thus she spoke:

"My sons' father speaks very wisely and must be obeyed. You, good brothers, are all over forty years of age. Certainly you should not be compelled to do what is against your wish. But it may be there are some among you in the village who

331

are young and who would benefit from a little learning—enough, say, so that you could cast up your accounts and see that you are not cheated in the markets."

She turned to Mr. Wu and said in her voice, which grew only more soft with age, "How would it be if we forbade our son to teach any who are over forty years of age unless that one wishes it himself?"

This was a fair compromise, and so it was decided. From then on the older farmers had their freedom from Fengmo if they wished, and none needed to fear that he would be held in less favour for rents and seeds if he wished to remain unlettered.

But Fengmo laughed when Madame Wu told him of the visit of the old farmers. "I have a way to win!" he cried, and he welcomed the difficulties. The upshot of his work was that even some of the old farmers began to want learning when they saw how the younger ones profited by it, and be sure that Fengmo lost no chance to make it known when a young farmer gained by knowing his letters, so that he could read a bill and check an account. It became the fashion at last to know letters, and other villages asked for schools, and Fengmo was so busy that months went by without Madame Wu's knowing how he did.

All this was very well for Fengmo, but it brought some disturbance into the house. Ch'iuming and Rulan moved into the village to live. This made Madame Wu uneasy, for Fengmo pressed them both into the service of his schools and how could Ch'iuming hide her love from Fengmo? Madame Wu grew exceedingly anxious, for, although Ch'iuming and Fengmo were of the same age, they were not of the same generation, and a very evil scandal would gather about the Wu name if there were any cloud about these two. But even while Madame Wu was anxious Fengmo came in one night to see her.

She received him willingly, for she knew by now that Fengmo had no time for anything except what he held important. She had a moment's fear when she saw him, lest he came to tell her what she did not want to hear about Ch'iuming. It was indeed about her, but this is what he said. He sat down squarely on his chair, put his hands on his knees, and began at once. His voice was steady while his eyes were rueful. She could not but admire his looks as he spoke.

The fresh village air had made him red and healthy, and the success of his work had made him bold.

"Mother," he began, "I do not know how to tell you what I must, but not knowing, I will begin anywhere."

"Begin, my son," she said.

He rubbed his hands over his short hair. When he had come home it was long and smoothly combed, but now he had cut it as short as any farmer's, and it was a brush of black.

"Is it about Ch'iuming?" Madame Wu inquired.

"How do you know everything?" he asked, surprised.

"I have my ways," she said. "Now, my son, what have you to say?"

The breach was made, and he could speak. "You know, Mother, that no woman can ever move me."

She smiled at his youth, and something in his serious young face touched her at the very centre of her heart. Ah, perhaps the old ways of love and marriage were wrong—who knew? She leaned forward a little.

"I can remember——" So she began and then checked herself. She could remember a day when she was no older than Fengmo, and she had wakened early in the morning and had looked at the sleeping face of her husband, and had known that never could she love him. And yet she had done her duty and was content and her life had had its own ways of happiness.

But the very youth in Fengmo's face stopped her. She leaned away again. No, she could not speak of herself to her son.

"What shall we do?" he asked.

"Let us consider what is most sensible," she replied.

But he had already a plan. "I ask your permission to take Linyi with me, and we will live in the country too."

This he said, and while Madame Wu could not but see the wisdom of it, she was sad to think of another empty court under the roof. Then she was pleased that he thought of Linyi as a safety for himself, and the more she considered it the more she became willing to do what he asked.

"I will agree to this," she said at last, "with one condition, and it is that when she gives birth to your children, you return here for the time of the birth and the few months after. The grandchildren should be born under our own roofs."

333

To this Fengmo agreed, and within a few days after that Fengmo and Linyi closed the doors of their court and moved into an earthen-walled house in the village. And Madame Wu was content to have it so. She pondered for a while whether she should not send for Ch'iuming and give her advice and some solace of praise, but she decided that she would not. The young woman must learn by life, as all must learn, what she could have and what must be denied to her.

So Ch'iuming learned. But in the year after this one, when
Linyi was about to give birth to her first child, a very strange
circumstance came about. It was the year of the great retreat,
when the enemy from the East Ocean islands won much
territory and drove many from their lands and their homes.
Through the city and the countryside these wanderers now
passed, and since the town where the Wu family lived was
in that region, many passed by there.

Among those who lingered was an elderly woman, a
widow, who with her son and his wife and children stayed
at the inn longer than the others. This son was now her only
child, and he told the innkeeper why they lingered.

"My mother lost a daughter here many years ago," he said.
"Is there any way of finding lost children?"

"Was the child not dead?" the innkeeper asked. The guests
were well-to-do, and he was courteous in what he said.

"She was not dead but cast away by my grandmother, who
had a fierce temper and was angry because my mother gave
birth to three girls one after the other," the man replied.

"How came you here in that year?" the innkeeper asked.

"It was an evil year in our region near the northern capital," the man said. "The harvests failed, and we moved to
these parts where food was plentiful. On the way, which was
here, my mother gave birth."

The innkeeper mused over this. "It must have been in this
very inn then," he said, "because it is the only one in our
town, and I have been here for my lifetime and my father
before me."

"It was in this inn, my mother says, and that is why we
have lingered. My two sisters are dead, and my mother still
yearns over the lost child."

"I will go and tell this to our gentry," the innkeeper said.
"If anyone knows, Madame Wu knows it."

So the innkeeper put on his best clothes, and one evening
after the guests had all been served he sent word to Madame
Wu that he had a question to ask her if she would receive
him.

She replied that she would, for the innkeeper's family had been old servants of the Wu family. An hour later he stood before her in the main hall, and this time she did not ask Mr. Wu to come to hear the man, for it was at a time inconvenient to him. Mr. Wu did not like to be disturbed after his night meal, and yet it was the only time when the innkeeper could come, so great was the rush of his guests now in wartime.

When he stood before Madame Wu he told his tale. She listened piecing all she knew together. She did not tell this man her thoughts. Instead she said, "Let the mother come to visit me and tell me everything."

"The very best thing, Our Lady," the innkeeper declared, and went back with his message.

The next day the son brought his mother. Madame Wu received the mother in her court, and the son waited outside in the main hall.

Now Madame Wu could not know what sort of woman her visitor would be. She had expected a woman of common origin, but as her visitor came in, leaning upon a maid-servant's arm, she saw this was no common woman, but a lady, though no longer young.

She gave greeting and asked the lady to be seated in the place of honour, which the lady refused until she was pressed. But at last both ladies were seated, tea poured, and everything prepared for talk, and Ying and the maid were at a distance too great to hear but not to be called.

After all courteous extra words had been said what the lady had to tell was this:

"We have come at some distance out of our way westward. Certainly safety lies very far from here, and we have come some two hundred miles farther than we need to come. But I have my reasons."

She wiped her eyes, one after the other, on a silk handkerchief.

"Tell me what you wish to tell me," Madame Wu said kindly.

Thus encouraged, the lady went on and told of the casting away of her child. "I know my child did not die. She was so healthy—more healthy than any of my others. And the child's father was not willing to have her killed, even at his mother's demand. He was a good man with an evil mother.

336

Alas, he died before she did, and he feared to tell me anything against his mother's will."

She paused to weep again. "How we were punished! One child after another died, girl and boy alike, until only my youngest son is left. Now I seek the child I lost, and that is why I have come so far."

"You know the child was not killed?" Madame Wu asked.

"I know that," the lady answered, "for even while I lay in bed after the birth I heard the son pleading with the mother, and she agreed at last that the child should not be killed, but only cast away over the city wall."

"Was the child wrapped in a red silk coat?" Madame Wu asked.

The lady stared at her. "In my old red coat," she gasped. "I thought if she were wrapped in it she might be seen by someone."

Madame Wu rose and went to the chest. There folded among her own garments was the one Ch'iuming had long ago given her to keep. "Here is the coat," she said.

The lady's face turned the colour of lead. "It is the coat!" she whispered. She clutched it in her hands. "But the child?"

"Living," Madame Wu said.

And then she told the story of Ch'iuming and how the girl had come into this house, and the lady listened, weeping and impatient and yet fearful. It was hard to tell that Ch'iuming had not pleased Mr. Wu and hard to tell how Madame Wu had allowed her to go to the village to live, though she valued her. The lady was grateful and yet reproachful, too, and at last Madame Wu said, "Let us go to the village to see for ourselves, and you will see that your child has been well cared for."

So without more delay she called for sedans, and the two ladies went at once to the village.

Now Madame Wu had long been saying she must visit the village and see for herself what Fengmo was doing, but what with cold winter, hot summer, and a slight ague she had, and her own love of being alone with her books, she had not gone. What she saw to-day amazed her. The village was clean and prosperous as it had never been. and the people looked healthier than ever they had. Children had clean noses and brushed hair, and the villagers pointed proudly at a new earthen building as the school. Fengmo had told her much, and she had listened and said, "Yes, yes, my son," but she had not comprehended all he had done.

Beside the school was his own house, and since a messenger had run ahead to tell of their coming, there all was ready for them. Linyi was with child, and this had been told to Madame Wu, but she was not prepared for Linyi's healthy looks. Her cheeks were red, her lips red without paint, and she had put on flesh as well as motherhood. The curled ends of her hair she had cut off, and this pleased Madame Wu as much as anything. But more perhaps she was pleased by the change in Linyi's manners. The girl was respectful and prompt, and her lazy ways were gone.

So they went into Fengmo's house and sat down, and Fengmo was sent for, and when he was come the whole story was told again, and Ch'iuming and her child were sent for, and Rulan came with her.

The moment that Ch'iuming came in mother and daughter looked at each other and knew who they were. No two could have faces so alike who were not made one of the other. All who watched burst into laughter at so magic an ending to a strange story, and if Madame Wu was the most silent, yet she was the most pleased.

"My mother!" Ch'iuming cried.

"This is my child," the lady said.

The two must weep, and the lady must embrace her grandchild, who by this time was big enough to be bold, and the child cried and kicked and Ch'iuming slapped her and the lady protested, and soon all was easy again. Of course the lady must have Ch'iuming and the child go back with her and join her own family. For this Ch'iuming must ask permission of Madame Wu.

"May I go, Elder Sister?" she asked timidly.

Now Madame Wu saw very clearly that Ch'iuming did not look well. In spite of the clean village air and the country food Ch'iuming was pale and her eyes were hollow as though she were sleepless, and Madame Wu saw that she kept her eyes away from Linyi. It would be well for Ch'iuming to leave the house of Wu. She gave her permission.

"If it were any other than your mother," she said, "I could not let you go, but Heaven has brought mother and daughter together, and how dare I keep you apart? You shall go, but not before I have new clothes made for you and the child

338

and such things provided as you will need on your journey. You must not go empty from our house."

The lady protested that this was not needful, but Madame Wu insisted. Then Ch'iuming and her child, after many thanks, returned with her mother to the inn, and from that time on they were parted no more.

And Madame Wu said nothing to this except that before they went she drew the mother aside and said, "Do not allow this child of yours to remain solitary. Find her a good husband and let her begin her life again."

The lady promised, and so Ch'iuming left the house of Wu, and after a few weeks when all had been prepared she went away with her mother. Madame Wu was glad that Ch'iuming did not come to bid her any private farewell. Well enough she knew the young woman's tender heart to know that this was not because she was ungrateful or forgetful. No, Ch'iuming did not come because there was no more to be said between her and Fengmo's mother, and she wished to spare her pain. Her love she carried away in her own bosom.

From that time on Madame Wu never saw Ch'iuming again. Once a year a letter came, written by a letter-writer and signed by Ch'iuming. In these letters, year after year, after greetings, Ch'iuming told her that she was well, that the child grew, and at last when the war was over that she was married again to a widower, a small merchant in Peking who sold native and foreign goods. He had two young sons whom Ch'iuming soon learned to love. Her mother died at last, and Ch'iuming had a son of her own and then twin sons. Her house was full.

These letters Madame Wu answered carefully with admonition and wisdom. And in each, from the kindness of her heart, she put news of Fengmo and his family.

. . . . . .

Yes, Fengmo's family grew also. Whatever his inner life, the life of his body was fruitful, and Linyi had children, a son, a daughter, and two more sons. For each birth she returned to the house of Wu, but when the child was a month old she went to the village again to take her place with Fengmo. She had no time for play or pouting or for curling her hair and painting her fingernails. Fengmo dealt with her sternly but justly. Well enough Madame Wu knew that he

339

would never love Linyi, but she knew too that he did not need love. He had other fires, and these flamed higher than love. He burned with zeal for the people. He was hungry for schools and more schools, and when there were schools, then he was not satisfied until he began to dream of hospitals. He had put aside all his silken robes. They lay in the chests in the storehouses of his family, and he wore plain garments cut like a uniform but without insignia or decoration. Something in his too-serious face reminded Madame Wu continually of André, but Fengmo was without André's humour. He was hard to his core, and his core he locked even against himself. Never had he written to or spoken again of the woman he had learned to love across the seas. Fengmo could do nothing partly well. His zeal burned in all directions at once.

This zeal all could admire until it touched the family itself, and then it was too much. Thus Fengmo was not content to teach the country folk, and even Yenmo, who loved him, but he must meddle with his elder brother; and this Liangmo would not have. The truth was that Fengmo could never find enough teachers for his schools, and seeing Meng, his sister-in-law, idle and fattening, he asked her one day why she did not help Linyi and Rulan with the older women who struggled to learn their letters and to sew more cleverly and such useful things. Meng opened her round eyes at him.

"I?" she exclaimed. "But I never leave our gates except to visit my mother."

"But you should, sister-in-law," Fengmo told her. "It is your duty. Your children are cared for by nurses, your eldest son is in the hands of his tutor, and your household is tended by servants. You should come for an hour or two each day and help us."

Meng grew very agitated. "I cannot," she exclaimed. "Liangmo would not allow it."

"But you have been taught to read and write," Fengmo insisted. "No one in our country who has learning ought to keep it for himself."

Meng listened, her plump face drawn in horror. Fengmo in these days had a loud and teaching voice, and once he began to preach what he believed, none could answer. Only his endless goodness saved him and made him still loved by those whom he taught.

"I will ask Liangmo," Meng faltered at last, and Fengmo went away satisfied that he had stirred her heart.

But Liangmo was only made angry when Meng told him, weeping, how Fengmo had spoken. "He made me feel wicked," she sobbed.

Liangmo took off the spectacles which he now wore and folded them up and put them in his pocket. Then he slapped the table with his hand. "Fengmo is really too troublesome!" he exclaimed. "He has put many ideas into the heads of the common people. Why, only yesterday the head farmers came to me to say that from now on they would have no middleman in selling the grain, but that they would sell it themselves. I asked them how they could do the accounting, and it seems Fengmo teaches them how to do it. How are the middlemen to eat and feed their families? Is there not a place under heaven for all men?"

He frowned awhile and then he said, "Meng, I forbid you to have any more talk with my brother. I will talk with him myself."

This Liangmo did, and he took time from the shops to go and see Fengmo. Secretly he was amazed at the cleanliness of the villages, for Fengmo's work had by now spread well over the region. But he pursed his lips and would not acknowledge his amazement. Instead he muttered that he did not know who paid for all this and that poor people should not be so clean as rich people in the very nature of life. Nor was there necessity for hospitals among the poor for there were too many people already, and why should so many live?

The end of the visit was that there was a great quarrel between the two brothers, and the quarrel was worse because Liangmo was outraged by Linyi's appearance, which he considered unfit for a lady of their family. She was dressed like any common schoolteacher and looked older, he declared, than Meng. Hearing this, Linyi was inclined to pity herself, but Rulan plunged into the quarrel on the side of Fengmo and the people. And Liangmo was the less pleased because he saw that Rulan was healed of her sorrow, for all her ardour was fulfilled in the work she did in the villages. The upshot of it was that all parted in anger, and Liangmo went to complain to Madame Wu.

Now Madame Wu in these days never left her own court except to visit the temple children. She had not added to their number. Whatever André might have wished, she had taken no more. One thing only had she done, and it was to give money to a Buddhist nunnery in the south part of the city, that they send each morning at dawn two nuns to search outside the city walls for such children as might be thrown out alive, and then that they bring these children back and nurture them. They were not to be made into nuns, Madame Wu commanded, but taught and reared and wed to farmers and such men as were good and kind. This she did for André's sake.

But André's children she kept in the temple, and as each girl became sixteen she betrothed her to a suitable young man, and such was the fame of these girls that there were always lists of young men who wanted wives from among them. Each time that a girl reached her sixteenth birthday Madame Wu called her to her side and spoke to her about the young men who were ready to marry her. Be sure there was talk enough in the city at such new ways, for Madame Wu did not only tell the name and the age and the qualities of the young men, but she showed pictures also.

"Shall only men see pictures?" she inquired when anyone spoke her wonder. "Shall it not be just for a woman to see also the face of the man?"

No one dared to judge Madame Wu, and so it became a matter for rivalry and honour that young men sent their pictures to her and she herself submitted them at the suitable time to the girls as they came of age. When the girl had chosen, she sent her picture to the young man, and such was the fame of the temple girls that never had one been rejected by the man she chose.

These girls Madame Wu came to consider as her own daughters, and to each she taught all that was needful for good relationship between man and woman. All were good wives, and Madame Wu became famous in that whole region for these girls.

It was her pride to give each of them a fine wedding, and she took the place of the mother. No one understood her smile or the look of distance in her eyes. But she did not need understanding. It seemed to her that André himself stood beside her as one by one she sent the foundlings who were his children into quiet and secure homes. For it was not enough for Madame Wu that she prepared the girls. She allowed

342

none to wed any man unless she herself had talked with him, and if he had a mother until she had seen and talked with the mother also. A bad-tempered mother-in-law was reason for forbidding the marriage, and three times she did so, and twice out of the three times so distraught was the young man over his loss that he himself departed from his mother.

This distressed Madame Wu, for well she knew a son must not leave his father's house, and yet André had once spoken of this to her.

He came to her mind more clearly than ever in these days as she grew older, and she remembered very well what he had said to her one winter's day, after his lesson to Fengmo. Snow had fallen in the court, and there were only his great footsteps across its whiteness. Fengmo as well as Ying had walked through the verandas, but André strode through the snow.

She had remonstrated with him. "Your feet doubtless are wet."

He had stared down at his shoes as though he did not know what she said, and without remark had unfolded his books, and then Fengmo had come in and he began to teach. She had sat near that day, listening and not speaking. But when Fengmo had gone she had put this question, "How far should a son be allowed to leave his father's house?"

For already she had foreseen that such teaching as his would lead to Fengmo's wandering.

"His father's house is his birthplace, no more," he had replied. He was setting the books in order, piling one on the other upon the cotton handkerchief in which he carried them.

"Is this to say that a man has no duty to his parents?" she had asked.

"I am the wrong one to ask that," he had replied. He had looked at her quickly and then away again, and his smile came out like a light upon his face. "See how far I have wandered! Yet I do not forget that my beginning was in a house in Venice."

"Venice?" she had repeated. He had never before given her the name of his birthplace.

"A city like Soochow," he had said, "whose streets are waterways, and instead of sedans we used boats, and I looked

343

out at dawn and sunset and saw the water change to running gold."

He had paused, staring at the blank wall before him, but she knew he saw those streets of golden water. Then he had brought himself back again and bade her farewell for that day.

In such ways had he broken down the walls of the compound in which she had lived, and now she held her peace when a young man left an arrogant and angry mother. The young man must live too. All must live.

This crumbling of the walls prepared her for Liangmo, when he came in with his lips pursed to complain of his brother Fengmo. She did not see her sons every day or even every month, and so each time they came inside her door she saw them freshly. Thus to-day she saw Liangmo as a prosperous man of affairs, the coming head of a great family, a merchant and a maker of money.

After greetings, Liangmo came straight to the heart of the matter. "My younger brother is becoming a fanatic," he complained. "Actually he wishes Meng to go out and teach. This is impossible. Linyi looks like a woman teacher. Her hair is cut off, and it has turned brown with the sun. Rulan looks like a communist woman. It is all hateful to me. Is this suitable for our family?"

Madame Wu smiled. "Did you not find the villages very clean?" she asked.

But Liangmo would not see any good. "I think first of our family, not of strangers and common folk," he said stubbornly. "The responsibility of the family rests upon me, Our Mother, after you and my father are gone."

Seldom did his sons speak of Mr. Wu. All knew that whatever had been his place it was all but empty now. He was drowsy and content and asked nothing but to be let alone. It is true that he was the beloved of his grandchildren. They went clamouring into his court, and he fed them sweetmeats and laughed at them and napped while they played, and Jasmine, feeling her childlessness, enticed them often and treated them as her own, so that the old man who protected her would feel no lack about him. The old must have children about them, she knew, to keep them from the fear of death.

But Liangmo was very proper as the eldest son, and he gave his father respect at all times, by mouth at least, and hid his

344

weakness. He now went on to complain further against Fengmo.

"And our youngest brother, Yenmo, is it fitting that he should not go away to school?"

"Yenmo does not wish to go," Madame Wu said mildly.

"Is that a reason why he should not be compelled to go?" Liangmo asked. "Does he look as the younger son in our house should look? There is no difference between him and a farmer's son."

"Well, well——" she said in her mildest voice.

Liangmo understood that she meant for him to be silent, and so he quenched his anger in a long drink of tea and sat with his face very solemn.

Madame Wu did not speak for a long time. She knew the value of silence. It was a soft grey day, the skies grey, the walls grey, and from the pool in the court a delicate mist rose from the cold water into air unduly warm for the season. The smell of earth hung about the courts.

"You are well pleased in your own courts, my son?" Madame Wu said at last.

"Certainly I am," Liangmo said. He put down his tea bowl. "I am obeyed there. My children are healthy and intelligent. Do you know, Our Mother, that the eldest has finished the lower school already?"

"Can it be so?" Madame Wu replied amiably. "And in the city, is all well?"

"Well enough," Liangmo said. "Markets are somewhat poor, perhaps, but not too poor for the season. Some foreign goods come in, now that the war is ended. The foreign hospital is raising a new building, and I hear new foreigners are coming."

"Is this a good thing?" Madame Wu inquired.

"Fengmo is pleased," Liangmo said dryly. "For myself, I can only say we are fortunate. Meng needs no foreign doctors, and the children are never ill."

"I remember I cured a grandson in the Kang house with our grandmother's herb brew," Madame Wu murmured. "I suppose he is a great lad now——"

The year before this Madame Kang had died. At this moment Madame Wu thought of her as she had seen her in her coffin. The coffin had been made twice as broad as usual, and there Madame Kang had lain, dressed in her satin robes,

345

her plump hands by her sides. After she was dead Madame Wu thought of her sometimes with old love still faintly sweet, and their friendship returned to its early days. Madame Kang had been a rosy, cheerful, hearty girl, sad only for such small things as that her nostrils were wide and her nose too flat between the brows. Mr. Kang had soon married a second wife, a young woman whose wilfulness stirred the great unwieldy household continually like a ladle in a pot of stew. But this was no matter of concern for Madame Wu, and no more than gossip for Ying, to which Madame Wu listened or did not, while Ying was brushing her hair.

Liangmo waited for his mother to speak. She drew back her thoughts at last and smiled at him her small, sweet smile. "Well, my son," she said. "The soul of every creature must take its own shape, and none can compel another without hurting himself. Live in your house, my son, and let Fengmo live in his."

"Teach Fengmo one thing, if you please, Our Mother," Liangmo said in anger. "Bid him keep his long arm out of my house."

"I will," Madame Wu promised.

So Liangmo went away, and when Madame Wu next saw Fengmo she taught him thus:

"Do you remember, my son, that once your tutor said to you that to teach is to invite the soul to Heaven but never to compel it?"

She saw by Fengmo's look that he did remember these words which André had spoken. The wonder of André had always been that his whole life was invitation towards Heaven.

Fengmo bent his head into his hands. "I know why you remind me," he said. "I know why I need to be told. The banked fires in me break out sometimes and I am driven by my own flames, and when I am driven I drive others."

She let him speak on, knowing that to someone he must confess himself, and to whom if not to her? Again she felt the strange impulse to talk to this son about André. They were very close, she and this son who alone had shared the wisdom that André had brought into the house. Again she refused herself. But she allowed herself this much comfort. She said:

"I often consider and ponder what it was that tall priest brought into our house. We are a family so old it cannot be

346

said we needed wisdom to live. We have continued as a family for hundreds of years, and our life goes on. He did not change us, and yet we are changed, you and I, and it is we who have brought change into the house. But what is this change?"

"We learned from him the right of the self to be," Fengmo said.

"How well and easily you have put it," she said. No one could have told from her voice at this moment that she felt André was here in this room, standing beside her son and looking at them both with ineffable love. She sat basking in his presence. He came so often to her alone, but never before had he come with another in the room.

"Had he lived," she said to Fengmo, "I think he would have approved all that you do."

"Do you think so?" Fengmo exclaimed. He sat up, and his pleasure in what she had said gave him new energy. "Mother, I am thinking of a new thing. What would you say if I persuaded the foreign hospital doctors to begin the teaching of country doctors, not too learned but able to cure the many usual diseases? Our people die so needlessly."

He went on, his voice bright and eager and full of life, but she scarcely heard him. She was thinking of André. She saw his great, beautiful hands. One of them, as so often it had been, was at the crucifix upon his breast. When his rosary broke he had tied it to a cord. The crucifix now was broken too. When the ruffians had killed him the crucifix had struck the stones where he fell. She had seen it so when she looked at him in his coffin.

"Good, my son, good," she murmured. "Good—good——"

Only when he rose to hasten away, full of his new plans, did she remember what she had promised Liangmo. She put out her hand and laid hold of Fengmo's arm. "Only remember this, my son—compel no one—not Liangmo, not Meng——"

"Oh, those two!" Fengmo cried. "I have given them up——"

He was gone and André was gone too. She sat alone, smiling to herself.

. . . . .

The years have passed over Madame Wu. She never leaves

347

her own gates. Yet somehow she knows enough and all of that which goes on. She is famed for her patient listening and her cool judgments, and many come to her for enlightenment. It is she who decides all great matters in city and country. It was she who decided, for example, what to do with the body of Little Sister Hsia when she died, one winter's night in her solitary house. The poor thin body of that one was brought to the Wu temple, and Madame Wu herself saw to the coffin and the burial. For Little Sister Hsia had separated herself even from her own kind. She had long quarrelled with the other foreigners in the city, who were from another country, and when she died it was with no one in the house except her old cook, and he alone mourned her. It was he who came and told Madame Wu that he had found his mistress sitting upright in her chair, wrapped in her ragged quilt, her holy book open on her knee.

There beneath the gods of clay, and beneath the picture of André painted upon alabaster, Little Sister Hsia lay in her coffin. The temple children were gone except for the young girl named Love, and she lit the candles. The old priest, now so old that he could scarcely totter, often let her help him with his duties, and the old nurse had a helper, for she could not walk easily any more.

Madame Wu had looked down at the bone-thin face of the woman who had left her own kind and kin, and tried to remember the prayer that Little Sister Hsia had used to say very often. But she could not remember it. She had forgotten it with all else she did not wish to remember. So she could only light a stick of incense in the pewter urn before the gods and ask Heaven to receive also this foreign soul. And Little Sister Hsia's coffin was sealed and set in a niche in the temple until a lucky day, and then it was buried upon a hill-side outside the city, and Madame Wu commanded that a stone be set up giving such few facts as she knew about her, so that if any kinfolk ever came to seek her they could find her.

She would have held this very unlikely except that a strange thing happened.

After the end of the war the whole countryside was in confusion, and many men came from over the seas to mend and to meddle in this confusion. It did not touch the house of the Wu family. Their city remained remote as ever it had been from the troubled regions. But foreigners continued passing through for one reason or another, and one of the reasons was that Fengmo invited them. Whenever he heard the name of a man from the West, Fengmo invited him to come and advise him about the work he did, and the men came, for the work was becoming known everywhere with not a little praise for Fengmo.

These foreigners, of course, Madame Wu did not receive, for she did not know their language, and it was too difficult to converse with them. Moreover, she declared, "My life is complete. I do not need to add another to it."

But one day Fengmo sent her special word that a man from across the ocean was come, and there was a reason why he wished to bring him to see her. She gave her consent to this, and a few hours afterwards Fengmo came and with him was a tall foreign man, young and dark. Indeed, he was so dark that, after greeting, Madame Wu looked at him and then turned to Fengmo.

"Is this man a foreigner? His skin is so brown."

"He is foreign," Fengmo said, "but his ancestors, indeed his parents, came from Italy, which was the birthplace, Mother, of Brother André."

How Madame Wu's heart now stirred! She forgot that she could speak no language but her own, and she leaned forward, her hands on the silver head of her cane, and she asked the young man, "Did you know the foreign priest?"

Fengmo stepped in quickly to translate, and then Madame Wu and the young man spoke through him thus:

"I did not know him," the young man said, "but my father and mother have told me of him, Madame. He was my uncle."

"Your uncle!" Madame Wu repeated. "You are his flesh and blood!"

She gazed at the dark young man and found one resemblance and then another. Yes, here were the dark eyes of André, but not so wide. Yes, here was André's shape of skull, and the hands. She looked at the young man's hands, more slender than André's but with the shape she knew. All was more slender and smaller than André, and the look in the eyes was not at all André's. The soul was not the same.

She sighed and drew back. No. the soul was not the same.

"You came here to find your uncle?" she inquired.

"I did," the young man answered. "My parents knew

349

where he was, although he never wrote to any of us in his later years. When I passed here I said I could come and see if he still lived and write home to my father."

"He is buried in our land," Madame Wu said. "My son will take you to his grave."

They sat for a moment in silence. Madame Wu struggled with a strange jealousy. She closed her eyes and saw André's face against the velvet inner dark. "You," she said to him, "you belong only to us."

She opened her eyes and saw his nephew sitting there before her. Ah, André had family and kin, foreign and far away!

The young man smiled. "I suppose you know, Madame, why he lived so far away from all of us and why he never wrote any letters?"

Fengmo answered for her. "We never knew."

"He was a heretic," the young man said solemnly. "The church cast him out as a renegade—homeless, without support. We never heard from him afterward. He sent back money we sent him—he refused to come home."

"But he did no evil!" Fengmo exclaimed in horror.

"It was not what he did," the young man declared. "It was what he thought. He thought it was men and women who were the divine. It seems hard to think this a sin, in our generation. But it was a great sin in his day. He felt compelled to write a letter to his Cardinal and tell him. In the last letter he wrote my father he told the whole story. We didn't know what he meant. My mother said she supposed he was crazy from living too long alone."

All this Fengmo translated for Madame Wu, and she listened and said not a word. They had rejected him—his own people!

She closed her eyes. "But we did not reject you," she told him in her heart.

She sat thus for a moment silent, her eyes closed, and the two young men stared at her. Fengmo moved, anxious because she sat so long, and she opened her eyes.

"Tell this young foreigner that it is a very long way to that grave," she said. "Tell him the road is rough and narrow. When he gets there it is only the grave, nothing more."

The young man listened. "If it is as far as that I had better not go!" he exclaimed. "I have to get back in time to catch the boat. After all, as you say, it is only a grave."

They went away, after farewells, and Madame Wu was glad to see them gone. She had need to be alone that she might comprehend to the full the knowledge she now had of André. All those years he had lived here, solitary!

"But not solitary," she thought. There were the children he had found and the beggars he had fed.

And she herself—how had she opened her gates and let him in? She would never know. He had been led to her, and she had opened her gates and he had come in, and with him he had brought to her eternal life.

Yes, she now believed that when her body died her soul would go on. Gods she did not worship, and faith she had none, but love she had and for ever. Love alone had awakened her sleeping soul and had made it deathless.

She knew she was immortal.